THE COLLECTION #2
EDGED

BLAKE BLESSING

Foreword

Hey, hey readers!

Like always, I'm going to keep this short and sweet.

This is a story about very troubled and toxic individuals who had no real role models in life. They basically had to come up with their own moral code and Beasty's is blaringly different from the boys for so many reasons.

You know what that does? It makes for a lot of conflict and sometimes poor decision-making. Some of it is juicy, and some of it is frustrating.

Just keep in mind that these are flawed characters trying to find their way, and it's all about the journey!

But don't worry. There's plenty of toxic love to fill your little black hearts. <3

With that said, this is book 2 in The Collection series. So if you have not picked up Snatched, STOP! Do not turn the page and do not collect $200.

Because this is an ongoing series about the same characters, you have to read Snatched to enjoy and understand this book.

This is also a why choose romance, meaning the female main character will not have to choose between love interests. Which is just the way I love my fictional worlds. ;)

Enjoy!

Warning

There are no new TW in this book.

So, I'm assuming if you're here, you enjoyed Snatched with no major issues! However, I'll drop the link here just in case you'd like to refresh your memory.

https://blakeblessing.com/175-2/

Remember, your mental health is always more important.

For those whose favorite book boyfriends are model handsome with an obscene amount of baggage and red flags, but are totally obsessed with you in an unhealthy way...

Don't worry, girlfriend. I got you.

Recap

At the end of Snatched, Beasty makes the decision that she wants to stay with the boys.

So all's good, right?

Absolutely, not.

While at the club, cops show up looking for Lake. Joaquin chats with them and discovers they're there about Stevo, whose head was delivered to the Pescis.

Meanwhile, Atlas calls Lake to the office, and with a little root cover up, he disguises his white-blond hair so he's able to sneak out.

So all's good, right?

Nope!

The cops show up at the house with an arrest warrant for both Lake and Joaquin. Unfortunately, Beasty is watching out the window as they're led to the police cars.

And she is pissed.

Now, you're ready to read Edged!

"What do you think she'll say?" Kim bounced his leg as he watched out the window. His deathgrip on the wildflowers almost crumpled them.

We were only about ten minutes away. Graduation should be well under way. Just as I'd planned.

Atlas and Kim had made it in the fashion industry. They were recognizable on the street in most big cities, and I was sure everyone in our old town would notice us walking in.

They were gossiping bitches and we never hid why or how we left, especially when it pulled them out of school.

What we didn't need was to be ambushed before we could find our seats.

"She might not say anything. We left her by herself for years." Atlas grouched, crossing his arms and glaring at me.

He'd excelled at modeling, and he supported Joaquin and me when we found our purpose in the group. But he'd never quite let go that I pushed them to take this opportunity.

I didn't regret it, but I'd be lying to myself if I didn't think he had a point.

We'd left. No goodbye. No notice. One day, we were just gone.

If she thought about us at all, it probably wasn't kind.

Like I said, I'd never admit it. Atlas would hold it over my head.

"I think she'll cry tears of happiness, then jump in our arms for a hug because she missed us so much." Kim bit his lip, looking at Joaquin and Atlas briefly before turning his gaze back to the outside.

Squinting at Kim, Joaquin mashed his lips together. "That's a good guess. We'll go with that. It's better than her spitting on us or just walking by without acknowledging us at all. Which, come on, why wouldn't she ignore us? We never talked to her."

"Kim could've," Atlas still griped.

The closer we got to the school, the more irritable he got.

He was about to get what he'd been craving for years. A chance to talk to Beasty. To see her. To take her with us and away from this place.

And he was focused on the negative.

My stomach soured as we rode through town. In the grand scheme of things, we hadn't been gone that long. But it felt like a lifetime ago that we left my rickety old apartment.

Our absence was long enough that the rundown buildings that needed a paint and power wash jarred my senses. It was downright depressing after being in the bigger cities with nice neighborhoods and manicured lawns.

The driver pulled up to the front of the school.

The large brown building was still standing strong, but

there was a drabness about it that seemed more like prison than school.

Taking a deep breath, I centered myself. The last thing I needed to do was let on that I was nervous as fuck.

Kim didn't wait for anyone as he jumped out.

"Kim!" I called, cursing under my breath. "I'm supposed to go in front of you." I kept my voice low, but it didn't hide the fact that he was being an idiot.

Joaquin and Atlas let me out, then as I took my place in front of them, they fell in behind me.

A couple groups of smokers huddled around the entrance. The adults gave us one glance then turned away. There was one group of high schoolers who immediately recognized Kim and Atlas. I glanced back to check on them.

Atlas acted like they didn't exist. Kim fidgeted and watched the concrete. He wasn't used to the mass attention yet. He could handle it when he prepped himself, but he was already so nervous about Beasty, he was screwed here.

For the most part, we made it to the top of the stands without any issues.

One girl tried to step out in my path, but I moved her out the way and kept heading up the stairs. Hearing her umph of indignation did feel good.

How the tables had turned. The outcasts were now desired because of our fame. Or Atlas and Kim's, mine by extension.

In the nosebleeds, there were more students and recent graduates but the lights were dim. Thankfully, no one tried to sit close to us, leaving a good three-foot buffer around us.

The person calling out the names were on the G's. We still had time. Shit, that had been close.

A side glance at Atlas glaring at the stage told me he understood just how close we made it.

But I didn't regret this either. It would have been a

nightmare to show up before graduation started, and get bombarded by people or have to listen to their whispers travel around the stands.

I watched the crowd for anyone who even hinted at coming too close, and looked for Beasty in the seats.

It was too hard to see her.

Then her row stood up and when they turned sideways, I picked her out.

My hands curled on my thighs as I held my breath. She was beautiful in a way that society didn't appreciate.

Her beauty was the very core of her being.

She was so strong. Fierce. Wild.

I smiled remembering how many fights she'd gotten into over the years.

The other guys gasped as they saw her. We all leaned forward, glued to her every move as she walked to the stage, then up the stairs. She held her chin up the entire time.

That's right, Beasty. Fuck everyone here. You're better than them.

"Cressida Hart..." the announcer said over the speakers.

We didn't plan it, we didn't even talk about it. But as soon as her name was called, we jumped to our feet, whistling, clapping, screaming. All for her.

For the first time in my entire life, everything was *right*.

Kim could be anxious. Atlas could be angry. Joaquin could placate both of them.

But I knew Beasty was going to say yes. She was going to come with us.

Then nothing and no one could tear us apart. We were going to make the world our bitch, and give everyone else a big fuck you.

Our life was starting now, with Beasty.

4

Chapter One

Joaquin hadn't been placed in the same car. They'd correctly assumed that we would have been able to communicate. Not that that really mattered at this point. We had too much experience working together, and our shit locked down too tight for this to be an issue.

"So," the man who'd introduced himself as Agent Barton started, "you don't seem nervous at all. Why is that?"

He was every stereotype in the book. Sharp eyes and coffee breath. Slight paunch and bad comb over. Agent Barton also had the stink of ambition around him. I bet he defined himself by the cases he closed, and his biggest failures were the cases he fumbled.

I could work with that.

One side of my mouth curled up into a slight smirk. I turned toward the window to hide it as his gaze burned into the side of my head through the rearview mirror.

What did he expect me to say? That I was a psychopath? I wasn't. Just the product of a fucked-up childhood.

"You're familiar with my past, correct?" I turned back, the expression wiped from my face. As much as this was bullshit, the last thing I needed was for him to peg me as a cocky little asshole. That would only make this farce ten times harder, and that wasn't the type of pain I was into.

"I am, Mr. Wright. It's hard not to be aware of the unfortunate start to your childhood when two of your friends are constantly in the public eye."

That wasn't true. Atlas and Kim did the bare minimum required in the spotlight. More like Agent Barton constantly saw them in ads and on billboards.

"Then you're aware that I was personally held by the Curator for years. At least two as far as I can remember." It wasn't a question, but I still paused.

"I am," he agreed.

"That was a living nightmare. I'm sure you can appreciate that nothing in my life after the day I was released has affected me as much as that. Any fear you're trying to lay at my feet, it won't work. You or your false charges, or even the veiled threats you're trying to dance around, can't scare me the way Gates did when I was a child." I clenched my jaw, my heart rate accelerated, pumping anger through my veins.

I itched to dig my fingernails in my legs but I couldn't. Not with them handcuffed together. I could pull on them though. Let the metal bite just the tiniest bit into my wrists.

"Lucky for you that the Curator is dead then, huh, Mr. Wright?" He shifted in his seat. It wasn't a movement of discomfort, but came through more as a thinking tick. He was thinking about how to spin this conversation to catch me up in a lie. "If the facts didn't state he was murdered when you were kids, you'd be at the top of our suspect list for that too. Not that I'd blame you." He shrugged. "The man was an evil the world is better off without."

I raised my brows. Did this asswipe really expect me to

say something that would put me in the shallow box he was trying to back me into? "If you're looking for sympathy on his death, I don't have it. If you're looking to characterize me by attempting to weasel out what I would do if I had ever met him as a man, I can't help you there either. I don't dwell on the past. No point in it."

He harrumphed. Barton didn't believe me. I didn't blame him, I didn't believe me either.

"Given the delicate situation of your...friends' success, we're not taking you straight to booking. We're going to have a nice chat at the station while my colleagues go through the club and your house."

I didn't respond.

The bigger question is why would the mafia set this up? There was a code among the syndicates I'd met. It didn't matter who it was. Cartel, mafia, the Network. All the different crime organizations left the law out of it. When there was a debt to settle, they settled it amongst themselves.

And Stevo? He shouldn't have mattered in the grand scheme of things.

The question was, why did *he*?

I caught Joaquin's eye as they led us in through security from the back entrance. Nice of them to protect our image. They would try to say it was kindness to get us to talk later.

Joaquin's gaze burned. He was pissed at me.

What the fuck ever. Nothing we could do about this now, except ride it out and figure out what the hell was going on.

Barton opened the next door leading to a deserted

hallway and ushered us in. My steps echoed as he lightly pushed me toward a room at the end.

One of the cops placed Joaquin into a room next to mine. His guy had a pep in his step that mine didn't. He must be fresh on the force.

There was still one door in the middle of ours. Probably the viewing room.

"Here, I'll unlock those cuffs while you're in here. There are men stationed outside, so don't try anything stupid."

"I wouldn't dream of it." I rubbed my wrists. The cuffs were nothing like the ones I'd used on Beasty. These hadn't been tight, but I was broad and my arms didn't like the angle of how I'd had to sit in the backseat. Yet the slight discomfort helped me keep a clear head.

I glanced around. This wasn't like the typical interrogation rooms I'd expect at the station. It was a regular office type setting, with wallpaper and cheap, hotel-grade furniture. The only thing separating this room from a typical conference room was the mirror behind Barton as he took a seat across from me.

He let out a loud sigh as he steadily met my gaze.

A scar marred the side of his top lip, and he'd done a piss poor job of shaving the underside of his neck. So, not as meticulous as I'd originally thought.

"What do you think my colleagues will find in their searches, Mr. Wright?" His eyes narrowed.

I shrugged. "Nothing. This is all a waste of time when I'd much rather be home with my family."

He chuckled. "Family. But none of you are related. And we've noticed a young woman in your care as well."

I tensed. I did not like this asshole even alluding to Beasty. No one fucking deserved to say her name. To breathe her air. They were so far beneath her, he shouldn't even know she existed.

But we'd never be able to lock her in the basement. Fine, we would deal with this shit.

"You don't have anything to say?" he hummed and leaned back in his chair, folding his hands over his stomach.

"What do you want me to say? Those men aren't related to me, but we were all in that house together, locked away by Gates. If that doesn't build an unbreakable bond, I don't know what does." I hesitated, gauging his reaction. I might as well put it out there. Chances were, he'd done background checks on all of us, including Beasty. "And Cressida is the girl who alerted the police. Why wouldn't she be part of our family? If not for her, my friends and I would probably be in shallow graves in the backwoods of West Virginia."

He nodded, like this was all exactly what he expected.

"I hear ya. I would have a hard time not hero-worshiping the girl who saved my ass too. You five together, you all pretty tight?"

"Of course. We've been together for years."

"But not Miss Hart. She only recently came to stay with you?"

"Yes." No harm in confirming this, but his time was coming to an end. I wasn't stupid. I needed my one phone call.

"Funny that. Because she and Stevo shared a history. I'm sure you know that." He paused.

I didn't confirm. "Listen. A deep dive into my family dynamics is a waste of my time and yours. I'd like my lawyer."

He pursed his lips, shifting to lean forward and brace his elbows on the chair. "I can't help you if you lawyer up."

"You don't want to help. I'll take that phone call now."

"Okay, I'll tell you what." He raised his hand and pointed to a camera in the top corner of the ceiling. The red light was on. He made some kind of hand signal to the glass and it kicked off. "The camera is off. I'm going to lay shit out for you, and after that, you can do what you want with it."

I waited. He was expecting an answer but huffed out a low laugh when he didn't get one.

"I don't think you're the bad guy here. Honestly, if this went to trial, you and Mr. Amaya have such a tragic back-story, as does Miss Hart, that you'd probably get off on self-defense, regardless that Mr. Anderson's head was delivered back to his hometown.

"Now, you and I both know that that kind of effort is not self-defense. It's anger, and it stinks of revenge. But I get it. If I'd lived your life, I wouldn't want to let anyone get the best of me for any reason. I'd want the control. I'd need the power to protect myself and the ones I loved."

He wasn't wrong. But he wasn't completely right.

"Then there's the very clear and unsavory ties connected to Mr. Anderson. No one liked him, no one is missing him. There's not a strong case. But..." He rhythmically tapped his first two fingers on the tabletop. "We're not really after your family. We're after much bigger fish."

And still, I gave Barton nothing. He made a scoffing noise in his throat.

"We've come to learn that your family has some very important ties. To some very big players. We want them. And your cooperation will make sure that your particular troubles will go away."

Damn, he really thought he was doing something.

I shook my head. "I would say I'd love to help you, but I think we both know that isn't true. Nothing against you or your cause, but I'm afraid you have me—and my family—all wrong."

"I don't though, do I? It doesn't take a rocket scientist to figure out that you sent Mr. Anderson back to notable men in the mafia. Or the fact that you have a silent investor that's almost impossible to find a trail on. Pay attention, kid. I said *almost* impossible."

The way he raised his brows and widened his eyes, he thought I was slow on the uptake.

"I can't help you. I want that phone call now. I have a lawyer on retainer who will clear this all up."

Barton's top lip curled and he pushed his chair back. He didn't bother with responding as he stormed out of the room.

Five minutes later, he came back and held the door open for me. Because I wasn't a complete asshole, I didn't gloat at cutting his fun short. I slid past him and waited for him to lead me to a side office. He pointed at the phone and crossed his arms.

I leveled him with a flat stare. The calls were recorded, but that didn't mean I wanted his eyes on the back of my head while I made the call.

After a petty huff, he shut the door behind him.

I dialed the number I'd memorized, and waited for an answer.

"Ms. Chen's office."

"This is Lake Wright. I had sent over an inquiry based on a referral by a mutual friend. I haven't heard back, and I'm afraid I've run out of time."

"Lake Wright," she repeated absently as she furiously typed. "Ah, okay. I see your inquiry. What is your situation?"

"My friend and I have been arrested. We're currently at

Rockford County Police Station. We need representation and to be bailed out."

"Lucky for you it's during the week and early to boot. Otherwise you'd be stuck there overnight." More typing. "Are you aware of the fees?"

"I am."

"And you agree to the terms?"

"I do."

"Perfect. I'll let her know." The line went dead. Real fucking nice, lady.

I set the phone down. I almost lifted it to make another phone call, but I didn't. Too many ears and not enough reason to hang myself.

I scratched the back of my head as I glared at the phone. Gio was going to have a coronary. I'd love to get his take on this and see if he'd heard anything, but that would have to wait.

Parker would want to know too. But I'd delay that asshole as long as I fucking could.

The last thing I needed was for him to decide we weren't worth the hassle and fuck us over.

Fucking Lake, letting his anger get the fucking best of him. He worried that I was the fuck up since I liked to drink a little too much when on the floor. But this shit?

I could barely raise my gaze off the table in front of us as the new attorney Lake hired argued our bail down. Not that it mattered. We had enough a hundred times over to make it.

If I looked at Lake, I'd strangle him. And he had the audacity to sit beside me with a calmness that he'd learned sometime over the last decade. Where it fucking came from, I had no idea. All I knew was that it was getting under my goddamned nerves.

"These are serious allegations," the judge hummed. He was an old man, bushy brows, and a slight accent like he was from the Midwest. Not the West Virginia twang I'd grown up with.

"And that's all they are. Allegations. The only thing the prosecution has is a handful of grainy images and a few...questionable testimonies." Ms. Chen made her loud opinion known in the tone of her voice.

I glanced up, and the judge flicked a quick glance at the DA before holding a paper closer to his face. "Considering this is their first offense and their commitment to the community, I'm sure you can argue their flight risk potential?" The judge asked, sounding bored.

Ms. Chen nodded. "No one is arguing their access to funds. But the life they've built for themselves is here. There is no reason for them to flee. Especially not based on the weak case against them."

The DA cleared his throat. "Since we're in agreement that they have the funds and the means, we're asking for five-hundred-thousand each."

"Very well. Bail is set for five-hundred-thousand each." His gavel banged against the desk, then I was pushing up out of my chair.

Ms. Chen led the way to the corner and stepped off to the side, in the faux privacy of an alcove. It was a joke though. Between the tall ceilings and the lack of floor and wall coverings, sound traveled at the speed of light.

"I'll get working on this. There are several motions I can file to get the testimonies and videos thrown out. In the meantime, stay away from any contacts who even smell like they could be attached to anything stronger than a parking ticket."

Yeah, right. With the club we ran, that was fucking impossible. But that was what we were going for today. Impossibilities.

She waved a young woman over. "My assistant will help you with the rest of today's process. Later this week, another of my associates will set up a meeting to review the case in greater detail once I've had time to do the proper research." She pulled a grimace like rushing through the back door on a new case wasn't her favorite.

I was right there with her.

She excused herself and I watched her strut to the doors leading to the hallway. She was about a decade older than us, but half our size. Yet her steel balls made her seem ten times that. The woman must have a reputation because men in high-powered suits leaned away from her as she breezed by and she gave them zero attention. She did not give the first fuck about any of them.

Out-processing was a fucking nightmare. But we made it with minimal headaches.

Lake tapped the back of his hand against my chest. "Let's go. One of the guys dropped my car out front."

I glared at him then and walked away. He caught up easily with his long-ass legs, chuckling under his breath.

"Stop getting your panties in a twist. They don't have a leg to stand on, and there's no way the Pescis are going to want to go to trial. They're trying to scare us, we just have to figure out why." Lake shoved his hands in his pockets and he cut his gaze to me.

I shoved the door open and stomped through. I hoped it hit him in the goddamned face.

It didn't, and in seconds he was next to me again.

His car was parked right on the curb. It wasn't allowed but no one had towed it yet, like the guard had been warned not to touch it. And there weren't any paps around.

Thank fuck. Our arrest hadn't gotten out. Even though we weren't as important as Atlas and Kim, we were still constantly hounded as a complete group of attractive and recognizable men. Fortunately, today wasn't a day where we were subjected to the same bullshit attention. Who wanted random fucking Sallys chasing you down the street because they knew what you looked like in underwear.

Fuck. I needed to grab a bottle and head to the club.

The car beeped as Lake walked closer. The power of fancy car technology. No keys were needed.

The seat was hot on my ass as I slid in. Lake closed his door, then we were driving.

"Drop me off at Snatched," I grumbled, strapping the seatbelt.

"No can do. It's probably still shut and I want to get back to Beasty."

"Now you want to get back to Beasty? Now? After you got bailed out on fucking murder charges!" I twisted my shoulders so I faced him. "And somehow, I got dragged into it with you."

Shaking my head, I dropped back against the seat. Our entire lives were centered around that girl. What we could give her, how we could make her ours. Once she was gone, it was like it just ramped up the fire under everyone's asses except for my own.

She fucked us over. Why the hell would we want her back? A tiny part of me could admit that maybe she was better off without us anyway.

And Atlas, he flipped the switch and got even more obsessed after she was gone. I was apparently the only one with enough brain cells to rub together.

Then Lake brought Beasty back, ignoring my strong arguments against it. But it worked out, and just when everything was starting to go our way, when I started to change my thinking, he got us fucking arrested.

I laughed, the bitter sound bouncing around the small cab.

Beasty was at our house. She wanted to be there. We wanted her there. For the first time in fucking ages, it seemed like everything I'd wanted in life was happening. A marble rolling around and around the bowl until it hit the bottom.

I just had to be patient. We all did.

Except now? Beasty had been pissed when I'd caught her watching us being escorted off the property.

We couldn't expect her to wait for us as we worked off a ten to fifteen year murder sentence. Hopefully, Ms. Chen was right and the charges would be thrown out.

"Come on. You were the one who escorted Stevo to the Gray Room. I was just the one who finished the job." His left knee started bouncing as we exited the highway. We only had another fifteen minutes of this torture and he'd already passed the exit for Snatched. I guess he hadn't been kidding when he said no. Apparently, we were both going home.

That was what I got for not arranging my own ride.

"None of us could have guessed that the Pescis would turn us in. If they even did." Lake sent me a quick glance.

"You know their play. They want Beasty. Hell, they probably thought she would have run after we were arrested. Were Gio and his guys even watching the property to make sure they weren't around?" I scrubbed a hand down my face.

It didn't take a rocket scientist to see this was for Beasty. And I'd gotten the same information that Lake had.

Stevo was an idiot they trusted with the wrong stuff. And he was the idiot who believed they wanted something physical. It was nothing that simple.

Information. Contacts. Names.

Nothing Beasty had.

But to the mafia, if they thought there was a chance she posed a threat, she'd have to go.

Lake made a disgusted sound in the back of his throat. "By now they know we have ties that go beyond the fashion industry. If they think we'll give her up, or that she'll go to the cops, we'll have to show them differently."

I was the first one to bend the laws or flat out ignore them when it suited us. But this wasn't the same.

"Yeah? It certainly didn't stop us from getting arrested. And it certainly didn't do us any favors with Beasty. You saw her when we left, didn't you?" I threw my hand out.

"Yeah," he grunted.

"And what, you think Beasty is just going to ignore the fact that we could get thrown in prison if someone has deeper pockets than us?" I shoved my hair out of my eyes.

"She's not going to run. She promised she was going to stay."

He was delusional.

"Is that really you talking right now? Are you that petulant?" I tossed up my hands. Lake was usually the voice of reason when Atlas pulled his shit and Kim withdrew into himself. I was a close second, but sometimes, I leaned on the cards a little too heavy.

I huffed out another laugh, except there was nothing funny.

We rode the rest of the way in silence. When we got to the house, Kim and Atlas both walked out to greet us.

Atlas tugged me against his chest and slammed his mouth down on mine in punishment, like it was my fucking fault I'd gotten arrested. I glared at Lake.

"The club has been cleared to open back up," Kim said quietly. "Even though they think it's the place of his death, they can't prove it and they didn't find the Gray Room. The tech guy also scrubbed the footage so they weren't able to recover anything past the previous twenty-four hours, and there was an unfortunate glitch in the private rooms."

He finished filling us in as we headed inside.

"Where's Beasty?" Lake asked, straining his neck as he searched for her. She wasn't going to pop out from behind the couch. You couldn't tell that from how his gaze kept moving around.

"She's been MIA since you left." Atlas pursed his lips on a scowl. "Kim tried to go talk to her, but she wouldn't open her door."

I gave Lake an 'I told you so look'. He ignored me and headed up the stairs. This ought to be good. I trailed after him, not because I was a masochist, but I really wanted to watch her flay him for being so fucking stupid.

Atlas and Kim apparently felt the same, because they followed behind me.

Lake didn't stop until he reached her door. He pounded on it then stepped back, tipping his ear toward her room as if he was listening for her.

Seconds went by, then her door opened.

My breath caught.

Her dark brown hair piled high on her head gave her an approachable air, even as the scowl on her face screamed back the fuck up.

She was beautiful. Just like this, and she looked even better in our house, and most especially after she'd let Lake and Atlas get close to her.

Beasty narrowed her gaze on Lake, before whipping her attention to me. The heat of her displeasure seared across my chest and a better man would have wilted. But I wasn't a good man, so I quirked a brow at her.

"What were the charges?" she snapped.

I turned to look at Atlas and Kim. Kim ducked his head

and Atlas returned her stare with a fierce one of his own. Ahh, she'd tried to get answers and they'd refused her.

That was why she'd disappeared.

"Murder." Lake didn't even sound like he wanted to soften the words.

"For Stevo." She nodded slowly as she took him in, then turned to me. Of course she did, I was the second idiot to get arrested.

"Did you do it?" she asked, shifting the door back and forth just a tiny bit before she shifted her attention to Lake. Beasty had apparently decided that he would be the one to give her answers.

Fine by me. I wanted no part of that shit show. I just wanted to observe Lake's crash and burn. Beasty's own version of the roadrunner.

"Do you really want the answer to that?" Lake's voice was quiet, yet still lethal. And it was clear, it was also a dare.

Beasty took a step forward, her fingers turning white as she gripped the door.

"What do you think?"

Chapter Three

KIM - AGE 20

The driver was a bad idea.

But I'd been outvoted. They said it would be better to talk to her if we could all sit around her. Where we could all see her. I knew what they were doing though.

You can't lie to a liar.

They had fear of missing out and they wanted a front row seat to how she reacted when we invited her to live with us. Even if they didn't want to be the ones to actually deliver the question.

I had zero room to talk. Not only did public speaking scare me but I was pretty sure I had something between my teeth right now.

Still, Beasty had said yes!

The butterflies taking root inside my heart were new. They flapped their joyful wings so hard, I felt like I was going to pass out. Especially when Beasty sent me sneaky looks every little bit.

The changes in my body were downright embarrassing.

Day after day, I was stripped, prodded, and groomed.

Tens of people, maybe even hundreds had seen my body, touched me, stood close to me and eyed me like a prime steak...Or surveyed me like a useful piece of land.

But each time Beasty's wild hazel eyes landed on me, I flushed so hot, I had to discreetly wipe my brow.

Like now.

She flicked her gaze to me, a mixture of disbelief and happiness radiating from her expression and I had to turn away. The weight of her stare was too powerful.

The driver turned down the road to our apartment building and I let out a sigh of relief.

I'd feel better inside once we weren't stuck in such a confined area. Right?

I just hoped today wasn't the day for a zombie apocalypse. That would add a whole new layer of problems.

Lake leaned forward, readying for the car to stop while shooting a look at us. I shrunk back in the seat.

Joaquin cleared his throat. "The apartment is nice. Real nice. But it's only four bedrooms. Atlas and I are going to bunk together so you can have your own room."

A sniffle came from Beasty, but otherwise, she'd dried up the tears.

I wanted to get another look at her, but I was too damn scared. It was strange this control she had over me just by existing.

The car jolted and Lake moved through the vehicle at a crouch and hopped out. He was always the first to get out of the car. After he decided he would be our bodyguard, he took the job very seriously. Now that Beasty was with us, I could only imagine how that was going to change him.

Atlas was next. When I peered through my lashes, Beasty cast an unsure glance our way, her mouth set in a frown.

She wasn't unhappy. I knew that. I might not have

watched her as much as Atlas, but I recognized that frown. It was her default expression when she was nervous. The shellshock must have worn off.

"Go on," Joaquin nodded toward the door right before Lake ducked his head down to see what was taking so long.

As if he lit a fire under her ass, she scrambled down the seat and kicked her duffle to the opening. Lake easily picked it up and then she was gone.

"You okay?" Joaquin muttered.

"Yeah," I breathed, then went next.

I gulped down a gallon of fresh air. Yes, this helped. Each drag of exhaust scented air cleansed the thick smell of Beasty from my nose. She was sweet, like she'd used some kind of floral soap and I hadn't realized how it had permeated the car until I stepped out.

Now maybe my racing heart would calm down.

The nice thing about having an apartment in the city was that people pretty much left us alone. We weren't really big names, but on some of the tours and shows, people got a little outrageous. Here, they gave us privacy as long as we returned the favor.

I was glad for that.

Otherwise, who knew what I would have done with people stalking us through the lobby.

The graduation at our old school had been bad enough. I hadn't hated school the way Joaquin and Atlas had, but I didn't really have any good memories there either.

Seeing kids crowd us who hadn't given us the time of day before, messed with my head. It was like standing in the Twilight Zone without knowing where the exits were.

Lake moved us through the lobby and into the elevator like nice little ducks. Still, no one spoke. We were silent, and not the good kind.

The lack of conversation was awkward, and uncomfortable. At least for me.

I peeked at Beasty, and she must have felt it too, because she fidgeted with the waist of her dress that was too big.

Finally, I let myself study her. With her facing the elevator doors, she couldn't see me. It was safe, but I didn't dwell on that.

The dress was shoddy. Second hand for sure. The shoes were old and didn't match. I could help Beasty with that. It was the blessing that came from being discovered. I found I had a knack for fashion and I leaned into it.

She'd never again scream backwoods West Virginia.

I'd already started filling her closet with pieces that would make her feel most comfortable. Now that she was here, I could do more.

If only the thought of talking to her didn't threaten to make me shit my pants. I smiled at her back. If I didn't get there on my own, I'd let her cut up Lake's Playboy collection. That would be one heck of a conversation starter.

Once the elevator doors opened, Lake pressed his fingertips to Beasty's stomach and she stiffened.

Did she not like touch either? Something ugly twisted in my stomach. What had happened since we left?

I searched every inch of exposed skin but there were no blemishes, no bruises. Nothing to indicate she was abused. My heart didn't care. Most people were smart enough not to leave physical evidence where the world could see it.

I told them we shouldn't have stayed away for so long.

Lake squeezed his large bulk around her and she relaxed. Oh, she didn't know he always wanted to be the first out of absolutely everything. She'd learn.

Even though my own shoulders dropped, the thoughts that she could have been mistreated while we were making a name for ourselves didn't leave. I should have been thankful. Every kernel of anger took up so much room inside my brain that the...

I didn't know what to call it.

Crush?

So that my crush on Beasty didn't reign supreme.

Lake unlocked the door and went in, checking all the rooms while we stopped in the tiny foyer.

We didn't normally do this. It was because Beasty was with us and she needed protecting. Why she might need protecting stuck like nasty glue in my mind.

I turned my head and clenched my jaw. No, I wouldn't start out this new chapter with Beasty with wild accusations of what did or could have happened. Forcing myself to let it go, I released a long breath, trying to calm my inner thoughts.

What would she think? Would she like it? Was this a place she'd want to stay?

I hoped so. I didn't think we'd be able to let her go now that we were finally letting ourselves have her.

As soon as the door shut behind me, all the anger evaporated. Gone. Completely.

I glanced at Atlas and Joaquin, unable to look at Beasty once again.

Atlas was calm and reserved, like always. That guy, when he was focused, nothing else derailed him. To Joaquin's dismay since we left West Virginia, he was usually focused on riling Joaquin up.

It was a small blessing that Atlas wasn't staring at Beasty outright, but we all knew he was watching. He just wasn't obvious about it.

Then there was Joaquin, scratching the back of his head in a rare show of confusion. Whenever he dealt in cards or numbers, you couldn't knock his confidence, and that had only grown since he started managing our money.

It tripled when he wrestled management away from the agency. He, more than any of us, bucked against authority and he was two steps away from becoming our keeper.

"Okay," Lake said as he came back into the living room. "Kim, why don't you show Beasty around?"

Then like hounds were on their heels, all three of those assholes disappeared without a word or a backward glance at Beasty.

Assholes. It deserved saying twice.

Beasty cleared her throat and I glanced at her, locking my eyes on her cheek.

"If you don't want to–"

"No." I shook my head. "I want to." Except it came out in a whisper. Who would believe that?

Come on, Kim. You're better than that.

I'd charmed the grumpiest designers and most entitled old ladies with stories of my time abroad and my useless study of foxes. This should be nothing.

I shoved my hands in my pockets and faced the open living room and kitchen. It was nice. Modest, but for a city apartment, I'd heard this was luxurious. We didn't have any art or anything on the walls yet. I'd spent all my time on our closets and not the decorating.

It hadn't bothered me before, but with Beasty taking it all in for the first time, I wish I had.

"There's not really anything to it. We have the living room." I motioned to the sectional couch to seat a good seven adults, then to the flat screen TV across from it. "The kitchen, which conveniently has a dinette." The kitchen had a small island and table in the corner. It wasn't big enough– the kitchen–to be considered a dining room, but it was big enough for us. Just the fact that it was ours made it a little slice of paradise. Who cared what we had to do to get it? "It doesn't seat all of us, not with you here, but we're on different schedules a lot of the time anyway. And if we wanted to eat together, I guess there's the living room..." I trailed off and stuck my hand back in my pocket.

Strolling forward, I stopped by the fridge. "Eat anything you want. We pay one of the agency's assistants to order food for us. We're on strict diets since we make money off of our bodies..." Shit, I was bad at this.

When I finally allowed myself to meet Beasty's gaze, she wasn't even looking at me. Her wide stare roamed over every corner of the kitchen. The awe on her face puffed up my chest and I had to admit, it felt good.

"You want to see your room?" Rocking back on my heels, I dropped my gaze to her feet.

"Um. Yeah. I guess that's where Lake dropped my bag."

Oh. Yeah. I forgot about that.

"Yeah," I croaked as I walked around her. She came with me and I slowed my steps so she could stay right next to me.

Soft heat from her body warmed my arm. I was dying to lean over and breathe her in, but I refrained. She'd slap me or think I was some kind of pervert. I'd been around enough of them, for too many reasons that I didn't want her to think the same thing about me.

Still, this was nice. If I could figure out how to talk to her, then this would be as close to heaven as I'd ever get on Earth.

The hallway was short, and we had two bathrooms. One for the suite and one in the hall. I was glad we'd decided to put her in the suite.

All of us sharing a bathroom with Beasty would be more embarrassing than the flush I got every time her gaze heated my back.

Beasty came with us. It was simply wild. I'd never expected it and now it was like a fever dream as I escorted her to her room.

"This is our bathroom. You're going to have your own."

"What?" She stopped and faced me. My heart, that had just started to beat at regular intervals sped up again. "Why would you do that?" Her voice whipped around the enclosed space. Her tone was almost hostile.

"What do you mean?" I scrunched up my brows, let out a slow breath, and locked stares.

Her eyes flicked back and forth between my own and I lost the ability to think.

She was so gorgeous.

No one back in West Virginia had thought so. But all the things that made her different were all the things I loved.

The minor scar across her cheek. The strong brows that the girls had hated because they weren't to trend. Her ears that stuck out just a little too far. And those were only a few.

The best thing about Beasty though? She was a hero. My hero.

I'd worship her until the day I died.

"Why would you all give me the suite? I should be in the smallest bedroom. Using the communal bathroom. I–" Her brows pushed together then up in that puppy-like expression I loved. I wanted to kiss away the wrinkle between them. "I just don't understand, Kim. Why did you all bring me here? I know what Joaquin said in the car but you never even talked to me growing up."

I choked on fear. I couldn't help it. How do you tell the shining light in the darkness of your childhood that you wanted to–ached to–speak to her but you'd been too anxious? That still, after all this time apart, she had the ability to steal my soul from my body with a look, and she didn't even have to try.

I'd hand it over willingly.

28

Instead of telling her the truth, I did what I was so good at.

"We had our reasons, Beasty, but let's not get into that today." I leaned around her to twist the handle on her door, giving her a sweet smile, and praying she didn't see the sweat on my forehead.

This close to her, I finally got another whiff of her floral scent. Outside of that, she was just Beasty, and it was the best smell I'd ever encountered.

"This is your room. We want to do this. You shouldn't have to share a bathroom with four guys. Don't argue with us, okay, Beasty?" The pleading in my voice must have gotten to her because she collected herself and nodded.

"Okay."

"We're going to order takeout from this fancy French place down the road. It's Lake's favorite. Mine too, really. I'll come get you when it's here?"

She shook her head as she passed me, not stopping until she was fully in the room. I was too much of a coward to follow her. She could figure it out anyway. It was pretty much just a bed, dresser, and standard bathroom. It wasn't anything like a luxury suite.

Although when we first moved in, it had been the ultimate sign we had made it. We'd all drawn straws to see who got it, and Joaquin won in the end.

Shocker.

"I just. I'm so excited to be here. Confused. But excited. I—I need a little bit of time to myself. I'm used to that, you know. Being alone. And today..."

"Today was a lot." I understood. It was like our drive out of West Virginia. Our first flight. When everything changed and you could only hold on and see where the bus took you.

29

"I'm not one for fancy food either. I like easy stuff. Simple."

Only because you've never had anything else.

But I didn't say that.

"I'll come out in a little while. Thank you...For everything." Then she shut the door.

I stared at the plain white wood for way too long.

We had everything we wanted, but she was still so far away.

Chapter Four

ATLAS - PRESENT DAY

I slammed the cabinet shut and would have smashed the mug into the counter if it wouldn't shatter. My goal wasn't to break it, it was only to get a little aggression out. I needed a release.

It wasn't the one I wanted, but that was what was available to me unless I wanted to hit the gym with Lake.

"Did you speak to Parker?" Joaquin asked Lake as he slid eggs onto his plate. He'd already made almost a dozen for the rest of us, including Beasty who hadn't come down yet.

The others didn't think she would.

But I knew different.

She would, because if nothing else, she was curious.

"No," Lake grunted.

I missed whatever he muttered under his breath as I poured hot water in my mug and grabbed a tea bag. I loved coffee, but tea was my preferred drink when I had a little too much anger swirling inside me.

Coffee only added to my rage, giving me a jittery sort of nervousness.

Tea leveled me out, letting me focus all my energy on whatever outlet I desired with a calmer and steadier head.

When I turned around, all three of my favorite assholes were seated at the table. Beasty's plate was even placed between Kim and Lake.

We didn't really have assigned seats, but since Beasty came back, they stuck to the same spots in case it made her feel more comfortable. Just like them, I claimed my place next to Joaquin.

She didn't need comfort. She needed to be pushed.

"I think he wants to avoid phone calls with us while our lines are most likely tapped," Lake finished as he stretched back in his chair.

"Smart of him," Kim added snidely as he stabbed his breakfast.

"Any issues on the news about the club having an unplanned closure?" I flicked a glance at Lake. He was our news man. Constantly worried about what would pop up, what wouldn't.

It was a terrible job and I was glad he was the one to do it and not me.

His nose crinkled like he got a giant whiff of shit. "The contrary. It looks like today we'll have record breaking numbers, which is saying something since our grand opening was a blow out. While our arrests weren't public, some kind of word has gotten out, and now we're even more exotic to the general public, and I think the celebs are salivating for a chance at a dangerous thrill. Like they don't know there are criminals in the private rooms." He rolled his eyes.

Kim set his fork down, tucked his hands in his lap and stared at his plate. After a minute, he glanced up, meeting each of our gazes. "What are we going to do about Beasty? If we're not careful, she'll get scared away by our fame."

Not our fame, but Kim wasn't wrong.

How Beasty handled the truth yesterday...

I didn't like it. She acted like she was some uptight priss who didn't understand why we did the things we did.

"She's not leaving." Lake sounded damn sure.

Joaquin raised a brow giving him that sexy, cocky look I loved so much. "You're sure? Because at this point, the only thing I'm sure about is that you're a damn idiot."

Grinding his jaw, Lake sat forward, ready to lay into Joaquin, but Beasty prowled into the kitchen stealing all of our attention.

This morning she was wearing a pair of old ratty jeans and a crop top. Nothing that we'd supplied her closet with. Her hair was a wild, tousled mess.

I couldn't look away from her if I tried.

"Good morning, Beasty." Lake acted like he was some refined pompous ass, not the guy who literally beheaded someone for doing nothing more than sticking his dick in Beasty.

I laughed under my breath. Sure, Kim, or Joaquin could argue that it was because he placed Beasty in danger. But we all knew better. It didn't matter who it was. If they touched her, Lake would kill them. And if he didn't, we would.

Since the day she walked up to that godforsaken chain-link fence, she was ours. She would always be ours no matter what she did or said or wanted.

If Beasty didn't have such a hold on my attention, I would have glanced at Kim. He could come across as sweet, but our Kim had a dark side.

Our feisty girl didn't say one word back. With her face set in harsh lines, she moved around the kitchen making coffee like she owned the place. It was an aphrodisiac to see her so comfortable here. One I didn't need, but loved none-theless.

"Beasty," I called.

She ignored me.

Of course, she did. Why would we expect anything different? When she asked for the truth yesterday, Lake gave it to her. To Joaquin's horror, he told her what he had done to that asshat.

Taking it all in, she watched him with a blank stare until he finished, then she shut her door in our faces, leaving us in the hallway like we were gum under her shoes that she couldn't even be bothered to scrape off.

Shit, I had to stop replaying that memory in my head or I was going to do something to piss the guys off. I gritted my teeth so hard, they were going to crack.

"Beasty," I called again, twisting in my seat.

Her shoulders stiffened, but that was the only sign that she heard me.

No, no. That wouldn't do at all.

The tension in my jaw radiated out through my body as I pushed myself up from my chair. Beasty was ours, and she wasn't going to leave.

I didn't give a fuck if she liked what Lake did or not. What I did care about was being ignored, discarded like I didn't matter. That wasn't the game I played with Beasty and I found I didn't like her version at fuck all.

"Atlas," Joaquin warned under his breath.

That didn't deserve an answer either.

I moved around the island on silent feet until I reached Beasty. She was facing the corner, spooning sugar into her coffee. When my shadow fell over her, she froze.

This was better.

I could work with this reaction. Any fucking reaction really, as long as she didn't pretend I didn't exist.

Pressing my palms against the counter on either side of her, I leaned in and gently rubbed my cheek against her hair. "You're not ignoring me, are you, Beasty?" I breathed out, continuing the short movements.

The last two fingers of her left hand rapidly tapped against the counter before she froze the movement.

"What do you want me to say, Atlas?" Her words were bland while her tone was angry. Beasty flattened her hands against the counter.

So slender and pale compared to mine. I covered her hands, threading my fingers between hers, locking her in place.

"How about start with a good morning? You grew up the same way we did. Doesn't it hurt not to be acknowledged?"

"Wrong thing to say..." I heard from behind me. It was a muffled whisper but I'd bet it was Kim. It didn't matter. I had Beasty right where I wanted her.

I stumbled back as Beasty shoved away from the counter. I caught my balance on the island behind me as she spun around, loose pieces of her hair flying in a halo around her.

She was pissed and the only thing it did was make me want to fuck her mouth. It would be a better use than whatever bullshit she was about to spew.

"Yes, Atlas. I know all about the loneliness of not being acknowledged. You know why?" She took a step forward and jabbed a finger at me, then at the guys. "Because you four did it to me my entire fucking life!" Beasty screamed.

Her chest rose and fell in exaggerated movements as a flush started to climb up her neck.

I blinked, then glared. I explained this to her. Our entire childhoods we thought she was too good for us. That we didn't deserve to breathe the same air. That wasn't us ignoring her outright. Hell, she was my entire fucking reason for existing.

Before I could argue my point, she kept going.

"All I ever wanted was to be with you four." Her voice dropped low, and somehow, her calmness after such an outburst seemed louder. "That was it. I wanted to be your friend. Hoped to be your lover. To *matter*." Beasty's voice cracked.

She brushed strands of hair out of her face with the back of her hand. "I know now that I mattered. But it doesn't change the fact that you hurt me. That you four ignored me over and over again because you were all too much of cowards to talk to me. But you know what else hurts?"

Beasty moved another step closer.

Her hands flew toward my chest and I caught her wrists, yanking her into me.

"That you all are fucking low-life criminals," she snarled.

At first her words didn't register. Then a blistering heat rushed from the top of my head, encompassing my body like a rush of lava. I shoved her away. "What the fuck does that mean?" I spewed.

One of the guys came up to my back.

Lake. Without turning, I could feel him breathing next to my ear.

She glared at me, but when her gaze shifted to Lake, the anger cooled to something I couldn't pin my finger on.

Shaking her head, she backed up a step, then another before she turned and raced from the room.

Kim was halfway through the door when he halted. His shoulders rose with each shaky inhale.

"Fucking bitch," I muttered, but I didn't mean it. As

much as I hated knowing Beasty wasn't who I thought she was, I loved seeing her as human. Approachable. Reachable.

"Good going, Atlas," Joaquin grunted as he brushed by Kim.

After one pained glance back, Kim left too, leaving me with Lake.

"I'm not letting her run away this time. The last time was a mistake," Lake said over his shoulder as he moved to make another cup of coffee.

The heat in my chest was leveling off, melting into something pricklier, like an anticipation under my skin that was biding its time. One last look at Lake, then I left, searching for Beasty.

I took the stairs two at a time.

What did Beasty think would happen? That we'd let her storm off? Sulk in her feelings?

The old compulsion reared its head and I didn't even try to ignore it. When we'd been kids, it had been impossible to think of anything else but Beasty.

Was she okay? Did she need us?

Even when I knew she was perfectly safe, I had these thoughts swirling around in my head.

What was she doing? Who was she talking to? What would it be like just to be close enough to smell her.

She never talked to people much. She had been a loner. Studying the world with bright, judging eyes, but still oblivious to so much around her.

Beasty had never even suspected I'd been watching her. I didn't give a damn what she said, she had no idea how many times I was there watching.

The door to her bedroom was shut. Without knocking, I twisted the doorknob and eased it open. The hinges were perfectly oiled, allowing me to enter silently.

I paused, waiting for some kind of noise to let me know where she was in the room. There was nothing but silence.

Then, when I stepped inside, I paused.

Sunlight streamed through the windows, making the dove gray and navy colors bright and enchanting. Beasty's favorite colors.

Kim had done a good job working with the decorator.

The bathroom door was open and no sounds were coming from inside. Beasty hadn't come to her room.

My first instinct was to go and find her but the stronger urge was to be in her space. That she wasn't here made it sweeter. How many times had I watched her as a kid, wondering what her room looked like?

I'd only barely restrained myself from staring into her window to see for myself. If I'd been caught doing that, I'd have been arrested and sent to juvie. There were too many cards stacked against me not to get harsh punishment for that particular crime.

Joaquin and the others would have been pissed. I couldn't do that to them, so that was the one limit I'd given myself.

But now, while Beasty was being such a little brat, I reveled in the privacy of her space.

I hoped she enjoyed her time away, because she'd never get that again.

My footsteps hardly made any noise as I padded toward her dresser. Her ratty old napsack sat next to it, half open with a T-shirt spilling out.

I pulled open the drawers. Artfully seductive lingerie was arranged in the top drawer, and it seemed as if she'd touched none of it. Then I opened the second drawer, and the third.

Beasty wasn't wearing anything we'd bought for her.

Well, outside of the outfits she wore to Snatched. Beasty probably only did that to avoid standing out.

As much as she put on a front about being who she was, there was a part of her that wanted to fit in. Maybe to blend in.

She may not have been who I thought she was, but I still knew her. I'd seen the longing in her eyes as she watched friend groups laugh and cut up together. I'd witnessed the uncertainty on her face when she'd look at what others wore and then glance down at herself.

The girl was gorgeous in an unconventional way. She'd never fit in. And she shouldn't want to. She should want to put all those assholes in their places and be who she was. Unapologetically.

I touched the edge of her pillow, shifted it to the side, and froze. I recognized that scarf.

"What the hell do you think you're doing?" Beasty snapped from the door.

Glancing over my shoulder, I smirked at the irate glimmer in her eyes. "You want me to answer that?"

"Stop being a creep and get out of my space."

What a fucking bitch. So nasty with her insults. A ball of tension in my chest released. Each time Beasty did something I didn't expect, she got closer and closer to our level.

She wasn't perfect. She could be crass and hurtful with her words. And I wanted to hurt her right back.

"You're breaking your promise, Beasty." I turned but noticed her pet case. I hadn't made it that far into the room yet. Quilliam was sleeping already and nowhere to be seen.

"You can shove your promises up your ass. I never made any." She stomped past me and rearranged her pillow to cover the scarf. When she was satisfied, she crouched by Quilliam's enclosure and ran her finger softly over the clear plastic.

"You said you wanted to stay, and you'd do anything to make me happy to prove it. Did you forget?" I goaded her on purpose. Beasty was proving to be just as much fun to rile as Joaquin. Maybe even more fun because I'd thirsted after this girl my entire life.

She choked and it put delicious images in my head. "I think Lake's and Joaquin's arrests wipe out any leverage you had." There was a note in her voice like she didn't think we deserved it anymore.

Grinding my teeth, I moved behind her, and ran my hand over the back of her head before cupping the nape of her neck. She tensed, but didn't shrug me off.

Bending over, I brushed my lips across the shell of her ear as I slid my thumb up and down. "You should still want to make me happy. But don't worry. You don't want us to hide, and I have every intention of showing you who we really are. It will be more enjoyable for you, if you want to make me happy."

Then I walked out, leaving a huffing Beasty on the floor.

R egardless of how I couldn't make any sense of my emotions, I trailed behind Lake into Snatched. He had so much confidence hanging from his shoulders like a long-ass cloak, I almost tripped on it.

Kim was next to me and each time he snuck a glance my way, my heart felt like it was trying to escape through my throat. He was silent, but he'd opened his mouth half a dozen times, then ended up shutting it.

Whatever he was feeling, he couldn't figure out how to express it.

Well, pot and kettle, because I had so many thoughts, and so much anger, bubbling just under the surface. Every time I tried to think of how to tell them exactly what I thought, it was like too many words were rushing to my mouth at the same time, and I just...couldn't.

Joaquin and Atlas followed behind us. They were several steps back, but their presence was so suffocating, I was choking from their gazes drilling into the back of my head.

The taste in my mouth was worse than ass.

Catcalls and whistles were thrown our way from the people standing in the queue. The guys ignored it.

I'd tried to search the news to see if anything about their arrest had gotten out, but nothing. It was like it never happened. They didn't act as if this was anything other than an inconvenience they'd already forgotten.

The bouncer nodded, and an attendant opened the door for us all to glide through. People treated them, and me by extension, like royalty and it was another needle on the stack of things that seemed surreal about being here.

I leaned toward Kim. "I'm heading to the bathroom," I shouted over the thumping music in the main club room.

He nodded, his lids down over his worried eyes as he met my stare. After a glance at Joaquin and Atlas, he followed me.

"I can go to the bathroom by my damn self," I snapped.

Kim flinched.

Shit, I rubbed my forehead as I stepped into the hall-way. There were less people here. The music was muted and outside of the creepy ass attendants lining the wall, it was like we had the space to ourselves.

Not waiting for him to say anything, and not giving myself an opportunity to apologize, I sped to the restroom and hit the door with enough force that it slammed against the wall before banging shut.

Checking the stalls, I let out a breath when I confirmed they were all empty.

"What are you doing, Beasty?" I said to myself as I braced my hands on the counter.

The lighting was low to set some kind of seductive mood. The air fresheners were just strong enough not to be overwhelming. Then there was me. Dressed up in another outfit from the closet.

Wide-legged, black slacks and a silky, white blouse I'd never wear. But I couldn't wear my ratty jeans and tees here.

Circles were almost noticeable under my eyes, but I'd applied a tiny bit of concealer.

Who was I?

Was I the woman who stood firm on what I didn't want my life to be? Who I didn't want in my life?

Well, that was fucking rich considering I'd let Stevo slide right in on a boogie board. He was the biggest mistake I'd ever made. To add insult to injury, I hadn't cared about him and he'd fucked my life up.

I swallowed hard.

Only for Lake to kill him. There wasn't even a bit of remorse there.

Not able to stand the sight of myself anymore, I left the bathroom. I hadn't needed to go, I just wanted a second to myself.

I'd always been alone. Always. And now with the boys trying to constantly force their way into my space, I couldn't breathe.

It wasn't that I wanted to be alone. I didn't. But how do you change everything you've ever been taught by life?

Kim pushed away from the wall and stepped closer to me. Locks of jet black hair fell into his face, giving him a boyish look. That and the large, puppy eyes he sported.

"Everyone is in the Gold Room." His voice was soft and angelic as he looked down, his dark lashes fanned out to hide his eyes.

I nodded, but he didn't see the movement.

The other night, I'd told them I wanted to know the real them. All of them.

The Gold Room, the gambling, that was part of it. I just didn't know if I wanted to keep going on this path.

"Let's go."

He glanced up, seemingly surprised that I'd agreed to go so easily.

Me too.

Hesitantly, he raised his arm, and I slid my hand into the crook of his elbow.

"I'm glad you're still here," he said so quietly, I almost couldn't hear him.

Releasing a long sigh, I kept my gaze trained straight ahead. What did I even say to that?

"Just talk to me, Beasty. Please?" he begged, tugging me to a stop just outside the Gold Room.

"About what? Whenever I do try to speak to you or them, no one listens."

Kim sucked in a deep breath. "We do listen."

"I can't." I shook my head and closed the distance to the door. I couldn't do this with him at the club. I wasn't even sure why I was here. "Look, I'm grateful for what you all are trying to do for me but... No, you know what? Let's talk about this later. Okay?" I added softly, looking over my shoulder to check on him as the attendant opened the door.

"Okay." He twisted his lips to the side and nodded for me to enter the Gold Room.

The noise coming out of the room was different from the others. Already this had a different vibe than the rooms with performances or dancing.

It was classy. And boujee.

Men laughed and women giggled. There was a tinkling of glasses sounding around the room that made this place feel...vibrant. Old school.

Even though the boys and I were dressed how we normally would for Snatched. Yeah, okay, they were dressed how they normally would, most of the other people–patrons?–were dressed like they were stepping out of the twenties.

Kim slid his fingers through mine when he stopped next to me. He froze, glancing down at our entwined hands.

My heart hurt for him. For me too, really.

Why couldn't we just live a quiet life meant for just us? Me and them.

No fame, no riches, for damn sure no murder charges. But they wanted something completely different than me and we were left standing on opposite sides of a chasm.

Giving Kim's hand a squeeze, I waited for him to look up. It took effort. He acted as if it was almost physically impossible to pull his gaze away from our hands.

When his eyes met mine, the world stopped. Only colors existed around us and the sounds died down to a muted buzz.

Kim's beautiful tilted eyes were so sharp in their sadness. I hated the way he tucked his chin like he expected me to pull away. To *push* him away.

God, why was this so hard?

I wanted them, didn't I?

I told them I wanted the real them. Right?

Something sharp, like an elbow, knocked into my back and I stumbled forward. Gasping, I tried to hold myself steady by using Kim's hold as leverage, but I tripped over my own damned feet.

"Watch yourself," Kim barked.

I would have been shocked if it wasn't for Joaquin pulling me into his chest and glaring over my shoulder. "He absolutely needs to watch himself or he's going to find himself on the banned list." Joaquin's voice was low, yet full of so much irritation and anger I almost flinched.

"Hey, now. That's uncalled for. I assure you, I lost my footing."

Twisting my head, I just caught which man was speaking. There were three of them. All tall, fashion-forward, and gorgeous. Exactly the kind of men I'd imagined the boys to be running with.

The man who had been speaking stood in the center of the trio, a little slimmer, his expression a bit more pinched. His gaze swept from Joaquin, then behind us, before landing on me.

"Funny, I thought Kim would be the one." His nose scrunched like he smelled shit.

Kim straightened up while staring at the man dead-on. But it was Joaquin who made the next sound.

He chuckled. It wasn't the funny *ha ha* kind of sound. More like, *you've got to be out of your goddamned mind* noise.

"Alfie, this is all beneath you. We left the fashion business. You can thank Lake for even allowing you on the property. What's your game by shoving Beasty?" he asked as if he really cared. But when I glanced up, a dangerous glint in his eyes said that maybe he didn't.

That this was about to be a whole different game to him.

Chills raced down my spine and arms as prickly tingles rolled up the sides of my face.

Alfie curled his top lip as he glanced at his friends on either side of him. Actually, they didn't look like friends so much as stone-faced bodyguards. I narrowed my eyes on him, as I twisted in Joaquin's arms.

Alfie did look familiar. I couldn't place him though.

"It was an accident. Don't worry, it won't happen again." He didn't spare me a glance, although he let his gaze trail over both Joaquin and who I assumed to be Atlas.

I snuck a glance over my shoulder. Yup, Atlas was standing so close to Joaquin, Atlas' chest touched his shoulder.

Joaquin's fingers twitched on my sides. "Now wait. You wanted our attention, right? I'm sure if I replayed the footage, your misstep wouldn't be a mistake at all." Alfie stiffened and his guards remained impassive. "You have it now. How about a wager?"

"I don't bet." Alfie frowned.

"Anymore," Kim supplied.

There was so much history and undertones, it was driving me insane. Like an itch inside my brain I couldn't reach. If they just said the right phrase, or gave the right look, I could figure out why this was such a scene.

The man had elbowed me, and I was pissed, but I wouldn't fight over it. Not without more provocation. There was no point. It was a waste of energy.

But for whatever reason, Joaquin was goading Alfie when he was trying to back down.

"Joaquin, it's not a big deal," I mumbled under my breath.

"What was that?" he asked by my ear, rubbing his cheek along my hair. What the hell was he doing? I glanced around the room, my gaze darting from one person to the next.

Joaquin was drawing a crowd and with all three of them clustered around me, facing off with this guy Alfie, people were literally pulling from their games to walk over.

I turned so he could hear me better. "It's not a big deal."

"That's where you're wrong, Beasty. It's a very big deal. And Alfie here has a gambling problem. Don't you, Alfie?" He stepped back and glanced at the tables.

"I beg your biggest fucking pardon," Alfie spat, his shoulders bunching up.

"Come on, Alfie. It's not like we don't know you." Atlas stepped up beside me, pocketing his hands.

They knew him? That comment...hurt.

Why did that one comment hurt? It didn't make sense.

Except they had some kind of history and I didn't have any of it. Wasn't *part* of any of it.

"And you're forgetting, I *know* you. If anyone has a problem, it's Joaquin." Alfie waved a hand toward Joaquin. "He—"

"We're not talking about Joaquin." Lake circled around behind him. The crowd pushed back, giving him a wide berth.

A woman off to the side reached into her clutch. The flash of her phone was just visible when Lake snapped and pointed at her. "Don't even think about it. You know what?" He put two fingers in his mouth and gave a sharp whistle. "Henry! Get this bitch out of here." Then to the crowd he said, "You're privileged enough to be in one of the exclusive private rooms of Snatched. These rooms are by invitation only. If I even get a whiff that you might be trying to record footage or any other items on the NDA you signed, we'll boot you out and place you on the banned list."

"What? I wasn't going to do that!" The woman spun away from the security guard, but he caught her and started carting her out.

"Now," Joaquin called as he strolled over to a table with different colored circles and a spinning wheel on the end. "How about Roulette?" He tapped two fingers on the wooden edge and raised one brow in a dare.

Alfie yanked at the bottom of his jacket and rolled his neck, seeming to pull confidence from the movements. Then he stomped over. "Fine, you want me to do this. Fuck it. I'll play, then I'm out of here."

One of the guards at his back pulled a tray of chips out of who the fuck knew where, and handed it to him. It wasn't the largest tray I'd ever seen, but it was decently full.

But shit, what did I know? Atlas placed a hand on the small of my back, shuffling me closer. Somehow, I'd gotten left behind as everyone else circled the table.

I'd been so caught up in watching Alfie, I'd spaced out for a minute. Stupid of me. I knew what could happen when you got lost in your head.

Atlas kept pushing me forward until I was next to Joaquin, and the table pressed into my stomach. He settled his hands on my hips and his chin on top of my head.

The dull roar of conversation was gone now as the attendant prepped the table.

The noise disappeared so completely, it made it impossible to ignore the rising beat of my heart.

Atlas' touch, the tension Joaquin was purposefully building, the way the boys arranged themselves around me...After the arrests, it was too much.

They acted as if there was nothing wrong. They were criminals and they embraced it.

These boys, the ones I'd idolized as a kid, were bad men, and they were going to pull me down, just like Books warned.

Breathing came harder and the edges of my vision started to waver, but I discreetly sucked in air. Then again, and again, until I wasn't going to make myself pass out.

"How's your career going?" Joaquin asked idly as he made his bet, sliding his chips onto a number on the board. At least, I thought that was what he was doing.

"Fine," Alfie bit out as he picked a different number. His gaze landed on me for two seconds. His top lip pulled back again, then he locked his gaze on the attendant.

This man was hurt. He was a grade-A asshole, but he was hurt too. Knocking me over? That was probably because he believed he'd been wronged by Atlas and Joaquin somehow.

"This wasn't in my plans for tonight, but I can't say turning you into my bitch is a bad ending." Joaquin shrugged as something mean glinted in his dark eyes.

Alfie pulled a disgusted face and reared his head back before collecting himself.

I started to twist around to check Atlas' expression, but his hold on my hips tightened and his head didn't move. In fact, he put more pressure on my head to dissuade me from moving, and one hand slid around to my lower stomach possessively.

My heart skipped a beat, but I didn't do a damned thing about it.

Causing a public scene in their club wouldn't do me any favors. I'd save that for later.

Instead, I focused on the scene in front of me. It was like a train crash I couldn't turn away from.

Joaquin and Alfie traded barbs as the attendant spun the wheel with the little ball bouncing around, searching for the place it would land.

Alfie grew more and more uncomfortable as Joaquin seemed to grow bigger with each snide remark and cutting glance.

When the ball landed, cheers exploded and I winced.

Joaquin smirked at Alfie, the devil in his eyes.

All the blood drained from Alfie's face as the attendant used a squeegee like stick to pull all the chips away. He'd bet his entire tray like a dumbass.

"No, no! I hadn't meant to put all my money on that. You distracted me on purpose, you fucking motherfucker." Alfie took a swing at Joaquin, but his guard caught him around the middle and pulled him back. Joaquin leaned away and avoided Aflie's fist by a good two inches.

"What do you think Dan is going to ask for when you

crawl to him, needing money?" Joaquin asked quietly as he stepped toward Alfie.

The guard still had Aflie in a vice grip, grunting as Alfie struggled to get out of his hold.

"You think this is funny! Is the idea of my cold dead body in the back of an alley exciting to you?" Alfie yelled, his eyes bugging out. "You toyed with me! Both of you fuckers did! You're evil! Exactly what everyone in the industry says you are!"

Atlas chuckled low and dark, the vibrations tickling my back. "We didn't toy with you. We fucked you. It wasn't special. Definitely nothing for us to consider a second round. If you expected more, that's your own issue."

He pulled me deeper into his body, unaware of the fury building inside me.

They slept with Alfie and from the sounds of it, together. That hurt as much as it burned the back of my mouth.

Fucking ridiculous emotions that were good for nothing. The guys weren't mine. What they did before didn't have anything to do with us now.

But more than any impossible infidelity, was the cruelty.

They were being cruel. Needlessly cruel. And for what? Because he shoved me?

"If you ever want to step foot back in this establishment, get him out of here." Joaquin nodded at the bodyguards with Alfie.

One nodded his head and the man still holding Alfie just grunted as he started to turn.

"You're sick, Joaquin! You're the one with the gambling addiction! You're the one who's going to run your friends into the ground!" Alfie was trying so hard to get the last word in.

Joaquin smiled at the guards' backs as they headed toward the exit. "It's only a sickness if you lose. Remember that, Alfie."

When he was gone, people lingered for a few minutes. Men straightened their shoulders, affecting smarmy expressions, as if they were waiting for one of the boys' attention so they could be part of the club.

Women squeezed their arms together to push their boobs up and sucked in their stomachs as they sauntered by.

Activity resumed as people moved back to their tables, yet I was frozen. Atlas didn't even seem to notice as he maneuvered us so his ass was to the table and we faced the room.

Joaquin slowly approached us, but his gaze was on Lake.

"You know you took his life savings, right?" Lake asked with an air of indifference. "He was here to get enough money to save his house from foreclosure."

Joaquin shrugged and Kim stepped up next to him, completing their circle with me in the middle.

"If he has to go to Dan..." Kim shot a glance at the door, then looked back at Joaquin.

"Dan isn't Gates," Joaquin growled as he bared his teeth in a nasty snarl. "Don't act like I did that to him. He made the decision to come here. There are three other casinos he could go to, or he could have gone to Vegas. He was the one who decided to be petty and knock over Beasty."

Each of them exchanged glances with various expressions ranging from anger, indifference, and uncertainty. The uncertainty was only on Kim, but I had a feeling that was just because of his comment about the man who held them.

The boys were cruel, maybe a little too cunning, and unremorseful.

I didn't know these men at all. Who I thought they were? Those boys didn't exist.

And they sure as hell didn't know me. We didn't have the same beliefs, and we didn't fit into each others' lives. Tonight just made me feel even further on the outside.

Which begged the question, what were we doing?

Chapter Six

LAKE - AGE 22

I'd never experienced anything so amazing and torturous at the same time.

"Do you want any coffee?" Kim asked Beasty in the cramped kitchen as he watched her from under his lashes. He was so fucking bashful with her.

That in itself was wild. The last few years, he'd really come out of his shell.

I wouldn't call him a social butterfly. He still retained that aloofness that was part of the drawl in the model world, but when he wanted to be, he was charming. Resourceful.

He'd learned how to turn it on at the drop of a hat.

Yet here he was, stumbling over his words and whispering to her like she'd hear what he said from across the kitchen.

Joaquin came around the corner and headed straight for the coffee machine. He shot a blank look at Beasty, opened his mouth, then thought better of it as he shook his head and fled without his coffee.

Atlas brushed by him as he was on his way out.

His steps slowed when he caught sight of Beasty standing at the sink, looking out the window.

She'd been here a week and we'd barely talked to her. She seemed to be excited to be here, but quiet. Real fucking quiet.

And she was also freakily clean. Cleaning up after herself and us. Every time Joaquin left a glass on the coffee table, it was gone before I'd even seen her breeze through. Like she had some kind of radar on our movements.

Impressive since Atlas grabbed the coffee that Joaquin had started before scooting out of the kitchen like his ass was on fire.

Those two did that. When they thought no one would notice, they did little things for each other. Sometimes for us, but not nearly as much as they did for each other.

Atlas walked to the table with thick, sludging steps. I had to smirk. He was being hella quiet. Peeking over his shoulder, he glanced at Beasty, who was still staring wistfully out at the ugly-ass building across the street.

He sat his ass down and watched her while pretending to study his coffee.

"We need to leave at ten," I said to Kim as I gripped the edge of the counter I leaned on.

Today, Kim had a job with Valencia, an Italian designer here for a low-key show. The last few years, Kim—and Atlas—had gained such popularity, they didn't have to do the small shows anymore. But Valencia was a big designer, and it was in the best interest of his career to take the job.

She also held a lot of sway in the industry and this was our bread and butter.

Kim nodded and turned his body toward Beasty without looking at her. It was cute as shit.

He was taking his time coming out of his comfort zone

where she was concerned. As infuriating as the slow pace was, I understood it. Hell, we all did.

We were all living vicariously through him.

"Beasty, do you want to come with us? See what I do?"

She startled, like she hadn't expected anyone to talk to her. Turning her head, she glanced at him, then me. I wasn't smiling when she turned to me.

Shit, I had a terrible dick face expression. I was going to scare her or piss her off.

Without blinking an eye, she glazed right over me to Atlas, then returned her attention back to Kim. That stung.

"Are you sure?" She chewed on her thumbnail, or what was left of it. Was she a nail biter? I didn't think she was.

Atlas had never said anything about it.

"Yes," Kim breathed, a giant smile sliding over his face. "I want you to see what I do. Maybe we can dress you up while we're there too, you know–"

"No." I didn't shout, but that was a firm *hell* no. They stripped the models down in the same room together and touched everything. A model had no secrets when they were being dressed.

They weren't getting within a foot of Beasty.

"I didn't mean that they would dress her. *I* would." His voice was stiff. Kim was miffed.

"Not a good idea." I held his stare and at first, I thought he was going to argue, but he relented.

His body softened and he canted himself toward Beasty. "I'd love for you to watch me work."

A soft smile broke over her face. "Sure. When should I be ready?"

"At ten," Kim repeated what I'd said minutes earlier.

She dipped out of the kitchen as Atlas finally faced her head on, even if it was her retreating back. We didn't say anything. Just exchanged glances like how the hell did we end up here? And not really caring because this was everything we wanted.

This was a fucking bad idea.

I ground my teeth as I stood off to the side with my arms crossed. Beasty was next to me, and if I thought she would be okay with it, I'd shove her behind me.

Valencia was a rod-thin woman over six feet tall, with the personality of a raging prickle bush. But she knew her fashion. And Kim loved her. Except today.

Every time he looked to Beasty, whether trying to speak to her or just to check on her, Valencia would go off on some kind of jealous spree.

The woman was old enough to be his mother and looked it too. With all the money she had, she chose to age gracefully, something that was controversial in the fashion industry. Yet she did not like that he brought a friend along.

"I can have Joaquin come pick you up," I murmured to Beasty without taking my gaze off of Kim.

I really didn't fucking like this. One of the other guys would have to come with me if she came to any more shows. The models and staff were eyeing her up like fresh meat, and that wasn't going to happen.

It didn't help that Beasty fit the model image.

Tall, slender. She wasn't conventionally beautiful. Not according to Hollywood's standards, but she was interesting. For some designers, that was like free cocaine on the buffet. They couldn't resist.

She also gave off a *'fuck you'* vibe. It was fake.

I knew it. Kim knew it. It was why he was trying so hard to bring her in and make her feel comfortable.

"No," Beasty snapped. Then gave me wide eyes. "I'm sorry, that was too much. I want to stay and watch. And I don't want to put anyone out."

"Beasty–" Kim called.

"I think these pants need to be pinned here." Valencia's heavily accented voice grated over my nerves. She stood to the side so we had a full view of her fingertips gliding over his ass.

Kim stiffened and his gaze became far off. I doubted anyone else realized what was going on or that there was even a problem, but I knew.

"You're crossing a line," I barked at Valencia. I didn't give a fuck if she thought she was a big fucking deal or not.

Beasty jumped at the crack of my voice but Kim was still dazing off into space.

The old hag laughed and the throaty noise grated over my ears. "Kim, your bodyguard thinks he has some power here." She straightened to her full height, and with her four-inch heels, she was taller than Kim. Almost my height.

Squaring her shoulders, she faced me. "This is my show. Either Kim follows my rules or he doesn't work for my brand. If you don't want to be the reason he loses work, then I'd suggest you do what guards do and pretend you don't exist."

Turning back to Kim, a deep frown tugged on the side of Valencia's lips.

When Kim looked back at me, there was finally some life there. Fire. That was better than whatever the hell he'd been exhibiting for the last hour.

"Valencia, you know I'm such a fan of your work. I've been following your career since before I entered middle school," he purred and she melted. It was missing his usual charm, but either she didn't notice or just liked the attention no matter how it came.

She snapped her fingers for one of her underlings, and the girl raced over with a cord draped around her neck with tons of extra pins. She handed a couple to Valencia.

Most of the color had drained out of Kim's face, but with his soft smile pinned in place, Valencia ignored it. She was happy to have his full attention again.

Kim met my gaze and shook his head. He was trying to say it wasn't worth the scene.

Old angers bubbled up under my skin. The kind that hadn't been there since Atlas and Kim first entered the industry, and we had to go through a monumental learning curve to see if they could do it.

A maintenance man passed through with a ladder and knocked the tail end into Beasty and she stumbled back into the wall.

"Watch yourself!" I yelled at the man, catching the end of the ladder before he could turn and take out a whole row of people. Glancing back, I made sure Beasty was okay. She was righting herself and didn't seem bothered. But I was, this guy was an idiot.

"Sorry! I didn't see her," he muttered and ducked his head, scramming before I decided to land my fist in his face.

Twisting my head to the right then left to crack it, I tried to release the taut tension that started building as soon as we stepped out of the car.

He *had* seen her, he just assumed she was unimportant. Otherwise, he would have taken out the two other models being fitted three feet in front of us. He chose the lesser of two evils to get by instead of acting like a human being and asking us to step back.

"I need to go to the bathroom." Beasty tugged on my arm.

Her eyes were pinched as she darted her gaze around the crowded room. It was a madhouse with different stations set up for fittings, makeup, and the line for the show.

Checking my watch, I sighed. They were running late. The show should start in ten minutes and they hadn't even gotten the full lineup yet.

I raised my chin at one of the security guys I'd made connections with. He worked for the agency and was often leased out to the venues given his expertise with running security at shows. It made everyone feel a little better to have a familiar face who knew event protocols.

"What's up?" Josh asked as he walked over.

"Beasty has to run to the restroom. Can you escort her there and right back?" I dropped my brows over my eyes and met his stare head on. He raised his own but didn't comment on the uncharacteristic action for me. I was usually a fly on the wall, just like Valencia expected of me and the other guards here with the bigger names.

"Sure." To her, he held out his arm so she could take his elbow. "Shall we?"

"No." I shook my head once and the grin died on his face.

"Yeah, ok." He pointed toward the back corner where the restrooms were. "I'll follow you."

Beasty tossed a confused look over her face before she led the way.

"All right people!" Valencia clapped. "Get in line! I'll reorder you if necessary but find a spot based on your number!"

I stepped next to Kim and lowered my voice, making sure not to touch him. He was always a little raw after a show or shoot, and today, it would be worse with all of Valencia's shit. "Are you okay?"

He nodded and swallowed. "I don't know why that got to me so much. She's such a bitch."

She was more than.

"I'll take care of it."

One of the other male models started crowding his back. He looked like he wanted to say something else but didn't. Instead, he took his place in line in the prearranged order.

Valencia stood at the front of the line so she could inspect and tweak each outfit before the models walked out.

I moved toward the back wall, close enough to the bathrooms where Josh would spot me as soon as he brought Beasty back, and where I could do a little of my own work.

The room started to clear as the models lined up. There were still stations set up so the models could be redressed and touched up when they come back from their first walk, but it was calmer than five minutes ago.

With my back to the wall, I kept an eye on Kim while actively searching for Valencia's assistant, Rich. He was a nasty weasel, but he had his purposes.

When he appeared around the corner, walking with his nose glued to his tablet, I whistled to get his attention.

Rich stopped and glanced up. A sneer started to form before it morphed into a cheeky grin. "Lake." He winked, like I didn't peg it for the fake greeting it was.

Everyone in fashion was fucking fake.

"Come here. I want to talk to you for a second." I kept my voice low so no one would notice. During a show, it would take a meteor crashing into the building to get these self-absorbed idiots' heads out of their asses, but I wasn't going to be stupid about it.

"I only have thirty seconds. You know how Valencia is during a show night." He rolled his eyes, showing exactly how he felt about his boss.

"About that." I took a small step forward to push us even closer. He tilted his face up, a coy expression lighting his features. I ignored it. "Remember when you did that hit and run last year, killing the elderly woman on a crosswalk?"

His eyes bulged and he started coughing. I caught his arm as he tried to bolt.

"That wasn't–That never happened," he choked out, trying to wave me away.

"Oh, but it did." I glanced around to see if anyone was paying attention.

Kim stoically faced forward, already in the zone for his walk. No sign of Beasty and Josh yet. As soon as Kim went out, I was hunting her. She shouldn't be taking this long.

"I swear!–"

"I don't give a damn about that." Not outside of using it as leverage for situations just like this. "What I do care about is finding out every dirty little secret on Valencia. You can help me do that, can't you?"

He wildly searched the room for her, and when he saw that she had her back to us as she fussed over the first model's outfit, he deflated. "I need this job."

"You'll keep your job. I'm just looking for a little leverage. I hate being called just a bodyguard." I raised one shoulder nonchalantly as if this was an issue with my ego.

I didn't give two shits about that. I cared that she was touching Kim when he didn't want to be touched. That she was abusing her power and treating Kim like he was some kind of doll for her pleasure.

Clamping my hand down on his shoulder, I pulled my wallet out of my pocket.

When I was sure he wasn't going to bolt, I let him go and pulled cash out. "Now. I'm going to give you three hundred as a show of good faith that I don't mean you any harm. Your secret is safe with us." I handed over the bills.

"Us?" He gulped.

"My friends. The four of us all know. We have no secrets

from each other. But, like I said," I dropped my head toward his, "we don't care about you. You have one week to get me a file of everything you can find on Valencia that even smells bad."

Movement caught my eye and I glanced to the side. Beasty was just a few steps away, and she eyed the money still clutched in his fingers.

"Call me." I gave him a warning look then stepped back. Beasty stopped next to me just as Kim walked out onto the stage.

Her lips twisted to the side and her brows pushed up in the middle as she watched him disappear. "I can't believe I missed his first walk. We can't sit in the audience?"

Stepping back, I leaned against the wall, letting my arms hang loose by my sides. You never knew when an asshole would pop up and try to sucker punch you. Which had happened more than I'd like to admit at these shows.

Especially, if there were new or useless security running the show.

"Afraid not," I grunted.

As much as I wanted Beasty to be able to watch Kim, and as much as I wanted Kim to have that too, it was just too dangerous for Kim if I left.

She braced herself on the wall next to me, and we watched the ever-rotating line of models. Once they started coming back, the place became a madhouse all over again.

The closing calls were being made and Valencia's voice could be heard over the speakers. Then without any fanfare like these snots were too good to be here, the models started walking back in.

Kim returned glowing. After every show he had this high about him. I liked that for him.

Sometimes out of all of us, he seemed the least fucked

up. This momentary euphoria he experienced made me believe that even more.

He beamed at Beasty and hesitated before he came right over. I glanced around for Valencia, but she was nowhere to be seen.

I wouldn't let that bitch ruin this moment for him. She'd get what was coming to her anyway.

Kim stopped when his toes almost touched Beasty's, simply smiling at her. She returned his dopey expression and my chest ached.

This was the normal I wanted for him.

The rest of us might be too fucked in the head, but I wanted this for Kim.

"What did you think?"

Her smile went lopsided, and some of the dreaminess fled her eyes, but she nodded. "It was great. I loved watching how everything worked. It's...a lot though."

"Yeah..." Some of his happiness died too, and I knew both of them were thinking of Valencia and her fucking ego.

"Maybe later today we can watch a movie or something? I'm a huge fan of rom coms." He pressed his lips together to suppress his smile.

I had to fight mine too, anger be damned.

"Kim," one of the other models called before he jogged over. "Are you going over to Valencia's after party?"

I think his name was Break. Breck?

He was the exact opposite of Kim and Atlas. Where Kim was the aloof untouchable fairy and Atlas was the daring asshole, Breck was a twisted ball of surfer sunshine with long, blond hair and light blue eyes. He even had sun-kissed skin.

This guy also ate up everything the fashion industry had to offer, including the drugs and partying.

"No," Kim answered, then turned back to Beasty.

I had to stop myself from reacting. He always put on such an act, I hadn't expected for him to be outright rude.

Breck turned to Beasty, and he made a show of slowly looking her up and down. "Well...who is this interesting creature?"

Kim and I both stood taller.

"Beasty," she said and held out her hand.

Breck grinned, grabbed hers and pulled her in for a full body hug. Her hands went to his side as he stuck his nose in her hair and took a long whiff. Beasty tried to push away from him, but he tightened his hold.

"We're all friends here. Don't you know that friends in the modeling industry are *very* close?" Breck's voice dropped.

I reached for Beasty at the same time as Kim, and we both pulled her away from him.

"Breck, that's enough. We're leaving." Kim positioned himself between Beasty and Breck.

Good, because if I could reach him, I'd throat punch him.

"Don't be like that, Kim," he huffed, good-naturedly.

Kim slipped his fingers through hers, and I almost tripped. He didn't touch anyone unless he had to. Everyone always touched him.

Beasty had no fucking idea how big of a deal this was. But Valencia popped up and her eyes narrowed on their joined hands. "You have one of my designs on, Kim. They're not leaving the building."

"Fine." He dropped Beasty's hand and started stripping down to his white briefs.

Josh appeared at my side with Kim's bag. This asshole Breck had me forgetting my job.

Kim tossed his outfit to Valencia, hitting her in the face with his pant leg.

The entire time, Beasty held her head up high, pretending that she wasn't affected. She couldn't hide the tremble in her hands though. Not when I was this close to her.

As I followed them out, I got distracted by watching her ass instead.

My gut clenched. When had Beasty grown up?

And what the hell was I doing checking out her ass?

Oh shit, this was all kinds of wrong. I'd watched over her just like the guys. I was so much older than her. Fuck.

Yet all evening, I sulked around spying on Kim's innocent interactions with Beasty.

She didn't even pay attention to the rest of us. We avoided her and she avoided us.

The sign that I had fallen from what little grace I had, was sitting in the hallway with Atlas as we watched the back of their heads while they watched a movie.

They were halfway through the movie when I couldn't take it anymore.

I still couldn't get Beasty out of my head as I drove, paid for the service, or when I stripped down in the room.

When Esmeralda, which I was sure was a fake name, walked in and slapped me across the face, the cool burn finally started to clear my mind.

Beasty was going to have a normal life. Kim too. I'd make sure of it.

One thing was for damn sure. She was too good for me.

Chapter Seven

CRESSIDA - PRESENT DAY

I checked my phone for messages as I finished brushing my teeth.

Last night was terrible. The rest of the night had gone by in a daze. I'd been lost in my own thoughts, and the boys hadn't been much better. They never left me alone, but they alternated between stewing in their own heads, and snapping at the patrons with rude and sometimes hateful comments.

I eyed them hard.

How had they gotten to be like this? Or maybe I was the idiot and they'd *always* been this way. I was just never close enough to them in school to see their true colors.

Sighing, I dropped my toothbrush in the fancy holder and left the bathroom.

Just like every time I had a minute alone in this room, which was all the damned time, I stopped and studied the decor.

It was still beautiful. The colors they picked were my favorite, but it wasn't me.

I wanted to be back in my tiny-ass apartment working at the bar, but they'd made it almost impossible.

Nothing was resolved with Stevo, and Lake made the situation worse by killing him.

"Dumb fucking Stevo," I muttered to myself as I snatched my T-shirt off the back of the chair and tossed it on over my sports bra.

One thing was certain, I couldn't continue like this.

Heading downstairs, I took the steps two at a time. Soft sounds were coming from the kitchen, so at least one person was up.

Turned out, it was two.

Joaquin and Atlas stood with their asses to the counter as they sipped on their coffee, talking quietly to each other.

For once since I'd been here, they didn't seem to be nitpicking at each other.

"Good morning, Beasty," Atlas purred as he set his coffee down and walked toward me. His eyes darkened as he got closer, his mouth almost a smirk but not.

"Stop." I held up a hand. Last night when he molded himself to my back, I'd been caught up in my feelings. I hadn't had a clear enough head to push him away.

His jaw clenched but he stopped. "What's wrong, Beasty? You were perfectly happy to let me put my hands on you yesterday."

Joaquin choked and the tips of my ears started burning.

"We were in public and I didn't want to make a scene." It was more than that. But it wasn't like I was ready to spill my heart out to him, anymore than he was ready to hear it.

Anger burned in Atlas' eyes. "Is that the way you want to play it? Like you don't crave my touch as much as I ache to touch you?"

The path I was on came to a screeching halt. *Back the fuck up.* "Are you trying to make this out like I'm the one toying with *you*?" He was out of his mind. Absolutely lost it if he thought I would continue to take their shit.

I was knocked off balance coming back here. The fact that they wanted me–*how* they wanted me, messed with my head and confidence.

But I'd had some time to process it, and while I was uncertain on how I felt after Lake and Joaquin were arrested, I remembered exactly who I was trying to be.

What I needed for myself. Letting Atlas be an asshole wasn't it.

"You've been fucking with my head since the second you came up to that fence, Beasty!" Atlas all but yelled. "How is this any different?"

I shook my head as my brows snapped together. "You're fucking delusional."

"We've already hashed out that I put you on a pedestal when you didn't need to be there. That's my fault, but you're still a compulsion I can't ignore."

"And you're blaming me for that?"

"I'm blaming you for–"

"Atlas, stop." Joaquin waded between us, giving me his back so he could face Atlas. He seemed tired and drained. Probably because last night after they kicked Alfie out, he got wasted.

It was the first time I'd ever seen him get like that and even though he wasn't wild and violent, he wasn't himself.

I tried not to be hurt that he completely ignored me to talk Atlas down from his tantrum, but it was impossible. All these boys seemed to know how to do was exclude me. I shouldn't even care. I was so fucking angry with them, for not having the balls to talk to me as kids, for not treating me like an equal and letting me be their friend, and for being the same type of people who I worked so hard to escape.

"No, Joaquin. She wants to play hot and cold and that

shit is not okay. She decided she wanted to be here. She decided she wanted to stay with us. All of us. And she," he jabbed his finger at me over Joaquin's shoulder without ever once looking my way, "decided she wanted all of us. The real us. Either she does, or she's a fucking liar."

"Why are we calling people liars?" Kim asked, his voice light as he strolled into the kitchen. His hair was ruffled and his eyes were soft from sleep. "We don't tolerate that around here. It's the worst insult."

Lake snorted as he came in right on his heels. "I heard all the shouting and came down. What's going on?"

"Beasty's being a bitch. Accepting my touch one second then throwing it away the next."

How...how was Atlas turning this around on me? I was the one who had the right *and* plenty of legitimate reasons to be livid.

Lake swung his hazel-blue eyes my way. His mouth pinched and I had a feeling whatever came out of his mouth next was going to piss me off.

"Is this true? You're going back on your word about wanting to be here?"

My eyes got so wide, they were going to pop out.

Fuck him. Fuck all of them. What right did they have to act like this? I hadn't had a normal childhood just like they hadn't but the way they thought, I just...

"Agh!" I screamed, gripping the hair on the side of my head. "You're asking me that when you assholes are literally criminals. When you throw so much shit in my face to see what sticks. Is this a test? Are you trying to see how far you can push me? To see what my breaking point is to make me finally leave for good?"

Kim's face fell, but the other three glared at me as if this argument was my fault.

I knew what I said was irrational. People didn't get arrested to test someone, but that was what this felt like.

How far can we push Beasty before she cracks? She's a dumb bitch who fell on our dicks and now we're going to have some fun and see what she'll take.

Lake took a step forward, extending his hand like he was going to touch me.

I slashed my hand down.

"No! You don't get to pin this on me. You don't get to act as if I'm the problem. Yes, I agreed to be here. I wanted to stay. I wanted to get to know you. Because the truth? I don't have a clue who you are." I heaved as I thought about how I wanted to get this message across. In the meantime, I stared each man down.

They met my stare, and for once, I had a kernel of power in a world where I had none.

"But you know what's even more obvious? You don't know who the fuck I am. I don't even know who I am. Growing up how we did, none of us got that opportunity. We—or I—because let's be real honest, I don't have a clue what your life was like at the Ramey Home. But I never got to be myself. I was always walking on eggshells, trying to stay invisible while still trying to matter. Do you know how fucking tough that was?" I screamed. "I know who I want to be. I know the kind of people I don't want to surround myself with. After you four—" I couldn't even say it out loud. "After you two got arrested," I flicked my gaze from Lake to Joaquin, "*that* changes everything."

"Beasty," Kim said with a steady, almost pleading voice. "You know us. You know *me*."

Tipping my head to the side, I studied him. "I thought I knew you, but if you're okay with murder, I don't know you, either."

"So what? You're leaving?" Atlas scoffed.

The desire to tell him yes, and let him watch my ass as I walked away, burned through me.

Drawing in a long breath, I let it fill my lungs and focused on my chest expanding while I thought over his question.

I *should* leave. I even glanced toward the front of the house. The boys stiffened but didn't move a muscle.

This was what had been taking up so much headspace last night.

Either I wanted to be here, or I didn't. At first, I wanted to be here because they were the boys I'd always wanted, who finally seemed to want me.

Now I realized the boys I'd built up in my head, even if the image was a measly, flimsy picture, were all a lie.

Yet, the thought about walking through that door and never seeing any of them again physically hurt. When I exhaled, it felt like needles scraping along the underside of my ribcage and up to my throat.

"I don't want to leave, but I can't go on like this either." I pressed my fingers into my temples, and dropped my gaze to the floor. "You all have this built-up idea of who I should be. Who you want me to be, and either you're punishing me for it, or you're pushing your wishes on me."

Kim made a slight noise, and I lifted my gaze to him. His dark brown eyes were glassy with emotion, and we held each other's stare for a moment.

"That's not true," he whispered.

"It is true." Now I just sounded defeated and that was fucking depressing. "Look at my room. Literally the only thing that says it's mine are the colors. You got my favorite colors right."

He snapped his mouth shut and I could see the wheels turning in his head.

Then addressing all of them. "I like working. I like

having a purpose. I want to work for my own things because it makes me feel good." I spread a hand out to encompass the fancy kitchen. "I could care less about luxury like this. It's nice. I'm glad you have it, but I was perfectly content with my little apartment because it was mine. This? This isn't mine, and I don't feel like I belong here."

"That's bullshit." Lake crossed his arms. "You belong here because we belong here. And we're not going to let you put shitty second-hand things in your room just because it makes you feel comfortable. You deserve better than that." He bent forward at the waist. "Think what you want, but we spent our entire lives trying to be worthy of *you*. To give you nice things because you deserved them. Don't spit on that."

Just like that, the anger that had started to cool ratcheted back up again.

"I didn't ask for this."

Joaquin held up a hand. "You wanted to know who we really are. We're letting you see it. We're also not going to throw away the house because it makes you uncomfortable–"

"I never asked for *that*," I repeated. He was twisting this all up, trying to make it sound like I was demanding they change who they were. I wasn't!

He glared at me for interrupting him. "I didn't say you did. I'm making a statement on what we're willing to do and what we're not. What do you need to stay here? You want to go back to believing we're America's sweethearts?" His face twisted up. "Unfortunately, that ship has sailed."

My breath started coming faster and my vision started to waver around the edges. I wasn't going to pass out. I was just suspended in this in-between place of what I should do and what I wanted.

I wanted to leave. Live the life I wanted for myself.

Yet, the very thought of walking out that door threatened to stop my heart. I could literally feel the fingers squeezing around my chest.

"Stay with us, Beasty..." The pleading in Kim's voice was the final cinch around my chest.

I was weak. I couldn't leave them. Not this time. Not until I tried to stay first.

Realizing that about myself was terrifying.

"I—"

The doorbell rang.

We stared at each other. Kim with his sad eyes, Lake clenching his jaw, Joaquin with a burning anger just below the surface, and Atlas? He was worryingly blank.

When a few seconds passed and no one moved, loud banging started filtering through the house.

There were muffled voices but I couldn't make out the words. The walls and doors were just too damned thick.

Lake glared toward the front, his jaw working back and forth but he didn't move.

"Are you going to get that?"

"Absolutely not," he snapped. "This is more important."

Was it? *I* was important? They were giving me all the signs that they cared, but my fucked-up brain still caught on all the ways their actions said they didn't.

"Fine." I spun on my heels to go answer it myself. Partly because I needed an escape, a way to get some of my wits around me again. And whoever was trying to come had a hell of a strong arm, and I couldn't listen to that sound anymore.

It was too jarring while my emotions were high.

Lake caught my bicep and moved in front of me. Joaquin took hold of my arms to stop me from going any further. He didn't hurt me, but he had a firm grip, keeping me out of sight of the front door.

I yanked my arms away but he held strong.

"Stop Beasty. We know who this is, and we don't want you to get caught up with them." Joaquin's lips touched the shell of my ear and goosebumps raised along my arms.

"Who is it?" I croaked.

"No one I want you around."

Atlas moved past us and stopped just behind Lake. Kim took up position beside us as Lake threw the door open.

"About fucking time, dumbass." A gruff voice with a strong accent echoed in the foyer. I wasn't great with accents, but I think it was from New York or New Jersey.

"Adrian, there's really no need for that." Another voice, same accent yet smoother, followed.

I strained forward, trying to see who it was, but Joaquin hugged me against his chest.

It didn't matter. The two men came around the corner with Lake on their heels.

"You should have called," Lake growled, his shoulders hunching up to his ears.

The first man to appear smirked, giving Lake a quick glance before turning toward us. "So you could ignore my call again? Forget about it."

When he faced forward, his gaze locked on me.

He was...gorgeous, but in a different way than the boys. Where my guys were handsome, almost to the point of pretty, this guy, with his head of styled curls, was more masculine. His dress shirt and slacks were fitted showing off his muscles, and he just looked like he smelled good.

The man on his heels showed all his teeth in his smile as he also zeroed in on me in Joaquin's hold.

"Well, isn't she...interesting. She comes across softer

than in her pictures." He smacked the first guy on the shoulder.

"Adrian," the man sighed and dropped his face, pinching the bridge of his nose.

These two were just as out of place here as I was, but in a different way.

"Who are you?" I asked. Shit, I hadn't meant to ask that at all. Kim angled himself to cover me, and I stepped to the side.

"They're not important." Lake walked around them and planted his feet apart as he faced them. Also trying to block their view of me.

"That's not any way to speak to your keeper, is it?" The more refined man tutted and stepped around him, ignoring all the warning vibes Lake tossed out. "I'm Gio. This is my good friend and colleague, Adrian. We're here to check on your boys."

The air clogged with so much tension, my throat started to close up. Gulping, I watched the boys for any sign of what was really going on.

It wasn't like I could trust them to tell me the truth. Even Kim was capable of hiding things from me.

"Parker sent you." Lake stated like he knew exactly why they'd show up, even if they hadn't expected them.

Gio rolled his eyes. "First, let's go into the living room. Your place is too nice to hang out in the hallway. Even with all the space, it feels a little cramped." He patted Lake's chest as he pushed by. He looked everything up and down like he'd never been here before.

Maybe he hadn't.

He whistled when he saw some of the vases and art pieces in the living room. He pointed to one of two women embracing. "Does Parker know you have that?"

"Parker can kiss my lily-white ass if he tries to take my

things. But we both know we're more valuable to him than that." Lake crossed his arms.

I guess seeing the guys sprawl out on the furniture set Joaquin at ease, since he loosened his hold enough that I was able to step away from him.

Slowly, I moved through the boys. They seemed to only be focused on Gio and Adrian, which was good. I took a seat on the chair and pulled my knees up to my chest, draping my arm over them.

These two men were another look inside the lives of my boys. I wouldn't waste this opportunity to get to know them better.

I opened my mouth and all attention swung my way. Immediately, I snapped it shut. I was going to ask how they knew them, but another point snagged in my brain.

"What did you mean, I look softer than in the picture? Do I know you?" I squinted my eyes. Gio stiffened for a brief second, but Adrian just grinned. Whatever reason they had seen pictures of me, Gio was either ashamed by it, or uncomfortable with sharing.

Adrian just seemed unrepentant. He grinned wider and shrugged.

"We have friends. You're welcome by the way."

"Adrian," Gio and Joaquin warned at the same time. Gio tossed an unimpressed glare at Joaquin before focusing back on Adrian.

"What, we saved her life. You can't even pretend we didn't. If we didn't tip off numb nuts here, she'd be in a lake somewhere." Adrian shifted back on the couch, getting comfortable.

"That's it. You're done." Lake reached forward and hauled Adrian up by the shirt. Adrian was a big guy, not much smaller than Lake. The looseness in his body posture said he allowed it.

"We came for a reason." Gio stood, angling himself toward Lake.

"Don't care. Call me."

"We have a job for Beasty," Gio said casually.

I perked up. The chances of these men being criminals was off the charts but I could use this. To push the boys, to give them a taste of their own medicine. I didn't want them in this world, and they didn't want me close to it if I read them correctly. This was also an opportunity to get all the answers the guys weren't willing to give me.

"What job?"

Joaquin exploded. "Absolutely not."

There it was.

"I realize you're sober for once, but that doesn't give you the right to speak for the lady." Gio raised one brow.

I rattled off my phone number and Adrian started repeating it to himself as he pulled his phone from his pocket.

"Send me the details and we'll talk."

They didn't get a chance to answer as Lake threw them out, all while Adrian laughed.

Turning to the guys, I raised my brows.

"You're not working for them." Atlas crossed his arms and leaned against the wall.

"I have to work somewhere. And I need answers. If you're not willing to give them to me, I have to hunt them for myself."

Joaquin's top lip peeled back.

I didn't give any of them a chance to argue as I bounded for the stairs. I paused midway up and glanced over my shoulder. "Either you help me or I take care of myself."

Chapter Eight

JOAQUIN - PRESENT DAY

Beasty's steps reverberated even after she made it to the hallway. Was the fucking girl stomping?

Then her door slammed shut.

Shaking my head, I went searching for Lake.

I didn't have to go far. He was facing off with Gio and Adrian out in front of the house but not far enough out that Beasty could see them.

"That was out of line. I should teach you a lesson for that." Lake clenched his hands into fists at his sides.

Since we partnered with the Castillo brothers, I hadn't met Gio very often. Maybe a handful of times. He preferred to deal with Lake. As someone who managed every fucking thing about Atlas' and Kim's career, that had been fine by me.

Gio had two buddies he worked with, and I'd never met either one of them in person. Looking at Adrian and his crazy eyes, that was a blessing.

"What the hell is this about a job? Beasty isn't a pawn for you to use with your fucked-up family." I rushed forward to get in Gio's face.

He narrowed his eyes on me as Lake threw out his arm to keep me from getting in Gio's face. Adrian still had on that irritatingly gleeful expression.

"Joaquin," Lake warned. What the fuck was he warning me about? He was out here doing the same damn shit. Why was it okay for him to get in Gio's face but not me?

"Not a chance, Lake. These assholes don't get to waltz in here and fuck up our lives just because they're Parker's little footboys." My temper flared hot. I knew it, Lake knew it, but there was nothing I could do to stop it.

Even the tips of my fingers tingled like I needed to flip my cards. I'd like to flip one straight at Gio's face. If done the right way, those things hurt like a bitch.

"Lake, if you don't want trouble," Gio turned hard eyes on Lake, "and you want to keep receiving tips that could save your girl's life, then control your dog."

"Dog?" This guy was fucked in the head. I launched toward him, but Lake caught me around the middle and slung me around.

"You're not helping!" Lake yelled at me.

Adrian laughed and braced his elbow on Gio's shoulder. "You didn't tell me that these guys were such a fucking razz of a time. I would have started going to meetings with you more often."

Gio sighed. "Lake, it's fine. Let him go."

He said that as if Lake was on his side. *This motherfucker.*

"I need to find out why they're here. Control yourself or go the fuck inside," he whispered in my ear. After giving me a tight squeeze around my chest, he pulled away and faced Gio and Adrian.

"Like we said, Beasty isn't a pawn. She doesn't exist for you. Hell, she doesn't exist for Parker. Is that clear?" Lake rolled his neck from side to side.

"We're not here to cause you problems. In fact, we're trying to help yo–"

"You help settle your own vendettas." Lake cut Gio off.

"The Pescis are our collective problem. You made it that way when you sent Stevo's head back to them." Gio sounded like that got under his skin.

Even though I felt the same way–it had been stupid of Lake–I had this sick satisfaction that we were causing trouble for Gio. I just wished I could drive that splinter a little deeper under his skin.

"I told you before, they're not going to actually move forward with the charges. They don't want their dirty laundry aired like that." Lake shook his head, showing great restraint when he tucked his hands in his pockets.

"Doesn't matter. They still want to ruin your lives for fucking with them. They're a vengeful bunch."

Adrian grinned. "But lucky for you guys, so are we."

Gio swung his head around to give Adrian another look. It went ignored.

If Beasty hadn't just offered herself up to men with mafia ties, I'd think their dynamic was hilarious. They were worse than brothers. But they didn't get that when they gave Beasty a way to fuck with us.

And that was what she was doing.

Fucking with us.

She wanted things. Things we wanted to give her, but we weren't doing it on her terms. So, the little shit was trying to force our hand and give us an ultimatum.

"We would only need her for a night. Maybe twenty-four hours, but I doubt it will come to that. Think about it." Gio turned and shoved Adrian's shoulder to make him start walking to their car.

"Don't forget," Adrian called over his shoulder. "We

have Beauty's number." They both slid into their car and slammed the doors shut.

"Did he just threaten us?" My voice went high at the end. That was the most ridiculous conversation I'd had in a long time. And my fingers didn't tingle anymore.

"I think it was a promise," Lake said begrudgingly. He watched them drive away as he walked back in the house.

Inside, the living room was completely empty.

"Where did they go?" Lake glanced around, scratching the back of his head.

"You missed all the fun of Beasty giving us an ultimatum. Either we give her what she wants or she's going to work with Gio and Adrian," I deadpanned.

He met my stare, understanding flared in his eyes.

"Beasty went up to her room," I added.

"Then where are Kim and Atlas?"

"I don't have a clue," I said as I listened. No sounds came from the kitchen or from the study. Atlas probably went to our room.

Leaving Lake behind, I headed to our room. Wherever Kim and Atlas were, I couldn't hear them from the hallway. We made sure if nothing else, we'd have complete privacy in our bedrooms.

I opened our door and harsh whispers cut short.

"Don't stop just because I showed up," I snarked as I headed straight to Atlas. I was impressed by how calm he stayed during that whole shit show. He was still much calmer than I'd have given him credit for considering Beasty's threat.

We should be thankful she didn't threaten to leave.

"What are you all looking at?" Lake came in behind me.

They glanced our way. Kim was guilty as hell, but Atlas...

Ah, he was furious. He just hid it better than I did. Atlas always had a cold sort of temper.

The tops of Kim's cheeks darkened as we got closer. "Did you know he did this?" He stared straight at me.

Furrowing my brow, I edged around the couch where they were sitting. On the screen of Atlas' laptop was a crystal clear, color image of Beasty.

She moved around the room and dropped something on the bed. The thing, which was some kind of hair clip, gave off a soft whooshing noise.

"You are shitting me," I said slowly, unable to take my gaze off of the screen.

He had surveillance on Beasty.

Lake didn't say anything as he bent over to get a closer look. Beasty moved over to Quilliam's enclosure and sat down beside it, running her finger over the plastic. He was asleep. It was still during the daytime, so he had no idea that his human waited for his attention.

It was like she chose a support animal that couldn't give her the emotional support she needed.

I barked out a laugh. It didn't take a genius to know that we were in the same category as Quilliam. She wanted answers, and we were reluctant to give them to her.

But not for the reasons she thought.

For me, I didn't want her to look at us like we were scum. Worse than that, what would stop her from walking out once she knew everything we'd done? If she felt threatened, she'd leave.

I didn't give a fuck that she said she wouldn't. The past spoke for itself.

"No, I didn't know he did this," I added, just in case it wasn't overtly clear that I had no clue he watched her. Not to this degree.

"This would have made my life so much simpler when we were kids," Atlas mumbled, turning back to the screen. He'd said something similar recently and I couldn't remember where or what for.

Then it clicked. This was new.

Lake slid by me and took a seat next to Atlas, bending close to the screen to see what Beasty was doing. "This is great quality. Who did the work?"

"I found someone in the Network who's good with computers and surveillance and shit." Atlas turned back to the screen and crossed his arms as he leaned back. Well, he was just fucking content to watch her like a creeper.

Sighing, I rubbed my forehead. Atlas wasn't a creeper. He was just misunderstood. Like we all were. Like Beasty was.

"We can't watch her like this." I dropped my hand and faced the guys fully.

No one answered me.

"Kim," I said, raising my eyebrows. He had always shown the most amount of conscience in his warped way. But the little shit didn't hold my gaze. He barely flicked me a glance before taking his undivided attention back to Beasty. "You can't seriously want to watch her this way."

"We need to know what she's going to do. You heard her. She hates that we work in a club with so many women. She'll leave if she thinks we'd cheat on her."

"I just, what?" That wasn't anything close to what she'd said. Or what bothered her. Kim loved his stories but this one was so far in left field, I had the need to call him on it. "That's not what she said and you know it!"

Kim spared me a brief glare. Atlas and Lake pretended like they weren't even part of this conversation.

I released a strangled noise in the back of my throat. Everyone said I was the bad egg. The alcoholic. The gambler. And you know what? I was those things, but I knew my limits, and I could see the world in crystalline clarity.

These idiots? They were going to toss everything good we'd built in our lives in a dumpster fire. Just by being idiots.

At the noise, Kim turned his head my way, finally giving me his full attention. But it wasn't the obstinate expression from before. His face broke into something painful to see.

"I can't lose her again, Joaquin. It will destroy me," he quietly pleaded.

Atlas sneered like I was the problem. "You can leave it all up to chance if you want, but I'm not going to let her walk away. She wanted us. Now she gets us. This need...this obsession to watch over her? This is who I am. And if she thinks she won't get punished for her shit, then she's got some tough lessons coming her way."

Neither Kim nor Lake objected to his crazy ass. What the fuck?

"We need to prove to her that we're not going anywhere. That she's important to us," Lake mused, like he had the universe figured out.

"I think she just wants to know that she's important to us, but she doesn't need us yet." Kim traced a delicate finger over the screen where Beasty was resting her head back against Quilliam's house with her eyes closed.

"We need to condition her. Train her to our touch and our touch alone. Drive her crazy until she's begging for it." Atlas started speaking faster as if with each word this idea was the gold that was going to go around her feet and weigh her down until she couldn't run.

"I like it. She needs to be just as obsessed with us as we are with her. Since she's been back, it's obvious that she's not as attached to us. We need to change that." Lake nodded.

All three idiots still stared at the laptop.

"It's settled. We'll edge her so hard, she won't be able to function without us. She'll need us, like we need her."

"God dammit," I grumbled as I spun around to leave them to their crazy. "I need a fucking drink."

Chapter Nine

BEASTY - AGE 18

I tugged on the hem of my shirt, trying not to make it obvious I was out of place.

Except I was. *Obviously.*

For the most part, I didn't care what people thought of me, but this was torture.

"Kim! Come stand over here! The sponsors will be here in ten minutes. They asked for you specifically." A young woman with a clipboard snapped her fingers at Kim and pointed to a high, round table. Then she searched the room and found Atlas. "Atlas, two of the designers love you. Stand over by that table. Pierre loves the finger foods. That way he can talk with you and eat at the same time."

Kim and Atlas moved to their respective corners of the private room and she finished directing the other models. Their agency had rented out a trendy yet elegant restaurant for tonight's event.

"It's a madhouse, isn't it?"

I jumped. Holy shit, that scared me. I turned and faced a guy around my age. He wasn't model pretty like the others.

No, that wasn't fair. It wasn't nice either. Joaquin and Lake were just as handsome as any model here. I guess models had a shininess to them. Like they cared a hell of a lot what they looked like and they had a whole team dedicated to making them look good.

A smirk tried to break free. What was the meme or saying from a few years ago? There were no ugly people. Only poor people.

This guy had scruffy hair and a fluffy beard that seemed more lazy than purposeful. There was also a mischievous glint in his eyes. He wasn't unattractive, he just didn't care. And that took balls. I envied that.

He raised his brows, a reminder that I hadn't answered him.

Any other time, I'd run. People didn't talk to me. I wasn't included.

Even now, I glanced over to see Joaquin and Lake walking away from a few guards. They stopped and huddled together. When the lady with the clipboard left, Kim and Atlas hurried over to join their conversation.

Then there was me. Along the wall. Awkwardly holding it up in my second-hand clothes.

So, this guy seemed like a good distraction. Maybe he had ulterior motives, but it was a brief way of pretending I belonged. It was more than I ever got in school.

I nodded, frowning as I faced the floor. Workers carried decorations and models were starting to congregate in closed circles. A pre-launch party seemed like a lot of stress. For the workers. Not the models. "Yeah."

"So, you're here with the wonder boys?"

I peeked over and the guy was grinning. One of his front teeth was crooked, but it worked for him. Made him seem happier or something? I wasn't sure. It just worked.

"You mean Kim and Atlas?" What initially was a way to

not feel alone, quickly turned into a nasty pit of suspicion in my stomach.

"Yeah, I saw you walk in with them. I'm with Lisbet." He motioned to a girl in the middle of a group of male models. She was stunning. Tall, slender, with golden skin and strawberry blonde hair. An unusual combination.

Then she turned our way and I sucked in a breath. She had catlike green eyes, upturned at the corners.

I thought the boys were the only ones with the ability to stop my breathing like that. Apparently, any gorgeous person did it.

"She's pretty." I sucked at small talk and this was more awkward than standing by myself. I let my shoulders slump. Maybe he'd take the hint and leave me alone.

"Anyway, she's got a thing for Atlas."

I straightened back up. That hit me square in the chest and not in a good way.

"Okay..."

The guy took a few steps closer until his chest was almost brushing my arm. "Oh, I'm Bryce by the way. Lisbet wanted to see if you had any inside scoop on how she can get close to him. He's pretty untouchable. And I thought..." One side of his mouth kicked higher. "Or hoped, that maybe we could hang out after this too." He touched my nape.

I didn't get a chance to react.

Lake barreled into him and pinned him to the wall by his throat.

"Lake!" I gasped, cutting my gaze around the room. Models screamed as staff rushed over.

Lake was an image of vengeance in his black suit and his slicked back, white-blond hair. The temperature increased tenfold as I stood there with my mouth open. The veins in Lake's hands popped out as he whispered to Bryce, but I couldn't make out what he was saying. There was so much going on, I couldn't focus on anything. Except how red Bryce's face was turning against Lake's paler skin.

Joaquin tried to wedge himself between Lake and Bryce, but Lake had so much more muscle than Joaquin had.

The girl, Lisbet, ran over on dangerously high heels, a look of utter horror on her face. She reached us at the same time Atlas and Kim did.

"What's going on!" she screeched, grabbing onto Atlas' arm like he offered some kind of support.

"Release him or we have to call the cops." One of the security guards for the restaurant came over. He didn't seem that concerned, more like this was an inconvenience of his time. "No one here wants a scandal, and if you want to keep your job, let him go."

Lake pushed away from Bryce while shoving him deeper into the wall.

"There's no problem. Right?" Lake yanked on the bottom of his suit jacket, straightening it out. He narrowed his eyes on a coughing Bryce.

At first, I didn't think Bryce was going to be able to talk. He coughed and sputtered while bending over, gripping his knees. He straightened, waving the security guards away. "It's fine. A misunderstanding."

"You're okay?" Lisbet asked, her hand still on Atlas as he watched me.

Did he think this was my fault? I hadn't done anything.

Pulling my shoulders forward, I stepped back. I hated attention. I hated *this* kind of attention, especially.

"Listen up!" The woman with the clipboard strutted back in clapping. "The designers are here! The sponsors aren't far behind them. Get back to your places! Act natural, and use that charm that got you here." She snorted.

"Or just stand there and look pretty," she muttered under her breath.

"Come on, Atlas. I'm in the same area as you." Lisbet tugged on his arm.

The woman with the power started hustling around the room yelling at models and Atlas let himself be led away. Joaquin and Lake huddled up and I could only catch clips of fast, furious whispers.

Bryce gave one last wheeze. He didn't even glance my way before he left the room in long strides. He moved like Hell was on his ass, but it was just Lake and Joaquin glaring after him.

I moved farther down the wall until I was nice and covered in the shadows and behind some kind of big leafy plant. The room was massive with tables set up everywhere and dim lighting. It wasn't hard to find a dark pocket.

Within minutes, there was tons of laughter and glasses clinking together. It was like watching the popular crowd on steroids in a warped reality. No one in West Virginia lived like this. I didn't think they did anyway.

There were so many snide smiles and hateful eyes. It all seemed fake, yet there was an energy in the room that was alive. It seemed like personal space didn't exist here either.

At one point, there was a man sliding a finger over Kim's shoulder. His smile dimmed, but he didn't remove it.

I itched to go smack the hand away, but this wasn't school. I couldn't just punch some guy in the face. Biting my lip, I moved further behind the plant.

About halfway through, Joaquin walked fast through the center, searching for something. Then when his gaze hit me, he changed directions.

"Hey, are you okay?" He stuffed his hands in his pockets. Joaquin seemed stressed, but calmer than Lake, who was still moving around the floor, watching everyone and everything.

"Yep." It came out snarky and I winced.

He turned and surveyed the crowd, taking in the same level of snobbery I'd been watching all night. Scratching the back of his head, he let out a slow breath. "This was a terrible idea." Then he leaned against the wall and bent his head closer. "These things are always dog and pony shows. Atlas and Kim are pretty much treated like pretty accessories."

I raised my brows.

Since they were discovered and left our small town, I had always been so jealous and envious. They left and were making something of themselves. They were important. Loved.

But the way Joaquin just made it seem, they were interchangeable. Treated as things and not people. Was that what they wanted? It couldn't have been.

"This blows for you, doesn't it?" Joaquin turned his head toward me, but his attention was on Lake on the other side of the room.

"It's okay," I rushed out. I didn't want them to think I was ungrateful. I'd been with them for less than two weeks and I was happy to be here. Grateful. "What...what happened with Lake and Bryce?"

His nose wrinkled on Bryce's name. "Nothing. Lake just has some issues. He's working through them."

I followed his gaze and found Lake having a heated conversation with a security guard. He was part of the venue with Staff written in bold block letters across his back, just like the man who intervened earlier.

"Do you want us to get you out of here? I can't leave, there's too much elbow rubbing left for me to do, but I can call a car for you and give you the keys. There's no need for all of us to have to sit through this hell." His lips twitched and I gave him a slight smile.

They'd kept to themselves so much since I'd been here, this was nice. To have a conversation. Maybe friendships just took time.

"I'm okay."

"You're sure?" He opened his eyes and it gave him a boyish look. I'd never seen him look boyish before. He always seemed so saucy as he was taking other kid's money.

"Joaquin," a man said in a nasally voice as he stopped next to him.

His entire demeanor changed from the boyish vibe to something darker and angrier.

"Matthew," he returned, pulling his hands from his pockets and straightening to his tallest height.

Matthew's mouth did some weird thing where his lips didn't press together but wrinkles appeared above his top lip. "We need to discuss the next contract. The brand has some demands and we'll need to negotiate."

"I expect to be part of those negotiations." Joaquin's tone was firm, confident.

Wow, he really had changed since we were in West Virginia.

"It's not necessary, I assure you." Matthew blinked a little too hard as his gaze swept down Joaquin's body.

I checked him out too. What was he looking for? Joaquin's clothes were just as nice as the others. It was even pressed. I was the one who stood out. Except here, I didn't stand out, I blended in with the wall and plant.

Invisible. I couldn't lie, I liked it better this way.

If people had been staring at me, I would have tripped or something.

Across the room, a waiter did trip. I caught it out of the corner of my eye, and as I faced the accident, a tray of red wine flew through the air, splattering Kim and the two people closest to him.

The woman screamed, outraged that her white outfit suddenly had maroon blotches.

Kim grabbed a couple napkins on the table, and started blotting her shoulder, smiling ruefully and speaking softly.

I couldn't hear what he said. I couldn't read lips and even if I could, I could only see the side of his face. But whatever he was doing, the lady calmed down, practically melting under his attention.

"Excuse me, Matthew. I need to check on Kim." Joaquin nodded his head at Matthew in dismissal. But he didn't walk away. He turned to me, dipping his head close.

The scent of his cologne tickled my nose and flipped my stomach. It smelled expensive. Foreign. Not what a boy from West Virginia should smell like.

What was I thinking? That was ridiculous.

"This might be what we needed. Stay here." Then he headed over to Kim. Lake joined him along the way, and Atlas was already by Kim's side. Lisbet was two steps behind them.

The entire room seemed to focus on their group. They talked to the models and adults around them. People laughed, and hung on their every word.

And here I was. In the corner.

I liked it here. It just...

Was coming with them a mistake?

Kim stepped back, bowed his head gently, then left the group and came straight to me. There were only a few people milling about and they parted easily enough for him.

His smile broadened when he got close. He didn't say anything though. He reached out, hesitated, then took my hand. Staring down at our entwined fingers, he seemed lost in a daze.

Matthew chortled behind him, talking to another man who probably worked in the same field. They gave off the same entitled energy, like they were lording over the attendees.

Snapping out of it, Kim led me out of the private room and through the back entrance. The staff stopped and said hello as we passed but no one tried to stop us. At the end of the back hallway, Kim pushed on the emergency door.

Cool air wafted over my face and I sucked in a deep breath. It hadn't felt stuffy in there until I came out here.

A car pulled up to the curb, and the same driver who brought us here jumped out and opened the back door.

"Thanks, Stan," Kim said as he stepped to the side, but kept tugging on my hand to let me know to get in the car ahead of him.

The back of the car was cool, like the driver had turned the air on ahead of time. How could he have known? Did he just sit with the car running in case one of the guys needed to leave?

I moved in to the other side and Kim slid in after me, leaving the entire middle section between us.

What had seemed normal on the way out, was now suddenly awkward. Both of us faced forward. Neither of us spoke.

The driver had the window up so we couldn't see him. Hopefully he couldn't see us either. I hated attention at the best of times, but someone having the ability to watch me, study me where I couldn't do the same to them, made my skin crawl.

We took a rough turn and I fell into Kim's side. He laughed under his breath as he steadied my shoulders.

"How bad did you hate that?" He grinned, like he already knew the answer.

I shrugged. Was I supposed to tell him the truth? I

hated lies and I'd seen just how Megan and her husband constantly lied to each other. It was slimy.

"Come on, you can tell me."

Pressing my lips together, I debated what I wanted to say. Honestly, I wasn't sure. The whole time I'd been with them was surreal. I'd never had any experiences like these, and it was nothing short of surreal.

"It wasn't the most terrible."

He laughed a little louder, and I pressed my lips tighter together to stop from smiling. It didn't work.

"It was terrible. And I smell like a winery."

Who even said winery? "I mean, yeah, you smell."

We both laughed this time, and it echoed around the space. Weird. I had never laughed with anyone like this and the sounds of our voices together, like they belonged together, in such a small space was nice.

And I was pathetic.

"Can you believe the lady next to me? She's been an alcoholic for over a decade but stopped because she can't control her obsession with geckos when she drinks. Even for the fashion world, it's really weird. And now I bet she's going to fall off the wagon." He grinned, but it suddenly died.

"What's wrong?" The way his personality dropped so quickly made me nervous.

"Nothing." He looked out the window.

This silence was different. Cutting.

Clearing my throat, I tugged on the collar of my shirt. "I think the worst thing is how different I feel here. I mean, I was always different at school. Even at home. Which is typical for foster kids, right? You never really feel wanted. I expected that here, but there's so much...money, maybe? I don't know how to describe it. It makes me uncomfortable."

Kim's head turned slowly as he listened to me talk.

"And I feel even more invisible. You guys all fit right in." I started to grin, but shit. That might sound weird, like I was comparing them to the people I was complaining about. Was I? "Not in a bad way. People just gravitate to you guys. They want to talk to you, be around you. It's really different from back home."

I winced. Why was I referring to that place as home?

"It's all fake. You know that?" His dark eyes glittered in the passing street lamps.

"You mean, you guys don't really like them and they don't like you?"

He slowly nodded. "In a way. It's not so much about *like*. The fashion industry, and a lot of others, is about who can help you get further in your own career. A designer could hate me, but if my name sells, they'll use me. Same for brands. And how we interact isn't real. It's all fake, small-talk stuff. We smile because we have to. We flatter each other, raining down compliments like it's our jobs since that's the way we get ahead too."

That was really depressing and sounded exhausting.

"You don't like it?"

I scrunched up my face. "No, not really. It's cool if you guys do, but I want something simpler for myself. I just want to be able to pay my bills, enjoy the things that mean something to me. And not be treated like I'm a disease to be caught." I tugged on the frayed hem of my sundress. I'd put on the same one I'd graduated in because I didn't have anything better.

"We don't think of you like that." His voice grew a little firmer, so different from the softness he usually spoke with.

"Yeah, but those people back there do. Everybody but Bryce gave me a wide berth." And I hadn't seen Bryce come back after he left. Kim opened his mouth like he was going to argue, but I shook my head. "It doesn't matter to me. I don't care about *them*. I was just kinda lonely in the corner."

His lips turned down on the side. "I'm sorry, Beasty. I'll talk to the guys and make sure you aren't separated like that anymore."

"It's okay," I said to shrug it off, but my heart swelled on the inside.

I had been feeling pretty alone. With just a few words, Kim reassured me that he didn't think I was on the outside. My chest was so tight, but in a good way. I dropped my hand to the seat beside me, the urge to fidget no longer burning.

He slid his hand over and touched his pinky to mine.

It was so small. So innocent, yet goosebumps rose on my arms and fireworks exploded over my head. I stood on the edge of so much of what I hoped for as a kid. This was what happy felt like.

And I think he liked me.

Chapter Ten

KIM - PRESENT DAY

The house was quiet as I tied my shoes.

Lake was off meeting with Gio. Parker wanted to chat with him and didn't want to do it on Lake's lines in case they were tapped. They probably were. That's why we used the secret burners, but Parker didn't want to listen to that.

Atlas and Joaquin were already at Snatched. Atlas had a meeting with a reporter, and she'd had a crush on Atlas for years. It worked in our benefit for him to meet with her.

And Joaquin didn't want to give him a chance to do something fucked up, so he'd tagged along to check on inventory.

Me? There was a staff meeting for the performers, and I was the best for that job. My chest expanded with the swell of pride.

Growing up next to the guys, I wished so hard that I could contribute somehow. They always seemed intent on babying me.

Fashion helped me find my place. More than that,

dealing with those snakes, I learned a better skill. Charisma. I was who I needed to be and I had a knack for making people feel comfortable.

I glanced up at the ceiling. Beasty had come down for breakfast, ignored all of us, grabbed a protein yogurt, and headed back upstairs.

She was pissed. I understood that.

Lake was an idiot for sending evidence back. He stupidly thought we were untouchable. We weren't, not completely, but we could take care of ourselves.

Beasty didn't know that though.

The hell of it was, I *missed* her. Every time I saw her and she didn't acknowledge me, I wilted on the inside. Soon, there'd be nothing left to nurture back to health.

I didn't want that. I was sure she didn't want that either. I simply had to make her see that she belonged here with us.

To do that, I needed her to actually spend some time with me. Arranging my face into a pleasant, but soothing expression, I walked to her room.

I rapped my knuckles against her door. My heart started to twist up into a beautiful little knot waiting for her to open it.

Then I heard footsteps. She was coming, and my heart soared.

She wanted to be here. I knew it with every cell in my body.

Beasty opened the door wide enough to show her body and not an inch more. Fire still burned in her eyes.

Now that it was only the two of us, I had more time to study her. To figure out what was in that smart head of hers.

How her brows pushed up in the center, the tightening of the skin under the eyes, it all told a story.

The truth, really. The eyes were the one thing about a person that didn't lie...

Unless they were a psychopath, which Beasty was not.

God, she was so far from that, I wanted to wrap her up. No, have her wrap *me* up, and lay in bed with her for eternity.

Firming up my spine, I nodded, more to myself than to her. I'd get us there.

I had to. Losing her wasn't an option. So I'd play Atlas' game, but we needed to get her on the board to make our moves.

"Hey," I smiled.

"Hey," she returned, but didn't smile back.

Baby steps.

"I'm going to the club. I have a meeting with the dancers, and I want you to go with me." Keeping that calm expression plastered on, I studied her.

When she narrowed her eyes, I almost broke it to smile.

"Is this some kind of suck up so I won't answer Gio and Adrian's texts?"

That wiped all the good away from my face. Damn it. I was better than this. Joaquin had a terrible poker face when it came to real life, but he understood the game better than everyone else.

I was the one with the constant facial control.

"You can text them if you want. I don't want to control you, I just want to spend time with you."

The skin around her eyes softened and I wanted to crow. It was all true anyway. I wished I could stitch Beasty to my side so she was never apart from me.

Atlas wanted to constantly watch her. I just wanted to touch her. But I couldn't yet.

"Kim..." She stepped back, opening her door.

Not giving her a chance to second guess her decision, I stepped inside. "Yes, Beasty?"

When she first came back to us, I was hesitant to push. It hurt so damned much when she left before.

"Nothing," she said as she shook her head. "I just need to get dressed and then we can go." She walked toward her backpack and sat down as she started rifling through it.

"Why don't you wear something that I bought you?" I crouched down on her level and caught her attention. When her gaze collided with mine, I fought hard not to rock back from the punch to the gut. Her attention was like a sledgehammer. So heavy, strong. Powerful.

In the past, I couldn't hold it for very long, but I gritted my teeth. I wanted her gaze on me. And I wanted to show her exactly how much I liked it. If I took a little more charge, maybe that would make all the difference this time.

Beasty's hand hovered over the top of her backpack. She had worn some of the new pieces to Snatched, so this didn't make sense.

"I don't fit in those. They're not me." She twisted her lips to the side and dropped her gaze.

Those few words followed up the sledgehammer with a hot knife. I had picked out all of her clothes. Every single one of them. Not the guys. Not the designers. Me.

With her body in mind.

"What does that mean?" I dropped back on my butt, lowering my head.

Raking her hand through her hair, she let out a frustrated noise in the back of her throat. "Kim..." Her top lip curled as she twisted and sat against the wall.

At first, she only looked at the ground, then she started to raise her eyes to mine and my heart thumped erratically in my chest, trying to break free of its confines.

Was this where she told me she was leaving? That she didn't feel the same intense connection that we did to her?

Lies. It would be *lies*.

"I don't feel comfortable in those clothes. I only wore them because I didn't want to embarrass you and the boys," Beasty sighed, beating her head softly against the wall. She closed her eyes and then I could breathe again, even as that hot knife twisted a little deeper.

"You could never embarrass us," I said with a little more force than I intended.

Her eyes popped open and her gaze roamed over my face, taking in every feature. Her wide mouth frowned, and I wanted to kiss the corner of her pink lips.

"It doesn't feel that way. But I like my jeans. I like my ratty old T-shirts."

"Beasty." I winced. "They look like they're literally falling apart at the seams. Your jeans have holes around the corner pockets and they're dangerously close to showing your crack. Which sometimes is a fashion statement but not with those pieces."

She busted out laughing, gripping her stomach and rolling over until her shoulder knocked the backpack sideways. "Sorry." She waved a hand and pushed herself up. "I just..." Rifling through her backpack, she pulled out a pair—which I only think she had two—of jeans and checked the back pockets. Then another round of giggling started.

Weirdly, the giggle was soothing where the laugh had been jarring.

"Are you okay?" I furrowed my brow, aching to reach out, but instead resting my hands on my knees.

Shaking the jeans at me, Beasty sat forward. "You know what's special about these jeans?"

"What?" I asked, turning my head to the side. This felt like a trick question.

"I bought them. I paid for them with my own money. I picked them out at the thrift shop."

I wasn't dense. She was trying to tell me something significant, but she was being ridiculous.

"They're falling apart." I stared hard at her. In no world would I let her walk around in clothes like that.

"They're *mine*," she fired back.

Now I made the choking noise in the back of my throat. Jumping up to my feet, I went into the closet.

It was a masterpiece with sections for each type of attire and all the trimmings, not only to make it aesthetically pleasing, but easy to navigate. I'd had it painted in neutral tones so she could really see how any outfit worked for her.

There was even an angled antique mirror in the corner for full body inspections.

All of the efforts currently wasted.

The very front right panel was loungewear, and the next was casual wear. I opened the second drawer in the second panel and pulled out a pair of jeans closest to the style she had. The material was buttery soft, but thick enough they weren't going to thin out after two wears.

On the rack above the drawers, I pulled down a white, fitted tee. A basic model outfit, but a classic.

When I turned, she stood in the door to the closet, her arms crossed.

I didn't like that. It wasn't an obstinate gesture. It was an insecure one.

As if I were approaching a wild animal, I moved toward her. No sudden movements, no loud motions.

"If you were starving and only had ramen, I wouldn't let you eat it if I could give you more nutritious food. Ramen does nothing for your body and it's high in sodium. Not to save your pride if it was hurting you." She opened her mouth, but I gave a slight shake of my head.

"Your clothes aren't hurting you, but there's no need to wear clothes that are so old, they should have been thrown away two years ago. I picked every single piece of clothing in this closet based on what I thought would look good on you. What I thought *you* deserved. You don't like it? We'll throw it out. It's uncomfortable? We'll find new styles, but please, Beasty, let us take care of you in this way.

"Let *me* take care of you like this. It's the only way I contribute to anything around the house."

She peeked at me as she took the jeans and tee from my hands, and moved her thumb back and forth across the material.

I hoped these were okay.

"You are a model, Kim. You literally made it possible for you four to get out of West Virginia."

Another twist of that fucking hot knife.

We got out, and she didn't. I heard everything she didn't say.

"Being a pretty face opened doors, but there's no talent in that."

Again, she opened her mouth to argue, but I shook my head. "All the guys are good at something that really helps us out. All I have is my face and fashion sense. Don't take that from me because you're stubborn." One side of my smile kicked up.

She left me in the closet and then the bathroom door shut.

That was a good sign.

Today was going to be great, I could tell.

When she stepped out of the bathroom, I lost my breath. Damn. It was such a simple outfit, but it molded perfectly to her body, highlighting every asset Beasty had. I did that. I picked out the perfect size and cut that did more than flatter her figure. Combined with her sharp gaze, it made her a goddess.

I held out my arm, but she walked past me. My smile dimmed but I didn't lose it completely.

It didn't even bother me that she refused to speak on the drive to Snatched. Much.

It was a short ride, anyway.

"This way," I nodded when we entered through the front. There was a small crowd in the main room since the bar was open and serving lunch.

Strange for a club, but it worked for us and pandered to the business crowd.

I led her through the back hall to one of the public rooms. This part of the club was closed during the day, so the halls were empty, except a few lone dancers straggling in.

This was only my third meeting. The third meeting with the dancers–period–outside of their training with the hired choreographer.

An extra pep was high in my step as I opened the door and stood to the side for Beasty to enter ahead of me. I may have had a hellacious childhood, but I had learned manners.

The dancers were laughing and chatting, lounging around the stage and platforms. When they saw us, it dwindled. Beasty slowed and let me pass by.

This time, it didn't seem like insecurity, but uncertainty.

"How are you badasses doing today?" I called out. I didn't even need to raise my voice that much, the acoustics were really well done in the room.

The women whooped, and the men laughed.

Beasty gave me a sideways look. She'd never seen me be anything other than my bashful self with her, or the smiling coy model for the fashion world. This would be a treat.

"We're doing just peachy," Rachel called from the back.

She was the second dancer we hired. Classically trained with contemporary roots as well. She fit right in for some of the more emotional dances we had planned.

"How have the last few days been since the...mishap?" I tapped my lips to only partially cover my smirk.

We hadn't made Lake's and Joaquin's arrests public knowledge, but the club had been temporarily closed for a short time during the search. We couldn't hide that. Although to the public, we covered with the story of a burst pipe.

Another round of snickering made its way through the room. All good-natured. Club and sometimes restaurant workers were usually nonplussed about shady business dealings. We also had every single employee sign an NDA, and they were paid handsomely for their skills. More than if they found other positions around the area.

"The tips are the best I've ever gotten. And I've worked some pretty crazy parties." That was Roddy. Also ballet and contemporary, although I think he'd done a stint with the circus.

"I mean, you *are* working the themed rooms. The requirements to get in are high. Just wait until you make it to the invitation-only rooms." Not that we had dancers in those rooms per se, but they didn't need to know that. They needed something to strive toward.

I swung my gaze around the room.

All the dancers were eager. Happy. It was just what I wanted to see.

"Now, we need to map out the dances." I searched for Andrea, finding her sitting on the edge of the stage across the room. "Andrea, do you have the rooms and assignments?"

"Yep! I have it all lined out." She hopped down and wove her way toward me. Andrea was the best choreographer on the east coast, and that was a feat. Yet, she was a tiny goth pixie. It was a conundrum my fashion brain loved, like a puzzle that didn't make sense, yet tickled the mind in just the right way.

"We have John and Lina performing the masks in Room One. Georgie and Tom are assigned to the feral dance in Room Two. Bobby and Sin are in Room Three for urban." She ran down the list, rattling off about ten names for the neon whips in Room Four. "We are down a dancer for the big performance next month. It's not pressing right now since we have so much time, but Alina found out she's expecting, so she's going to take some time off." Andrea tapped her thumb on the edge of her tablet, thinking.

"I—" I started to jump in but Beasty walked up next to me, completely focused on Andrea.

"Do you need dance experience?"

Andrea's head shot up, and a condensing look fell over her face like a closing curtain, but her gaze flicked to me as she rearranged her features.

I wasn't intimidating. I was likable, but I still held her job in my hands just like the others.

"Obviously. We're performers." It was as close to the snark line as she was willing to get.

Beasty nodded, not caring about her attitude. That was what I loved about Beasty, even when she was alone in foster care, she'd seemed so strong.

"I'm a quick learner, and I work hard. Is there anything you'd be willing to teach me or where I could fit in?" She held her chin up as she looked down on Andrea.

Andrea was so tiny, and Beasty so tall, I was almost surprised Andrea didn't get angry for Beasty flexing her size on her.

But Andrea was a bit of a battle-ax. She didn't give two shits about anyone.

Raising one pointed eyebrow, she perused Beasty's figure, never once glancing my way. Ballsy.

"You have the right body type. That's half the battle for some disciplines. You can come in for a few training sessions for a trial. If you're as quick a study as you say, I'll give it a shot. If not, then no hard feelings. Maybe Kim will let you run drinks in the main room." Implying that was all Beasty could be good for.

"I'm sorry, Andrea. What kind of authority do you hold here?" I mused softly, the edges of my lips curling up when I really wanted to snarl at her.

Beasty wanted a job. I could maybe work with dancer if she was out of touching distance.

There was no way in hell that she'd run drinks and get groped or worse. Lake would constantly be in and out of jail until they just tossed away the key.

Andrea's shoulders climbed up to her ears before she slowly canted her head toward me. Everyone else cut all the noise. They weren't even breathing.

Andrea and the dancers needed just a teensy bit of a lesson.

"Just the choreography," she gulped. No way would she want to lose her very generous pay for something so stupid as a flippant comment to try and cut someone down.

She wasn't like that, not really, hence her giving Beasty a shot. But she was still part of a very catty world. Dancing was just as bad as modeling. Maybe worse.

"You know my backstory, yes? All of our backstories?"

She nodded and I stepped closer, edging Beasty out of the way. I didn't bother lowering my voice. I wanted everyone here to hear every word I said.

I wanted them to commit it to memory.

"Beasty is important to me."

Someone snickered in the back.

I snapped my gaze around the room, searching for the person too stupid to live. "Is that funny?" I called out. "Does someone have an issue with my *friend?*"

The culprit didn't need to give himself up. The other dancers stepped away as if he was contagious. Glancing around nervously, he tried to smile but it was more of a wince.

"No, Mr. Kim." He was getting formal. Funny since I'd never asked anyone to call me that. "She's beautiful." He ducked his head to hide his smirk. "I'm sure she'll do great. It's just a terrible name." He wiped his hands on his thighs. "Why would you call someone you care so much about, Beasty? It's not very nice."

I frowned. He was trying to placate me and mock me at the same time.

"Let me tell you a story, Mr..."

"Roberts," he supplied, his voice only slightly shaking.

"My friend here, *Cressida*," I stressed her name as I laid my palm on the nape of her neck, "was homeless as a child."

I wasn't sure if Beasty would take offense to that or not, but she stayed relaxed. Unbothered. And I reveled in the slight skin to skin contact so much, I almost lost my train of thought.

Almost.

"Through no fault of her own, she was put through hell. Do you know how hard it is to be hungry, or alone, or cold?"

The young man shook his head.

"Good. I wouldn't recommend it. But my good friend, my best friend and *lover* really–she knows." Beasty stiffened but didn't interject. Good. There was hope. "That's how she grew up. Everyone called her Beasty because she was wild." I smiled, nostalgia hitting my chest for the beautiful girl with a mess of tangled hair and dirt smudges on her cheeks. "She was happy. Yet she threw away her own version of safety to save my friends and me from the Curator. I'm sure you've heard of him?"

No one twitched. Not even Mr. Roberts acknowledged my question.

"It was terrible nasty stuff being imprisoned by that man. It was Beasty who saved us. So, I will take no criticism on her name. That is who she is. Because she's wild, and brave, and fierce. Nothing like the rest of the world. She's better than everyone else. That's fact. Not opinion."

I turned to Andrea.

"If she wants to dance, she dances. If she wants to pop balloons with forks she holds between her toes, she can. We'll put her on the main performing stage and call it modern art. No one will bat an eye and they'll rave about the genius of it all. Understood?"

Beasty snorted and tried to cover it as Andrea nodded so hard her teeth clinked together.

"Great!" I widened my smile and curled my arm around Beasty. "We have some big visitors coming soon, and we need to make sure we have all performances nailed down before then. I'll be walking through the rooms tonight to check everyone out. Beasty will be my date, won't you Beasty?" I nuzzled the side of her face with my nose.

She pulled back and glanced at me, her eyes brimming with emotion. I'd like to think it was a step in the right direction. Then she narrowed her eyes. "Maybe."

Laughing, I tugged her around so we could leave. I was done with this meeting.

"You all will do great! I have complete faith in each one of you. You were hired for a reason. Oh, and Andrea." I stopped us, turning to the side to give Andrea a warning glare.

"No more veiled comments to break Beasty's confidence. I won't like it, and you don't know it yet, but you don't want to get on Atlas' bad side. As soon as his meeting is over, I'm sure he'll be watching footage of this one."

She blanched. Good.

Now we just had to break it to the others that I set Beasty up with a job as a dancer. But I'd die on that hill.

Better a dancer on stage than running drinks in the crowd. Or working for Gio.

Chapter Eleven

ATLAS - PRESENT DAY

"I'm sure this will be a headliner," Marie said smugly as she started packing her notes away.

I glanced over my shoulder at the camera in the corner. Joaquin was most likely watching. He always had a stick up his ass when I met with anyone who stank even the slightest bit of media. It scared him shitless that I could make one wrong comment and blow our lives up.

Foolish man.

I never said anything by accident. Anything that blew up was intentional. And I only instigated scenes that would get him hard.

Harder for me, I should say.

"I hope so." I threaded my fingers together as I leaned back in our favorite VIP booth. It was actually a smart move to do our meetings here. Everything in this corner was recorded in case anyone tried to fuck us over, but it was also in a prime location where the patrons meeting here for lunch could get a good look at us.

It was good for business.

"I'll let you know what Tommy says, but I don't see any

issues." She grinned and hugged her bag to her chest, one minute away from getting out of the booth.

She lingered, like most people did in our presence.

But today, I didn't rush her away. The goodwill was necessary just in case word got out about Lake's and Joaquin's arrests. So far, so good. Except for Joaquin griping about the pendulum swinging over our head.

The man was too stressed. I'd fuck it right out of him later.

"Sounds great." I pressed my stomach into the table top as I glanced around the room.

About half the room was full as a few servers bounced from table to table, dropping off plates and refilling drinks.

The dance floor sat empty. I'd have to talk to Kim about bringing some of the dancers out during the day. Nothing crazy, just something subtle to give a high-end vibe. Something to set our club apart from all the other restaurants in town.

Hell, maybe we could even close the room down to the public during the day and make it part of a membership. A good ninety percent of the people here wore business attire. They could afford it.

"Okay, well, I'll be in touch." Marie fluttered her eyelashes as she slid out of the booth. She had an extra sashay in her step as she descended the stairs out of the VIP area.

I flipped off the camera and smirked just for Joaquin.

I didn't waste any time heading back to the office. Pulling my phone out, I started to check the home surveillance to see what Beasty was doing, but there was a message in the group chat instead.

KIM:

> Beasty and I are heading to the club for
> the staff meeting.

That was thirty minutes ago.

Slowing my steps, I accessed the club surveillance. The club rooms were all empty now, except for some of the dancers practicing their performances.

But the office...

Joaquin wasn't watching me because he was watching Beasty's ass as she looked through the meaningless knick knacks on Lake's desk.

The thought of her leaving us was still too hot as it cut through my chest. Joaquin thought I was crazy?

I was strategic.

The one way to ensure Beasty would never run was to make sure she was just as obsessed and addicted to us as we were to her.

It was too one-sided. I didn't give a fuck what Beasty said. It was what she *did* that I paid attention to. It was what *I* always did.

Watched.

Snorting, I picked up my pace down the long hallway.

Beasty was on point with one thing. I didn't really know her. She'd never really spoken to anyone when I stalked her before.

And I said stalked because why pretty it up. I was her biggest stalker.

I knew every expression her face could make, her mannerisms, her habits. But without the conversation piece, her mind was just out of reach.

We'd have to change that.

The door behind me slammed and I twisted to see who was following me.

Lake stomped down the hallway with a thunderous expression darkening his face. Without any of the mood music, his footsteps bounced off the walls.

"We have to make some calls." He clipped my shoulder as he brushed by.

I reached out and grabbed his arm. "What are you talking about?" I didn't have time for this. I wanted–needed to be where Beasty was. I ached to make her squirm.

"Parker's pissed. He's planning his trip out." He glanced up and down the hallway. We were alone, but it was second nature to scan our surroundings. "Gio heard from one of his contacts that the Pescis are going to hit the club. They're miffed we aren't getting the bad press they expected us to."

"They could always leak it." That would be unfortunate for us, but it would get the end goal they wanted. Or at least move the needle in that direction.

Lake gave a gruff shake of his head, and turned toward the secured entrance to the offices, staring holes through the door that led to where Beasty was. He would have seen the text. He'd know that was where she'd most likely be, even if he didn't check the cameras.

"No, they wouldn't. They already pushed the line of getting too much attention on themselves. Gio thinks one of the idiots in charge got the bright idea to hit us that way because of who we are. They have no idea we don't give a fuck about the fame."

That was a conversation for another time. "What kind of calls do you need to make?"

"We're calling in some favors. Gio doesn't know when they plan to make a mess so we need to be prepared and have some people on staff or at least watching." His lips thinned. "For the unforeseeable future, Gio and his two friends are going to be staples in the club."

Lake would hate that. To him, Gio was only minutely more tolerable than Parker.

"Like you haven't seen Adrian slipping in and out the back entrance."

No way Lake wouldn't have noticed. Since he'd decided to be our bodyguard, he leaned in on every possible tool to know everything that happened around us. He had the security footage on his phone just like I did.

Except, I zeroed in on Beasty. Lake watched everyone else.

It worked, because between us, we had all avenues covered.

"Beasty is in the office, so unless you want to air our dirty laundry..."

He pulled away from my hold and headed straight to the doors.

"No, we'll take Guy's office. You can join me."

I cursed as I followed him. We paused long enough for him to scan his keycard access, then passed through to the holding room. He scanned his card again, then passed our closed office door and went to the next one.

"I need this room. Out." Lake rapped his knuckles on the wall just inside the door.

The man behind the desk was Lake's head of security. We didn't have friends, but this guy was as close as Lake had ever gotten.

He jumped up, knocking his chair back. "What code?"

"No code," Lake headed to the security cameras and started hitting buttons to change the angles and perspective. "I just have to make a phone call and I need privacy. There are too many people in my office."

Guy relaxed and snickered. "I told you the true head of security needed his own office."

Lake sighed, but it was packed full of frustration as he

kept tapping buttons. "I don't normally need privacy. My friends and I share everything. This is just a one-off that has to be handled delicately."

Guy hummed as he rounded the desk and sauntered out. What did he think this was, some kind of lover's spat or something?

He was too amused for me.

Walking over, I slammed the door on his retreating back and twisted the lock.

Lake deflated and he slowed down on pushing the buttons so fast. "Okay, I don't recognize any of the men here. Or women. Gio showed me a whole catalog of who to watch out for."

"Do you need me here?" I glanced at the door.

"Yes," he snapped, not looking at me as he pulled out his phone. "I need moral fucking support. I don't like some of these assholes. If I step over a line, I need you to pull me back."

"Hell," I muttered as I walked closer to him. He leaned his ass on the edge of Guy's desk and hit call.

Crossing my arms, I tucked my chin. There were so many things I'd rather be doing right now.

"Yes?" A voice hesitated on the other end.

I knew that voice. And I hoped to never hear it again.

"Rich," Lake barked. "I need to call in a few *favors*." He made it sound like Rich had some power here. As if he had the ability to back out. But he didn't. Especially since he'd handed over so many juicy details on Valencia.

"What are they?" Fear trilled in the high pitch of his tone.

"We need at least five models at the club in the VIP Room every night. We'll comp their visit. Free drinks. Good press for them. But, if I need it, I need a scene. A messy one. Which is still good publicity for them."

I sneered. I hated that saying. All publicity was good publicity. What a crock of shit.

"I don't know if I can do that. There aren't any shows around DC for a few months. Most models are in New York or LA," Rich rambled.

"I don't give a shit. You have access to Valencia's database and funds. Make it happen." The implied threat was there. If he didn't do what Lake wanted, with minimal benefit to him, Lake would destroy his career.

They hung up.

Then he made another call. This one to a few security companies he'd worked with in the past.

He arranged for extra plain clothes to be there.

It was the next call that really made my blood boil.

"Bryce," Lake said as the man answered his phone, his top lip curled in disgust. "This is Lake."

"Who?" As if he didn't know who Lake was. He wouldn't answer his phone if he didn't know the number. No one in this industry did.

"The head of security for Atlas and Kim. I'm sure you remember. A few years ago, you attempted to help Lisbet out by trying to maneuver our best friend out of the way."

"We don't fucking need him," I growled, grabbing Lake's wrist and squeezing.

Lake hit mute and looked up at me. "If worse comes to worse, we need a fall guy." Then he unmuted the phone.

"What do you want?"

"Funny you should ask that. I have some...fascinating information about you regarding a beach house six years ago..."

The line went silent.

"Good. I'm glad to see I have your attention. Here's what I'm going to need from you..." He outlined exactly what he wanted to happen, but I stopped listening.

All I saw was his skeezy ass leaning into Beasty. Whispering to her. Acting like he wanted her. Like she was nothing but a cunt to fill.

When Lake had pummeled him into the wall, a burst of excitement flared through me. Bryce had deserved it. He wasn't worthy of her.

We hadn't been either, not until she fucking left us.

"Are you okay?" Lake shook off my hold.

I hadn't even realized I'd still been holding onto him. "What?"

"Are you okay?" He peered into my eyes before he took in the rest of my face.

My jaw clenched so tight my gums ached. I relaxed it and sucked in a deep breath.

"Fine." I rolled my head from side to side, the cracks from the movement giving a different kind of satisfaction. "I'm done here. I'm finding Beasty."

"I'm not done, you jackass! I haven't even gotten to the ones I really hate!"

"Don't care!" I called over my shoulder as I unlocked the door and threw it open. Guy was nowhere to be seen. I scanned my badge to get into our office, and stopped short.

Beasty wasn't looking through Lake's knick knacks anymore. She was in the chair in front of Kim's desk, angled toward Joaquin as he worked. Kim was behind her, massaging her scalp like he did this on the daily.

What the hell happened between the hallway and here for him to give her a scalp massage? What happened for her to want to let him?

My stomach still burned like acid, and seeing Kim touching her only added to it.

Beasty cracked her eyes when the door shut behind me, but she didn't acknowledge me.

Fuck her.

Fuck her right and proper. If she was going to act like I didn't matter to her, then she could start her punishments now.

I quickened my pace until I was right in front of her and dropped to my knees. Her eyes snapped open, but I didn't say anything.

Unbuttoning her jeans, I shoved my fingers under the band of her jeans and underwear and yanked them down. She screeched and slapped my hands away, but I was too much of an expert at stripping jeans away. Joaquin put up a harder fight than she did.

"What are you doing?" she screamed.

Once the pants were around her knees, I gave a sharp slap to the side of her ass, ignoring the revulsion licking up the small of my back.

She yelped, but when she didn't try to push me away anymore, I smoothed my hand down her thigh until I reached the top of her jeans. I slid my thumbs over her soft flesh and wedged my fingers under the band again.

"You said you'd take your punishments anywhere and anyway I wanted to give them to you. That you wanted to be here and you'd prove it." I didn't raise my voice even though my brain was imploding from thoughts of her with other men.

I needed to erase every memory she'd ever had of anyone who wasn't us.

Flicking my gaze at Kim, I measured his judgment. His eyes were dark and hooded as he gazed at where my hands met her thighs. I'd have no problems from him.

Joaquin huffed, but he could suck my dick. And he would later.

Beasty's eyes blazed with hate and anger. Delicious emotions I wanted to see on anyone who wasn't her. I didn't want her hate. Or her anger.

I wanted her love.

Her *obsession*.

I wanted us to be her reason to breathe, and without us, she'd crumble from withdrawal.

Those were the kind of feelings I wanted from her, and right now, we were going to start her training. Her conditioning.

"Do you want me to stop?" I asked, my voice a warning.

She'd given her permission in the club and now she was taking it back.

As much as I wanted to take exactly what I wanted, I wouldn't do that. Not to her or anyone.

If she pushed me away...This was done. I wouldn't fuck with her anymore. It would be the final nail in her coffin with us.

Beasty's nostrils flared and she turned to Joaquin, then twisted back to see Kim. It was all so fast, like she needed to see how they were reacting to my stripping her.

I couldn't see Joaquin, but I could see Kim. And when she faced me again, her eyes were wide and her chest rose with each quick inhale. I smirked. She hadn't expected to see that much desire on Kim's face.

"Well?" I mimicked moving her jeans down just a hair, then tugged most of my fingers out.

"No," she gritted out. "I don't want you to stop."

Like she was moving through sludge, she curled her fingers around the sides of the chair. Once she was still, I pulled off her shoes, then removed her pants.

At first, she pressed her thighs together. I raised a brow. I didn't want to be mean to Beasty, but I couldn't stop it. I taunted her. Used the power of my expressions to call her a coward.

She huffed and relaxed her thighs.

Cupping her knees, I pushed them open. I held her gaze

as I spread her wide. I wanted to see her pussy, but I wanted to watch the emotions rolling over her more.

As beautiful as I was sure her cunt was, they were all mostly the same. But there was only one Beasty. No one had her face. And that was what I wanted to devour.

She bit her lip and a blush stained her cheeks. It stretched down her neck and her chest. So red.

The office was cool, but here Beasty was, burning up.

Her legs trembled and when I finally dropped my gaze, I stopped breathing. Maybe they didn't all look the same. She was so wet, a bit of her arousal trickled out.

I hooked my hands under the backside of her thighs and jerked her to the edge of her seat.

She yipped, her fingers turning white where she gripped the chair.

Kim reached out and held her shoulders back. Probably to comfort her, but also to hold her still.

God, she smelled delicious. I slid my hands up the inside of her thighs, and when I reached her apex, I used my thumbs to spread her lips apart.

Just a little bit of hair. She trimmed, kept herself neat, but didn't wax.

Leaning forward, I blew across her clit and she whimpered.

"What should I do Kim?" I glanced up. Kim leaned over her shoulder so he could see exactly what I was doing.

"I want you to tease her." His voice was deep, deeper than I'd ever heard.

I chuckled as Beasty moaned.

She didn't like that. "I want you to make me feel good. If you're going to be there–"

Beasty didn't get to finish her order. I slapped the inside of her thigh. Immediately a bright red handprint appeared.

I grinned. Where was Lake? He was going to be pissed he was missing all the fun.

"Nothing else from you. This is for us, remember? Your punishment. Call it hazing if you want. Whatever you need to tell yourself to sit through it quietly and be a good girl." I glared, daring her to argue.

If she did, I'd leave her right here. Alone and untouched.

That wasn't what I wanted, but it would still be a different kind of edging.

"I won't talk," she groused. It was so irritable, it was adorable.

"Good. Now, Kim, you said tease her." I rubbed circles with my thumbs, leaving her exposed but causing enough movement it would be a delicious sort of torture. "What did you have in mind?"

"Lick around her hood." His voice quivered as his eyes darkened. He was so eager. Of course he would be, Beasty was still his one and only.

Rolling my lips together, I dropped my gaze. I didn't know who was more worked up, Beasty or Kim.

At least Joaquin wasn't trying to place a stop to this, afraid that we'd hurt Kim's feelings. But Kim was over the shock of us sharing. From the look on his face now, I'd think he craved this as much as Beasty did.

Slowly, drawing it out so painfully long, I lowered my head until my mouth was right there. I kissed her clit, amused at her soft intake of breath, then I used the tip of my tongue to circle the sensitive bud.

It pulsed and I pulled back.

"You're not ready this quick, are you?" I grinned. "How embarrassing."

She scowled and tried to close her legs. I just squeezed in warning.

"That's nothing to be embarrassed about," Joaquin barked from his seat.

I glanced over to find him reclined back, his cock so hard there was a massive tent under his slacks. He pushed forward, wincing, but still able to narrow his eyes on me.

"We will never shame Beasty for what she feels. If you do, we have a problem."

Most of the time, his chastisements were as much fun as his anger. But this one got to me. I was being nasty, but there were lines to my meanness and this crossed one of them.

I took a moment to collect myself, and turned back to Beasty. "There's nothing to be embarrassed about. It's flattering that you'd be so aroused by my touch, you're seconds from coming. I'm sorry."

She blinked, like she wasn't sure what to do with that.

I knew what to do.

"Just sit back, I won't let you come," I murmured as I dropped my head. She leaned back in the chair, unaware that I wouldn't let her come at all today. Not until she needed us with the same desperation.

Licking around the bud, I pulled it between my lips and sucked gently on it. Her breath quickened, and I didn't have a hope of staying soft. Already I strained against the seam of my pants.

I worked her with my mouth, splitting my time between her clit and slit. Every once in a while, I shoved my tongue inside her tight pussy.

She'd quake and I'd back off, go somewhere else. Except now she trembled so hard, I sat back on my heels. She stared at my chin, seemingly mesmerized, as I massaged the sides of her lips again, absently pulling her open and giving her just the tiniest amount of friction.

At some point she'd moved her hands to grip Kim's

wrists. Beasty's mouth was slack as she dropped her head back against Kim's stomach, rolling her hips like she needed more. I was sure she did.

I grinned at her tortured look.

When her legs stopped shaking, she started making noises of irritation. Then I started my ministrations all over again.

I kept her face in full view as much as I could. It was like a new religion watching this side of Beasty.

How her face showed pleasure was unlike anything I'd ever seen before. With me between her thighs, she was a new person. A sweeter one. Less prickly.

More mine.

I hummed and she jerked against my hold.

Yes, she was more mine this way.

"Tongue fuck her." Joaquin's voice was guttural and closer than it should have been.

I glanced over my shoulder, and there was Joaquin. His chair was at the corner of his desk, only a few feet from us with his arms crossed and his hard cock still causing a scene.

Who was I to argue?

I didn't when they had actual good ideas.

Kissing my way up the inside of her thigh, I worked her back up, massaging her clit with small motions as I fucked her with my tongue.

She was so wet, and tasted so goddamned good.

"She loves it," Kim whispered, his voice strangled. "Do you love it, Beasty? Is he fucking you so good with his fingers and tongue."

Beasty grunted, shifting her hips to try and ride my face. But I pulled back.

No way in hell was I going to let her ride her way to completion.

"What the hell, Atlas! This is enough. You've teased me enough," she wheezed as she pushed hair out of her face.

The door clicked and Lake walked in. It took a minute for him to see our positions. Then he skidded to a halt and shoved his phone in his pocket.

"*This* is why you left me?" Lake pursed his lips and his eyes flashed from me to Beasty.

I dropped my head and gave Beasty one more lick before resting my cheek on her inner thigh.

"I was helping Beasty with a few things." I couldn't lose the grin as I let Beasty's legs drop and started putting her panties back on.

"What are you doing?" She kicked me away.

"We're done, Beasty. Now that Lake's here, there's something else that needs my attention."

Joaquin grunted, but I ignored him. There was desire rolling off her. She wanted me. And the physical evidence was the salve I needed.

Kim removed his hands and stepped back. He adjusted himself in his pants and rubbed a hand down his face.

I started to give her another bullshit answer when she jumped up out of the chair and hopped around to finish pulling her panties and jeans on.

"I can't fucking believe I let you touch me. You fucking asshole. *In here.* In front of everyone." Her voice was strangled.

Fuck that. We weren't going to act like I defiled her.

Pushing to my feet, I caught her in my arms and held her tight, even as she struggled.

"I told you, you'd be punished. After the way you've been acting, like we're less than the dirt under your shoes, you deserved this." I pressed my lips together as I flicked my gaze between both her eyes.

Beasty stopped, tipping her head back. Shock slackened her face.

"Being with us, any of us, wherever we want, however we want, isn't shameful. Not between us." I pressed her against my chest, drilling home with my gaze exactly how serious I was. "Is that clear?"

Her face screwed up like she wasn't sure if she should be livid, confused, or maybe a mixture of both. She settled on somewhere in between.

"I don't deserve a punishment."

"Then call this a courtship," I snarled, too angry to soften my words. Beasty, the girl I'd chased after my whole life was treating *me* like the bad guy. Like someone who would hurt her just because I could.

She needed to look in the mirror.

"You're so fucked in the head, you don't even realize it." She elbowed me in the ribs and broke my hold.

Then she raced to the bathroom and slammed the door.

"I told you this was a fucking mistake," Joaquin said, as he moved his chair back in place and grabbed his keycard. He stopped at the door, staring at the wood as his card hovered just outside the range of the keypad. "If she leaves, this is on you. Because of your fucked up ideas on how to make her yours."

"Like you're any better." I scoffed. "Your idea of dealing with a problem is to spend money on the floor while drinking yourself into a stupor."

"Which I haven't done since Beasty came back."

"You've drank since she came back," Lake said.

A sad smile ghosted over Joaquin's face. "Okay, that was a lie. But I'm doing my best to change. I know it's fucked. But I don't want that side of me to touch her. And what you're doing, Atlas, you're fucking *with* her. Making her hate us and question us, when you should be wanting to build her trust."

"She wants the assholes," I argued, wiping my chin on my sleeve.

Joaquin barked out a laugh. "Beasty doesn't want the assholes. She just wants *us*. But honestly, I'm doubting that. You guys continue to play your messed up games. I'm heading to the Gold Room."

"Just like you always do! You're no better than I am!" I called after him, but the door already shut behind him, and it was sound proof. "Fuck!" I yelled and kicked the chair Beasty had been in.

He was wrong. She needed this. *I* needed this.

Otherwise, we'd never know she wanted to stay with us.

He was wrong.

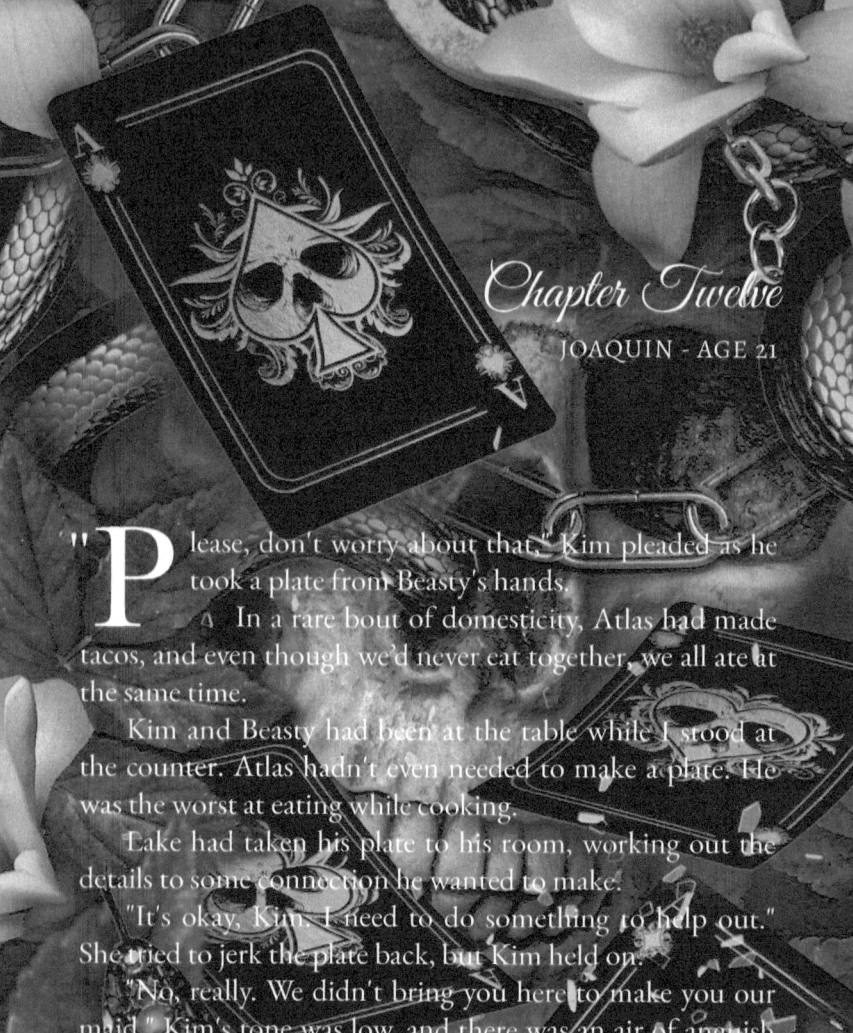

Chapter Twelve

"**P**lease, don't worry about that," Kim pleaded as he took a plate from Beasty's hands.

In a rare bout of domesticity, Atlas had made tacos, and even though we'd never eat together, we all ate at the same time.

Kim and Beasty had been at the table while I stood at the counter. Atlas hadn't even needed to make a plate. He was the worst at eating while cooking.

Lake had taken his plate to his room, working out the details to some connection he wanted to make.

"It's okay, Kim. I need to do something to help out." She tried to jerk the plate back, but Kim held on.

"No, really. We didn't bring you here to make you our maid." Kim's tone was low, and there was an air of anguish I'd never heard in his voice before.

"Kim, I need to do this, I–"

"Really, Beasty. It's not–"

Somehow, the plate slipped from both their hands and all four of us watched it fall.

No one moved to catch it, although there was shit all I could have done from the kitchen.

Time slowed just before the plate crashed. The sound exploded, cracking through the room like the warning notes of thunder, seconds before the plate seemed to break into a hundred pieces.

As shards flew across the floor, Beasty crouched down. "Oh no!"

"Stop. *Stop*!" Kim grabbed onto her shoulders and tugged her up. "You're going to cut your hands and your feet."

Her face turned red as her gaze darted to every piece of cheap porcelain that she could see. Kim gave her a soft shake.

"Hey."

She tilted her head to the side and cut her gaze at him. I turned to hide my smirk.

This wasn't funny. Beasty wasn't settling in with us, and she had a bunch of numb nuts who didn't know how to act around her.

Her anxiety was so smothering, I was damn near choking on it.

And still, how she glanced at Kim, like she was about to punch him in the gut instead of the contrition I knew she felt, was hilarious.

"Carry Beasty out of here. Joaquin will clean it up." Atlas jerked his chin toward the hallway.

"Fucking excuse you?" I pushed his shoulder and he grinned.

"I cooked. You can clean up the mess. It won't hurt you to clean up after Beasty either." Beasty stiffened and Atlas didn't even see it.

"What the fuck is your problem?" I slapped both of his shoulders this time and his lower back hit the counter.

"Take Beasty out, Kim," Atlas called while keeping his gaze locked on me. He was being an asshole and from Kim's frown and Beasty's ducked head, everyone knew it except for him.

"Come on Beasty." Taking her elbows, Kim used his fingertips to pull her arms away from her body. He was probably trying to figure out how to pick her up with the least amount of touch. Actually...

I turned to face them.

It was a miracle he was even touching her like this.

She yelped as he bent down, hugged her under her ass and lifted her in the air with a low grunt.

Atlas glanced over his shoulder at the sound, a dark smile curling his lips. "I didn't know Kim was that strong."

I thought I heard Kim muttering under his breath, but they were already around the corner and out of sight from the kitchen.

"You dick." I shoved Atlas again because I needed to do something with my anger. If I didn't get it out this way, I'd turn around and punch the wall. Atlas deserved the hurt more.

Except, it didn't hurt him. He just laughed.

I opened my mouth to tell him every which way he was an ass, but he grabbed my face and roughly pulled me to him as he slammed his mouth down on mine. I bit his lip, and he laughed harder, his body shaking as he dug his fingers into my cheeks.

Using his brute strength, he walked me backward until I hit the wall, molding his body to mine. Knowing exactly what pushed my buttons, he rubbed his hard cock against mine, pressing so deep into me I fought to breathe.

For a second, I forgot about his remarks and reveled in the feel of him. Of all the partners I'd had, no one compared to Atlas. No fucking one.

He smelled like home, but spicy like a thrill of betting large, knowing there was every chance I would lose huge and doing it anyway.

Atlas was everything to me.

Except, he wasn't.

The other guys mattered.

More than that. Beasty mattered. She was more important than all of them, and he'd just made her feel like an irrelevant shit. Nice to have, but not important.

Using all my strength, I shoved him away. He grunted as he stumbled back a few steps, using the back of one hand to wipe his mouth.

The bright, fluorescent lights overhead washed out his gorgeous skin and cast long shadows over his face. But that didn't take away from any of his beauty.

Asshole.

"Do you know what you just did!" I whisper-shouted, injecting every ounce of disgust I could in my voice as I pointed toward the back of the apartment.

His lips twisted to one side before his smile soured. "I gave Kim a reason to be alone with Beasty. Isn't that what we wanted? To give him a chance to get closer to her."

He was on crack. There was no other way he'd find what he did an acceptable reason for spewing the shit he did.

Flaring my nostrils, I took two steps forward, getting in his face. "The way you taunted Beasty...You didn't see the way she deflated. You made her feel terrible. Like she's a klutz or something."

For a second, he wavered, but then any bit of remorse disappeared. "Kim will fix it. This is the opportunity he's been looking for." Atlas turned away and moved his plate to the sink. "Are you going to clean that up?"

I peeled back my top lip and fisted my hands at my side. What had gotten into him tonight?

"What's going on, and what did you do to Joaquin?" Lake asked drolly as he brought his own plate back.

He never fucking did that. Just like all of us, we were trying to catch a glimpse of Beasty without being in her face.

"Beasty and Kim dropped a plate. I told Joaquin to clean it up." Atlas rounded the counter and headed out of the kitchen, carefully stepping to avoid getting porcelain in the soles of his shoes. "You're more than welcome to clean it up too. I cooked so you all are on your own."

"That's not what happened," I seethed. It didn't do a damned bit of good. Atlas was gone, and Lake sighed as he left and reappeared with a broom and dustpan. Where both Kim and Atlas tried not to track shards through the house, Lake was barefoot and didn't seem like he gave a fuck if he shredded his feet or not.

"I can clean that up. That wasn't the point."

Lake raised one brow as he crouched. "Then what is the point?"

"Beasty isn't settling in. Atlas isn't making it easier." I hesitated. I could share what he'd said, but we didn't need Lake in Atlas' shit. He enjoyed stirring trouble too much.

"This is just a new change for her," Lake said as we swept up the last of the plate. Except, he missed several pieces around the edges of the room. Once he stood up and dumped it, I took the broom from him and started collecting all the stray bits.

"It's not just that it's new. She doesn't like being here with us." I punished the floor with hard strokes of the broom.

"She likes it just fine," he argued and I stopped, dropping my forehead onto the end of the handle.

I

Lake could be just as thick-headed, but in a different way from Atlas. It was no wonder I went out most nights to drink.

"How? Tell me how she likes it just fine here when she's depressed and antsy all the time." I resumed cleanup as Lake crouched down and held the dustpan for me.

I brushed the last pieces into it as his jaw worked and he studied the floor.

"It takes time. She's been with us just a few weeks."

Yeah, and in those weeks we'd taken her out a handful of times and she hated it. The people in the fashion industry weren't for the faint of heart. They were scheming, narcissistic, petty asses. Coming up through foster care, I'd–like the rest of the guys–thought she'd understand that they didn't matter.

Their opinions were shit. They weren't worth the air she breathed.

She'd never admit it, but they bothered her.

"You remember how it was when Kim and Atlas first started working. It was a shitshow. This life takes an adjustment period." Lake raised his gaze, confident that he finally had a good answer.

But he forgot I knew his tells. It took him way too long to come up with that answer for me to believe it as truth.

"It sucked balls for me and you. And we eventually found our place. What's Beasty going to do? The best way for her to settle in is to find a purpose. She's not going to be our fucking maid," I griped, but it was lost on Lake. He hadn't been here for that conversation.

"She *is* our purpose."

That was it. He and Atlas were hitting the hard stuff when I wasn't looking.

"I can't with you right now." I propped the broom

against the wall as Lake dumped the last bit of porcelain in the trash.

Walking through the empty living room, I headed for the room I shared with Atlas.

He was reckless kissing me earlier. Beasty could have come out. It wasn't that I cared about her knowing we fucked. I wasn't sure she'd understand it.

We grew up in West Virginia for fuck's sake. They had even less tolerance for gay men than for people who didn't look like them.

It wasn't blatant, more of a subtle behind the scenes kind of intolerance. It was in their looks and backhanded comments.

Beasty wasn't like that. Most kids who grew up how we did knew there was more to the world than that. But some of it could have still rubbed off on her without her even knowing.

We just needed her to be here a little longer before we sprung it on her. And Atlas was trying to fuck it all up.

We were supposed to make Beasty's life easier. Lake was right in that was what this was all about, but Atlas was trying to make her fit us instead of the other way around.

I needed to go out for a few hours. That was it. Play a few hands of whatever game table was open. I wasn't picky.

If it included cards, I loved it.

Our bedroom door was shut. We kept it that way. Beasty would have questions on why there was only one bed, but she had no reason to be in here, and she wasn't a snoop.

Inside, Atlas had the air return cover pulled out of the wall and he laid on his back with his head next to it. He was the image of relaxation. His eyes were closed and his hands were threaded over his chest.

But this wasn't an isolated image.

He was spying.

Cracking open an eye when I walked closer, he scrunched up his nose like I was the fucking problem.

All of those heated emotions that had started to calm, swelled right back up to the point that I ached to just shove my dick in his mouth to keep him from talking bullshit.

That was what he wanted, so I refrained.

"What are you doing?" I mouthed as I got down to my hands and knees.

I wasn't above spying either when opportunities were handed to me on a silver platter.

Atlas had been worse here than before when we were kids. It was like those years apart broke him, and now he was a stalker on steroids. At least she'd never know.

He placed a finger to his lips and gestured toward the hole with his head.

Leaning down, I breathed as quietly as possible and listened.

"I'm not sure this is the place for me." Beasty wasn't sad, or angry. But she was resolute.

Panic sparked in my chest.

"That's not true, Beasty. If I belong here, so do you. Where we don't belong is in a small town where people look down on us." Kim's hushed whisper was almost unintelligible. It was probably only from years of living with him that I knew what he said.

"You belong here because you're beautiful," she sighed and her defeat had my fingers curling tight into the carpet. "I'm not, and they do look down on me."

"Okay, I know exactly what you're talking about with the people here. I had that too. Consider it a type of hazing where they test to see if you have staying power, but..." he trailed off.

Was he not going to address her putting herself down? Even Atlas stiffened.

"Did you say you're not beautiful?" Kim asked with a hint of a growl.

I grinned. He couldn't muster up a true growl if it slapped him in the face.

Next to me, Atlas tipped his head back and scowled at the hole, his nose crinkled up in disgust.

"Kim." She sounded peeved. Exasperated. Especially when it was followed by a chuff of air.

"Beasty." He returned her same energy and I grinned. *This* was what I wanted for her.

I was stupid jealous of Kim, but this easy conversation was miles better than the uptight girl in the kitchen.

"My nickname is even Beasty." I imagined her rolling her eyes. "I don't care. Beauty isn't all it's cracked up to be. I realize it causes more problems than it helps, but..."

"Stop that," Kim snapped.

"What? It's true. If I was pretty, who knows what would have happened when I was growing up."

There was a pause. Did she shiver? Was she gazing at him or was she turned away to hide herself?

Shit, my palms started sweating, and little beads gathered at the base of my neck. This must be a tiny taste of that compulsion Atlas lived with.

"You're being–" I bet Kim was going to say stupid, but he stopped himself. "If no one touched you, that's a blessing. It doesn't have anything to do with how you look."

She snorted. "Kim, I don't care. I really don't. I'm just pointing out, it makes me stand out in a bad way."

"You're interesting, Beasty. You give off a *fuck you* vibe to people who don't know you. And that makes them fear you. I promise. Your name? I love it. It's who you are. Not what you look like." Kim started talking faster, his tone rising. "I don't want to hear you put yourself down anymore."

"I wasn't," she deadpanned. "I was stating facts."

"I don't care. I don't like it." His heavy breathing echoed through the wall.

Something rustled. Clothes? Them? Who fucking knew. I shoved my face a little deeper into the hole. Maybe I could see through the vent on the other side.

Atlas yanked me back by the shirt and I sneered at him.

"Okay, Kim. I'm sorry. I won't say anything like that again."

When I glanced down, Atlas snickered. Beasty was humoring Kim so he didn't get upset.

"Want to watch a movie with me in the living room?" Kim was back to being bashful.

There was only about a two-second pause. Then, "Sure." She was also shy.

It was cute that they were circling each other and didn't have any fucking clue what they were doing.

Good. I wanted that for them. For them to be the firsts for each other.

Their footsteps padded away, and then the sound of Beasty's door shutting came both from the hole and the hallway.

I picked up the return cover and fixed it back.

Sitting on my ass, I steadied my breathing, forcing myself to let go of all the anger and jealousy. It was pointless, but I tried.

Then Atlas opened his fat mouth.

"Joaquin, did yo–"

I didn't give a shit what he was going to say. It wasn't important. And it would just fire me up. That was what Atlas did and who he was.

I loved him, but fucking hell, did he get on my nerves.

Slamming his shoulder back into the floor, I worked my pants down and he grinned. Atlas needed his face fucked, and Beasty would never hear.

Chapter Thirteen

LAKE - PRESENT DAY

It was barely after nine, and the club was in full swing.

Not unusual since we opened. Which was fantastic.

Usually.

Right then, so many people packing the place from wall to wall made my scalp tingle to the point I wanted to rake my nails over it. Turn my white-blond hair red.

Gruesome, but the violence running just skin deep couldn't be ignored, and the easiest way to deal with it was to turn it on myself.

Scrubbing a hand over my face, I leaned my ass against the railing and crossed my arms. I should be in the office, scanning the cameras and flipping through different angles. But Guy was doing that.

I was better off showing my face. On the off-chance the Pescis sent underlings to cause a scene, they'd think twice if I was visible.

I set the other guys on touring the club rooms.

Joaquin was pissed. It had been too long since he sat a

game in the Gold Room and instead of getting his fix, he was trolling the Black Room.

Atlas was in the Gold Room. Kim had Beasty with him as he walked the performance rooms.

We'd switch in a little while, but I was the most intimidating, so I'd prop up the front most of the night.

A man walked through the crowd, his spiked black and red hair covered one eye, giving him a sinister vibe. That and the millions of piercings he sported.

He was naturally blond, so the dark color against his skin gave him a ghostly appearance.

I sighed.

Calling in reinforcements sucked ass. Especially when Parker ordered Gio to participate.

What did Gio do? He sent his third man.

The one who was even more unhinged than Adrian.

Smiling, Storm used his tongue to twist the bar sticking through his lip. The ball in his mouth flashed when the lights landed on him before moving across the crowd.

"Lake." He turned and hopped up on the railing, letting his feet dangle.

Why the hell had Gio sent this goth reject? He was the complete opposite of Gio and Adrian's refined taste. Well, Gio's at least. I had theories that he forced Adrian to dress the same. Storm was probably just beyond his control.

"See anyone you recognize?" I stopped my perusal of him and turned back to the crowd. The bartender caught my eye, and I paused on him, but he was gazing at Storm, not me.

That proved it. Storm was too much of a distraction for the staff. That said something considering the place was co-owned by two models and celebrities frequently visited Snatched.

"Nope." He popped on the 'p'. Cutting me a sly glance, he rolled his hands over the railing. "Where's the girl?"

"None of your fucking business."

He laughed, the sound scathing.

My phone buzzed and I pulled it out of my pocket.

KIM:

There was something I forgot to mention...

ME:

And that would be?

ATLAS:

If it's about Beasty, I already know. I watched the footage.

ATLAS:

I'm on my way.

JOAQUIN:

What's that supposed to mean?

At first, Kim didn't say anything. Then the dots started to jump.

KIM:

We're in Room Two.

Pocketing the phone, I pushed away from the railing and descended into the crowd.

People had their hands up, and they swayed to the thumping music and pushed into each other, yet never falling into my path.

One side of my mouth tipped up. I hated how white my hair was. After getting out of the club before the arrests, I had a serious moment about incorporating that damned root spray into my morning routine.

Coffee. pre-workout. Workout. Shower. Root spray.

But it was messier than I liked and I didn't have time for all that.

Then there were times like this where people avoided me like the plague. They saw my glowing, white hair under the club lights and knew I owned the place. So, it had its perks.

"Where are we going?" Storm shouted as he fell in line next to me.

"I'm going to meet up with my friends. You're staying your ass here." I picked up the pace, hoping to leave him behind.

He didn't get the hint.

"Yeah, okay, but let's talk about that girl."

"Nope." I dipped my head in acknowledgement to the attendant at the mouth of the hallway. The overpowering music dimmed, and soft, elegant piano notes trickled through the speakers. I sighed at the pleasant change.

"I'm sorry, sir. You don't have the proper stamp."

I grinned, not glancing back.

"Stamp? Lake, tell her I'm with you," Storm grunted behind me.

"No can do! I'll see you back in the front room in thirty. Keep watch for me."

If he really wanted back here, he'd do it. This wasn't the exclusive hall. But, he'd lose sight of me to do that and then he'd have to hunt through every room to find me.

I glanced back to see the door shutting in Storm's face. One angry eye visible through the shocks of midnight-black and blood-red hair. Then he was gone.

Perfect timing.

The attendant to Room Two opened the door.

A rap song with instrumentals played overhead, and all the platforms were taken by women dancing provocatively with their neon whips. They slithered like snakes around their body as they spun this way or that.

This was probably one of the most mesmerizing rooms that we had in the club. We kept the lights almost too dim for the standard, but the glow from the whips helped.

I stopped, searching the room.

At first, I didn't see Kim. Then Atlas' tall frame appeared between two groups of people along the wall.

His stalker ass would know exactly where Beasty was.

Just like in the main club room, my hair seemed to glow, and a path straight to Atlas opened up.

There was Kim. And Joaquin.

But where the fuck was Beasty?

I hastened over to them, barking the question before I was even close enough for them to hear me.

Then I saw Andrea with a group of women off to the side. Beasty right in the center.

She was easy to see because she was a good two inches taller than the other girls. That wasn't what made my blood boil.

It was the whip in her hands as she ducked her head to listen to something Andrea said before turning to study the closest woman on a platform.

I started to push away from the guys when Joaquin caught my arm. I twisted to break his hold, but he just caught me again.

Shaking his head, he mouthed no and motioned for me to come closer.

"Listen to what Kim has to say."

I shot Kim a glare. He didn't seem the least bit repentant, so whatever he was about to say, I didn't give a fuck.

"What?" I still asked.

"Beasty needs a job." His words were slow and measured, making it a little easier to hear him over the music.

"She can work–"

"Adrian and Gio have been texting her." Kim took a step forward, and we all leaned our heads together. "If we don't give her an opportunity to work, she's going to take them up on it."

Joaquin raked a hand through his hair as he shook his head. "That's not why she's going to take them up on their offer."

Kim pressed his lips together and glanced at Beasty.

I looked over my shoulder, and got caught. She wasn't paying attention to Andrea anymore. She stood there with the whip between both hands watching us. The light reflection on her face wasn't enough to give her expression away, but her posture said it all. She didn't like that we were huddled together.

Well, too fucking bad.

If she didn't want us watching, then she needed to stop whatever stunt she was about to pull.

"Let her."

Atlas was the supporter here? That didn't make any sense.

"This is the hill you want to die on?" I asked, bending toward him.

"Atlas is right. I already ran through all the jobs she'd accept. She was a bartender before. She could bartend or run drinks, but I don't want her that close to other people. I'd rather her be on the stage where the patrons can look but not touch." Kim smiled behind me.

Like a lovesick idiot who couldn't not know what happened, I turned back to see Beasty relax her shoulders and join the group Andrea was now addressing.

"What's going on?" I decided to focus on the immediate issue.

As much as I wanted to toss her over my shoulder and cart her away, Kim was right.

I wanted her untouchable, and if I couldn't control everything, I could at least control where she worked in the club.

No one answered as the music quieted and someone tapped on a microphone.

"I hate this," I grumbled.

Joaquin nodded, his mouth set in a grim line.

Andrea walked the girls on the stage along the back of the room, lining them up with Beasty on the end. Three other girls next to her.

Once she had them in place, she hustled to the side, grabbed a mic from one of the staff, and rejoined the girls. The music cut down to almost nothing as a light appeared on Andrea.

It was bright and harsh and hurt my eyes after being in the dark room for a few minutes.

"Ladies and Gentlemen. You've come to the right place at the right time." Cheers went up and I sneered. These idiots. They were too drunk to realize that wasn't anything clever. "At Snatched, in the themed rooms, we do amateur night once a month, and you've made it to the very first one."

I turned back. "We do fucking *amateur* night?"

Kim nodded. "It was part of the initial plan."

Fucking hell.

"We're going to have a bit of friendly competition, and lucky us, all four owners are here tonight. Boys, are you willing to judge?" Andrea smirked against the mic.

I was going to kill this woman. We didn't have time for this. Not when the Pescis could fuck with us at any second.

"Two of you judge. One of you, come with me to keep an eye on the club." I swirled my finger around our circle, encompassing the group.

When I started to spin on my heel, Andrea tutted over the microphone. Grinding my jaw, I paused. This was so beyond disrespectful, I'd have words with Kim about her behavior. If I wasn't satisfied with that outcome, I'd take matters into my own hands.

"Come on, boys. For our very first amateur night, you have to participate. The crowd demands it, don't you?"

Women hooted while the men hollered. Drunk fools.

"I'll judge," Kim called as he stepped forward. "We don't need all four of us on stage." There was a dark threat under his light tone. One look at Andrea said that she heard it, but didn't care.

Kim should have picked his staff a little more carefully.

"I'll judge." The words rang out through the room, and I twisted. Like hell would anyone else get up on stage with Beasty. Kim's whole point was to give her a chance on stage where she would be untouchable.

The man who'd spoken slipped through the crowd. I was just able to see the top of his head as he squeezed between people. I'd had point-two seconds to see his face before I locked up.

Donnie Pesci was in our fucking club.

Where the hell was Storm and why hadn't I let him follow me around like a damned shadow? It also meant he got past the bouncers, and I'd sent each one of those dicks pictures of the brothers.

This guy was one-hundred percent recognizable from his fashion picks alone. He was some Peaky Blinders wannabe with his old-fashioned suit. It was ridiculous on him. Mostly because he was a dweebie-looking man. Nothing like Gio or his crew.

Except there was a maliciousness in his eyes that reminded me too much of Gates.

"Perfect!" Andrea beamed and someone next to me whistled.

Damn it. I couldn't kick him out now without a scene.

"Joaquin, go grab Storm up front. The three of us will judge." I didn't glance at any of them. My focus was lasered in on Donnie.

He smirked as he approached us, patting his stomach in a weird-ass way. "I've seen pictures of you sweethearts, but none of it prepared me for what you'd look like in person." He bobbed his head like he was confirming something for himself. "But man, you four are pretty."

Donnie was one word away from getting my fist in his face, consequences be damned, but he stopped there.

Atlas and Kim stepped up beside me as Joaquin started walking to the side exit. Donnie glanced over my shoulder and pouted. "Aw, he's not going to stay for the fun? That's a shame. I'm impressed with this place." He made a show of eyeing every nook and cranny. "And the ladies really know what they're doing." The conniving smirk on his face as he bent forward might as well have been knives scraping down my chest and up the sides of my neck for how much it irritated me.

"Come on, judges. Get up here. We've arranged chairs for you." Sweeping her hand toward the stairs on the side of the stage, Andrea stepped back. Then she turned off her mic and huddled the girls.

I made eye contact with Beasty, doing my best to warn her not to do anything stupid. But what did that even mean? Even if it was bright enough for her to see the nuance of my expression, just being here on stage was already pretty fucking stupid.

We made plenty of money. Enough that the club was

more of a pastime than a required revenue stream. A way to keep ourselves busy.

Beasty could do whatever the fuck she wanted. That shouldn't involve dancing for horny men and women.

Especially when it put her in close contact with the Pescis.

"I'll go up first." Donnie grinned and stuffed his hands in his pockets as he walked toward the stairs.

I put a hand out to stop Atlas and Kim. They hadn't seen all the pictures I had. They didn't know who this man was. Why hadn't I shown them all the goddamned pictures? That was right, I was the dumbass who thought they'd send a lackey to cause trouble.

One look at Kim's and Atlas' faces, and they'd figured it out. Or at least that this man was a threat.

"That's the youngest of the Pescis. Watch him. If he tries to make a move, I don't give a fuck who's here, he doesn't touch her," I whispered.

Atlas nodded, but he was already moving swiftly to the stage. For once, his gaze was on Donnie and not on Beasty. Thank fuck. I knew it was a good call to have him here instead of Joaquin.

Joaquin was solid, but Atlas would go fucking crazy over Beasty.

Kim was less intense but just as crazy.

The four chairs Andrea mentioned lined up across the stage. To go with the theme of the room, they were white, high-end, faux-leather chairs with high backs. Artsy but also easy to clean up.

Pulling Andrea close to me, I glared, digging my fingers into her arm. She whimpered, but like a true performer, showed nothing in either her face or body language.

"The girls do not touch us. Which should be no problem for the type of dance they're doing, correct?" The whips were used in artistic dance. Yes, it was provocative, but these rooms were open to the public, not sleazy back rooms where lap dances were tossed out like Skittles.

"Got it. That wasn't the plan," she rushed out as she turned her head away.

Something about that motion said that was exactly what she had planned.

"Judges, take your seat," she called over the microphone.

Donnie took one of the center seats just to be an ass. I took the other middle, Kim grabbed the end chair next to me and Atlas placed himself on the other side of Donnie. We had him surrounded.

The heat from the spotlights warmed my skin almost uncomfortably as we waited for Andrea to get her shit together. She had one final huddle with the girls, then snapped her fingers toward the DJ box.

Darkness descended as the lights flipped off. A soft intake of breath rolled through the crowd. With heavy shades draped over the windows and the whips turned off, no one could see a thing.

Then slow, instrumental notes of a rap song spilled from the speakers, and as if choreographed, one whip turned on. The second followed a beat after, then the third, and finally the fourth.

Beasty was easy to spot.

She was also in front of me. Not touching, but damn close. Close enough that if I leaned forward, I could skim my fingers through the luminescent strings of the whip.

Whatever girl was in front of Donnie was even closer and he did reach out and touch her.

Asshole.

Since Beasty wasn't in front of him, I leaned back, gripping the back of the chair by my head.

I might as well enjoy the show.

Beasty wasn't a dancer. She wasn't comfortable with the movements, and she was far from fluid. But she was fantastic with moving the whip around her body. The intense look of concentration on her face only added to the appeal.

She was in the zone. From all signs, she was loving it.

Then they swapped places and she moved in front of Donnie. I leaned forward and glared at the side of his head as he reached out a hand to touch her thigh.

"Don't think about it." I caught his fingers and bent them backward. He cocked an eyebrow and pulled his hand back, shaking it out when I let go. The light from Beasty's whip highlighted tiny scars and imperfections on his face. I memorized each one.

The girl in front of me made a noise like she was trying to get my attention, but I never once glanced at her. I kept my gaze locked between Donnie and Beasty.

They rotated again and Beasty was in front of Atlas. He loved it a little too much as he bit his lip, completely forgetting about the threat between us.

One final rotation of dancing, and the song notes trailed off. The lights came up and Andrea clapped, the noise thumping over the speakers since the mic was turned back on.

"What a great performance! What do you say, give a round of applause for our ladies!" She tossed one hand up in the air like she had been the one to perform.

The crowd obliged.

Donnie stood up, adjusting his tie as he nodded toward Beasty. "She's got my vote. Could use a little work on the stiffness though. I hear that can be taught with the right partner." He winked and Beasty stiffened.

He walked toward her and the three of us stood up.

"Relax," he mocked. "I'm just taking the stairs off stage." But he stopped next to Beasty and I stepped forward.

Before I could get there, he jumped out of my reach. "You really were too good for Stevo. He should have brought you around. It would have saved all of us—including Stevo—a lot of trouble." He dropped his easy-going facade and with one deadly stare toward Beasty, he left.

The room was silent except for his footsteps. Once he was almost to the door, I jumped into action, grabbing the whip from Beasty's hands and tossing it at Andrea.

It smacked the other woman in the face and I wished I was in a better space to find the karma in it. Instead, I cupped Beasty's elbow and started moving her toward the stairs.

"Beasty wins," I said to Andrea, then the four of us were off the stage.

I glanced at Beasty and wished I hadn't.

Her face was pale, and she stared after Donnie with too much thinking happening in that brain of hers.

We were going to regret tonight. I could feel it.

Chapter Fourteen

CRESSIDA - PRESENT DAY

Holy shit.

That man. I hadn't paid any attention to him as the guys made their way up on stage. Instead, the initial fear of performing trapped me instead my own head.

But I'd seen him before. One time.

With Stevo.

That guy had to be in the mafia.

Shit.

Lake led us in the opposite direction than we should be heading in. That man had answers. I could convince him that I didn't have anything. Stevo had only ever given me a cold. They sure as hell wouldn't care about that.

Logically, I knew the mafia was dangerous, but this was as close to neutral ground as possible. I took a step away and Lake gently, but firmly pulled me back. Then we were in a back hall and moving faster.

Joaquin appeared at the end of the hall, out of breath. He ran three steps in and the door swung so hard behind him, it almost hit a man in the face.

I gasped.

"You're a real dick, you know that?" the man grumbled.

"What happened?" Joaquin panted, jogging to meet us in the middle.

There was no one else here. How strange that they had back hallways the staff didn't use during the busy times.

"Donnie was one of the judges for amateur night," Lake spat, tugging me closer. "He didn't try anything. Just made sure to let Beasty know about Stevo. Then he left through the room's main entrance."

"I'm on it. I'll meet you in the office." The man with Joaquin was decked out in all black with dramatic, spiked hair. He took off at a sprint like he knew exactly where he was going.

Was he staff?

"Let's head to the office." Lake still held onto me, but he pulled his phone out with his other hand and sent off a text.

The guys took up positions around me and somehow, we made it back to the office without ever passing another person. I needed a blueprint of this club.

"Who was that?" I asked just because I needed to. Just in case I was wrong. But in my gut, I knew I wasn't.

Lake stuck his tongue in the side of his mouth and narrowed his eyes. I didn't think he was going to answer me, then he said, "Donnie Pesci."

"And that is..." I trailed off, my heart thumping erratically against my chest.

The dance had been amazing. A high of adrenaline like nothing I'd ever experienced and I couldn't even enjoy it before something fucked up with the boys came back to bite me in the ass.

Shit, this wasn't all them, though. Was it?

I was the one who got mixed up with Stevo in the first place.

"One of *the* Pescis. Atlas, did you have the cleaners here today?" Lake leveled a serious gaze on Atlas.

"Of course." He raised one brow in calm defiance.

Releasing a breath, Lake took a seat and leaned back as he faced us. He seemed wired but worried. Tired but ready to go at a moment's notice. For the first time I could remember, Lake looked his age instead of several years younger.

"The Pescis are the mafia. The mafia *is* the Pescis. Donnie is the youngest brother." Lake narrowed his eyes on me as if he was measuring my reaction.

I nodded. Right. "We should have talked to him. He wouldn't do anything while we're all in public–"

Joaquin barked out a laugh and bent over to slap his knees. "Beasty. You're not this naive. I know you're not."

I scowled as he slowly straightened. "What's that supposed to mean?"

"Come on," he said in exasperation.

I wasn't stupid, and I didn't appreciate him acting like I was. I wanted a way out. A way to live my life on my terms. And as long as we treated these guys like they were the big bad boogiemen, then that was what they'd be.

You had to bring your monsters into the light to kill them. That was the only way.

"They need to know I'm not a threat." I balled my fists up at my sides.

Kim–Sweet, sweet, Kim, came close, holding up his hands. "That man, he has a penchant for starving kittens. He's known as the Backroom Bandit because when he's not hurting innocent kittens, he's torturing people unfortunate enough to get on his nerves." Kim nodded, like he could see the disbelief in my expression. "You think someone like that is going to care that you're not a threat?"

"You can't be serious." I raised both brows.

Joaquin sighed, pinching the bridge of his nose. "Beasty, the mafia doesn't care about threats. They care about reputation."

Some of the antsy energy slipped through the cracks of my system. That...made so much fucking sense, and I didn't like it.

It made everything I'd been hoping for either a non-option, unpredictable, or both. Actually, definitely both.

"Because you killed Stevo." I turned to Lake.

"Shhh." Joaquin flapped his hands. "We had the place cleaned but you never know if there's something we missed."

"Sorry." I winced. I wasn't completely behind what they were doing, but I didn't want to be their downfall. I couldn't be. "There has to be something we can do. I can't live under this threat all my life." I brought my palm up to the side of my head.

I'd had a couple years of freedom after foster care. I hadn't come this far just to shut myself away in a box.

These boys? They were used to it. Locked inside a glass cage because Atlas and Kim were famous. They had to constantly worry about who had access to them because people were crazy.

"I just, I need some air." I started moving to the door, but Kim intercepted me.

"Beasty, what's wrong?"

"Everything," I said, but my own voice sounded as if it was down a wind tunnel. Shaking my head, I rubbed my forehead. Everything was wrong.

How did they live like this? They didn't say it so much as broadcast the tension in their body language and ticks.

Joaquin's hands twitched as if he wanted to shuffle his deck of cards. I glanced back at Lake, and he wasn't any better. His nails were digging into his thighs. He probably had indents in his slacks.

In front of me, Kim rolled his lips together as he watched me.

The only one not moving was Atlas. He was eerily still. No expression. No blinking. Just observing me.

"I need air," I repeated. "Please," I begged, knowing Kim would understand.

"Okay, yeah, okay." He pulled his keycard out of his wallet and scanned the pad next to the door. It unlocked and he tugged on the handle before it could relock.

Even that small thing. I didn't have a card with access. I was stuck where they wanted me. Did they not think about those things?

Were they oblivious to the fact that I was at their mercy or did they want it this way?

I didn't want to think bad of them, but the more I knew them, the more I realized their capacity to...

Nope, I wouldn't voice those thoughts, even to myself.

The door swung open and we just stepped into the holding area when someone started banging on the next door.

"Open up! Police!" The words were just distinguishable through the thick door. And they sounded like they came from the ceiling.

My heart exploded in my chest and I stumbled back.

Hands caught me and passed me off to the next set of arms.

Lake prowled toward the door, scanning his keycard with angry movements.

"Not fucking funny," he berated before the door was all the way open.

Adrian stood there, grinning with his hands on his hips. The other man, the one with the black and red spikes in his hair stood behind him, a slightly amused expression softening his face. Gio was the only one of the three who didn't look happy to be there.

His face was red like he'd ran five laps around the club.

"Kim, take Beasty home."

"No," Kim said and Lake twisted to glare at him. "Who knows what they have planned for tonight? For all we know, he could have clowns hanging out in front of our house. I'm not leaving the club unless we *all* leave the club."

One long beleaguered sigh, then Lake motioned the other guys to go into the office. "Fine. Main dining room only. That's the safest place."

Atlas watched me as he leaned against the office doorframe. Joaquin opened his mouth like he was going to say something. He was the one who spoke to me first when they picked me up from graduation. He was also who made me feel wanted at one of the first jobs they took me to.

I waited, my chest swelling for some unknown reason. Hope maybe? He might not care, but sometimes his actions said otherwise.

Joaquin just shook his head and turned back to the room. I deflated, and everyone noticed.

I hated pity. As much as I hated attention, I'd rather get laughed at than pitied. My shoulders curled forward and I spun toward the next door.

Lake didn't have any issues doing what he wanted. He caught my arms, holding me still as he dropped his mouth to mine in a fiery, brief kiss. I grunted when he bit my bottom lip.

His lips smiled against mine, and he laved the hurt with his tongue.

"Stay with Kim. You want to ask questions later, fine. But not here," he whispered, then let me go.

I couldn't tear my gaze away from his back as he sauntered into the office. Joaquin and Atlas were already deep inside where I couldn't see them, leaving Gio and his two friends in view.

Soon, Lake's body mass covered any glimpse the three men had of me.

"Come on, Beasty. If you want, I'll have the bartender make a strong drink for you. I want to tell you how beautiful you were while you danced–"

I almost snorted but I held it in.

"–and you can tell me if you liked it or not." Kim plucked my hand from my side. Then he lifted it, playing so carefully with my fingertips.

This was Kim. He always touched me so sweetly and marveled at the image. I had too, when I was with them before. It had been obvious no one touched him. Hardly ever, even at most of the events I went to. That he was comfortable touching me, and that he wanted to, had always been a high.

That thrill and wonder had been missing when Lake brought me back.

I was scared to want things I'd thrown away. It was strange. I was still in a weird place, stuck between what I wanted and knowing what was good for me. Yet, the gentle brushes of his fingers against mine set off a light tingle in my stomach.

No one else but Kim had ever sparked that reaction in me before.

Until Atlas had created a need so intense and frightening in the Black Room, it was like hot needles jabbing my lower stomach and inner thighs.

Then Lake short-circuited my mind, melting me into a puddle with the power he showed me I had.

"Let's go," Kim repeated as he opened the next door and led us to the club.

I was so lost in my thoughts as I trailed behind him that the trip to the VIP table was all a blur. One second we were standing in the in-between room, then Kim was sliding me into the booth.

"Good evening, Mr. Kim. What can I get you?" A server dressed in their crisp black uniform stopped at the edge of our table.

"I'll just have a sparkling water. What do you want, Beasty?" Kim slid into the other side of the round booth, immediately picking my hand back up. His long fingers warm against my palm.

"Just a water too. Thanks," I mumbled through a weak smile, plucking at the edge of the shorts I'd worn for the dance. Andrea had been so kind as to supply an outfit for amateur night.

"You know, I think you have a real talent for dancing," Kim said as he pulled my hand to the tabletop in front of him. He turned it over and started tracing the blue veins in my wrist.

"Don't lie, Kim." I rolled my eyes, some of the intense emotions clearing the longer I was away from all the tension in the office.

He froze, then smoothed his fingertips farther up my arm.

"I thought you were beautiful, that's not a lie. That's so far from a lie, it hurts not to speak it." He wasn't loud. Kim never was, but tucked back away in the corner of the VIP section, I could still hear him and a pleasant rush floated up my back.

"We've had this conversation before." Didn't he remember?

"And I thought you were beautiful then too." He slid his gaze to my face, and one side of his mouth tipped up. "Beauty isn't skin deep, anyone ever tell you that?"

Snorting, I curled my fingers into my palm. I wanted to pull my hand back, but I couldn't break the touch. The tingles sliding up my arm and resting deep inside my chest were too addictive.

"That's hilarious coming from a man who makes his living from his face."

He nodded, his expression turning somber as he broke eye contact.

"Kim, I–"

I could kick myself. How many times had I thought how horrible his life was because of his beauty? He'd been taken by that horrible man because he was pretty. And now I was rubbing it in. I couldn't win for spewing shit that didn't matter.

"It's fine, Beasty." He said something else, but I glanced out at the crowd.

A man was walking through. There wasn't anything that stood out about him. He was mostly in the shadows anyway, but he turned to look at the stage, and in that second, my breath caught.

Yanking my hand back, I sat straighter.

There was no way he'd be here. Why would he? Did he work with the boys somehow?

All these questions swirled inside my head that I didn't have the courage to ask. I couldn't move.

A brief swell of shame soured the back of my tongue, and I was horrified I could even feel that about being here with Kim.

Yet, I couldn't deny the emotion.

There, walking out of the club, was Books.

Chapter Fifteen

BEASTY - AGE 18

T his was downright pitiful.

I glanced at the few outfits I had brought in my duffel bag that were hung up in the closet. A couple pairs of old jeans, ripped from wear and not from fashion like the guys' pants. A few plain T-shirts and one that said Moe's Minions from the shelter I used to work at.

The sundress.

A couple big T-shirts for sleeping. They should have gone in the drawer but the closet was so sad with only a handful of items hanging up. This way, they wouldn't get that drawer smell on them anyway.

Sighing, I grabbed the pair of jeans I'd worn almost daily since I got here and the Moe's Minions T-shirt. The boys hadn't said anything about my clothes, but they noticed. Each time their eyes would linger on my butt where the pockets were starting to get holes, or on my side where the seams were starting to loosen on my shirt, I'd heat up and turn away.

They'd been gentlemen and hadn't said anything. Maybe that was worse?

163

After getting dressed and running a brush through my hair, I left my bedroom and headed to the kitchen. There were enough noises coming from that direction that they all had to be there. They weren't that quiet, but Atlas and Kim kept different schedules.

Rounding the corner, I gave Joaquin a little smile. "Morning."

"Morning." He nodded, his gaze dropping to my T-shirt and jeans. Immediately, my face started to flush just like I knew it would.

Lake turned around from the stove where he was making a massive amount of scrambled eggs. Atlas was sticking bread in the toaster on the other side of the kitchen, yet he glanced over his shoulder too.

I shifted my weight on my feet as I suddenly had all their attention. This was one of the first times I'd been in the same room with all of them outside of joining them for their jobs, and the weight of their attention was a little terrifying.

"Good morning," Kim said softly, grinning as he set his tea on the counter. I'd learned that about Kim. He liked tea. All kinds, but a spicy chai was his favorite.

"We're all off today, and I thought we'd go out and do something," Lake said as he turned to the pan. He rolled the spatula back and forth in his hand.

"To do what?" I'd been here over a month and I still didn't have a purpose. I was just kind of floating through.

I could ask, but what if that got on their nerves? Or reminded them I was here?

That was stupid. They knew I was here, but when I was coasting along with them, I didn't cause any trouble, and I wasn't extra work.

If I started asking for things, I'd start creating more headaches. That was Foster Care 101. To stay in a house you liked, you made yourself as small and invisible as possible while balancing it out with being useful.

"We're going shopping." Kim grinned wider, like he was proud of the announcement.

"What for?" I asked in a measured tone. I had a sinking suspicion, but what else was I supposed to say?

"Clothes," Kim answered, the one word a happy chirp.

"Clothes?" I swallowed.

"You need some new things. We're going to get them for you." Lake still spoke to the skillet as he picked it up and divvied the eggs between five plates.

Not four. Five.

They'd planned this.

Anxiety ridden butterflies took flight in my stomach at the same time it decided to growl. Loudly.

Atlas glanced over and raised a brow.

How damned embarrassing. And what did I do? I laughed like Steve Urkel. Clamping my lips shut, I walked to the counter and picked up the plate with the least amount of eggs.

But Kim took it out of my hands and scooted another plate toward me. One that had at least four eggs worth of scramble on it.

"I have to keep my figure for the shoot next week." He lowered his voice like he was sharing a secret with me. "I make just as much money off of my body type as I do my face."

Kim backed away and went to the table as I snuck a quick glance at his body. He was tall, taller than most Asians, and I think he'd even grown a little since I'd been here. When did guys stop growing?

Joaquin choked, and when I turned to him, he rushed to set his mug down and grabbed a paper towel to clean up the coffee on the counter.

Picking up my plate, I carried it to the table and then went to get a cup of orange juice. For a bunch of guys, they had so many groceries. The good kind. Not tons of off-brand cereals or boxes of Mac-N-Cheese. It was kind of weird, but I was happy they got to eat so well.

A memory of Aunt Erin flashed through my head.

"Food is food, Beasty. We have to be thankful for what we get. Don't bite no hands that feed."

Weird that that popped up in my head. It didn't matter here at all, but the short fragment tightened my chest. I couldn't even remember Aunt Erin's face clearly anymore. It was all fuzzy pictures with a dark blurry hole in the middle.

Of my favorite memories, I remembered her hands, the concrete, or her tent, but not her face. I must not have looked at her face much.

"Are you okay?" Kim tapped the table next to my plate.

"Hm?" I jerked my head up. I'd taken a seat and hadn't even noticed. "Yeah, just wool gathering."

He shook his head and gave me a wistful smile before he started in on his breakfast. It was good. But they didn't taste like the eggs Megan made. She smothered hers in butter, but these were...savory. Salty and tasted like they had garlic in them.

Conversation was quiet while we ate. Atlas and Joaquin talked about an upcoming job. Joaquin ran through some quick numbers with Lake and Lake talked about a new idea for security.

But, overall, it was sparse.

The lack of noise only made my own chewing that much louder in my head.

I pushed my plate back when I finished it, my stomach protruding from eating every bite.

"Ready?" Lake asked Kim. Kim in turn raised his brows at me.

"Yeah." I shrugged. I'd already brushed my teeth and if they wanted to go now, I was ready.

They weren't ready. I waited in the living room for fifteen minutes as they went to their rooms to get dressed. When they came out, they looked as haughty and well-dressed as I expected of any models.

In the SUV, I took a window seat in the back, with Kim in the middle and Atlas on the other side.

Lake had at least turned the music on to cover the sound of our silence. Before long, we were pulling into an upscale mall that made me more uncomfortable than their quick looks at my clothing choices.

"Who are we shopping for?" I asked, tugging on the hem of my shirt as I stood next to the car.

"You, crazy." Kim laughed.

Dread weighed down each step as we walked to the entrance, even with Kim next to me the entire time. The other three fanned out behind us. It was early, barely a few minutes after ten and we passed two people.

Okay, this might not be bad if the place was empty.

It might even be kind of nice.

The smell of the mall always fascinated me. I hadn't gone that much as a kid, but I'd been. And it always smelled the same, like there was some secret air freshener all malls kept on hand all the time. Like they used the same cleaning supplies, which was ridiculous.

"Let's start at Macy's." Kim pointed to the end. "It's not the boutiques I like, but they have some decent brands." His steps picked up with his excitement.

It was cute. He seemed really excited to be around so many clothes.

But he didn't head to the men's section. He zeroed in

straight on the women's. A part of me had hoped he'd get distracted.

"Kim, what are you doing?" I slowed my steps like that would force him to go at my speed. It didn't. He made it there, then doubled back only to zing away again.

My steps lightened and I bounced as I walked, mirroring Kim. His excitement was contagious, even as my anxiety started to soar through the roof.

Some of the attendants at the perfume counter turned our way, their gazes pausing on the boys, before coming to me.

One woman's nose wrinkled when I turned to look at her.

I knew why.

I was an ugly duck. It didn't matter that Kim said he thought I was pretty. The rest of the world didn't think we matched. We weren't compliments of each other like most couples were.

While it didn't bother me for the typical reasons, the attention was still uncomfortable.

Glancing away, I focused on Kim's back as he stepped on the escalator. If I couldn't see their judgment, it didn't affect me.

Except whispers started at the bottom floor by the jewelry counter.

I glanced down at a group of employees huddled where they could see us. One young girl, maybe around my age, pointed at Kim, then pointed across the floor.

Without thinking too much about what she could be pointing out, I glanced over.

My heart skipped a beat.

In the men's section, was a giant advertisement of Kim. Did he know that was here?

He had to, right? Yet, he was so focused on getting up the stairs, he either didn't know, or pretended not to.

"We'll start over here. You have a great body type, Beasty. You're well-proportioned. Have a nice shape. Best of all, you have long legs. You would hardly need anything hemmed if we get lucky." He dropped my hand to start rifling through some clothes on an interior rack.

Jeans. He was moving through jeans.

Atlas leaned against a wall nearby, expressionless as he watched us. Or me, really.

But when I made eye contact with him, he shifted his gaze to Kim.

Where did Joaquin and Lake go? They were literally just here.

I glanced around. This early, the store was empty except for some employees. And somehow, we'd lost two of us. They were on the escalator behind me. I was sure of it.

Leaning to the side, I glanced around the middle display. There they were. But they weren't alone.

Another man stood with them. A shady looking man. If I'd seen him on the street in our old town, I'd walk on the other side.

He was too thin, gaunt cheeks, and when he glanced at me, there was a glint in his eyes. One that I'd made sure to avoid when I was on the street with Aunt Erin.

I sucked in a breath, and Atlas stepped in front of me to block my view.

But he wasn't quick enough to hide the fact that Lake handed that guy a wad of cash.

"Beasty," Kim said, a note of exasperation in his voice. "Are you listening?"

I jumped and turned. "Yeah, sorry. I wondered where the guys went."

Kim glanced around, like he hadn't realized we were two short. Then he shrugged. "They know how to take care of themselves. We don't have to worry about them. Not since the time that little old lady tried to get Lake's number."

Atlas snorted.

"What?"

"It was nothing. You know how horny some ladies can be when they see big muscles." Kim held up three pairs of jeans. "Let's go try on these styles. I have an idea of what would look good on you, but I want to confirm it."

I nodded slowly, fighting the urge to glance back at Lake and Joaquin. "Yeah, sure."

Kim was a great distraction, but it wasn't enough to get the picture out of my mind. Lake couldn't be a drug dealer. They had too much to lose. And that would be stupid.

None of the boys seemed like they did drugs anyway. I'd seen addicts before, on the street when I was young, or even on the street when I'd walk through town. They had none of the signs. That didn't mean that they didn't take steroids. Or that Atlas and Kim didn't need help to keep their model bodies.

That wasn't fair of me. I was judging based off of a two-second view of something that could be completely innocent.

But that niggling in the back of my mind said that wasn't the case.

I made it all the way inside the dressing room with Kim before I came to my senses.

"Here, try these first." Kim handed over a faded pair of wide-legged jeans.

I took them, staring at him. He was inside the room with me. And the curtain was closed. Did he want me to change with him right here?

Swallowing, I glanced at the jeans, then at the curtain.

"Oh. Oh!" A rosy pink tint suffused his face. "I'll wait out there with Atlas. Open the curtain when you're done. I want to check their fit." He ducked out of the room, and he started whispering with Atlas. Their voices echoed, but not loud enough for me to make out the words.

The entire time I stripped my pants and put on the pair he'd handed me, I couldn't get Lake and Joaquin out of my head.

What other reason could they have for meeting a guy like that, here of all places. If it was something illegal, they wouldn't meet in a store where there were cameras. Right?

My brain started to spin looking for scenarios but I couldn't come up with one good reason why they would meet with a man like that.

Books words floated through my head.

"Your life started out as shit, and if you get sucked into the wrong crowd, you'll continue to live in shit."

These boys, they were the only people I ever wanted to truly be friends with. They ran from me so much that when they finally came back for me, it seemed like a dream come true.

Yet there was a voice in the back of my head that said maybe this wasn't what I wanted it to be.

Books wasn't part of my life. He didn't know me. And he certainly didn't know them. But bad people were bad people. That was who he was talking about.

And if I didn't distance myself from that behavior, I would never break the cycle.

I needed to. For myself, I needed to prove that I wasn't my childhood. I could choose to be whoever I wanted to be.

If the boys were doing drugs or selling them...

"Beasty, are you done yet?" Kim asked as he tapped his fingers on the wall next to the curtain. His voice didn't sound right.

I pushed the curtain open and cleared my throat. "I'm done."

My arms hung awkwardly at my side. The jeans felt like heaven. Thick, soft material that stretched perfectly across my hips. I'd never worn anything like this. I wasn't sure I liked it.

Kim fidgeted as he bent to the side and checked out the back of the jeans. I tried not to flinch. He was right there next to my ass.

Then I saw them. Hovering at the entrance to the changing rooms were a group of women, young and old. All smiling, with their phones out. Every single one of them eyed up Kim and Atlas like they were pieces of juicy steak.

Atlas didn't seem to care. He ignored them and kept his attention on us.

Kim twirled a finger for me to turn.

I did, but I glanced over my shoulder. "Are you okay?" I whispered. His finger was shaking.

He nodded, then shuffled closer. "People in crowds like this are unpredictable. Sometimes they try to touch us, and when I'm not prepared for it..." He winced.

"Then let's get out of here." I stepped back to change. I didn't want these clothes anyway. They were nice. The gesture that they wanted to buy things for me was sweet, if uncomfortable, but this wasn't me.

"Can I..." He motioned to the room.

I gulped. I'd never changed in front of anyone like this before. Except that would be easier than letting him stay in view of the women watching him. They were by the door now, but what if they got bold? "Yeah."

He grinned. "Don't worry. I'll turn my back. And I still want to see you in the other pairs. I'll just order what I want once I have a better idea of your size."

I didn't tell him that I knew my size, and that I had my

own money from Books. Instead, I changed, and he took a few minutes to check each style.

The longer we were in here, the more at ease he became. And then we were done. All in all, we might have spent five minutes trying on the two other pairs of jeans.

When we walked out, Lake stood at the entrance to the changing rooms speaking to a security guard. They'd gotten the workers to head back to their stations, but now there was a small crowd of female shoppers.

As soon as he glanced back and saw us coming, he said a few words to the security guard and the man started guiding the women away.

Joaquin took the lead and walked at a clipped pace as Kim, Atlas, and I followed. Lake took up the rear. I guess to keep people away. They acted like this was normal and I couldn't quite wrap my head around that.

But the bigger thing bothering me was the question Kim asked Lake as we passed.

"Did you get what you needed?"

Lake nodded and then they moved like nothing had happened at all.

I hated that I was cynical. But how could I not be?

It was only the desperate hope that I was wrong that allowed me to pretend I hadn't heard it.

But desperation breeds idiocy.

Chapter Sixteen

KIM - PRESENT DAY

Somehow, I lost Beasty.

She was sitting right next to me, but she was somewhere else. And from how her eyebrows edged upward in the center, I didn't think it was a good place.

I'd made a study of her expressions. The subtle nuances of her emotions once we had her close to us. It was sublime, having such close access.

Her expression right now was pained and blank, all at the same time. Even her jaw was slack as she stared out into the crowd.

I followed her gaze, but didn't see anything that should have affected her so strongly.

Shifting in my seat, I tried to get my hard-on to go down.

When we had the discussion before about sharing Beasty, I was on board because I would rather have a piece of her than not have her at all.

Yet watching Atlas eat her out...

I groaned softly and pinched my pants at the knees to tug them down.

Add that to how she danced for me, and I was a goner. I was constantly irritable. I could be like Lake and beat off every chance I got. Or like Atlas and Joaquin and find release in someone else. But I wouldn't do that.

I didn't want to touch another person for any reason. I also didn't want to touch myself.

The ghost of her hand coasting over my shoulders as we made love was still the best thing I'd ever experienced in my life. And I'd be damned before I chose a cheaper option just because I was horny.

Fuck that.

I wouldn't come until Beasty was the one who helped me with my very hard problem.

"Beasty?" I reached out and touched the back of her hand.

She turned to me, and her eyes flared. Did she think I was upset that she made a comment about how pretty I was?

I didn't give a fuck about that. It was the thing that gave me a purpose in life. That made enough money for us so that we could take care of her. The way she deserved to be taken care of.

"I can't do this, Kim. I need to know that I can live my life without living in a glass box like you guys do."

Ouch. That stung, although Beasty didn't seem to want to hurt my feelings. But she was right. We did essentially live in a glass box. We couldn't take her out like ordinary people. We'd tried that once, and people get crazy if they recognize you.

I'd gotten better at it though. I'd conditioned myself to accept light touches. To smile and take pictures. It had all been a grueling process, but I'd done it.

Not even for myself. I did it in the hopes that one day Beasty would want to be with us again.

"What do you want me to say, Beasty?" Most people said that because they were assholes or they wanted to be combative. Sarcastic.

I just wanted to know what she wanted. What she needed to hear. Whatever it was, I'd tell her that lie so she'd feel good about being with us again. There was no harm in that.

"I want you to tell me that you'll figure out what it's going to take for the Pescis to leave me alone. I want you to tell me that you'll make it right so I don't have to hide." She drew in a shuddering breath, then released an equally shaky laugh. "I'd also love for you to tell me that you four are going to stop associating with crazy dangerous people."

All impossibilities. One, men like the Pescis didn't just forgive and forget. They were slighted by us, and as long as we were winning, they'd never kick Beasty off their radar. Beasty didn't seem to understand that this had nothing to do with her and everything to do with their egos.

Because of that, there wasn't anything we could do short of playing their game. And the only way to do that, was to fight fire with fire.

The illegal kind that came from knowing all the right people.

That alone meant we couldn't leave the crime life behind or our associates. But there was another, bigger reason. Lake was more the driving force behind it, but I believed in his brand of logic.

Men like Gates were a dime a dozen.

They took, used, abused. Did any fucking thing they wanted. To anyone they wanted.

That would never happen again. Never.

The one way to ensure it wouldn't, was to know every player on the board. To know their secrets and their lies. To be in a position to use it against them, was to be on the board with them.

I wanted Beasty. At any cost.

But this one.

We just had to make her see that.

"We hate living in a glass house too. No one likes it. But it's a necessary tradeoff for the success we've had." I placed my arm along the back of the booth and turned into her. Discreetly breathing in the delicate scent of her skin. She hated perfumes. Beasty only ever smelled like soap and herself and it was intoxicating. "But we can make this right with the Pescis. We can make it so that you don't have to hide and you can live your life. You only ever have to tell me what you need, Beasty and I'll make it happen. That's how much you mean to me."

Her gaze flew back and forth between my eyes as her mouth curved down on one side. I grinned.

This was the expression that said she was gauging every part of my face, looking for the truth. Smoothing my expression out, I gave her a sincere look.

"You'll stop doing bad things?" she pushed.

My heart cracked. Something about the way she said that reminded me of when we were kids. Which was odd, because outside of the one interaction, I never spoke to her.

I touched her jaw, and slid my finger along the under-side until I tipped up her chin. Her mouth was so sweet. Plush and soft. The barely there freckle over the right side of her lip caught under the club lighting. I wanted to lick it.

Leaning in, I left only a few centimeters of space as I stared deep into her eyes. Just when her chest rose from a soft inhale, I veered to the left, slowly heading toward her ear. Outside of my fingertip under her chin, I didn't touch her.

I couldn't.

I wanted her to touch me first.

But I could do this. Tease her in my own way. Not Atlas' blatant, aggressive style. My way was more enjoyable. A slow burn.

"Kim," she panted.

I blew on her earlobe, the gentle breath moving the hair that had fallen into her face. Then I directed the stream down the column of her neck.

She shivered and I strained even harder against the zipper of my pants.

"Beasty, you're all I've ever wanted. You know that, don't you?" I asked.

"Is that enough?" she returned, but she sounded as if she were speaking on autopilot.

"It has to be. Because I can't take it if you leave again." I swallowed. All night, I'd been so confident, high on the fact that I'd given Beasty something she wanted. An opportunity to earn money. But the quick reminder that any minute Beasty could walk out—not from the Pescis' schemes—but just her lack of desire to be with us anymore, and my heart fluttered wildly and weakly all at once, as if warning me we wouldn't survive without her.

Releasing a breath, I dropped my head to her shoulder, all thoughts of seduction forgotten. "Please don't leave me again."

We were back in my room, her cuddling my back, refusing to answer.

"Kim." She reached up and grabbed my hand, pulling it down to her lap where she cupped it with both her hands. They were soft and warm, cradling me with a delicacy that was foreign to Beasty when it came to anyone or anything, except me.

All of us saw it, how she was with me, and I guarded it like a starving Rottie over a fallen rabbit.

I craved this from her. She knew it, and yet she still had the ability to leave me.

Atlas was right. She didn't just have to want us. If we wanted to keep her, she had to need us.

"Beasty, lovely to see you."

Damn it. I sat up and glared at Gio. He was dressed into an expensive suit. Not the slim-fitted kind that we wore, but an expensive as hell brand that most business men wore. And he was pissed if the pinched way he held his mouth said anything.

He adjusted the cufflinks, dropping his gaze for a minute before giving me his focus.

Adrian and Storm stood sentry behind him. Adrian grinned like a clown as he studied Beasty and me. Storm watched us curiously, but didn't give off the same loud energy. His was much cooler.

"Kim." Gio raised a brow.

"Gio." I dipped my head. They should be going after Donnie or making a plan. Why were they here instead of with Lake?

Just when I had Beasty to myself, on the tip of a new precipice, they interrupted.

I glanced behind him, looking for any signs of Joaquin, Atlas, or Lake, but it was impossible to spot anyone when the crowd was now packed shoulder to shoulder. I couldn't even see the hallway.

Sliding out of the booth, I removed my hands from Beasty's, and stood up to block her from their view.

She didn't like that, or maybe she didn't like when I did it. Gio turned and watched her step down from the booth on the other side.

"What can I help you with?" I wanted to bring their attention back to me. I didn't mind these three, not that I'd had much interaction with them, but Beasty wasn't for their eyes.

"We have a lead on another of the Pescis and we need your friend here to help. Do you prefer Cressida or Beasty?" He angled his shoulders toward Beasty.

I think the fuck not.

Sliding in front of her, I raised a brow at Gio. "We're not going to do this here."

"And what is *this*?" Gio gave me a bored look and Adrian popped up over his shoulder with maniacal glee written across his face.

"Kim," Beasty sighed and pushed to her feet.

Shooting my hand back, I trapped her behind me as I gripped her shirt in my fist.

"You're being ridiculous," she huffed.

"Please, Beasty." I wanted to shout at her to stop being naive, that if she didn't want us to go down the crime path, to stop throwing herself onto it too.

But I could never talk to her like that. It would push her away and I wanted to hold her close. I needed her to trust me in a way I no longer trusted *her*.

"Gio, you should speak to Lake. Leave Beasty out of your plans."

Adrian draped his arm around Gio, making a show of shaking him. "What's up with these guys?" he asked in a loud voice. He wanted us to hear.

"Adrian," Gio warned.

"No, I really want to know. Color me curious." Adrian twisted his mouth to the side as he framed his jaw with his thumb and forefinger.

Storm stepped up on the other side so he could see what was going on. Whatever had happened after we passed him in the hallway, he was no longer in a good mood. He was now downright diabolical with the silver from his piercings glinting every time the club lights flashed over us.

"It's a secret." I gave him the sweetest, softest smile I had in my arsenal. Then I leaned toward them like I was going to let them in on it. "And we don't tell our secrets here. We have a special place for that."

"A room. We know all about it," Adrian snickered and Beasty stiffened.

Ice licked up the back of my neck as I lost my smile. Who the fuck did this guy think he was?

He had no idea who we were, and he didn't want to.

But no one made me look the fool in front of her.

I grabbed Beasty's hand and played with her fingers in what I hoped was a soothing motion. "We're pretty easy-going guys. We have to be in our line of business," I said absently as I took in the crowd before bringing my attention back to the three assholes in front of me. "We're the Fashion Boys, after all." I shrugged, using the name Parker had coined for us. "But we're not just pretty faces. We have a mean streak, and what I think you'd do well to remember, is that we've tasted shit before. More than you probably ever will in your life."

I took a chance and pulled Beasty against my back. Latching onto her other wrist, I wrapped her arms around me, savoring the feel of her pressed against my back. I loved being the little spoon with her. We just fit.

"That goes for every single one of us, including Beasty. We're not going to let her be a party to your schemes that will not only put her in danger, but even more firmly on the radar."

There was just so much Beasty didn't know, and I wasn't about to let her do this to herself.

"If you keep pushing, we'll push back. *I* will. And you won't like how I do it. I might just have to bring out the roadrunner treatment." Watching their expressions harden with each word that fell from my mouth was exhilarating.

Scrunching his face up, Storm narrowed his eyes on me. "Okay, I'll bite. What's the roadrunner treatment?"

I shrugged, giving them a closed-lipped smile. They couldn't dim my happiness, not when Beasty was plastered to me and showing no signs of pulling away.

It didn't even bother me when Adrian dropped his gaze to my erection.

Sex was dirty. Nothing would ever change my mind. Except with Beasty.

She was so clean and pure, I couldn't feel the revulsion of my body's reactions when it came to her.

Gio dropped his gaze, and before he could make a smart-ass comment, Lake pushed through the crowd. I'd been so engrossed in watching these three, that I'd completely missed him coming into the main part of the club.

Lake glanced at me. "Joaquin and Atlas are bringing a car around. We're done here for tonight." Then he leveled Gio and his friends with a stare so harsh, it should have melted their skin from their bones.

That would have been a lovely picture.

"Gio, if I have to tell you one more goddamn time that Beasty is off limits, you'll regret it," Lake growled.

Gio frowned at Lake like he was an annoying, kid brother instead of a dangerous man laying a threat between them. "You've got this all wrong. We're on the same side—"

"There are no sides," Lake spat. "We have business acquaintances that we have to do business with because we can't do it all on our own. But make no mistake, if you stop being useful to me, or working with Parker no longer bene- fits us, this relationship is done."

Adrian and Storm both snorted and Gio raised a hand

to silence them. "You don't just stop working with the Castillo Cartel."

"I don't give a fuck." Lake tossed his head to the side like they could kick rocks. "Try me and find out how serious I am." Lake held his arm out for Beasty, and I sighed when she untangled herself to step closer to him. "Stay in the club and make sure it doesn't burn down, or leave. Whatever. But we'll have words tomorrow about why you went behind my fucking back after I just told you to leave Beasty alone."

Lake took Beasty's arm and started weaving through the crowd to exit the club.

I winked at the guys on my way out.

Maybe it was time for us to reinvent ourselves our way.

Then we could get Beasty completely on board and stop pretending to pander to everyone trying to get their slice of us.

Just fantasizing about what that would look like left a dopey grin on my face as we left the club. And no one blinked at us twice.

Chapter Seventeen

JOAQUIN - PRESENT DAY

"A re you going to move at any point today?" I passed Atlas on the sofa in our bedroom as I headed to the closet.

I'd already gone down for breakfast and came back up while he hadn't moved. He was in that exact spot when I got up this morning too.

"No," he grunted.

Stopping, I backtracked to peek at the screen.

"She's awake, she's just not leaving." Those dreaded elevens popped up between his brows as he studied the laptop. "She's going to need breakfast."

There she was, just like he said. Awake and whispering to her hedgehog.

Sighing, I scratched the back of my head. It was a sad day when I was the voice of reason. Not that I was raging out of control or any shit like that. Outside of Atlas, we were just all very thoughtful and conscious of how we wanted our lives to be, and we worked hard to get there.

What was I thinking?

We weren't thoughtful, but we weren't idiots. Yet,

Beasty being here really brought out the ass and idiot in them, making a bad blend enabling bad decisions.

The back of my mouth watered. A drink sounded really fucking nice right about then, but I didn't have time for that.

I was supposed to go to Snatched today and check the books. We were also supposed to meet with our attorney to review our case.

Fuck it. Lake could handle the tiny dynamite attorney. I had a feeling the charges would be dropped soon anyway. And I was always right about those feelings.

Like the feeling that how they handled Beasty was all wrong.

"I'm heading out for the day. If you need me, call Lake." I grabbed a fresh fit, one picked out by Kim. His style wasn't exactly mine, and he did try to include pieces I liked, but every once in a while, I humored him by wearing something he specifically bought for me. That I would never wear on my own.

I stopped to check it out in the corner mirror. White linen pants with a matching, collared button-up.

It was stylish. It looked damn good on me. *If* I were on the beach somewhere instead of just outside of D.C. But whatever.

Kim constantly lectured us that we set the trends, we didn't follow them, so who cared?

Atlas cursed and grumbled under his breath as I walked by, but he had already forgotten me by the time I got to the door.

I smirked to myself as I stopped outside of Beasty's room and knocked.

Atlas would now know that I was getting ready to whisk away the object of his obsession.

Take that, asshole.

Just like the other times, silence initially reigned. Then I knocked again, and there were faint movements.

When the door opened, Beasty eyed me up like she wasn't sure if she wanted to stab me in the eye with a needle or...well, I didn't actually see any good intentions, but she was still here. So she had them.

"I'm taking you out of here for a little bit. Put on your shoes." I held my breath, not because I was nervous, but shit was so precarious with her right now—for good reason—that I didn't want to make a wrong move and scare her away.

"Why? You all have made it clear the outside world is dangerous for me." Her tone was flat. Unimpressed.

"You need some time away, and I could use it too. I'm also one of the best bets for you to hang with and go unnoticed." I rocked back on my heels. Lake wasn't famous like Kim and Atlas, but he was recognizable with his white hair.

One of her eyes squinted in distrust. Did she know that she wore her emotions on her sleeve for all the world to see? Kim could teach her a thing or two.

"Okay..." She drew her answer out, watching me instead of getting her shoes.

"Or you could stay here..." I taunted.

"No, I want out of here." Beasty left the door open as she went close to the bed and picked up her tennis shoes.

Hell, I hadn't realized it on the screen, but she was wearing one of the things Kim bought her. That was progress.

She touched the edge of the hedgehog's house and walked back to me, wearing a plain, tight tee and a pair of jean shorts. Nothing fancy, and definitely something comfortable.

"Where are we going?" She stepped past me, holding the heel of her sneakers on the tips of her first two fingers.

She didn't have to put her shoes on or take them off at

the door. We had a cleaning service. But now wasn't the time to make that argument.

"I thought we'd go to The Cakes Place. It's not far from Snatched, but it's out of the way of general traffic." I waited by the front door with my hand on the handle as she sat down on the stairs and slipped her shoes on.

Twirling my keys, I took a second to appreciate the moment.

Beasty was here. We were all together, and in a way where there could be an us. Not just a her and Kim.

I had to squeeze my eyes shut to get the image of Atlas with her out of my head. Fuck. I wanted to fuck him while he fucked her. I wanted to spear her on both our dicks. There were so many positions we could arrange her in.

Over us, under us...Between us.

Fuck. I groaned.

Shaking my head, I opened my eyes. Beasty stood two feet in front of me, staring at me like she wasn't quite sure what to make of me.

That was fair. I had no fucking clue what to make of her either.

"I have my car outside." I opened the door and cursed at myself. Of course, my car was outside.

There was zero room to call the others idiots.

She made a soft, choked noise in the back of her throat, but she didn't say anything else to further embarrass me. Kind of her.

I approached the head of the car, and I almost walked to the driver's side, but at the last minute, I pivoted to go to the passenger's side door. I beat her there by ten seconds and got it open, just barely missing her.

Beasty scrunched up her face and it was cute as hell, as she slid inside.

This wasn't so bad. Already some of that dark cloud that had been circling her head seemed to clear.

"You want some music?" I asked as I turned on the car and immediately started backing up. She jerked in her seat from my hard stop and huffed. "Sorry." I grinned. "I'm used to Atlas riding with me, and he lives to make my life a living hell. I try to return the favor where I can."

She didn't respond, and some of my good mood fell.

Clearing my throat, I adjusted in my seat and turned on the radio. If she didn't want to pick the music, I sure as hell would. I couldn't sit here in silence with her and my thoughts. That was too nerve-racking. How did Kim do it?

Low, slow notes of Radiohead started creeping out of the speakers. It was my preferred style of music. I'd have to get Kim to change the playlist in one of the numbered rooms one night.

The drive was peaceful at least. We finally pulled into the diner and I shut the car off.

My thoughts bounced around inside my head, and my hands trembled against my thighs after I turned the car off.

The sounds of the engine cutting off echoed through the cab, adding obvious attention to the fact that we were both still sitting in our seats.

This wasn't like me. I didn't get nervous. I got angry. I got frustrated. I got high on a win.

I did not get nervous. But this was the first time I'd been alone with Beasty. If you didn't count a few random conversations we'd had on the side of the room during different events. Those were different though.

This was intimate. Serious.

I rolled my head on the headrest until I faced her. She was already turned my way.

"Ready to head inside?" I raised my brows.

"Sure," she rasped, pink hitting the tops of her cheeks.

188

Grinning, my mood swung right back up where it had been. I could work with this. And hopefully, the fucker would stay in one spot.

Out of the corner of my eye, I caught the security guard discreetly pulling in. Lake had security on all of us, so the Pescis shouldn't get anywhere near us while she ate lunch.

A gum-smacking, middle-aged woman glanced over her shoulder from the counter where she was pulling food out of the window. "Just two?"

"Yup," I called out. The few tables in here ignored our exchange. Either used to the routine, or too hungover to care. From the looks of one man, who I'd seen at the club at least once, I'd say too hungover.

"Take a seat anywhere you want, hun." Then she forgot about us as she balanced several plates on her arms and started walking them out to a table of four.

"Over there?" I pointed to the back corner by the window. She shrugged. *Noted.* She didn't give two fucks about seating arrangements, so I'd stop asking.

I pulled the chair out, waited for her to sit, and then took my seat on the other side. I'd taken the corner, so I could see the rest of the diner. If for some reason one of our enemies came through the door, I'd see them.

Stretching my legs out, I leaned against the wooden back and let my gaze rest on her.

She fidgeted, glancing out the window, then adjusted the placement of her napkin-wrapped silverware. She'd flick her gaze to me every few seconds.

"What?" I cleared my throat.

"Why are you doing this?" Her voice was low, like she didn't want anyone else to hear our conversation.

"Doing what?" I teased, but I knew exactly what she was asking.

"Taking me for breakfast. Holding doors open and

189

pulling out my chair." She twisted her lips to the side and widened her eyes as she looked at me. Not in shock or surprise. More like she was serious and she was trying to get across just how serious she was by not blinking.

Sucking my tongue over my front teeth, I thought about it. Why was I doing this?

I was still pissed at her. Really fucking pissed that she just walked out before. But then I saw her with Kim while Atlas' lips were on her. Hell, even just being in her presence soothed some of the hurt feelings until I wanted to forget I was upset with her.

But I couldn't. Digging deep inside my chest, I did my fucking best to hold onto those feelings while also enjoying the moment. It was confusing as fuck, but I was trying.

"Extending an olive branch," I finally settled on. Then I stretched my hands across the cheap Formica tabletop. I didn't touch her, but I took up space. Lots of it.

Dropping her gaze, Beasty nodded like she was working it all out in her head.

"Aren't you going to say anything else?" I asked, but at that point, the woman walked over, still smacking her gum, and dropped two plastic menus on the table.

"What can I get you to drink?"

"Coffee for me. Black." I looked at Beasty.

She pushed the menu back. "Coffee for me too, and a stack of pancakes, side of bacon, and one egg over medium."

"The Total package then. Anything for you?"

I shook my head.

The woman nodded and snatched the menus back off the table.

One side of my mouth kicked up. "You didn't want to look at the menu?"

She smiled. "These diners all have the same thing. I

knew what I wanted and I didn't want to waste my time searching for the combination."

"Smart." I liked that she knew what she wanted, but damn, she'd changed in such a short time. When she was with us before, she hadn't been so decisive. She hadn't been so confident either.

It looked good on her, even if it roused the anger inside me all over again. Kim should have been there to see her come into herself.

"Why didn't you order anything?" She rested her elbows on the table. For a second, I let myself get lost in her gaze.

I was yanked out of my haze when the waitress set both mugs on the table. Beasty startled too.

"I had breakfast already. You still needed to eat, and you weren't going to come out of your room anytime soon," I said wryly.

Her lips pressed together. Was she amused? Affronted? Both?

"I would have come out when I was hungry."

"This way you didn't have to and you got out of the house."

She released a long breath and sat up straighter as she looked around. A soft smile on her face reflected in the window as she gazed outside. "This is nice. I feel normal right now."

"We're not normal though."

"You're not. But I am." All of that said in a matter-of-fact tone.

"No, Beasty." I tapped my fingers on the table to bring her attention back to me. "You're not. You and us? We're the only ones who matter. It's okay to not be like other people. I actually enjoy being smarter than most of them."

Her eyes lit up.

Gotcha. *See, Beasty. I could make you smile.*

I swallowed down the anger enough to ask the next question. "What did you do while you were gone?"

We held each other's stare. The sunlight hit her irises just right, bringing out the patterned emerald and gold as they contracted around her pupils.

"Why do you want to know?" She was no longer happy to be here, she was suspicious. My chest tightened because that wasn't what I wanted either.

"I'm not going to hold it against you." I tapped on the table with both hands now. When I glanced back at her, I committed all of her features to memory. The angle of her long nose. The width of her mouth that could give her a harsh or serious edge.

The strong angle of her chin was also new. It showed just how stubborn she'd grown to be.

Sighing, I scrubbed a hand over my face as I scooted down even further in the seat. "I don't know you. You're right. You also don't know us." I thought about how to say this next piece without either one, getting her hackles up, or two, scaring her away. "When you were gone, you changed. You grew up. I want to know what it was like and why you wanted that life so much."

Beasty softened right before my eyes. I leaned forward, pressing my chest to the table, getting as close as I could. Like magnets coming together, she did the same.

"Okay," she agreed. A tight coil inside my chest relaxed. Good. We were both going to ignore the elephant in the room. "I'll start with the CliffsNotes. For the first time in my life, I was independent. I took care of myself and that, above anything else I think, made me feel good."

"And before, when you were with us, you didn't feel like you could take care of yourself." She wasn't wrong, but I couldn't imagine any world where Lake or Atlas would let her run so much of her own life.

"No." Her mouth formed a small 'o' on the word. Then she licked her lips, and I was fucking mesmerized. It was like watching card shuffling tutorials. They just captivated me.

"And you don't think you could be happy with us?"

"I didn't say that," she hedged, and my gaze snapped back up to her eyes. "But I don't want to fall into the cycle."

"The cycle of what?" I furrowed my brows together, trying to piece together what I'd missed while I was stuck on her luscious lips.

"The cycle of life. The pattern of low-life people gaming the system and mistreating others. Whatever cycle people are born into."

What. The. Fuck.

"There's no way you could fall back into that cycle."

She licked her lips again before rolling them together, lowering her eyelids just enough so that her eyelashes covered her eyes. "I wasn't talking about me."

The floor literally fell out from under me. That was what she thought? I sizzled from the rage suddenly coursing through my blood. "You think we're going to be like Gates? You think we want to hurt little boys?" I growled.

"What?" Her eyes popped open in panic. Her ponytail swung behind her as she shook her head. "I'd *never* think that." She threw her hand on top of mine and squeezed like she was desperate for me to believe her. "But you're still falling back into the cycle. Don't you want to get away from all that? Be someone better? Not turn out like the people who raised us?"

She was fucking shitting me.

"You think we're evil? Is that it? You think we're damaged because of what happened in our past?" I yanked my hand back. She was backtracking now, but that wasn't what she'd *said*.

"No." Her nostrils flared as she pulled her hand back. "That's not it."

"You know what? I don't give a fuck what it is. There's a security guard in the lot. He'll take you home when you're done." I tossed cash on the table and stalked out, struggling to breathe.

Fuck this shit.

All these memories swirling inside my head. I hadn't thought about them in years, and now flashes of Gates stormed through the barriers of my mind like it was all yesterday.

His smell. His touch. His smile as he caused us pain.

And Beasty thought we were falling back into the cycle. Her backtracking didn't matter.

She compared us to that disgusting pig.

That was unforgivable.

Days had gone by since we'd tried to take Beasty shopping. I couldn't get out of my head enough to talk to her.

She wouldn't hold my issues against me. I knew she wouldn't.

Of anyone, she'd understand that I didn't like touch and attention. And all of those women would have touched me if given the chance. If I was caught off-guard, it messed with my head.

Still, it was embarrassing how I needed to be out of their sight. Beasty must have understood, since she let me stay in her dressing room.

But my brain didn't know that. My brain said I'd shown weakness to her and now she'd laugh at me. Or worse, be ashamed of me.

So, like any other person with messed up issues, I avoided her. I'd seen her in the kitchen a couple times, and once in the living room, when I came through, but we hadn't spoken other than a few polite words.

It had been easy.

I'd had a new string of jobs and so did Atlas. She opted to stay home, telling Lake she didn't fit in and needed a break before she tried it again.

Lake and I walked in the door, and the house was quiet. Almost too quiet.

Atlas and Joaquin were gone. Beasty should be here.

"Do you hear anything?" I asked Lake. He shook his head, then put a hand up, signaling for me to stay by the door as he went to check the apartment.

This was silly. He never found any boogiemen. Except for that one time, but it was just a cum sock of his that got kicked under his bed.

He came back, not alarmed, so he had to have seen Beasty.

"She's reading in her room." He smiled. "You should hang out with her."

"Why don't you?" It wasn't a whine. It was avoidance.

Lake paused, and the look he sent me was nothing short of scolding. Good thing I wasn't afraid of him like everyone else in the fashion world.

"We've had this discussion a thousand times. You're the one who's good for her. You. Not us. We're..." His face twisted up as he searched for the words, but he shook his head.

Lake's sudden foul mood set off a bomb inside me. "If you want someone to hang out with Beasty, you do it!" He was being too much of a martyr for no reason.

Walking toward me, Lake lowered his voice. "Look. This is how it has to be. I love that she's here, but this is as close as I'm ever going to get. Joaquin and Atlas too. This. Is. As. Good. As. It. Gets. For. Us."

"Why? You're not making any sense!" My voice started to rise until I clamped my lips shut.

"What's your fucking problem?" He cocked his head to the side.

I couldn't pull in a full breath. Just like when I was younger, anytime I tried to talk to Beasty, I couldn't think or breathe or do anything other than give her a weak smile. "This girl—She tears me up, Lake. I can be whoever I want to be. I can put on any face I need to, but not with her. Literally the only thing I can do is smile because she strips me bare."

Didn't he understand that? He had to have noticed it.

"There's no other choice, Kim. It's you or none of us. Is that what you want?" he whispered furiously.

"No!" I shot back. "Of course not, but I can't be the only one to be friends with her." I was already messing it up. Just look at how I almost had a breakdown in Macy's. I would have if she hadn't let me catch my breath in the dressing room with her.

Lake sighed, glancing back at the hall before completely turning away. "I'm going to go shower. Get Beasty to watch a movie with you or something," he muttered, leaving me standing in the doorway as he stalked off toward his bedroom.

How was I supposed to talk to her when I couldn't even look her in the eyes for more than a few seconds? This was insane. Lake should be the one taking charge. Or Joaquin.

Beasty came out of her room while I flapped my hands like a lunatic. She skidded to a stop, her finger stuck in the middle of a book.

My heart went into overdrive under her scrutiny.

"Are you okay?" She canted her head and peered closer.

"Fine. Just having a conversation with myself." I grinned, clasping my hands together.

The weight of her stare was heady as she shuffled closer.

She gave me a sheepish smile as she took in my outfit. "Was the job fun?"

I'd gotten to keep the pieces from the shoot. It wasn't often, but sometimes the designers wanted us to take the items we wore, hoping we'd get photographed in them and give them a boost of free advertising.

Well, not free. They paid me for it. And today's ensemble was a black pair of slacks, white dress shirt, and a black floral scarf tied around my throat. It was masculine while just on the right side of delicate. I hated the job but I loved the spoils.

I laughed, then regretted it when her face fell. I wasn't laughing at her. "It's a job. A necessary evil to be able to do all the things I want to do." *Like take care of you.*

"Then why'd you laugh?" Her frown was magnificent. There was just enough fire under the uncertainty, like she wanted to call me out for making her feel bad.

I glanced at her through my lashes.

Maybe Lake was right. I should hang out with her. Not avoid her because I was hung up on my own embarrassment.

"Do you want to watch a movie with me?" It was the hesitancy in my voice. The vulnerability that drew her in.

It was a gift in my personality to appear meek and sweet. I could be. When I wanted to be. It conquered the fashion world, and now I'd use it to conquer Beasty. But I didn't want to own her.

I wanted her to own me.

As soon as I had her under my spell, I'd wrap up the singed and damaged pieces of my heart in a big navy bow and gift it to her.

Her entire demeanor softened, from the set of her wide lips, to the slack in her shoulders. Even the skin around her eyes seemed to melt with the effect I had on her.

"What did you want to watch?"

"A Disney movie?" We'd never really watched them growing up. I'd seen some since Rosie had played them on holidays, like they added a little extra cheer, but I experienced most of them as an adult.

And there was a darkness to them that I didn't think others saw. It fascinated me.

"Okay." She mashed her lips together. "I can make the popcorn if you put on the movie. Or you can make the popcorn?"

"I'll make it and you pick something. Doesn't matter what." I almost skipped to the kitchen, all the anxiety that had festered under my skin for days suddenly gone, as if a bubble popped, leaving behind a lavender mist of giddiness.

I turned the stove on and added the oil. I couldn't cook, but I could make popcorn. And making it ourselves was better for us. Less calories and bad stuff.

I hated that I couldn't see the living room from where I was. Every second the kernels didn't pop, I got deeper and deeper into my head.

What if Beasty changed her mind?

What if she didn't want to watch a movie anymore? I couldn't even change out of my work clothes in case she disappeared while I was locked in my bedroom. Even my magnificent efficiency with changing outfits took time.

I poked my head around the corner and sighed. There she was, sitting on the couch, her back to the arm with the lamp turned on behind her, reading her book.

Atlas had never told me she liked to read. It made sense though. She spent enough time in the library to get away from her fosters.

The popcorn finished popping and I seasoned it to perfection before balancing the bowl and a couple waters in my hands.

"It's ready," I said quietly as I came around the corner.

Beasty sat up, set her book on the end table, and pulled the blanket off the back of the couch. She held it up like she was waiting for me to sit.

My heart thumped erratically as I took the cushion next to her, close but not touching.

She dropped the blanket, covering both of our legs, and then grabbed one of the waters from my hand. All without touching.

I hated touch. I always had.

It tore at my skin like a rusty cheese grater, leaving behind a slimy residue that never seemed to wash off.

Yet, Beasty's touch didn't.

Hers felt so good, it was like a balm to my soul. I craved it.

She seemed to want to respect my space, maybe because of what she'd seen others do? I wanted her to forget all that. To touch me like she wanted me.

To touch me like I was hers.

"Are we sharing?" Her question jolted me out of my thoughts.

"Yeah, I thought we could." I settled the full bowl between us, half on my thigh and half on hers, although she was sitting crisscrossed. "What did you pick?" I asked.

I glanced at the screen and laughed. This time, Beasty shared the humor with me.

"Beauty and the Beast?" I asked, deadpanned.

She grinned, a mischievous glint lighting her eyes. "Yep. I thought it was fitting. Remember when I first met you? I asked why you all were so pretty. You still are, you know. You four are the most handsome men I've ever seen."

The glow from her words suffused every cell in my body. "You're biased because we grew up together."

"Nah." She shook her head. "I'm being honest. You're all crazy attractive, but in different ways. You all always stood out."

I raised a brow. "That's because there weren't many ethnic people in West Virginia."

She snorted. "Yes, there were, just not as many as the big cities. You still stood out. And my nickname is Beasty." Beasty playfully tapped my shoulder, then pulled back her hand as if she startled herself.

I caught it, and pulled it into my lap, careful not to knock the popcorn on the floor.

Her fingers were long and slender, and her skin a little chaffed, but soft, like she'd started applying lotion recently. So different from my own.

"Is this okay?" I whispered.

Swallowing hard, her gaze locked on our intertwined fingers. She didn't answer, just turned on the movie.

Cheerful notes from the opening song started to play. Beasty clicked the lamp off and we were left in the dark, with only the light from the TV.

I wanted to stare at her so bad. I ached to turn my head and look.

Nothing in the movie registered, although this was one of the few I'd seen before. Instead, I focused on her breathing, on the feel of her skin against mine.

Every sensation was so vivid and electric, I clenched my teeth.

I was sitting here with Beasty. She was holding my hand. Spending time with me.

She fidgeted just enough that I allowed myself to turn my head.

At first, I studied her profile. The different light played over her features, highlighting different micro-expressions.

She cut her eyes at me and froze.

A slow smile took over my mouth as she shifted enough to face me.

"What?" she whispered.

"I really like you, Beasty," I blurted it out. Just spilled my guts right there on the couch. I got so hot, I started to tug on the scarf with my free hand.

Her eyes widened to round moons, and then she swallowed again.

"Do you like me too?" I asked. Her cues filled me up with golden courage.

Beasty's lips trembled and her tongue snuck out to lick across the bottom. Orange and blue light flickered across half of her face, reflecting from her eyes.

It never made sense before. Our obsession with this girl who saved us.

It did, but it didn't.

Right then, gazing into her eyes, everything clicked into place.

She was mine. I wanted her to be only mine and I would be only hers.

"Do you like me, Beasty?" I asked again, leaning in the barest amount. Her reactions said she did, but I wanted to hear her say it.

"Yes."

My eyelids fluttered closed. That one word washed over me, pushing away so many of my hurts.

"Can I..." I shivered. "Can I kiss you?" I looked deep into her eyes.

Beasty bobbed her head, meeting me halfway.

There was no rush. No pressure. Just a gentle brush of lips that turned into more.

I tingled where our skin touched. Little fireworks

exploding inside my chest and mind. Using my thumb, I rubbed circles on her inner wrist, just as captivated by her warmth as her taste.

My first kiss. It was perfect.

She grew bolder, leaning deeper, sliding her tongue along my lips until I opened my mouth and let her in. Pulling the scarf from my neck, I slid it around hers, holding her to me. It smelled of me and I wanted to claim her for my own.

I groaned as my dick hardened.

Then she jumped and tried to lean away. Letting go of the scarf, she moved back at least a foot from me. It took a few seconds to catch my breath.

What had just happened? The first crushing thought was that she regretted the kiss. But she wasn't looking at me at all.

Beasty stared at the door, biting her lip. A key scraped against the lock, then Joaquin walked through the door.

My pulse pounded in my ears and I swallowed the sand in my mouth.

She acted like we'd been caught doing something wrong. Hell, I felt like we'd been caught doing something wrong. But we hadn't.

This was the most right thing that had ever happened to me in my life.

I'd live every single moment over again, a hundred times more, to reach this moment.

"I'm sorry. I need to go to the bathroom. I think I should just go to bed," she stammered as she knocked the bowl into my lap. I caught it before it spilled, but she was already gone.

Glancing up, Atlas and Joaquin were in front of me, fury and desire etched into their faces.

"You were making out?" Atlas' voice was gravel. Yearning. Desperate.

I shook my head. A denial was on the tip of my tongue, but squeezed my eyes shut.

There was nothing wrong with kissing Beasty. Nothing shameful in it.

It was beautiful.

"We kissed," I croaked. Knowing it was okay and confirming it, and putting it out in the universe, were two different things.

Atlas dropped to the floor, sitting in front of me, and Joaquin raked his hands through his hair as he glared at the hallway.

He wasn't angry though. He was tipsy. The alcohol leaked from his pores.

"How did it happen?" Atlas watched me with serious, unblinking eyes.

My mouth suddenly watered from my nerves but I ignored it. Nodding, I took a breath and reminded myself of who I was.

I was Kim. A master of expressions. A great storyteller. The calm in the middle of a raging storm.

"She told me all about her childhood. We traded stories, the light ones. We started with looks, until she reached out to hold my hand." I set the bowl of popcorn on the end table. "And when the movie was playing, we turned toward each other, like we were on the same page. Completely in sync. And we kissed."

"Kim," Joaquin groaned.

"You're going to make me install cameras." Atlas' brows pulled low over his eyes. "That's not a bad idea anyway."

"What else do you want me to say?"

"Does she like you?"

I nodded, bringing one hand up to touch my smiling lips. "Yeah. She does."

"Does that mean you're together? Does she want that?" Joaquin squinted at Atlas as if to gauge his reaction to my answer.

"I hope so." I really, really did.

"We need cameras," Atlas muttered to himself again.

Chapter Nineteen

LAKE - PRESENT DAY

"I left Beasty at the diner," Joaquin slurred over the other end of the line.

Jumping up out of my chair, I cursed when my phone hit the floor. "What the fuck does that mean?"

"I don't know what you want me to say..." Joaquin trailed off, clearly lit off his ass.

"And where the hell are you? Who's watching her?" Someone better be fucking watching her. I grabbed my keys off the corner of my desk and ran from the office. For some reason, I'd decided to work from home today. That was a mistake.

"I'm at Snatched in the Gold Room. We've got a helluva game playing right nah." More slurred words. He was smashed.

"Who is with Beasty?" I demanded, enunciating each word.

"The Cakes Place. Rory is in the lot. He won't let her out of his sight." He snorted. "I don't know why we're even bothering with her. Why have we ever?"

"What happened?" I tried to lower my voice, but every

alarm bell was shooting off inside my brain. Beasty alone outside of our house was asking for disaster. Donnie's presence at the club was just confirmation that they weren't going to let this go.

I was supposed to be meeting with Ms. Chen in one hour. That wasn't going to fucking happen now.

"She thinks we're scum, Lake. We're no better than Gates." Joaquin could hold his liquor when he had a mind to it. For him to let himself deteriorate this much meant he was fucked up in the head before he ever started drinking.

"Statistically, what she said makes sense. But weren't Gates. Not even close. We're survivehs."

"*You're* not making any fucking sense." I slammed my car into drive and sped down the driveway, tires squealing.

"I don't have time for this shit," Joaquin grumbled, now actually using real words. "She's at Cakes. Go pick her up, then take her somewhere else. I don't care where. Just don't let Atlas see her." The line clicked.

"Fucking hell." I hit Rory's number as I took the turn that would lead me to the breakfast diner. It was just past Snatched, so it wouldn't take long to get there. Not at my speed.

"Boss." Rory sounded strangled.

"Where is she and what is she doing?"

He coughed. "She just left the diner. She sat there for a good thirty minutes crying. No one noticed at first, then some lady named Bertha came over and patted her back, handing her wads of napkins."

"Where is she now?" I snapped. Why the hell did I have to repeat myself so much today. With my free hand, I dug my nails into my thigh, needing that little bit of pain.

"She's walking on the side of the road—"

"Why didn't you put her in the car?" I yelled. My vision started to cloud with red around the edges and my nose closed up making it harder to breathe. All it took was one stray bullet, one deep slice of a knife, or worse, a moment of distraction to be thrown in the trunk of a car, and we'd never see her again.

I needed more pain.

Curling my toes in my shoes, I raked my nails along my jeans. Stupid me, thinking I didn't need slacks today, but I did. I really fucking did.

"I tried." Kudos to him for remaining calm in the face of my anger. "But I'm following her. Even though she keeps turning back and screaming at me and flipping the bird." A thread of amusement hung in his words.

But that visual didn't spark any humor for me. It turned my rage cold. Joaquin better have a fucking good reason for leaving her alone.

I didn't give a damn if she thought I was the devil. She was going to be safe or I was dead. Those were the only two options.

"What road are you on?" I barked and floored the pedal until the trees were a blur as they passed.

"County Road 6. She's heading deeper into the country instead of toward Snatched. I thought she'd have a–"

I hung up on his ass. I couldn't listen to his voice anymore.

Beasty was about to get her ass spanked. That was her only option.

I didn't give a fuck if Joaquin left her there–although I'd take my grievances up with him separately.

She was at the club. She saw Donnie. The stupid girl was smarter than to take off on her own. Her self-preservation was stronger than that. I'd seen enough with my own eyes during our teen years.

It wasn't long before I came up behind Rory's SUV creeping along the dirt road. I passed him, and there Beasty was, stomping like a damned elephant as she flipped the bird over her shoulder.

I swerved to a stop in front of her, swinging my door open and hopping out.

Her hand was pressed to her chest as she stumbled back. "You scared the shit out of me!" she screamed.

Tears tracked down red cheeks, and her bloodshot eyes were swollen from crying. Hurt feelings didn't matter when it came to her safety. She goddamned knew better.

"Rory." I snapped my fingers to get his attention.

He hung his head out of the driver's side window. "Yeah, boss?"

"Park at the end of the road. Watch for trouble." AKA the Pescis.

He glanced at Beasty, humor lighting his grin, and ducked his head back inside. He didn't waste any time flipping a bitch and heading back toward the diner.

I stormed toward Beasty, and she violently shook her head as she backed up, tears still tracking down her face.

Jesus Christ. Even her neck was flushed and wet, either from sweat or tears.

She was furious and hurt and fucking gorgeous.

Collaring her neck, I walked her backward. "What the fuck are you thinking leaving the diner by yourself?" I growled, getting so close in her face, my nose brushed the side of hers.

Beasty shoved at my chest, but I was stronger. "What do you mean what was I thinking?" She yelled. "Ask your asshat friend why he left me there in the first place! He's a fucking baby throwing a temper tantrum," she snarled, even as tears built in her eyes.

This poor girl. She probably couldn't even see me.

"He didn't go walking down the side of the street where he could get snatched up by our enemies."

"Enemies?" she huffed, her voice thick. "*Your* enemies, not mine."

"That's how you want to act? Like you didn't learn anything as a kid? Or even out on your own. You've seen bad people, right Beasty? Or were you too sheltered for that?"

"Too–To–" Her top lip peeled back and she banged against my chest with all her might. "*Fuck you, you fucking dickhead!* I'm in this goddamn mess because of you!"

That was e-fucking-nough. I bent and picked her up over my shoulder and carted her into the woods.

There were no private property signs here, and there was no fencing. Nothing to show that this was owned by someone else.

If I remembered correctly, this was all state land.

Perfect for teaching her a lesson.

She thrashed and screamed over my shoulder but I landed a hard smack on her ass. The sting on my hand was so delicious, my eyes rolled back in my head.

Once we couldn't see the road anymore, I dropped her in a small grove of trees.

Catching herself on my arm, she dug her nails in to hurt me, but I grabbed her arms and pulled her in close. "Don't forget my kink, Beasty."

"I didn't forget," she snarled, then her hand cocked back and she slapped me across the face. I groaned, clenching her to my chest as I dropped my head back.

This was how she wanted to play it?

Fuck, yeah. I was game.

I shoved her against the tree and pulled her shorts and panties down as I crouched in front of her. She didn't need any coaxing to fist her hands in my hair and yank just right.

The sting on my scalp sent goosebumps down my arms as I propped one of her legs over my shoulder. I could smell her sweet, tangy scent from here. Using my thumbs, I pulled her open, her lips flowering out with the little nub on top.

Fucking beautiful.

I leaned forward and wrapped my teeth around it, glancing up at her as I bit down the tiniest bit. I didn't want to hurt her. Much.

I wanted to use the threat of pain to bring her more pleasure. To tease her. To level her down from her big emotions the way pain did for me.

Beasty's eyes were wild and her top teeth dug into her bottom lip as she glared down at me. She yanked a little harder, jerking my head back. I groaned and she yelped. Her clit was still between my teeth, and I wasn't going to let her go. Not until she begged.

Or came. Whatever happened first.

I curled my fingers over the leg on my shoulder, using my nails to cut into her skin. Not enough to break, but enough to mark.

Then I worked two fingers of my other hand inside. With how sopping wet she was, it wasn't hard. It was almost too easy.

But I didn't give her gentle, and I sure as hell didn't give her loving. I gave her intense, brutal thrusts as I circled my tongue around the bundle of sensitive flesh caught between my lips, massaging it, coaxing it.

"I hate you. I fucking, *fucking* hate you," she gasped, grinding her hips against my face. I chuckled under my breath as I slammed my hand against her harder, making sure to curl my fingers against her g-spot.

My cock was hard enough to break up concrete and every time it pulsed, my vision darkened around the edges.

The urge to pull back and tell her to show me exactly how much she hated me was so strong, but it wasn't stronger than the craving to help her. To break her apart in my hands.

"All of you. You're so...so..." She tipped her head back, releasing a long moan as she started to clamp down on my fingers. That was the sign. She was close.

I released her from my mouth and pulled out my fingers. Beasty didn't let me go far. She scratched her nails against my scalp and I shut my eyes. These trickles of pain were everything, but still so far away from what I actually wanted.

A small appetizer. A tease.

"Wha–" Beasty clenched her leg on my shoulder, trying to pull me against her.

I laughed again. "You're a brat, Beasty. I didn't know you had this side of you." As much as I hated brats, I loved Beasty in any form she came in. And I couldn't hate that she'd given me a reason to give her a tiny taste of pain.

Her face darkened with the dangerous scowl. The pretty flush had transformed into a livid red. Beasty was pissed. And now that she had sufficiently lost her orgasm. I dove back in. This time sucking her clit with more force than care and shoving my still wet fingers back inside her.

She cried out, and tried to edge backward, but there was nowhere for her to go with her back against the tree. "Too much, too much, too much," she chanted as she beat against my back.

I stopped for just a second. "It's not too much. It's perfect. Because you're perfect, Beasty." I licked around her nub then bit it again. She was so hot, and already she was starting to pulse around me.

Backing off again, I shot her a grin. As she lost another orgasm, anger vibrated through her. I didn't even see it coming when she landed her next slap.

Damn, she cut my lip on my tooth. I stuck my tongue out, tasting a tiny drop of blood.

"I'm sorry!" She tried to drop her leg but I held her firm.

"Stop!" I barked. "Don't start that shit." It came out harsh, but shit. We were just starting to have a good time. Now she was acting like she'd had a bucket of cold water dumped over her head.

"I didn't even think—"

"You don't think with me. I don't want you to. Your body knows what I need just as much as I know what you want. This between us, Beasty, it's never bad. The hurt is good. Not everyone understands it, but we do, don't we?"

The excitement seemed to leak out of her and a dark cloud gathered over my head. No. Fuck no.

I angled her hips so I could watch her as I brushed my nose against her, then I licked up her slit. Her breath quickened, but she didn't say anything. Didn't give me the satisfaction of any of her noises.

"We understand each other, don't we, Beasty?" I tried again, kneading her ass as I worked her over with my mouth, desperate to get the fiery, spitting kitten from a few minutes before.

"No," she panted. "I don't understand any of you. You're all..." she swallowed as I inserted one finger, more gently this time. "Assholes. You're all assholes who don't care about anything but yourselves."

"Not true." I worked my second finger back in, and instead of thrusting, I curled them rhythmically inside her to consistently hit the spongy spot that would have her in a puddle before too long. "We care about you, Beasty. You're all we care about."

"Funny way of showing it." She huffed, dropping her head back again as a soft noise fell from her lips.

"Funny that you don't see it," I murmured back.

She stopped trying to talk to me, lost in the sensations I was pulling from her body.

Like she knew what I needed, she grabbed the sides of my head, angling me where she needed me most and using her nails against my scalp. I groaned, and continued my ministrations until she once again started to close on my fingers.

This time, I didn't stop. Fuck Atlas and his idea to edge her. We could edge her in other ways than to have her hate us.

Beasty groaned, and dropped her head, showing me those beautiful hazel eyes. Her mouth parted as she panted and rocked against me.

Not changing my movements, keeping the same rhythm the way women needed, she came apart in my hands. Her eyelids drooped, and she bit her bottom lip even though it didn't do anything to stop her from vocalizing her pleasure.

When the tremors started to subside, I pulled my fingers free and lifted them to her lips, sliding them into her mouth so she could taste herself as I worked her down softly with my mouth.

She shuttered, closing her eyes.

The moment was like nothing I'd ever known before. Beasty was it for me. For us.

It didn't matter what she thought, we'd bring her to our way of thinking. We had to. There was no other option.

When I sat back, I lowered her leg and let her get her balance before I helped back into her panties and shorts.

"Come on." I stood and held out my other hand as I sucked any remnants of her from my fingers.

She eyed my hand like a snake in the grass before stopping on the tent in my jeans.

Shaking my head, I snagged her hand. "I'm fine. Let's go. We've already been out here too long."

Beasty didn't put up a fight as I placed her in the passenger seat. She didn't attempt to talk about what bothered her on the way back.

I didn't either. Not that I was afraid, but she was sated and calm, and I didn't want to rock that boat before I figured out what the hell happened with Joaquin. Just looking at Beasty, I knew it wasn't what he thought.

Sighing, I turned down the driveway.

My own reflection didn't last long because there was a black SUV in front of the house that certainly wasn't any of ours.

Chapter Twenty

ATLAS - PRESENT DAY

That fucker.

He didn't even ask me if I wanted to go.

I opened my bedroom door, ready to head downstairs and grab some food. I bet Beasty already had her food by now. He at least could have taken her to Snatched where the surveillance fed right to my phone.

All the doors were shut. Lake was in his office, and Kim was in his room. He got food earlier so who knew what he was doing.

I didn't have any interest if it didn't involve Beasty.

But Joaquin would pay for this. Maybe I'd take him to the Black Room and get him up on the platform. If I could get Beasty on board, I'd have her edge him until he never tried to keep me out again.

He'd hate it.

At the bottom of the stairs, I still had one hand on the banister when the office door slammed and Lake came barreling through the house. He didn't even glance at me as he raced out and slammed the door shut behind him.

That couldn't be good.

But again, not my concern. My concern was in a diner where Joaquin was with Beasty.

After I'd eaten, my phone dinged and I checked the screen. Security.

SECURITY:

Someone is on their way up the driveway.

Irritation scratched the inside of my chest. Joaquin and Lake took care of business. I was the pretty face. It worked for me, allowing me to spend most of my time doing the things I loved.

With the club, I pulled my weight in different ways. Handling random house calls on a weekday wasn't part of it.

It wasn't like we could have security stop them either. Not if it could be the cops or feds. That would be too fucking suspicious.

I pulled up the feed from the doorbell and watched the SUV pull up. The door opened and a dainty foot in a clog stepped out.

Well, well. The Mediator was here.

Sonia slammed her door shut, righted her rainbow overalls, and pushed her sparkling sunglasses on top of her head. Her expression was pained as she walked up the steps. She didn't like me much. Thought I had bad energy.

Snorting to myself, I opened the door before she had the chance to knock.

"What a surprise." I smirked.

We'd been working with her since about a year after we left West Virginia. We made an acquaintance of an acquaintance who introduced us to Sonia. For the most part, she was a nice woman.

For what she did.

Every time I'd seen her, she was dressed like a 70's reject and acted like a cuckoo bird. There was no way this was who she was. As she did jobs for us, it would have gotten around that a woman in rainbows and sparkles gave ultimatums that people couldn't resist.

That hadn't happened yet, so there was more to Sonia than what met the eye.

"Lake here?" She asked, her voice light but blunt.

"Well, hello to you too."

"No? How about Kim? Anyone but you, really. I guess Joaquin is okay, but he still owes me fifty bucks." She sniffed and glanced around the foyer as I shut the door behind her.

"He won that money because you're terrible at Blackjack," I said as I walked by her. We might as well have this conversation in the living room.

"You don't steal money from a lady," she returned hotly. But it wasn't serious. It never was, otherwise, she would have stolen the money from him a few years ago. Or added an extra fee on her services.

"Right..." I humored her. "Lake called you?"

"Joaquin, actually." She flopped down on the couch and one of her clogs fell off her foot. "A few days ago. He said you needed my services."

Shit, that could be anything. Or anyone. The judge, the Pescis, Adrian because he got on Joaquin's nerves. But that wasn't his style. My money was on the judge.

"He didn't give me any information. I'll call him." I held up one finger and dialed Joaquin. He answered on the second ring.

Loud chatter was in the background as an attendant called out a number.

"Tell me you're not at Snatched." I wished I was upstairs so I could get my laptop and pull Beasty up on the cameras.

My phone was okay, but I preferred the largest screen possible.

"What the hell do you want?" It was almost unintelligible.

My stomach dropped to the floor. There were many things that would get Joaquin shitfaced, but there were only so many that would push him to this when he was out with Beasty. I didn't like any of them.

"I'll be right back," I tossed over my shoulder at Sonia as I ran upstairs. I pounded on Kim's door and when he opened it, he gave me a bleary-eyed stare as if he'd been sleeping. I pointed downstairs. "Sonia is here. Go watch her."

She was a smart woman. She knew we had cameras up, but if Kim was there, she'd be less likely to snoop or cause trouble.

Kim didn't need any other prompting as he made his way toward the living room.

Inside our room, I put the phone on speaker as I sat on the couch, pulling up the footage for Snatched on my laptop. The Gold Room was the only place Joaquin would be.

"Where's Beasty?" The Gold Room was up. There was Joaquin, slumped over at a Blackjack table with an empty glass in front of him.

"Gone."

Jumping up, my laptop fell to the floor. "What the hell do' you mean gone?" I shouted. Air stopped flowing as I tried to swallow and my vision started to go black.

"Left her with Rory. She's fine. Lake's on his way to get her." And that asshole left without me?

Everyone was going to pay. This wasn't part of the plan.

I opened my mouth to spew some shit at Joaquin, but I snapped it shut. He'd be handled later. Right now, there were more important things to deal with. "Why did you call Sonia?"

"Oh," he grumbled. "We got the file on Danny Pesci. And Stevo."

Sonia wasn't going to help with Stevo. Stevo was fucking dead and she worked with breathing clients only.

"What was the point of that?" I asked, opening my laptop and checking the GPS on Lake's phone. He was about five minutes from Snatched on a back road.

I texted him while I waited on Joaquin.

"Just to have more info. Lake has some on Donnie. But I have the file on Danny."

"And what is Sonia here for?" I gritted through my teeth. Dealing with a plastered Joaquin was worse than getting a newbie make-up artist who had no fucking idea how to work with different skin tones.

"To work on Danny."

"Where's the file?" Lake hadn't responded. What the hell was he doing? He hadn't moved since I'd pulled up his location. I sent a text to Rory next.

"In my bag."

"Got it. We'll chat about this later."

"Yeah, whatever," he snarked.

Pulling the phone away from my face, I looked at Joaquin on the screen. What the hell was wrong with him? He hadn't done this since before the club opened. He was lucky Parker Adair went to his damned rescue. Otherwise, he could have been chewed up at that Viper's nest.

And the fucker hung up on me.

Grabbing the file from his bag, I checked my messages again. Still nothing from Lake, but Rory had responded.

RORY:

Lake is with her. She's ok, just upset.

Dropping my head back, I rolled it side to side in controlled movements, enjoying the cracks. She was fine. Lake would bring her home, then I would barricade her in my room and demand answers.

She might not give them willingly, but that was what I hoped for.

I flipped through the file. Danny was a busy guy, hanging out at Mary Sue's, one of the Pescis' hangouts. Original name. Not.

He had a baby with an ex. Nothing crazy there. Rumors that he was a wife-beater. I didn't need to check the facts, he had that look.

The last page was a black and white image of Danny with a woman, hitting it from behind while he pulled her hair to tip her head up.

In black sharpie, there was an arrow drawn to her and the words, Donnie's wife.

Hell, yes. Exactly what we needed. Which resource did Joaquin tap to get this gem?

I checked Lake's location one more time before I left the room. He was still in the same spot. Sonia would only take a minute, then I'd go to that location and lay my own eyes on her.

Already, my nerves were starting to fray at the edges just knowing she wasn't in view of any of the cameras. Now that she was back and we had surveillance everywhere, the compulsion to watch her was almost unbearable. I needed to see her, or at least know where she was at every second I was awake.

And this? I knew where she was at, but not knowing what happened or why she was half a mile from the diner, was a poison working through my blood, leaving my skin hot and itchy.

Downstairs, Kim sat on the arm of the chair across

from where Sonia sat on the couch. Kim, the subtle flirt he could be, had Sonia giggling like a twelve-year-old schoolgirl.

"I'm telling you, Snatched is the place you need to be. You'd fit right in in the Urban Room, and the performers are absolute artists." He leaned in, not even caring about his ruffled bedhead. "And it's quite seductive. If you love that, we have other more...*private* rooms for our favorite guests to enjoy." He winked and she giggled, tapping her bare feet on the rug.

She glanced up when I rounded the chair and cleared her throat. Oh, she really did not like me.

"Well?" Sonia asked primly.

"I have a file on Danny Pesci. He's fucking his brother's wife." I walked over to hand her the file, and once she took it, I sat in one of the other chairs. My hands itched to check Lake's location, but I could wait a little bit.

Sonia whistled. "The Pescis, huh? I've heard plenty about them, but they're out of my normal territory. Does this have to do with Lake's arrest?"

She knew enough people in the law circuit, so it wasn't a surprise she knew about his arrest. Interesting that she didn't mention Joaquin's. "We've made them a little angry by taking away one of their toys." I traced my fingers over the seam at the end of each arm. "They surprised us when they went to the cops."

Kim glanced at me and back to Sonia, his smile completely gone now.

Flipping through the file, she stuck her tongue out to the side. Then she hummed when she got to the last picture.

Sonia closed it and set it down across her thighs. "You know that they're never going to take this to court. They're going to drop the charges, and from what I hear, there's not enough evidence to make the charges stick. You sure you want me to take this job? Seems like a waste to me."

I wouldn't bother with it, but Joaquin thought it was important, and I never doubted him on things like this. He was too good at stacking the odds in our favor.

Shrugging, I raised a lazy hand. "I don't question Joaquin."

We spent the next several minutes ironing out how she was going to position this and what our preferences were on the interaction. I didn't have any and if Joaquin wanted a say, he should have fucking been here.

The front door unlocked, and footsteps echoed through the house as they drew closer.

Anticipation lit up in my stomach and my head snapped toward the hall.

Lake came through first, thunder in his expression until he saw Sonia sitting on the couch. His posture loosened and he stepped to the side.

I expected Beasty, but she didn't come through.

"Where is she?" I demanded, standing up.

"Leave her alone for a little while." Lake scrubbed a hand over his face. Then he glanced at Sonia, completely disregarding me. That was fine. I enjoyed the few times I blended into the background.

But Lake was high if he thought I was going to let Beasty be alone.

"What's today's call for?" He addressed Sonia directly as he walked deeper into the room.

"Oh, you know, a job that's not worth the money."

I didn't wait to hear the rest of the exchange. I ran up the stairs, taking them three at a time. At the mouth of the hallway, I slowed down. Instead of knocking on her door or heading straight to my room, I pulled up the video feed on my phone, making sure it was silenced just in case she was talking.

The rooms were soundproof, but I hadn't gotten as good at watching Beasty by being thoughtless and making assumptions.

The video was clear, yet Beasty's body language was all wrong.

She had her back to the stand that held her pet, slumped over her knees with drooping lines. There was so much despair rolling off of her, I couldn't stand it.

Beasty needed to be punished. She needed to pay. But on my terms. Not like this.

My heart twisted inside my chest as I fisted my free hand. Just like when we were teenagers, the best thing I could do for her was let her know she wasn't alone.

I opened her door and her head popped up. Beasty should have locked it if she wanted to be alone.

She didn't say anything, just looked off to the side, like she didn't mind me here as long as she didn't have to acknowledge me.

Sucking in a shallow breath, I walked closer, getting a good look at just how devastated she was.

There were no tears, but there had been. Her face was blotchy and the skin under her eyes was swollen. Even her lips were puffy like she'd bitten them too much.

If Kim were here, I doubt he could pass up the chance to photograph her. This was exactly his vibe.

Scratching the back of my head, I slipped my phone in my pocket and took a seat against the wall, only a few feet from her. I reached out a hand, then froze. What the hell was I doing?

Pulling it back, I dropped it to my lap.

It seemed wrong. I only touched her when I wanted to fuck her. Or when I knew she wanted to fuck me.

Right then, she was fragile. Brittle. One wrong touch and she could break.

"Whatever it is, it's not worth the energy."

One side of her mouth slid up as if pulled by a loose string. "Joaquin isn't worth the energy?"

I knew that motherfucker was the reason for this as soon as I heard how plastered he was. I'd get the information from him when he was sober. Then I'd decide the best way to fuck him over.

But for now, I shook my head, trying not to clench my teeth.

"You're worth ten of that asshole, Beasty. I promise."

Her eyes widened, but she remained frozen. We stared at each other until I couldn't take it anymore.

If I stayed, I'd end up punching a hole in the wall, and that wouldn't help either of us. I preferred my bad behaviors to manifest in different ways.

I hopped to my feet, glancing at the quiet enclosure. I'd have to meet this pet of hers someday.

"Atlas..."

"It will be okay, Beasty. Whatever it is, as long as we're together, it will be okay."

Then I left her on the floor, not sure if I was saving us trouble or causing her more pain.

But I didn't leave her alone completely. I set up my laptop in my room and took a seat on the floor against the wall. Then I watched her process her thoughts.

Just like I'd always done before.

Chapter Twenty-One

JOAQUIN - AGE 21

The sounds of chips hitting the table and cards shuffling was my happy place. It was familiar and just itched that perfect spot inside my head.

A dopamine rush like nothing I'd never experienced.

This room was better than the last couple I'd found too. A backroom of a gentlemen's club where the men were in suits, instead of stained tracksuits and holey T-shirts. Part of it was because I was semi-famous as the manager for Atlas and Kim.

Which was a fucking fight. The agency thought I was a kid with no business sense. Then I fleeced the owner from a substantial amount of money during a card game one night.

Then I did it again. And again.

Once he realized the head I had for numbers, he told his minions to let me be their manager. There were still bumps in the road, but nothing major.

The other part of the invitation to the better rooms was my wider range of connections.

Know more people, get better invites.

Know the right people, sit at the most lucrative tables.

The cards in front of me were the nine of clubs and eight of hearts. I'd observed enough of the cards played in the last few rounds to know most of the larger weighted cards were sitting in the used stack.

"Hit me." I tapped the felt table next to my cards. The attendant nodded and flipped over a four of clubs.

I broke out into a wide grin that was absolutely not contagious when I glanced at my table mates. It wasn't even the alcohol lifting my spirits, I only had one drink tonight.

Beasty didn't know this side of me, at least the drinking side. And I'd like to keep it that way. If I went home one too many times with glazed eyes and alcohol on my breath, she'd notice.

That was something I couldn't handle. Not until she was firmly ingrained with Kim. Then maybe I'd be able to slip up every now and again.

A man caught my eye across the room, and I grabbed the hard-won chips and gave a two-finger salute to my table mates.

"It's been a pleasure."

They grumbled and the attendant eyed me with disdain. I'd get maybe two more times in this room before they kicked me out. They hated card counting. I could prolong it with a few poker games because the management didn't care if I took the patron's money. Just not theirs.

The man I approached smiled, leaning back on the counter to prop himself up on his elbows as he twisted his stool from side to side.

He wasn't anything to write home about. Not really. Average features. Brown hair. Large glasses.

At least until he smiled, then he could give even Atlas a run for his money.

"Ratio." I tapped my fist against his as I slid onto the

open seat beside him. "Strange to see you in my neck of the woods."

"These places are going to get smart one of these days. You're too obvious." He grinned, turning to face me. This guy was the picture of normalcy. But I didn't buy it. It was too suspicious how he came into my life. Yet I couldn't get too upset about it.

He helped us out in a big way when we first left home. Saying it was a favor to a friend.

"Just because you have a math related nickname does not make you smarter than me." I scoffed. He was good. Scary good. The one time I played against him—which was the only time—I almost didn't win.

A sobering reality to find myself in.

He hadn't asked for a rematch and that made me suspicious. For men like us, who understood numbers more than the written language, gambling was an addiction we couldn't shake.

It worked out because my gambling was the second reason we were as independent as we were.

The first? Was help from Ratio.

"The humble ones are the ones you have to look out for." He touched the side of his nose like he was letting me in on a secret. "They don't even see me and don't realize I won until I'm gone. But you," he raised his voice, "you're loud and they see you coming from a mile away. They keep playing you, hoping to get their money back, but someday they'll get wise and walk. Or kill you."

He said that last bit with a smile that was so unbothered, it made the hairs on the back of my neck stand up.

"What are you doing here?" I changed the subject. Philosophical conversations weren't my thing. I'd rather have fun taking men down a notch at the tables.

"I got a lead on another treasure. Thought I'd pass it

along." Ratio faced the room, looking for all intents and purposes like he hadn't rocked my world yet again.

The first time? After I'd taken his money, he'd pulled me aside and told me where the Ming Dynasty vase was.

"Why are you telling me this?" I narrowed my eyes. This was too fucking suspicious. The first time, fine, he wanted to help us, even though I couldn't figure out why. This time? Too fucking weird.

"Let's just say, I know a man who hated the Curator. He likes to right wrongs where he can."

"So this is a tip from him?" I pushed, hoping he'd give me more information than last time.

"Nah, I hadn't talked to him in a while." His face darkened, then cleared right the fuck up. "I caught wind of this lead. I don't need the money, and I'm sure you get more *fuck you* satisfaction out of his stuff than I ever could."

"That's a fair assessment." I grinned. I still didn't trust him. "What is it and where?"

"Just some old books someone traded for his services."

That was all it took for sweat to break out across my face and my throat to close up. I couldn't fucking breathe.

"You okay?" He eyed me with so much intelligence in his eyes, he had to know exactly what his words just did.

Fucked me up.

Because I was a pussy who couldn't stand reminders of being kidnapped and abused.

"Yeah," I coughed, blinking. "I got something in my eyes."

Ratio sighed. "I left the details in your car. But I hope you're not driving back."

I didn't answer. I'd only had one drink. I had fully planned on driving home, but now? I might need a fifth just to function.

"I'm watching. Don't drive." He hopped off the stool

and sauntered through the tables toward the exit. Not a damned person looked at him.

Me? Several men glanced at me, either cutting their eyes in jealousy, or with thoughtful, curious expressions.

I couldn't blend into a crowd if I wanted to. Neither could the others. For the most part, it was the reason we were as successful as we were. I wasn't about to start hating our blessings now.

Somehow, I'd cashed in the chips, got confirmation of the electronic transfer, then left through the back. I could have walked out the front, but I needed air.

My tongue was trying to climb up my nasal passages.

The door banged shut behind me and instantly the world was forty percent quieter. Only the distant sounds of male laughter and cars revving were present. They weren't even bouncing off the brick alleyway because they were too far away.

My phone buzzed and I glanced down.

ATLAS:

Kim and Beasty are making out in the living room.

Nothing else. No emojis to share how he felt about that. But I knew. He was burning up with jealousy and deliriously happy.

Kim was the best of us. The most controlled. The least problematic...For the most part.

He deserved Beasty and if they were together, it meant we'd be able to take care of her indefinitely.

Yet my fucking heart blazed from the brand of pain.

I didn't respond. There was nothing to say.

There in the front seat of my car was a black folder, blending in with the black seats. Anyone walking by wouldn't see it. One, it was dark, and two, my windows were tinted.

Once I was in the car, I turned it on, and started the AC. I could look at the folder now, or wait until I got home.

The hairs on my arms stood up as I debated how fucked up I was. Glancing around, I caught a glimpse of Ratio at the corner of the building. He leaned against the wall, just to the side of the light. Not enough in shadow to purposely be in the shadow, but not in the center of the light either.

I should learn a thing or two from him.

Shaking my head, I said, "Nah."

I tossed the folder in the passenger seat and headed home, forcing my thoughts on Beasty and Kim.

It was no hardship. The image of them together turned me on like nothing else. One of us with her.

Atlas and I almost saw them together before, but they jumped apart.

Lifting my ass in the seat, I shifted, trying to make my jeans more comfortable, but damn. I was thinking myself into a hell of an erection.

Even though I couldn't sit comfortably, I could breathe better.

And damn it if that wasn't a win.

I expected to see Kim and Beasty on the couch as soon as I walked in the door. I wasn't disappointed.

Kim had his hands on Beasty's waist and his tongue down her throat as she lay on him. When the door shut behind me, Kim jumped and tossed Beasty away.

I stifled my laugh.

Flushed faces and outrageous gasps looked good on them.

Kim had never done anything. With anyone. Was as

virgin as the fresh snow, our childhood excluded. I ground my teeth together. Why had that thought popped up?

I knew. It was everything Ratio had dredged up at the club. He hadn't even known it. He was too nice of a guy to mean it.

No, Kim was untouched in all the ways that mattered. I was happy for them that they got to explore this together. And frustrated as hell.

"Oh, um. I should go to bed." Beasty clumsily pushed herself up from the couch and stumbled down the hallway, like her legs didn't work right.

Kim was left on the couch with a dopey grin on his face. "That was..."

"Hot?" I supplied.

"Mind blowing. It's just so...different with her," he whispered, slowly climbing to his feet and stretching his arms over his head. "Everything is." His smile of genuine happiness almost cleared my thoughts of their agitated state.

"I'm glad, Kim."

I passed him to head to my room, folder in hand. I still didn't want to look at it. I'd have Lake take care of it. He was good at these things. The man channeled his pain a different way that worked for him and us.

Kim followed on my heels and when I opened my door, Atlas kneeled on the floor in front of the air return, the cover once again discarded to the side. This time, he was trying to look through it, instead of just listening.

I knew better than to ask what he was doing. If we could hear what happened in Beasty's room, she could hear us.

Dropping the folder on the bed, I joined him on the floor. I didn't need my head in the hole to realize what was happening. My spine stiffened and I almost let Kim push me out of the way as he tried to wedge himself between us.

"Hey..." Lake popped his head in, but I waved a hand and shushed him.

Beasty panted, soft and fast. My eyes rolled back in my head imagining what she was doing.

"Mm..." she moaned, but it was shaky like she was rubbing herself fast and furious. Then she groaned, but it didn't sound like pleasure. It sounded like she was irritated.

Before long, she moaned again. This one quiet.

The four of us gathered as close to this hole as we could. It wasn't easy. Lake had triple the mass that we did, and Atlas wasn't small either.

Beasty was masturbating. Right after a makeout session with Kim.

My body tingled with liquid fire as I dug my fingers into the carpet. Atlas still fought to see into the room, never mind that it was impossible.

We were perverts, but Beasty belonged to us, so that made this okay. She was taking care of herself because of Kim.

A sharp inhale was barely audible.

Snapping my head toward Atlas, we exchanged heated glances overtop of Kim's head. His eyes were full of desire and his pupils contracted with Beasty's next breath. We'd be fucking this out tonight.

Then another louder groan filled the air and Kim whimpered. He dropped his head in his hands, like he didn't know what to do. But the tent in his pants said otherwise.

Her breathless moans grew louder. She was getting close. When I turned to see what Lake was doing behind us, he had sat back, cupping his nape with one hand and biting his knuckle on the other hand so hard it almost looked like blood around his teeth. Yet his eyes were closed as if he was savoring every sweet sound that fell from Beasty's lips.

What was going to happen when Kim and Beasty finally starting messing around? This was going to be torture. I'd be putting in an order for better insulated walls in our next house.

"Kim..." Beasty breathed out in a voice deep with pleasure. *Goddamn.*

There was nothing else after that. Just the soft puffs of her breathing.

I rested my forehead against the wall, my heart pounding out of my chest.

Fuck. That was wild. We all just listened to Beasty come.

I waited for the nastiness and guilt to wash over me, but they didn't.

The only thought crossing my mind was why couldn't that have been us with her?

Chapter Twenty-Two

CRESSIDA - PRESENT DAY

Quilliam was just starting to stir when my phone buzzed.

Damn it. I hadn't been able to spend as much time with Quilliam as I wanted to lately. He still came out of his enclosure almost every night, but I wanted more time with him than that.

> **ADRIAN:**
> Hey hot stuff. How about a night out?
> We can even go to Snatched.

This guy was insane. I didn't for one minute believe he had any interest in me. More like, he liked to get on people's bad sides, and Lake seemed to not care about being on their good side either, so it was this constant back and forth.

> **ME**
> No. Unless you want to tell me what's going on with the Pescis.

ADRIAN:

> Hey, hey, hey. Let's not get crazy and start incriminating ourselves in text messages. Good thing this is a burner and you don't know my real name. But you, my friend, you'll be in prison before the IT guys pluck all the packets out of the air for that internet message.

That didn't make any sense.

ME:

> Not interested.

I should have put my phone down. After Joaquin shattered me this morning, I didn't have any desire to go out just to fuck with them.

There was no energy for it. All my spoons were in the sink, dirty, and caked with nasty-ass shit. I was hollow inside.

ADRIAN:

> We could still talk about that job...

ADRIAN:

> There's a nice payday in it for you...

As much as I abhorred money—How could I not when greedy people were responsible for all the bad things in my childhood?—I needed it. To be safe, to have food, and a roof over my head.

In case the worst happened and I needed to run, I had to have a stash to get me out of here. Even the sturdiest houses would fall when built on sand.

Swallowing hard, I stood up and wandered into the bathroom.

In the mirror, I leaned forward, really studying myself.

The harsh frown, the brows that needed to be plucked. A smattering of freckles dotted my cheeks and nose since no one had ever told me I needed to use sunscreen.

Who was I?

I'd used Books' words as a guiding light because they'd made sense. But I'd seen him.

That *was* him. Just a little older, barely changed at all. There was no chance that it was someone else.

Why was he there?

I started laughing, and my face split into some demented version of myself. Why did I listen to him? He was in this world. He's the very person I shouldn't listen to.

My phone sounded again.

ADRIAN:

> Tell me what you want most and we'll make a fair trade.

I didn't even need to think about it.

ME:

> I want to know who I am. I want the

I started to type Pescis, but shit, he was right. I didn't have a burner. My records would be there for anyone to pull.

ME:

> I want to know who I am. I want to be able to live my life without looking over my shoulder.

ADRIAN:

> Ah, young grasshopper, you want your freedom. We can give that to you. Last chance. You want answers or not?

The boys thought it was dangerous to get mixed up

with these three guys. It probably was. Yet they were the only ones trying to give me answers instead of discounting my feelings and stuffing me in a room.

I was fucking tired of it. Of *their* hurt feelings, *their* assholishness, *their* overbearing treatment.

In a weak moment of frustration, I yelled. "Arghh!"

Slamming my hands on the counter, I leaned toward the mirror.

"No. I'm not going to let them treat me this way."

But do you want them? That was the question.

My snarl morphed into a pained wince. It was like watching a movie. I saw the expression. I understood it, but I was disconnected from the emotion.

We didn't match. The boys and I didn't make sense in any universe. But I couldn't turn off the feelings that bombarded me every time they were around. They were mine in a way nothing else ever had been.

Not for the first time, I just had to figure out how to get them to understand I wouldn't live under their bed, tucked away and controlled. A precious item that no one was allowed to touch.

ADRIAN:

> G said he'll answer your questions and he wouldn't even make you work for it. Not if you do this for us.

ME:

> I'll meet you, but not at Snatched.

I raced around the room, grabbing my shoes, and hunted for my wallet. I hadn't needed it since they brought me here.

My chest squeezed. Already I was changing, even if I'd barely unpacked any of my stuff.

When I opened my door, I almost barreled over Kim. He raised his hands to catch me, but I stopped short.

"Beasty," he said softly, tucking his chin and giving me a bashful look. "I heard what Joaq–"

"Not important," I snapped. Kim flinched.

That was fucked up of me. Of all the boys, I'd wronged him more than he'd wronged me, and I was lashing out at him.

I switched my phone from one hand to the other. "I'm going to meet with Adrian and his friends," I said in a measured tone. "They're going to give me answers."

"Beasty." Kim's voice took on a pleading tone. "Please don't. We can give you answers. There's nothing they know that Lake and Joaquin don't–"

Holding up a hand, I gave him one firm shake of my head. "I'm not talking to Joaquin. He has his own issues to work through. And Lake had his chance. I'm getting answers in the ways that are open to me." Breathing in deep, my chest expanded as I thought out my next words. "You can go with me, but I'm not staying here."

The olive branch.

Kim meant the world to me. If they would just listen when I tried to talk to them, we wouldn't have any of these issues.

He glanced over his shoulder, staring toward the stairs for more than a minute. Then his shoulders slumped and he faced me again. "Okay. But we're not telling the guys we're gone until we're already there. And we take the guard of my choice."

My brows climbed my forehead. They had more than one or two guards?

I knew they had a full staff, I just didn't like to think about it. It made the divide between us too wide.

"I told them we're not meeting at Snatched." That was just asking for trouble.

"That's the best option." He stepped back for me to pass him. "Being around so many beautiful women makes Adrian twitchy. He has a shoe fetish and tries to get them to slip off their heels."

"Really?" That shocked me, but I could also see it.

"Yes." He used exaggerated movements to glance at my feet. "Tennis shoes. Good choice. He won't ask for those, and if we need to run, you'll be good."

I nodded because there was no room for humor. I had answers to get and only so much time before Lake or Atlas barged in. I couldn't be certain that's how they'd respond, but I assumed.

"Tell Adrian we'll meet them at The Hot Spot." Kim nodded as if he was trying to convince himself that this was a good idea.

I exhaled through my nose. He was helping me. Not standing in my way like Lake would have, or Atlas might have.

The warmth of happiness exploded in my chest and for a second, my eyes welled up. I could count on one hand the number of times I'd felt *like this* in my life.

When I read Books' note and got the gift card.

When the boys offered me a home with them after graduation.

When Linda hired me.

And now this.

I laughed, the sound thick from my crazy emotions. I did realize how sad this was that Kim giving in to what I wanted changed my entire mood. But I was only human.

If Kim didn't hate touch so much, I would have thrown my arms around him and kissed him.

Except he did hate it. And even if he didn't hate it

with me, I couldn't shake the feeling that I'd fucked up when I left. That maybe he didn't welcome my touch anymore.

If given a do over to leave or stay, I'd do it again in a heartbeat. I learned so much about myself while I was on my own. But maybe I should have done it differently.

This time? I was doing everything different.

Stepping into his space, I placed a soft kiss on his cheek, then stepped back. "Thank you," I said quietly.

He placed his hand over his cheek and closed his eyes before nodding some more. "Let's go, Beasty, before we get caught. Lake likes to read BDSM erotica to those who go against him."

I wanted to savor the moment, but a snort escaped, and I slapped my hand over my mouth. "You're kidding." He had to be.

He just grinned and started walking.

While I texted Adrian, he sent a message to someone else.

When we stepped out of the house, a black SUV was there waiting. The man in the driver's seat was a different person than the man who had gone with Joaquin and me to the diner. This man seemed kinder somehow, even though he didn't smile at us.

It must be in the eyes.

Kim opened the door and I climbed in the backseat. As soon as he joined me and shut the door, he smacked the back of the passenger headrest in front of him. "Let's go, JJ. Lake's going to have a conniption when he finds out we left."

JJ grunted, but didn't make any remarks.

The drive was farther than I expected. Did Kim pick this place on purpose, so it would take Lake longer to get to us?

I couldn't keep the goofy grin off my face at the thought.

When we pulled up outside a concrete building, I shot a questioning look at Kim. I thought The Hot Spot was Pho or something. Not an electronics store out in the middle of nowhere.

He smiled and got out. "This is a...friend's place."

"I'll be parked to the side. Text me when you're ready to leave, and I'll drive to the door." JJ cut his gaze at us. He must not be a fan of this place, he seemed too jacked as he surveyed the parking lot.

How did Kim meet this friend? It couldn't have been through modeling. There were bars on the doors and windows, and that didn't scream fashion.

The bell on the door chimed, and a gust of cold air hit me in the face.

A man about thirty came out from the backroom. "Welcome to The Hot–"

When he saw Kim, his eyes widened and his mouth made an 'o' shape. Sweat beaded on his forehead and his face drained of blood. He couldn't have been a friend of Kim's.

I sent Kim a sidelong glance, and he just kept that calm smile on his face even as he stretched taller and pulled his shoulders back. There was a different aura surrounding Kim. A confidence that didn't match the smile on his face.

"Dan, nice to see you again." He strolled forward, touching phone cases along the way like he was browsing. He turned his head to the box he was touching and his smile morphed into a small smirk. Then he was moving forward again with so much ease he practically glided across the floor.

Something was off about this. Shifting on my feet, I stayed right where I was by the door.

"Yeah, it's great," Dan answered with a thin voice. I was shocked he wasn't pulling on his collar with how uncomfortable he was.

"Some friends are going to meet us here in a few minutes. We need to use the backroom." Kim pulled a tissue out of the box on the counter, then handed it to Dan before he pointed at his forehead.

Dan just crumpled it in his fist as he stared hard at the glass countertop.

Kim glanced over his shoulder. "Are you coming, Beasty?"

I jolted forward. Once I was on my way, he faced Dan again.

"Yeah, sure. I'll make sure all footage is off and the scrambler is on." Still not looking at either of us, he pointed to the door behind him. "You know which room it is."

"Great. Point them our way when they get here, yeah?" Kim reached out and took my hand as he led me through the back.

What in the world?

Who was this man? This wasn't the sweet and soft Kim I knew. First, he was like this at Snatched during the staff meeting, but I thought that was a fluke or something. Like he was acting that way because Andrea was nasty to me.

But this was too much of a coincidence for his behavior to be a one off. Right?

Kim steered me into a small conference room with one round table and four chairs. Nothing on the walls. No art, or anything in the room. There was one tower in the center of the table with the cord running down through the middle and plugging in at an outlet in the floor.

"What is that?" It definitely wasn't a phone.

"It's a scrambler. We have a couple at home and in our offices at Snatched. They basically prevent good recordings.

If anyone is recording, they'll only hear static." He pulled my seat out and pushed it in when I sat.

He never did that for me before. The action now seemed uncomfortable. When did Kim learn manners and who taught him?

A mound of jealousy sat heavy in my stomach. This was ridiculous. I shouldn't be jealous over something like this.

Except I was.

"We don't have to do this if you don't want to, Beasty. I'll make Lake answer your questions." Kim took the seat next to me and leaned close. Not touching, but still close enough that I could smell the clean scent of cologne on him.

"No, it's okay," I rushed out. This was not the time to get stuck on things that didn't matter. Pursing my lips, I racked my brain for something that would change the topic, but I was saved by a knock on the door.

It opened a couple inches. "Cressida?" Gio.

"It's us," I called out.

"Good." The door swung open and Gio walked in. Adrian and Storm followed. Adrian wore that shit-eating grin that he seemed to have permanently stamped on his face. Storm was less ecstatic to be here as he walked in last.

Where Gio and Adrian were exactly what I'd expect mafia men to look like, Storm seemed like he'd be more at home at a goth rave.

"How did you manage to get away from your keepers?" Gio asked as he took the seat next to me. Adrian claimed the final seat and Storm leaned against the wall, not too upset he missed his chance to be at the table.

"Let's not start antagonizing each other. You wouldn't want us to think you're trying to cause a rift, would you?" Kim's tone matched the same slithery charm he'd had out front, but the smile on his face was as serene as I'd ever seen.

Gio quirked a brow. "It's not antagonizing. It's a legitimate question."

"It doesn't matter. What I want is answers. You want my help. If you explain exactly what you want, then maybe I'd be willing to help you. *If* you tell me what's going on." I rested my elbows on the table, turning my head slightly toward Gio.

Glancing at Kim, Gio stuck his tongue out of the corner of his mouth like he was working out a puzzle. "You don't want to get your answers from the Fashion Boys?"

What?

"The Fashion Boys?" I parroted. Why did that sound familiar?

Gio grinned and Adrian outright laughed. "Our mutual acquaintance and business partner came up with the nickname. It fits, and they're the only ones I work with connected to the fashion industry, so..." His shoulders raised in a slight shrug.

Kim snickered. Clearly, he wasn't offended.

In fact, he sat up a little straighter like the name made him proud.

"I want your side. Why are the Pescis after me?" I dove right into the meat of it.

Gio set a hard glare on me. "Are you sure you're ready for those answers?" Then to Kim, "Are you sure this is a secure room?"

"Absolutely. We have more than enough leverage and goodwill on Dan to ensure this meeting never surfaces. And we buy all our equipment from him." Kim pointed at the scrambler in the center. "They're the best. We've tested them."

My mouth dried up listening to their exchange.

Just when I started to get my head on straight about what I wanted, something was shoved in my face that reminded me that the boys were involved in things I wanted nothing to do with.

Gio turned back to me. "Okay, Cressida, or do you prefer Beasty?"

"Cressida is fine." I didn't really care one way or the other, but for such a serious conversation, Cressida felt right.

"Cressida," he repeated. "What did Stevo tell you about the Pescis?"

I swallowed. Just thinking about him twisted a hot poker in the center of my chest. Over the last several days, I'd tried to forget about his death. I fought with myself to ignore the fact that Lake had killed him.

Because of me. *For me*, so he said.

Doing what I did best, I forced everything about Stevo's death to the back of my mind except for what Gio was asking.

"Nothing. I had no idea he was mixed up with anything bad at all. He was an idiot but that was it." Then because it might make a difference to the conversation I added, "I had already broke it off with him before I left town with Lake."

Kim sucked in a sharp breath and regret sat sourly at the back of my throat. I shouldn't have said that. It was an ugly reminder of something he'd probably like to forget.

Who was I to get jealous over him pulling out a chair? I was so fucked in the head.

Gio rested one arm straight on the table and the other on the back of his chair. "You know he was a lackey for them? You know what they do?"

I hesitated, then nodded. Lake had explained at least that much, sparse as the information was.

"Then you know they believe you have something you shouldn't have." One side of his mouth shot up in a smile, but it wasn't nice. It was bitter and hateful.

"But I don't. He never left anything at my place, or in my car. It was such a shallow, pointless...thing," I spat out the last word, hoping like hell I'd picked a word that wouldn't further hurt Kim.

"Doesn't matter. These guys? They're pretty much wastes of space with too much ego and power to use logic for anything other than to wipe their asses."

I furrowed my brow. That didn't make sense, but I didn't say anything, letting him talk.

"With them, it's not about what you actually have, it's what they think you have. And that's where the danger comes in, because what they think you have isn't something you can just give back." Gio started tapping his fingers on the table.

"What's that?" I twisted deeper toward him, caught up in his words.

"Knowledge." The words dropped like a bomb between us.

"But—that's—stupid!" I sputtered. "We didn't do fucking pillow talk!"

Kim made another noise and I hated myself for my outburst.

Pulling in air through my nose, I squeezed my eyes shut.

"Like I said, they're not the brightest, but they're powerful."

There was a pause and I opened my eyes.

Across from me, Adrian lost his smirk, instead glaring at the table like it offended him. Storm's body now wired tight.

"Shortly before you disappeared with Lake, they figured out Stevo was searching everything he delivered. He was reading documents, documenting shipments. For all intents and purposes, he was collecting leverage." Gio's gaze skirted to Kim.

"I don't have any of that," I whispered. But there was no way for me to prove it, was there?

Was I destined to live my life between the boy's home, massive as it was, and Snatched? That sounded miserable. It *was* miserable.

"Lucky for you, I don't care for them much. I'd like to help you with your problem, but we need your help." The conversation lightened to a perky tone.

"How?" I asked woodenly.

"They won't put themselves within ten miles of us. We're happy to help you take care of your problem, but you'll have to draw them out."

"Absolutely not." Kim peeled his lip back. "Beasty is not bait."

Gio rolled his eyes. "We're what we have to be when we need to be it. She wants freedom, she has to do her part to help us. We've been trying for years to take care of this our way and we can't get close enough."

"Absolutely not," Kim repeated. "Come on, Beasty. You got your answers. It's time for us to go." He stood and held out his hand.

I sat there. Torn.

"You're too important to us to risk your life for Gio and his friends to get revenge. You're too important to *me*. Please, Beasty," he whispered.

His eyes were dark and intense as he stared straight into my soul.

This was Kim. My Kim. The boy who was my first kiss, my first everything really.

My will to stand my ground crumbled right underneath me, and I fell into his trap. Sliding my hand in his, I let him pull me from the chair.

I didn't even say goodbye as Kim led us out the back.

There was nothing out here, just a field. Pitch black with no light even from the front.

"Beasty, I need you." Kim reached for me, cupping the sides of my face and pressing his lips to mine. Kisses were different with him.

Tender, intense, and soul searing. Kim kissed me with lips and tongue as if he was literally touching my soul. Taking pieces and merging them into himself.

Then he dipped his head and trailed wet kisses along my neck as he trapped me against the wall. "I need you. Only you. Only ever you." His voice was as strangled as his touch was gentle.

"Wait," I panted, cupping his shoulders.

He fell back a few steps. The lack of his touch left me cold. "Sorry. I'm sorry, Beasty–"

"No." I spun us around until his back hit the wall. "I want you Kim. Let me do this for you," I whispered as I leaned up and placed a lingering kiss on his lips. He whimpered as my hands trailed down his chest and waist.

His abs contracted and he tipped his head back. His response to my touch was potent and intoxicating. This heady feeling coursed through my blood. I'd never experienced this kind of power, not even during our first time. He placed his hands flat against the wall as he let me explore his body.

I unsnapped the button on his pants, lowered the zipper, and reached inside. Brushing my nose along his neck, I breathed in. He loved a clean scent and it suited him so well. He swallowed when my fingers closed around his cock.

He was hot and hard. So fucking hard.

I pulled my head back slightly to see a look of euphoria and need dance across his face. He wanted me. No matter what bullshit sat between us, my leaving, his choices, our beliefs. None of it changed the fact that we were explosive together.

Nothing ever would.

I started to lower to my knees as I pulled him out, then his phone chimed. Not the regular sound of a text, but an angry, blaring alarm.

"Fuck, fuck, fuck." He pulled me back up to my feet. "That's a code red. We have to go."

Code red?

My body trembled from adrenaline.

Go where?

Chapter Twenty-Three

CRESSIDA - PRESENT DAY

"What's going on?" I asked Kim as JJ sped back to their house.

Kim had been on his phone non-stop and I was afraid to look over his shoulder. Would I see more dead body confessions? Something even more sinister?

That they were capable of any of it made me sick, but I couldn't stop the thoughts from banging against the recesses of my mind.

It wasn't that they couldn't do it or that I thought they were immoral or anything like that.

Just that they could be sucked back into the kind of life we wanted to escape. Thinking they could be so greedy, they could fall to their lowest looking for handouts and taking advantage of good, innocent people scared the shit out of me.

I didn't want that life for them, and I sure as hell didn't want that life for me.

If Joaquin had just let me explain that to him...

My palms were sweaty as I gripped my knees. Kim

hadn't answered me and as a result, I was running through a thousand different scenarios of what a code red could mean.

We pulled up at the house, and Kim bolted from the car, racing inside. He popped back into the doorframe holding out his hand.

"Please, Beasty?" he pleaded. But why? What was he pleading for?

It wasn't even in question if I would take his hand or not. Together, we sped through the house, finding the other three in the living room with the news on.

No.

The volume was down, but the caption was scrolling across the bottom of the screen.

Valencia, renowned fashion designer, arrested for laundering among other charges.

Wait.

This wasn't the video footage Kim had been devastated about. This was something different?

Something that didn't even have anything to do with them?

"What's going on?"

Lake stood with his back to us as he watched the news. He tensed. That was the only sign that he heard me.

Joaquin sneered from his place on the couch as he swayed back and forth. He was plastered. More than plastered. Whoever had been serving him should have cut him off at least three drinks ago.

Atlas was the only one who seemed mildly unbothered. He slipped his phone back in his pocket as he glanced up at me. He was in the chair, like he didn't want to be anywhere close to the distillery that was Joaquin.

"This is only the potential for trouble. I told Lake not to send out a code red to Kim." His lips turned down in a frown. "But I'm not sorry you're back where I can see you."

I..."What do you mean, potential for trouble?"

Kim was pale as he went around me and perched himself on the arm of the couch. He finally looked up at me, acknowledging me for the first time since we left The Hot Spot.

"Valencia was a designer I used to work with." He swallowed hard as he turned back to the TV. "You remember? You were there at one of the shows."

I did remember. I didn't remember her name, but I vaguely recognized the glamorous, yet stern woman who flashed across the screen. And how she ran her hands across Kim. I swallowed.

Was that the event where Lake slammed that man into the wall? I couldn't remember. I'd only gone to a handful of their events over the course of my time with them, and it was all such a blur. I had constantly been overstimulated from so much new stuff.

"What about her?" I took a seat between him and Joaquin.

Making a sound of disgust in the back of his throat, Joaquin got up and walked to the kitchen.

My cheeks burned. Glancing at the others, I waited for their disdain, but it didn't come. For once, their attention was focused somewhere not on me.

Atlas plucked the dangling remote from Lake's hand and turned the volume up.

"Valencia Mositano, arrested after whistle blower reported her illegal activities. This comes on the tail end of her most recent fashion week where she wowed the crowds with her edgy designs."

"Give me that." Lake snatched the remote back, turned the volume off, and sat on the coffee table as he started typing furiously on his phone.

"Why is this an issue for you guys?" There was a giant

puzzle piece missing, yet I had no idea what shape it was since I couldn't see the puzzle picture.

It was infuriating and frankly a little scary.

"Because." Lake pocketed his phone, then swung his legs around so he faced me and Kim. "That man..." Lake pointed at the TV where a man's picture took up the other side of the screen. He was familiar too, but I couldn't place him. "We know him. He's been a source of information for us, which in itself isn't bad. But depending on why he talked—he wouldn't have willingly—we don't know what else he would have shared."

"What Lake isn't saying is, with the current issues going on, this could just pile shit on top of shit," Atlas deadpanned.

It still didn't make sense. Was I just this stupid, or were they speaking a different language. Then it clicked.

"He has information on you." I scratched my neck, suddenly itchy inside my own skin.

"I wouldn't call it information, not specifically," Lake tried to argue like there was a difference. There wasn't, not in things like this. A red rock and a red seashell were different on the surface, but they were both the same color. Red.

Lake's phone rang and he pulled it out of his pocket. His other pocket. Since when did he carry two phones? He picked it up on the second ring.

"What?" he barked.

"My, my. You're so testy." The sound of the man's voice coming over the line gave me chills. I couldn't even explain it. The voice was smooth, charming, yet something told me that he was very, very dangerous.

But was he dangerous to us?

"Now isn't a good time." Lake rubbed his forehead as he

closed his eyes. He seemed like the weight of the world was on his shoulders.

"It's never a good time. Every day you make me question if this was a good investment for me." The man tutted, but I could almost swear I heard the smile in his words.

"Then you're welcome to pull out. We'll pay you back with interest. Honestly, it's no skin off our backs."

The man snorted. "I heard you're on your way to making Gio an enemy. Stupid that, since he's one of the few men I have employed who can watch you without fucking with you."

"He does fuck with us. He's trying to get Beasty to work with him," Lake growled.

Sighing, the man carried on like Lake hadn't spoken. "I heard about your new issue. Do you need help taking care of it?"

"Absolutely not," Lake snapped. For a second, I was transported to the conference room of Kim saying those very same words with just as much feeling.

A hum came from the phone. "I hear Ms. Chen is working hard for you? Glad that referral played out well."

Lake just grunted.

When I glanced over, Atlas was watching me so intently, I wasn't sure he was even paying attention to the phone call.

"Well, there was another reason I was calling. I was going to help you with your fears on the latest scandal to touch your doorstep, but it's not really your scandal, so I'm not sure you're going to go for it."

"What is it?" Suspicion coated Lake's words.

This conversation was painful. Was this how he always talked to this man? It had to be the silent investor. There was no one else Lake would offer to buy out. Not that I knew of.

"There's a small statue that I want. *Need,* really. At a museum in DC. Right in your backyard."

The guys exchanged glances as Joaquin wandered back in. More like stumbled with amber liquid sloshing over each side of his glass.

"You're not even going to ask questions about it?"

"No, Parker, I'm not. You'll tell me without me stroking your ego." Lake sneered at the phone.

"Fine, fine. There just so happens to be a charity event happening there this weekend. And you know what kind of event it is?" He paused for dramatic effect. "Fashion," he said with so much pizazz it sounded weird in his voice. Then Parker chuckled. "Right up your alley."

"So with our arrests, the recent news—which I don't know why you think I'd care about that, and issues with Gio's friends, you want us to help you acquire a piece of art?" Shaking his head, Lake glared at the phone. "What makes you think we'd need to do this for you?"

Atlas sat forward, bracing his elbows on his knees as Joaquin caught himself on the back of Atlas' chair. Next to me, Kim had his arms crossed, curling into himself as he listened, not looking at anyone.

We all held our breath, waiting for Parker to answer. This guy seemed a little crazy. I couldn't pinpoint what it was, but there was just something about his tone that scared me.

"Consider this. You may not care about burning bridges, but it never fails to come back and bite you in the ass at some point. All of your actions have consequences. And it would be far better for you if I—and my brothers—were in your corner." A woman called his name in the background and he laughed. "I have to go. Little Love will have my balls if I don't jump to her every whim."

A distinct click ended the call.

"What does he want you to do?" I felt weird, like my skin was disconnecting from the muscle. I had an idea about what Parker was asking, I wasn't stupid, but I just needed Lake to say it.

The boys exchanged glances, except for Joaquin. He stared at me with so much contempt, a nasty chill started to shake in my chest.

"We're not doing it." Lake placed his phone on the table beside him with enough force that it audibly clattered.

Twisting his lips to the side, Kim leveled Lake with a serious stare. "Parker's a bigger threat than the Pescis," he insisted. "We should at least consider it. It's not like we couldn't do it."

"We have Beasty now. Do you want to place her in danger like that?"

"What's the danger?" Atlas asked. It didn't sound like a sarcastic question.

"Outside of getting caught by the museum guards and getting arrested for theft? Think about the additional exposure to her. Because of the active arrests on Joaquin and me, there's a good chance they'd throw us in jail until the court date, and then she'd be less protected. I only trust the guards so much." Lake gripped the lip of the coffee table next to his legs so hard his knuckles turned white.

"We need answers about why Valencia's assistant ratted her out. As far as I know, he wasn't into hard stuff."

"You're not answering me," I said louder, the tips of my ears starting to burn the longer they ignored me.

"What, Beasty?" Lake snapped as his head swung my way.

I jerked back while Atlas reached forward and shoved Lake's shoulder. Hard.

"Leave her the fuck alone," Atlas returned with a sneer on his lips.

Joaquin released a peel of laughter as he slapped a hand on Atlas' shoulder. "Don't take up for this cunt."

I jumped at the insult and my mind went blank.

"What the fuck is wrong with you?" Kim stood from the couch, placing himself in front of me.

"Me?" Joaquin stood, and so did Atlas and Lake. They all faced off with him, blocking my view, but I didn't want to see him.

"This bitch," he slurred, "she thinks we're scum. Pedophiles. She thinks we're just like Gates." He laughed again, but it broke off into something close to a sob.

I covered my ears with my hands. I didn't think that. I had never thought that. I wanted to stand up, to take up for myself, but as they started to yell at each other, I couldn't.

Someone touched my shoulder, but I twisted, getting out of their reach.

This was unsafe. This was bad. I hated confrontation like this. Without allowing myself to think too much about what they were saying, I ran to my room. To *their* room, in *their* house, that I was just using.

Tears streamed down my face as I shut the door and locked it.

If I wasn't there, I could pretend it wasn't happening. Tomorrow would be a better day. I'd tiptoe down, pretend nothing happened.

Quilliam was out of his little house. He grunted at me as opened the top, and he made little sounds of protest as I picked him up and curled him against my chest. He immediately rolled into a half ball. Not tight like he was afraid, but just enough like he was reading my emotions and didn't know what was happening.

Holding him, I focused on the warmth of his body and weight in my hands. It helped.

Then knocking started at the door.

"Beasty?" Kim.

But I didn't answer him. My voice was literally paralyzed.

After a few minutes, he sighed and there was a thump like he dropped his forehead against the wood. "My door is open if you want to come see me." There was nothing happy in his voice. But he wasn't angry like the others had been.

Fuck, that was rough. Why did that bother me so damn bad?

Sitting here, holding Quilliam, I recognized I should have stood up for myself. Shit, how many times did I get into fights over the years? At least until the guys left, then my perspective started to change.

Why had I changed?

My voice was fucking frozen and I couldn't talk. I could only get the hell away from that room.

The tears didn't stop for hours. Not until I had Quilliam back in his enclosure and the covers pulled over me.

The hallway remained silent and no one else came to the door.

I was glad they left me the fuck alone, but I wasn't. If they wanted me, they would have tried harder to check up on me. Wouldn't they?

Shit, I didn't know and that made it all worse.

Chapter Twenty-Four

BEASTY - AGE 18

I opened my door and paused, listening to see if anyone else was up. I'd had my alarm set for six since I'd been here.

They were doing so much for me and I was basically being a freeloader. I needed to do my part. Pull my weight.

More than that, I enjoyed being in the kitchen when no one was up. It was finally starting to feel normal, instead of like I was a customer in a business when all the employees walked out.

I was lucky I was starting to feel comfortable here at all. At Megan and Ed's, I never settled in. Life was constantly walking on eggshells.

And I'd only been here three months, instead of the years I'd spent there.

When I didn't hear anything other than typical house sounds, I released a breath and padded as softly as I could to the kitchen.

Kim was a big part of why I was doing so well.

He was sweet, kind, and attentive. He looked at me in a way no one had ever looked at me before.

He really saw me.

Catching my reflection in the glass on the microwave, I chuckled under my breath. I had the dopiest smile on my lips. It wasn't like any smile I'd ever had before. The boys probably thought I was weird.

They were all so...

Not exactly like what I had expected. They still didn't talk to me much, but they didn't seem to mind that I was here.

I hated coffee, but I made a cup anyway. They all loved it, except Kim, and I wanted to try it. There had to be something good about it.

Three times. If I couldn't get the taste for it after three times, I'd give up. They didn't know I was testing myself anyway. It wasn't like I'd ever had the chance to drink it before. Starbucks was too expensive, and Megan and Ed only made enough for themselves.

One thing coffee had going for it was the smell. It was rich and heady. That was what was addicting about coffee. If only it would taste as good as it smelled.

"Morning," a gruff voice came from behind me.

I jumped, banging my toes on the cabinet underlip.

"Shit," I gasped, hopping around, holding my foot.

When I turned, Joaquin stood in the doorway, hand frozen on his bare chest like he'd been mid-scratch when he greeted me. I dropped my gaze to the ridges along his stomach, then flicked it back up.

Damn it, I hoped he hadn't noticed that. They didn't really walk around without clothes on, and I'd never been around boys like this. It was hard not to look. Impossible. Yet, I was immediately flooded with guilt as soon as I failed my own test.

His face scrunched up uncomfortably as he dropped his hand. "Sorry."

"It's okay." I straightened, blinking the tears out of my eyes. "I was um...just making coffee for you."

I grabbed the cup that was now brewed and held it out to him.

He eyed me, not taking it. I wouldn't believe me either. Why the hell would I make him coffee this early in the morning when it was barely light outside.

I glanced at the window and saw the pale gray that happened just before the light blue started to brighten the sky. Joaquin was also never up this early. That was Kim and Lake.

"That's okay. You keep it." Then he skirted around me and started making his own cup.

Standing there, still holding the hot coffee, I stared at him as his hand hovered over the cabinet like he was debating something.

It sounded like he said 'fuck it' under his breath as he pulled down a second mug. If he felt my gaze on his back, he didn't say anything. A mutual awkward vibe was in the air but I couldn't look away.

So many years I'd wanted to talk to them, and three months into living with them, and I still wanted to talk to them.

All of them except for Kim. He was the glue holding me to reality. Or maybe my sanity, because it still didn't feel real.

With one cup in each hand, he spun. And there I was, shifting on my feet, holding the still full, aromatic cup of coffee in both hands. It was comical. I held it like I was in the North Pole trying to warm myself up, yet we were just at the end of summer. It was still hot.

"You okay?" Joaquin cleared his throat.

"Yeah," I said.

"Good." Then he skirted around me and left.

I sighed. That was weird, and I was the one who made it that way.

I sat on the stool and watched the sun rise over the building next to theirs. The window over the sink was small, but it was a nice view. Better than anything I'd had before.

Forcing myself to take tiny sips, I was mostly able to not pull faces.

There was sugar and milk, but I didn't want to use it. The coffee pods were expensive and I didn't want to take more of their groceries than I needed to.

I finished off the cup, feeling the mild jolt of caffeine. It would hit harder in about fifteen minutes, and that was what really kept me coming back to try it.

I had just washed the cup in the sink when Kim's reflection appeared over my shoulder.

"Beasty, good morning...Is this okay?" He slowly moved my hair off my shoulder before dropping a kiss on the crook of my neck. My cheesy grin stared back at me from the window.

"It's more than good." I nodded and Kim gave me a goofy grin of his own.

We were riding the high together. He'd never said he hadn't done anything, but I was pretty sure he hadn't. And it seemed rude to ask. I hadn't, and he probably knew that since everyone had treated me like a pariah at school.

"What are you doing today?" I asked as I turned and rested my hip against the counter.

He hummed as he filled the electric tea kettle up and turned it on.

"We have a photoshoot and a couple auditions. Do you want to come?" He raised his brows.

I hesitated. Since that last night when Lake had punched a man, I hadn't gone to any more of their jobs.

And after our shopping experience, I tried to steer Kim toward spending time with me here at their place.

"It will be fun. Fashion shoots are way less intense than a show. And you can stay in the lobby for the auditions. Nothing crazy will happen, I swear." His voice got louder with each word, which was regular volume because he was soft spoken.

So different from Lake's rumbling barks or Atlas' deep baritone. Joaquin talked too fast to compare.

I didn't fit in at those places. And quite honestly, I didn't like them as much as they didn't like me. It was just like growing up in West Virginia, except the mean people had access to money and fame. The attention got to them, the same way that greed got to the people in foster care.

Kim reached a tentative hand out and stopped my hands from twisting around each other.

"Please, Beasty? After all these years, I just really like having you close." His eyes were so open and earnest, I fell right into their depths, willing to give him anything he wanted.

"Why didn't you talk to me before? When we were kids?" I couldn't hold the question in. Not anymore.

Kim was the closest to me in age. I'd see him sometimes in the hallway and after school. Of all the guys, it would have been easiest for him to talk to me.

I had always thought he just didn't like me, but that didn't match with the person standing in front of me now.

He rolled his lips together, dropping his gaze from my eyes to my chin. "I wanted to."

"Then why didn't you?" There was a pleading note in my voice I hadn't heard before. Not even when I went to see Books. "Just help me understand. Was I not worth the trouble? To be seen in public?"

The questions kept rolling from my tongue. Why did I need to know? Why now?

Like the dim morning was just as good as the cover of night, I suddenly needed to know why I hadn't been good enough growing up. None of their excuses made sense when they just couldn't acknowledge that I was a real person.

His eyes seemed to frown, but eyes couldn't do that. Yet I couldn't argue the sadness that was clear to see. "I wanted to, Beasty. But you understand, the way you found us," he sucked in a breath, "we were damaged, you saved us."

That didn't make any sense. "I didn't save you. The police officer did. Anyone would have."

He shrugged and looked anywhere but at me. "I'm not shy, not really, but I just could never talk to you. It wasn't because I didn't want to."

I deflated, not satisfied, and the awkwardness he projected tore at my heart. I wasn't trying to upset him. He didn't deserve that when they'd taken me in and didn't ask me to do anything other than just be here.

"I want to get a job or something. Okay?" I flipped my hand up and cupped his wrist.

"Where did that come from?" Kim tilted his head to the side.

The caffeine must be doing it. Making my thoughts travel down several different competing paths. I just had so many thoughts and my feelings seemed bigger.

I'd never paid attention to my emotions before. I didn't let myself. Otherwise, I never would have made it out of Megan and Ed's.

"I–I don't know," I said softly.

Kim shifted to hold my hands in his, and his gaze was glued to where his thumbs slid across the back of my hands.

"None of that matters. Only right now."

That was true. The past did not define us.

But it didn't take away the ever-present sting of old hurts either.

"Sorry," I breathed.

"Don't be sorry." He leaned forward, waiting.

Kim did that. He moved slowly. Never touching me without making it clear he wanted to, or asking permission. It was sweet and heartbreaking all at the same time.

Tipping my face toward his, he brushed his lips across mine.

Butterflies erupted in my stomach and I tightened my hold on his hands. With a gentle force, he tugged me closer to him.

When he broke away, he looked me in the eyes. "I don't want to go without you."

"Okay." There was nothing else to say. Not since I'd caused a scene.

Except, I should have listened to my gut.

On the way to the photoshoot, Lake took a detour, pulling off on a side street that went between a few industrial buildings. He stopped at the corner, and Kim grabbed a package from the back of the SUV.

It was the size of a notebook and about half an inch thick. Maybe it was a file or something? It was plain cardboard on the outside with no writing or other clues about what it could be. It didn't appear heavy, either.

He handed it up to Lake.

"I'll be right back," Lake said as he exited the car and walked to one of the building entrances. The door opened, and a beefy hand stuck out.

Lake took something from it before slipping the package into the hand.

I cut my gaze to Kim, but he watched Lake with bright interest. This didn't look innocent. As far as I knew, there was nothing they would be exchanging in an industrial part of town.

I'd been homeless. I'd been in foster care. I'd been exposed to some very shady people.

My gut was telling me something was off, but I didn't want to believe it. Not about them.

The boys had everything I wanted for myself. They made it out of our town. They were able to support themselves. They were making their own happiness. And our history meant everything to me as pathetic as it was.

Yet I couldn't shake the feeling they achieved so much by falling into the cycle instead of breaking free.

I was going to be sick.

Chapter Twenty-Five

JOAQUIN - PRESENT DAY

The room swirled as bouncing colors of bright white and gold lights danced around me.

Fuck. I used both hands to rub my eyes. How was I supposed to play cards like this?

I blinked. Then blinked a couple more times in rapid succession. I think that was a five of diamonds and a two of spades. Wait. There were two of the twos. When I reached out to touch the card, there were two of my hand. I wasn't using both hands.

Holding them up, I nodded. Right, I had four hands now, so there was only one two.

"He's done."

I didn't need to turn to know it was Lake, his voice was too familiar. The snake.

He thought he could just barrel over us whenever he wanted and we'd fall in line? Fuck him.

Fuck him right up the ass with a fork. Nah, that bastard would enjoy that too much. He'd ask for more just to feel that bite of pain.

"Of course, sir." The attendant bowed his head. There were two of him too.

"I'm en ownah too.." Okay, I was plastered. It was time for me to quit. Lake didn't give me a chance to speak my realizations out loud as he hauled me up by my arm.

"Stop," he growled in my ear. "You're making a scene and you are an owner. That means people here *know* you and *will* remember you."

The words were familiar, but they didn't penetrate the thick wall of vodka-soaked cotton surrounding my brain. I should write them down, then I could figure them out later.

"Do ya ave a pen?" I turned my face up toward his.

He didn't glance down at me, keeping his gaze straight ahead with a fierce expression on his face. Once we were in the office, I tried to recount our steps here, but there were none. I was pretty sure I floated.

That or Lake carried me bridal style. Either was possible.

He slammed the door shut. I glanced down and found my ass in a chair. Made sense.

The room trembled as Lake stomped like an elephant until he reached the wet bar, then he poured a drink. Interesting that he'd want to drink after yelling at me. But whatever, I wasn't his keeper.

Then a glass appeared in front of my face. "Open," he demanded.

My mouth popped open on command, and he shoved a couple pills in my mouth. "Drink."

The glass was pressed against my lower lip and cool bubbly liquid flowed inside as I tipped my head back.

Once the pills were gone, he set the glass down and pointed to it with three fingers. "Finish that."

"I don't lie sparkling watah," I argued, just to be an ass.

If I had to deal with his asshole ways, he had to deal with mine.

"Drink it." He was so sure I was going to listen..

There was a headache starting to form at the edges of my mind. The medicine would help, but I'd drank enough alcohol in my life to know that hydrating myself was the best chance I had at not feeling like a total bag of shit the next day.

He busied himself at his desk while I sat there nursing my water. An unmentionable amount of time passed, mostly because I had no fucking idea what time Lake brought me in here. The only thing I did know was that with each step down the drunk ladder, my mood became sourer and sourer.

Images of Beasty across from me, telling me we were following the cycle, plastered themselves right in front of my eyes.

Then images of Beasty's face as I tossed cash on the table. Then Beasty two nights ago as she ran upstairs.

Best part? A sprinkling of Gates' ugly face was mixed in with it too. I glared at Lake across the room. How the hell was he blocking it out right now? I didn't need to ask. I knew the answer.

Let something else hurt and the original hurt is forgotten.

Great advice except I couldn't control my brain any more than I could control my way with numbers. It was just there, a part of me all the goddamned time. I looked at objects and saw ratios, I saw numbers and picked out patterns.

When something had the smallest reminder of my childhood, there was Gates' face over me.

I wished like hell that I was more like Lake, fucked up kink and all. It would be a hell of a lot easier to deal with than constantly being tempted to stab forks through my eyes.

My stomach rolled with each aching second. Standing, I had to use two fingers on my desk to make sure I didn't topple over. Once I was good, I refilled my glass at the wet bar.

"Are you back?" Lake was pissed. He didn't even deign a look my way. He watched his computer, giving me the back of his head.

"I never fucking left. That's the problem," I grumbled and stumbled my way back over to my desk.

Now that the glow of a drunken stupor was fading, I was hollow inside with my feelings on the floor. This fucking sucked. But the short escape of a few minutes or a few hours was worth it.

Who knew? Maybe I'd hit the bottle as soon as Lake said whatever fucked up piece he had to say.

"Beasty has barely come out of her room." This time he spoke so conversationally, like he was telling me about his favorite cane.

As much as I wanted to block it out, his words were a punch in the gut. "You think it's my fault."

"I know it's your fault. You were the one who left her in that fucking diner." He spun in his chair and stabbed his finger on his desk. Heat had already climbed up his neck and jaw, making his hair appear even brighter. "And you were the one who spewed bullshit at her the other night. Now you want to hide out in the Gold Room, drinking, and gambling away your fucked upness?"

"You didn't hear what she said to me!" I screamed, flinging the glass across the room. It shattered against the wall and the fizz added to the ear-splitting sound.

"Because you took her where there were no cameras!"

He stood, bracing his fists on the desk and bunching his shoulders up like some kind of gorilla.

Since when did he turn in to fucking Atlas? "Are you obsessed now too? Fucking loser. She was feeling suffocated. I thought she'd want a few minutes away from you asswipes." I panted, my chest rising and falling rapidly. His nostrils flared and I stormed over to him. "She doesn't want to be with us, Lake! She thinks we're scum! Worse than scum! She thinks we're just like Gates because of what we do! I can't fucking–" I clenched my hair in my fists and screamed my frustrations to the ceiling. "I can't fucking live like that. With someone who thinks of me like that, not after he...Not after..." Shit, I couldn't even get the words out.

Lake shook his head one time. "You're wrong. I don't know what she said or how she said it–because she won't talk to us–" He narrowed his eyes. "But Beasty would never fucking say that shit. You have to have misunderstood. Or she misspoke."

"You're fucking wrong." I paced away a few steps. I didn't have anything else to say to this motherfucker. I wanted to go back to the Gold Room. Drown my sorrows in a fucking bottle while I fleeced the house and other assholes out of insane sums of money.

Good times.

The keypad beeped, then the door swung open. Guy stood there with a grim frown slashed across his face.

"Boss, there's been a news break that you need to know about, but I don't think you should see."

Lake straightened up and steadied himself while smoothing his hand down his dress shirt. "What is it?"

Guy darted a quick glance at me before placing all his attention on Lake. "Maybe you should come to my office."

"Whatever it is, just spit it out. If it's on the news, I'm

going to know about it sooner or later." I waved a hand, still agitated.

He waited for Lake's nod before he continued. "There's been a video submitted to the national news outlet. It's unclear where it originated from, but they showed a fragment on the evening news just now."

I froze, then tilted my head.

What video?

"Fuck!" Lake cursed, then he exploded into action, pulling up the news on his computer.

There were so many options of what a leaked video could be, and none of them good. Not for us or our image. Or our pockets. Hell, maybe it *would* be good for our pockets. I was half-tempted to talk to Lake about the release of our arrests.

People would flock to Snatched.

Lake pulled up a search, then read the screen, his eyes and lips furiously moving. Spinning, he punched the back wall as he bellowed. There wasn't a beam there, so he made a nice fist-size hole in the plaster.

Guy stepped inside and shut the door, leaning his back against it as he watched Lake.

Whatever the video was, I didn't want to see it. Not if it pulled that kind of reaction from him. More sober than I wanted to be, I shuffled forward, my feet with a mind of their own.

I kept my head turned to the side, but my eyes were glued to the monitor. Each step brought me closer. And closer.

A grainy color video played, and my stomach rolled. Oh, shit. I recognized that wood paneling. That pillow on the floor.

And more than that, I recognized Atlas.

Then the clip ended, and I squeezed my eyes shut, baring my teeth.

No, no, no, no.

I couldn't stop repeating that word in my head, like a broken loop I couldn't break out of.

Were there more videos? Of me? Of fucking Kim? Of Lake?

How did anyone get those? And why release them now after all these years? Fucking, no, no, no.

More streams of that word. That fucking, fucking word.

Lake started raking his nails down his arms, then slammed his fist on his thigh. He screamed and raged, but somehow the sounds just got quieter and quieter.

Turning, I stared at the screens on the wall. The volume was off, and my vision was blurry. I could just make out the Gold Room. The main club floor. The entrance.

I needed to get out of here. The air was stale and a musty scent started to twine around me.

I just needed to leave. Once I had fresh air and a new bottle in my hand, I'd feel better.

In the next blink, I was in front of Guy. "Move," I demanded.

He started to shift, but it wasn't fast enough. I slapped my hand on the wall by his head, the sting waking me up. "Fucking move!"

"Let him go," Lake said from behind me, a lot of his rage gone.

Guy almost dove out of the way, and I scanned my card to get out, then scanned it at the next door. I didn't remember getting my card out, but I clenched it in my fist until the edges cut into my palm.

The wall art blurred as I headed toward the Gold

Room, but my steps slowed as I reached the attendant. She started to swing the door open, but I raised a hand.

I couldn't go in there. If that video was on the news, it would already be circling the masses. Those assholes would stare at me, and try to steal my money because they'd think I was fucked in the head.

I was fucked in the head, but the idea of letting them look at me turned my stomach even more.

"Mr. Amaya?" She asked as she held the door open.

Two men passed by and turned to stare at me.

I took a step back, then another, before turning and sprinting down the hall. I couldn't be here. I wanted to be home with Atlas.

We needed to check on Kim too.

At the back entrance, one of our guys waited with an SUV. He opened the door, not saying a fucking word. Good. That was good. I couldn't talk to anyone right now.

I climbed in the back and rested my head against the headrest. I must have dozed. In what seemed like three minutes, the door opened next to me.

Jerking up, all I saw was Atlas' young face before I wildly glanced around. Shit, I was back home. That was all.

"Thanks," I muttered as I rolled out of the vehicle. The house seemed dark, and when I opened the front door, it was deathly quiet.

I walked through the house, not really sure where I was heading.

In the living room, Beasty sat in the corner of the couch. No lights or anything, like she'd been waiting for someone. How long had she been there?

I tried to muster up the anger and betrayal I'd had for her a few hours ago, but it was gone, replaced with vile memories of my time before I knew her.

"Where's Kim and Atlas?" I asked, rubbing at my chest, desperately trying to quell the pain of the past.

"Kim went to bed early and I don't know where Atlas is." She stood, her brows dropping low over her eyes as she took a step toward me. She was livid.

Then I understood.

They didn't know. None of them knew about the video. I only knew because I was in the office with Lake.

I breathed a sigh of relief. It shouldn't have made a difference. Except there seemed to be space around me now. A nice little bubble before everything burst.

I'd never handled this kind of shit well, and this was a small blessing.

"We need to talk," Beasty said, fury whipping through her voice. Even her chin was set in defiance.

Nodding, I removed my suit jacket then unbuttoned the top of my dress shirt. She wanted to fight, this was better than talking about the video. Then holding Kim together as he fell apart.

The one saving grace was that it was Atlas on the clip. He didn't give a fuck about that kind of stuff. He showed his issues in other less damaging ways. Like attaching to Beasty.

"Talk." I stepped forward.

"I'm not your enemy." She tipped up her chin and took one more step forward. The pale blue moonlight fell in strips across her face, giving her a deadly, ethereal glow.

Beasty was strong. And fierce.

Sometimes, I think the only person who didn't see it was her.

I snapped a hand out and fisted the hair at the back of her head, tugging back just enough to tip her face up. Her eyes flashed, and she dug her fingers into my ribs, trying to push me away.

But I held her still.

"Shh." I shook her hard. Beasty stopped, but she still glared at me. The heat of her gaze spread warmth through my body that was ice just seconds ago. I closed my eyes and reveled in it.

This was what I wanted to get lost in.

Beasty. Even if she was a fucking cunt.

Tonight, she could be mine.

"You're the best kind of enemy. We love you so fucking much," I crooned. She sucked in a breath but I kept going. "But you don't love us at all. You love your ideas and logic. That's what this is, right? You think we're bad men, because we were exposed to a bad man in our childhood?" I chuckled. "There's a sad sort of poetry in that warped symmetry, don't you think?"

She started struggling again. "What the hell is wrong with you? You don't love me. You don't even know me! Just like I don't know you!"

I grunted as her thumb dug deeper into my sides and I used my hold on her to trap her against my chest. "Pain is Lake's thing, not mine," I murmured against her temple.

Yanking her head to the side, I bit the slender column of her neck. "But that doesn't mean I don't want to hurt you."

"You're a fucking asshole!" she screamed in my ear.

I winced and loosened my hold enough that she threw herself out of my hold. Out of nowhere, she slapped her hands on my chest with enough force that I tripped over my foot and fell back on the chair.

I grunted, but she was already working my pants undone. Holding my hands up, I swallowed, clamping my lips shut. I didn't want her to stop.

"You four think you can upend my life, and mess everything up for me, and treat me like this?" The righteous indignation coming off of Beasty was an aphrodisiac I never knew I needed. "I've done a lot of thinking the last couple days. I see where I went wrong." Her voice lowered like she was talking to herself. "You don't respond to conversation. You respond to sex and hurt feelings."

She got my cock out, hard as fucking steel in her cool hand. I bit my lip to hide a moan as she stroked me from root to tip.

Fuck, I had no idea what to do with my hands and they hovered in the air. As she started to lower her head I threaded my fingers through my own hair. Better to not force her away when she offered exactly what I needed.

"You're not my goddamned enemy. If you were, I wouldn't do this." Sucking the tip into her mouth, she worked the base with both hands. My vision went white and I arched my back.

Then she popped up. "You're not a bad man. You're a troubled one."

Her words doused the edges of my arousal, but as soon as she lowered her head and swirled her tongue around the tip, I pushed her words away. She hummed, and sucked, and licked, until she was the only thing on mind. Nothing else.

Beasty worked me over like someone who enjoyed giving blowjobs. I pressed my toes into the floor, then heels, repeating the cycle over as she built a blistering pleasure inside me.

She looked so good with my dick in her mouth.

Then she pulled away again, and her hands stopped working.

I groaned.

"It's not fun to be edged, is it?" She smirked, then licked from the base to tip.

Taking a chance, I reached out a hand and caressed her cheek. "I love it. If you didn't, then Atlas didn't do it right."

"That's uncalled for, I've edged you plenty." Atlas strolled in, bare chested and only wearing pajama pants. He was fucking delicious.

Until the video clip flashed through my head. *No, no, no.*

I squeezed my eyes shut. That memory wasn't allowed here, not now.

Beasty froze.

"What's wrong?" I asked her. The euphoria of her hands on me with Atlas here was exactly what I needed.

Everything was different this time than when she walked in on us before.

She shook her head, her gaze locked on my twitching dick. Atlas got to his knees next to her, and goosebumps trailed down my arms. This was every wet dream I've had.

"We're going to torture the shit out of Joaquin. He deserves it for being a prick to you, doesn't he?" Atlas cooed, using two fingers to shift her hair off the shoulder closest to him. Then he cupped her neck and turned her to face him.

"Yes," she whispered, her gaze roaming all over his face. "I want him to understand that he hurt me."

Atlas nodded. "This is the best kind of hurt you can give him. The good kind." He kissed Beasty, tangling his tongue with hers, tilting his head to take the kiss deeper.

It was the most erotic thing I'd ever seen and it was just a kiss.

He pulled away, just enough to press one lingering kiss on her lips, then pressed his forehead to hers. "You're so delicious, Beasty. I've never tasted anything as good as you."

I tried to move Beasty's hand off my cock so I could stroke it myself, but Atlas slapped it away. "This is your punishment. Not your reward."

Raising my hands, I relented. This was their show, and I needed someone else to be driving right now.

Atlas guided Beasty's head down, and then they were kissing over the tip.

"Oh, fuck. That's so hot." I couldn't resist. Reaching out, I cupped the sides of each of their heads.

This was perfection. Nothing in life could compare to this. Not the best drink, the best game. It all came back to Beasty and Atlas.

Together they jacked me off and sucked my cock, their combined wet mouths getting me hotter together than each of them alone.

"God," I wheezed, mesmerized by the way Atlas controlled Beasty. He twisted his hand and Beasty mimicked him.

"That's it, just like that," he murmured between kisses. "You're doing such a good job. You're driving him crazy." Then he licked from my tip to her mouth.

She didn't need any more urging as she shifted her head to meet his kiss.

That asshole was showing her exactly how I loved to be pleasured and she was soaking up every lesson. Beasty moaned as Atlas continued to divide his attention between me and her. He shouldn't have been able to do it. But his skill at working us both up was unparalleled.

"Such a good girl. You're a natural. Look how crazy Joaquin is for you." He continued to talk her through it with a low, rich cadence to his words. Beasty glanced up at me, and satisfaction flared in her eyes.

I'd had many blowjobs from Atlas to compare to. But both of them together was mind-blowing.

That tingle started at the base of my spine and I jerked with a grunt.

Atlas, that fucker, pulled Beasty off until neither of

them touched me and my cock bounced against my stomach.

He laughed under his breath as he turned Beasty to face him, and started making love to her mouth. Holding her head still, he kissed her how they were meant to. This should have been their first intimacy, not the Black Room.

His hands cupped her face and she gripped his sides, their fronts plastered together.

Beautiful.

Stroking myself, I was almost there when Atlas broke the kiss and stopped my hand.

"We're going to have to do this over and over again, Beasty," he panted. "Until he learns his lesson." The mischievous glint in his eyes sparked. I loved and hated this side of him.

Beasty's eyes were glassy when she glanced at me again. Then disentangling herself from Atlas, she flattened her palms on my thighs to steady herself.

Atlas was right, this was the hurt I wanted. The torture that lasted hours, and drove me out of my mind until nothing existed, except for them.

"No." Her mouth pursed.

It took a minute for my brain to register. By then, she had already stood up. Ice trickled down my back from the vicious determination on her face.

"I'm returning the favor. He'll get nothing else from me until he comes to his senses and stops being a shithead." She stalked out of the room with stiff steps, like it was just as hard for her to leave us as it was for us to leave her alone as kids.

My cock softened the longer I stared at the doorway.

I'd finally broke through with Beasty, just a little bit, and she fucked me over.

Only this time, I didn't blame her.

"Y ou deserved that." The nice thing to do would be to stay here and finish Joaquin off, but he had been an ass to Beasty.

Getting to my feet, I pulled out my phone as I walked toward the stairs.

Beasty was in her room, pulling the covers down to climb in. I could watch her for the rest of my life and never get bored. Would she care if I snuck in her room and slipped under the covers with her?

Would she notice if I waited until she was asleep?

Of course she'd notice. There was no way she wouldn't notice. Everything I'd ever observed about her said she had a light reflex. She was a light sleeper.

Sighing, I returned to our room.

A message popped up on top of the screen.

LAKE:

Is Joaquin there with you?

ME:

> Yes. He's on the couch with a bad case of blue balls. Do you want a pic from our security cameras?

LAKE:

> I'll be home in five minutes. Get Kim and meet me in the study with Joaquin.
> CODE RED

What the hell was wrong now? I told him we didn't need to worry about Valencia's assistant. If we could figure out what to do with Beasty, I'd say we'd take the job for Parker and let him handle the problem for us.

But there was nowhere I'd trust her to be safe. Not if I couldn't be with her.

Leaving my room, I knocked on Kim's door before I opened it. He was asleep in his bed, flat on his stomach.

"Kim," I whispered, bouncing the edge of the mattress. I'd shared a room with him before, and he always needed a soft wake up. Back when we were kids, I was happy to do that for him. He was like the little brother I'd never had.

As adults, I always slept with Joaquin. Lake usually grabbed Kim if we needed him.

He sucked in a breath and his eyes popped open. Then he started breathing normally when he saw it was me. "Hm?"

"Lake needs us in the study." No need to tell him it was a code red. I'd let him have a few minutes before Lake's stress weighed us down.

"Fine," he grumbled. "But if the lizards bite his ass, it's not my fault."

I smiled. It had been a hell of a long time since I'd heard those kinds of things from Kim. So fantastical. He was usually more realistic now.

It took him a second to stretch. "I'll see you in the study."

Joaquin was still on the couch, but he'd at least tucked himself away. He stared at the wall like he was in a trance. Walking around behind the couch, I squeezed his shoulders. "Lake wants to see us in the office. He said it's another code red."

At first, Joaquin didn't give me any sign that he'd heard me. Then he tipped his head back, glancing up at me with beautiful brown eyes full of pain that hadn't been there earlier.

"You know," I accused. "What's the code red?"

He shook his head. "Atlas..."

"It's a real code red?" I pushed my tongue into my cheek as I studied him. All it would take was one twitch and I'd know if he was lying. There it was. His cheek under his eye pulsed.

This was real. Whatever it was, he didn't want to tell me.

"I–" he started to say with a wince on his face, but Kim entered. Joaquin got to his feet and backed up. His eyes widened as he glanced between me and Kim.

"What the hell is it?" I gritted my teeth. I hated fucking secrets. "Spit it out."

"There's footage. From when we were at Gates' house in West Virginia." He shook his head so violently, his hair whipped around his head. Then he fled to the kitchen.

He was getting a drink. I wouldn't see Joaquin this sober for days now.

I turned to Kim.

All the blood had drained from his face, making his black hair appear almost blue. He started to go down but I jumped forward and caught him. "It's okay, Kim. He's not here. He can't hurt us anymore."

"I don't want...I don't want anyone to see us like that. Beasty was bad enough at the fence." His voice was reed thin as his fingers fluttered over my shoulder.

The room was so goddamn hot and still smelled like Beasty. I needed to get Kim to lay down, but not here where just minutes ago we'd sucked Joaquin off. These memories couldn't be mixed up together.

It would fuck with my head.

Swinging Kim up into my arms, I walked us to the study, nudged the door open just enough to get through and laid Kim out on the couch. "If Beasty sees, she's going to see just how dirty we were. We were disgusting."

I should have argued with him. I should have, but I couldn't.

We weren't worthy of Beasty. I'd said that from day one. But Beasty wasn't this perfect hero standing on stage anymore. She was level with us. Fucked up, like us.

It was more perfect this way.

Beasty wouldn't care about any videos. If Kim asked her not to watch them, she wouldn't.

If I asked, she would just to spite me, but she'd listen to Kim.

The stomping alerted us to Lake's approach before his appearance did. No one stomped like that raging bull.

He cut his gaze to me, then Kim before making a beeline right to the desk. This room was dark and full of books and leather. Everything a gentleman's library should be. But Lake was the only one who used it.

Lake sat his ass on the edge of the desk and rubbed one eye as he crossed his other arm over his chest. He looked beaten.

"Did Joaquin fill you in?" he asked.

"I didn't fill them in on shit. I was doing my fucking best to manifest it into another reality." Joaquin appeared in the doorway, a glass filled to the brim with vodka in one hand and the bottle in the other.

"That's going to give you alcohol poisoning if you drink all that." Lake raised his brows in warning at Joaquin, but he was so far past giving a fuck, I couldn't think of a single thing that worked on snapping him out of his head when he was like this.

Joaquin shrugged. "Like that matters to me." He took another gulp while holding eye contact with Lake.

"What was released?" I crossed my arms. I didn't care if people saw it. The attention would only make Snatched more popular. That was a lesson I'd learned early on.

Scandals were a cash cow. A scandal where you were the victim? That was like a golden ticket to fame and fortune.

What I did give a fuck about, was Kim curling in on himself and Joaquin drinking himself to death. He tried to raise the glass again, but I closed the gap between us, and yanked it out of his hand.

The sting of Vodka hit my nose as it splashed over my shirt. "If you take another drink, I'll beat your ass."

He sneered, his eyes already glassy. "Like you'd risk your money maker."

"It's not my money maker anymore, you dumbass. And I would risk everything to keep you from killing yourself."

His mouth clamped shut.

"What was on the footage?" Kim asked.

I glanced over at Kim and red colored my vision. His shoulders were hunched and he'd brought his knees up to his face, hugging them. He wouldn't even look at us. He rested his forehead on his knees.

When Lake didn't answer, I turned to him.

He was staring at me, an apology written on his face.

"Don't fucking say it." I curled my lip.

"It was a short clip. Nothing inappropriate on the video that's circling the news. But you're on it."

My heart started beating in my throat.

"I don't give a fuck about this small clip," Lake continued. "I'm more concerned about what else is on that video, and if it will be leaked. I've already made calls about squashing it if it appears online. I've pulled in favors and made promises. So far, the only thing out there is the clip that the news is showing."

"National?" Kim asked.

"National," Lake confirmed.

Fuck. I didn't care about this shit. But me? I was on it?

Shaking my head, I set the glass next to Lake on the desk, he wouldn't let Joaquin touch it, and I fell into one of the leather chairs.

The sound of a cap twisting came from the corner. Joaquin had the bottle.

I jumped up and grabbed that from his ass too. After tightening the lid, I tossed it to Lake, and took my seat. I was woozy and the room started to spin. If I hadn't sat down, I'd have ended up kissing the floor.

We sat in silence, none of us able to look at each other.

Like all the years and distance disappeared, I smelled that nasty couch he had in the living room. The hot summer air that pressed in on us because we didn't have air conditioning.

We didn't have any hope and hardly any happiness there. There was nothing to cling to except each other.

"What's going on?" Beasty asked from the doorway.

Fuck, she couldn't be here. I was with Kim on that.

"Get the fuck out of here," Joaquin slurred, waving a hand her way.

"Joaquin!" Lake barked. None of us, except Joaquin, missed the hurt crossing her face before she set her jaw.

"You're an asshole, but something is clearly upsetting you. What happened?" she demanded, stepping inside the room.

Kim slightly turned his head and watched her, the pieces of his broken heart in his eyes. Lake's expression was drawn as he frowned.

Joaquin started to bluster. "No. You wanted to punish me? Then this is my punishment. You don't get to have any hand in it. You don't get to *see* it."

"See what?" Her brow furrowed and she positioned herself between Joaquin and Lake, right in the center of the room.

Fuck it. She could watch it if she wanted to. She could know all my secrets if she never left my sight again. Just drinking her in soothed something in my soul. The new jagged pieces from the news weren't so painful when she was here.

I didn't even need to talk to her. Just watch her.

That was all I needed to know everything was going to be okay.

"A video was released to the news," Lake said.

Her mouth popped open as she darted a glance at Lake then Kim.

"It's real," Kim turned his face further so his cheek now rested on his knee.

She nodded and gulped, moving her gaze to stare at the corner of the desk. I narrowed my eyes on her. She didn't look as in the dark as she should be. Beasty seemed to know exactly what was happening.

"You don't know who it was?" Rubbing her hand over her chest, she swallowed again.

Was her mouth watering like mine? There was a good chance I was going to be sick.

"No," Lake sighed.

Glancing at Kim again, she pursed her lips. "Do you want me to hold you?"

"You're not asking to see it?" There was a note of hope in his voice, and it distanced me from the past just enough. We didn't have hope there, but we did now.

"Not if you don't want me too."

"Then you can let me hold you." Slowly, Kim rearranged himself until his feet were on the floor. He held his arms open and Beasty sat lightly in his lap. He didn't waste any time before wrapping her up in his arms, and burying his face in her hair. His shoulders started shaking as he held onto her like a lifeline.

Joaquin stared at them, fury and pain stamped in the brackets of his mouth and the faint lines around his eyes. He was too young to look so old right then.

"Do you want to watch it?" Lake asked me.

I shook my head. "No. There's nothing on it I need to see."

Joaquin relaxed like that was an answer he hadn't known he'd needed.

"I'd rather shave my head than relive anything in that house," Kim mumbled into Beasty's hair.

"Then we're set? We're not watching it?" Lake asked, standing up.

"I already saw it when you watched it. I wish I hadn't." Joaquin leaned his head back to look at the ceiling.

"Then tha–"

Lake's phone chimed.

He glanced down, then his entire body went rigid.

"What is it?" Beasty asked, innocent to pretty much everything in our lives.

"Someone saw Donnie Pesci chatting up a reporter today." Lake shot Joaquin a look.

"There's no way he had access to something like that," I argued. No fucking way, actually.

"Who knows what they have access to." Lake started pacing back and forth around the room.

Why the fuck was this happening just when Beasty came back to us.

Fucking Stevo. He haunted us from his grave.

Chapter Twenty-Seven

KIM - AGE 20

"Are you seriously asking this?" Joaquin whispered over the table.

I sniffed. "Beasty's been with us six months today. We should celebrate."

"No." He shut the conversation down so hard, his teeth probably rattled. Atlas next to him raised one brow as he glanced between us.

"What did you want to do?"

I bounced in my seat. "I thought we could all go out to a nice dinner."

Atlas shook his head. "No, people recognize us too easily now. You remember the mall."

Licking my lips, I ignored the churning in my gut. I'd had nightmares about that. Strangers trying to touch me. I wasn't sure how I managed it on the job, except I was prepared for it. I expected it. I was compensated for it.

In public, people just wanted to take because they thought they could. It made me break out into a nervous sweat just thinking about it.

"What can we do then?" I dropped back and thumped

against the chair. "We can order baked spaghetti. Of all the things Beasty eats, that's what she eats the most of."

"Why not get something nice? Like something from Atelier?" With his arm around Joaquin's chair, Atlas played with the ends of his hair.

I loved that they were starting to get more comfortable with Beasty here. When she first came, you wouldn't know they were friends much less lovers. Like they were afraid of what Beasty would think.

"No, that won't work. You remember that one event we did and they served fancy stuff? Beasty ended up spitting it out in the corner when she thought no one was looking. She hates fine dining." I tapped my chin.

"Maybe we can do a movie night." Atlas raised his brows at Joaquin.

"We're not doing a movie night." Joaquin scrunched his face. "We're not friends like that. We promised to take care of her. Not to be her besties. That's what you're for." He smirked to soften his words and it worked. But I knew him better than he thought and I knew how hard this was for them.

Beasty and I were going at a glacial pace. Kisses mostly and some heavy petting. It wasn't that I didn't want to go further, and I think she did. I just enjoyed the ride.

It was nice. More than nice. Perfect.

"You really won't do something nice with me?" I sighed. These guys could be asses. I'd already tried to get Lake on board and he wouldn't budge either, stating he didn't think she liked them like that.

Like what? People?

Joaquin pinched his lips together and looked at Atlas. Atlas met his stare with a calculating one of his own.

"Fine, we'll order in her favorite meal. Once we eat, we'll

leave you two alone. Don't force what isn't there," Atlas warned.

I grinned. "I don't know what you're talking about."

Of course, I knew what they were talking about. They treated Beasty like she was poison, but really pretty poison. They liked to watch the way she shimmered in the sun, or lounged around our apartment in this case, but they were frightened of getting anywhere near her.

Wait. That was a terrible analogy. They were the poison and they didn't want her near them. But we weren't like that. Beasty wasn't like that. The guys just needed to come to terms with it.

The front door shut then Lake came around the corner into the kitchen. His hair was soaked from his run. He took one look at us and frowned. "What's going on?"

"We're doing a nice dinner for Beasty. Today's the six-month anniversary since she's been with us." I preened, even as his expression grew darker.

"Is that so?" he asked Joaquin and Atlas.

"Apparently." Joaquin glanced up at him.

"Shit." Lake scrubbed his brow as he retreated from the kitchen.

This wasn't awkward at all.

We sat around the table picking at our food. I'd carried the conversation a little bit, but Beasty seemed uncomfortable, and the guys had no idea how to talk with her if it didn't include, *don't worry about him*, he's *an asshole*; or *we'll be leaving in a minute*; or even *Kim really wanted you to stay in this spot so people leave you alone*.

"Atlas, tell Beasty about that time you fell into the

Komodo dragon enclosure." I pointed my fork at him across from me.

He gave me a half-lidded look that wasn't impressed.

"Really?" Beasty asked, cutting into her spaghetti.

"Yes, he's always had a thing for lizards." I snapped my lips shut. It was just second nature. But I took a breath. I didn't want to do this with Beasty. I wanted her to see the real us.

"That's cool." She peaked at Atlas from under her lashes. If the lighting was better, I'd say she was blushing. I wasn't sure if I liked that or not. "What's your favorite?"

Atlas cleared his throat. "The gecko."

"The gecko? I thought you liked the iguana because they have a cool spine going down its back?" Joaquin shoved a bite in his mouth and grinned at Atlas.

"No, you're wrong. He never liked the iguana. It was always the gecko. He had a thing for the one on TV that wore khakis." Lake caught my eye and winked.

They were playing along for me. It worked because Beasty lost some of her unease. As much as they were scared of her, she was rigid when they were around too. Like she was afraid of doing or saying the wrong thing.

"You know, at this one foster home I lived at, there was this blue fat lizard that hung out on the steps. I used to talk to him sometimes." She smiled wistfully, not noticing the dour looks we tossed around the table.

I didn't know about the guys, but I'd like to forget Beasty was ever in a different home than ours.

There was a knock on the door. Rapid. Like someone was in a hurry.

Lake excused himself and like magnets drawn to his back, we all watched him leave. Joaquin and Beasty were both chewing their current bites.

"Hey." It was one of Lake's sources.

"I told you not to come here," Lake returned, keeping his voice low. Only the apartment was so small, we could all hear what he was saying, even if we couldn't see him.

"This is about that package that Joaquin sourced. It's going to take some greasing, or some sneaking, but we can ge–"

"I think I heard my name." Joaquin stood and tossed his napkin on the table.

Their conversation stalled, and then Joaquin said, "Let's take this conversation to the hall."

Beasty was so focused on the bits of conversation as the door closed, it seemed she was trying to see through the wall. A frown tugged her lips down on both sides and her eyebrows went up in the middle. Not in a sad way, but one that spoke of concentration.

It was a cute look.

Yet, I still had an uneasy feeling in the pit of my stomach. Atlas didn't seem to notice because he kept eating and sneaking his own glances at Beasty. But to him, he just seemed happy to watch her, not really caring what look was on her face, or what it meant.

"Beasty, can you believe you've been here for six months?" I asked, smiling.

She tried to return the smile, but it was brittle and forced. "It's crazy." The door closed again, and she shot a look to the entrance of the dining room.

Lake and Joaquin walked back in like nothing had happened. They took their seats, and picked up their forks.

"Are you doing something illegal?" Beasty flat out asked.

"Absolutely not." Lake set his fork back down and faced her.

Atlas and Joaquin were slower to lower theirs, but I just held mine suspended in air. Would we really be able to keep

Beasty forever if we didn't let her into at least some of our lives?

She squinted one eye. Beasty didn't believe a word that came out of his mouth. I didn't blame her, Lake was a terrible liar.

"Beasty, why would you think–" I started.

"I saw the money exchange at the mall. I've seen other things too. I–" Sucking in a deep breath, she let it out slowly. "Please tell me you're not doing anything dangerous." She leaned to the side, toward Lake, like she was trying to get across just how serious she was.

"We're not doing anything we shouldn't be doing. That's the truth," Lake said softly.

Studying him with hard eyes, she nodded. "Good. Because I couldn't stay here if you were." Her voice shook as she held his gaze, then met Atlas' stare, then Joaquin's and finally mine. "I can't live like I grew up."

We couldn't tell her. She'd leave and just the thought of her not being here when I woke up in the morning tore me to shreds.

I wanted her here when I went to bed. When I was done with a job.

I needed her.

My hand started trembling so hard, I laid my fork gently across the plate. I'd only eaten half, but I couldn't eat anymore.

Joaquin caught my eye and then nudged Atlas. "You once asked about college. Is that something you still want to do?"

If Beasty was caught off guard, she didn't show it. Nodding, she shifted in her seat. "Actually, I think I'd rather just get a job. I've been here for a long time now and I feel like I'm taking advantage." She bit her lip.

"You're not taking advantage." Lake wiped his mouth

with his napkin. "We're happy to take care of you while you figure out what you want to do."

This time she didn't just frown but a line appeared between her brows. "I just..." Beasty glanced at the ceiling as if she was trying to find the right words. "I just need to feel like I can do this myself. At least a little bit. A job would help."

"What do you want to do?" Atlas asked, his gaze locked on her as he made lazy circles on the table with his fingers.

She shrugged, seemingly forgetting her comment from a few minutes ago. I was glad she could. But I couldn't. It was the only thing running through my head.

"Maybe I could apply at the gas station on the corner or the grocery store. I don't know what else I could do." She avoided their gazes and she put the next bite in her mouth.

"Also a hell no," Lake snapped.

"Lake," I hissed. He was going to make her want to leave us.

"No, Kim. I have to keep all of you safe. You're my family and that's my fucking goal in life. I can't keep Beasty safe at a gas station." His top lip curled, showing exactly what he thought of people who worked at gas stations. Or maybe not them, but Beasty. "It's beneath her."

Definitely about Beasty.

"It's not beneath me," she murmured.

"It is. I'll put the word out with some of our contacts and see what's available in a place that's appropriate."

She didn't say anything.

That was where conversation died. Each bite took us closer to the end of dinner, and the closer we got, the worse my thoughts. Reaching under the table, I cupped my hand over hers, and she smiled over at me.

It was tiny, but her attention gave me some confidence

back. Except when we were clearing the table, all the desperation came back again.

"We'll clean up," Lake said, taking Beasty's plate from her hands.

"No, I can–"

"You do too much already. Let Atlas do the dishes. He needs to prove he's more than just a pretty face." Joaquin had jokes as his gaze darted to me before smiling at Beasty. "Go hang out with Kim."

I could do this. It was nothing.

"Do you want to watch a movie in my room?" I held my breath as she startled. I'd never had her in my room before. We'd always watch movies in the living room. It just seemed like a lot. And I enjoyed being with her where the guys could see her if they went out or to the kitchen.

If she was in my room all the time, they'd never see her, and I couldn't do that to them.

But now, I needed her in my space. I needed reassurance.

"Sure."

"Go on, we got this," Joaquin urged. Then the three of them started cleaning up.

I reached out and took her hand, leading her to my room. Did she say something? I glanced back, but she wasn't looking at me. Maybe I imagined it. The pounding of my heart was all I really heard anyway.

Inside my room, I flipped the switch.

It was neat. I wasn't a messy person, but my bed wasn't made. "Yeah, so...this is it." I turned to see Beasty staring at the door. "Close it?" I asked.

She nodded and shut it.

Then we stood there, facing each other. Time was suspended in this moment. If she thought about the conversation at dinner, she hid it well. But there was still a wrongness in her expression.

If I could, I would freeze us here. Stop her from asking more questions. Stopping us from lying to her anymore.

I don't know what happened between one blink and the next. One second I stood there, wondering how to make her stay, and the next, she was in my arms, our lips locked together in a sweet, sensual tangle.

For the first time, I let my hands glide down her back without checking with her first. She was soft and molded so perfectly against me. Tilting my head to the right, I deepened the kiss as my breath quickened.

Yes, Beasty wanted me just as much as I wanted her. When we were like this, nothing was wrong between us.

I hardened and my entire body tingled, but most especially the places where our skin touched.

Sliding one hand under her shirt, she stopped me. "Wait, what are we doing?" she rasped, and it stroked my ego to know how much I affected her.

"Beasty." I kissed her again, catching her top lip between mine. "I want you." I kissed her yet again, this time sucking her bottom lip. She moaned softly against my mouth. "I...I've never been with anyone before. You know that?"

She nodded, watching me with wide eyes. "I know. Me neither. You're my first kiss even."

I smiled, diving in to brush my lips along the corner of her mouth, then trailing a kiss to her neck. Gripping her hips, I urged her closer to me.

"I want you to be my first. I want to be your first. This is right, isn't it, Beasty?"

I didn't plan for this. It was so far from my mind as I enjoyed the slow burn. But after what she said...

Her breathing was loud as she held me just as tightly. I couldn't pull back and see her face, just in case she said no.

But I wanted this with her so bad. To seal us together, so I was a part of her forever. Seared into her memories like she was burned into my soul.

"Please, Beasty..." I wasn't above begging. But if she said no, I'd stop. I would never ever force her. Just the thought gave me chills.

There was no answer. That was my answer.

I pulled back and Beasty cupped my face, looking between my eyes. The emerald flecks in her own were so mesmerizing.

"You really want me?"

How could she doubt that?

"More than anything," I breathed. "More than everything." I needed her in a way I had never needed anything else and I wished I could burn every second of this in my memory. Especially the way it was remaking my very being.

"Okay," she nodded, kissing me. "Okay, yes. I want you too. I want you so much."

My chest expanded.

I stripped her shirt off, then her pants while she worked on my shirt, then my pants, all between passionate, sweet kisses. We fell into my bed in a tangle of limbs, laughing.

The light was bright, highlighting all our skin, and I didn't care. I wanted Beasty to see me. I wanted to remember everything about this moment.

Sitting back, I took a second to really see her. Creamy skin with a smattering of freckles across her chest and shoulders was on display. She had gentle feminine curves. But it was her expression that always drew me back in.

Her brows furrowed as if she didn't like the wait, and her teeth made indents in her bottom lip as she studied my body too.

Thousands of people had seen me because of modeling. Backstage, during shows, in commercials, and ads. But here with Beasty, it was like the first time I'd stripped in front of anyone.

The way her gaze roamed my torso and down to my dick built an unparalleled confidence inside me. My shoulders pulled back and my chest puffed out. But that was enough of this. I wanted to make Beasty feel good.

With me. In my arms. Bending down, I traced my tongue around her nipple, excited from her whimpers. She spread her legs and cupped my shoulders. I rose back up and settled my hips between her open thighs.

Beasty gazed at me with such beautiful, half-lidded eyes. We were high on each other and suddenly, all my fears vanished. There was just her and me enjoying each other the way people in love were meant to.

Reaching down, I slid my fingers through her slit and my eyes rolled back in my head.

She was wet. For me.

"I–Beasty–I don't want to wait. Do you need–"

She slid her hands around my back, curling them over my shoulders, as she locked her ankles around my hips. "I don't want to wait, Kim. I want to feel you," she whispered in a tortured voice, as if she was as desperate for this connection as I was.

"Oh, damn." I reached for the nightstand, grabbing a condom from the box Lake had given me, just in case.

It took three tries to get it on, my hands trembled too much.

We laughed, and when I glanced up, Beasty watched me with a soft smile.

My heartbeat slowed and pounded in my ears. We were going to make love. Beasty and me. Every hope for us I ever had ended and started right here.

She was mine. I was going to cherish her forever.

"I love you, Beasty," I choked out.

"I love you too, Kim." She pressed her fingertips to my chest, then trailed them down. "I know you don't like to be touched, but I love touching you like this."

"Not you, Beasty. You don't count. I want your hands on me all the time."

She furrowed her brow like she didn't believe me, but I didn't give her time to think. I adjusted myself, then leaned over her, pushing my hips forward just enough to get the head in.

Beasty was hot and wet, I could feel everything through the thin latex.

When she didn't move, I pushed further, a slight gasp falling from her lips.

"Are you okay?" I asked, strained.

"It's perfect, Kim." She cupped my cheek, and looked so deep into my soul I forgot to breathe.

"You're perfect, Beasty."

"Only to you." She grinned.

"I'm the only one who matters." Just like Lake said to do, I snapped my hips forward, drinking in her cry through a kiss. I waited until she relaxed.

It was torture. It was exquisite.

Once she returned my kiss, I started to move. I was only three pumps in and the orgasm was coming.

"No, no."

"What's wrong?" Beasty asked, her brows furrowing in that way I loved.

"I need you to come." I found her clit, massaging tight circles. Then I dipped to gather some of her wetness to glide easier across that sensitive bundle of nerves. Her breath quickened, and she started to rock her hips.

Good. This was a good sign.

She had to get there. I wasn't going to last long.

Close, she was so close. She whimpered and her breath

continued to catch. Moving her hands to my neck, her fingers flexed and bit into my skin.

Just when I couldn't stave off my own pleasure anymore, she clamped around me and cried out. Her head dropped back as her eyes fell closed. She was the vision of acute and rapturous pleasure.

One pump. Two. Then with a broken gasp, I stayed planted on the third. Careful not to crush Beasty, I rested my weight over her, our sweat soaked skin cooling in the open air.

"Nothing matters more than you, Beasty. You're the most important person in the world to me." Pushing my face into her neck, I mouthed, "To all of us."

She traced small circles on my back, and before I knew it, I was asleep in her arms.

Loud voices pulled me from the drudge of sleep. Heavy, hot cobwebs seemed to stretch from one ear to the other inside my head. But it was the hard, expanding plane under my cheek that took all my attention.

Shit. That was a chest.

There were hands on my thighs that couldn't possibly belong to the chest either.

Blinking the blurriness away, the room came into focus. It was early. Asscrack of dawn kind of early with gray light filtering through the window.

Last night, after I'd barged into the study, I'd been so ready to confront the guys. So ready to throw down, but holy shit. That video was real. I'd never in a million years thought it was real.

But it had been my first thought when Jake called the first code red.

Joaquin had already been plastered out of his brain and the other guys started drinking too. Even Kim.

I took the bottle when offered to me, because shit. It

just sounded like a good idea. I needed a way to get out of my own head. I'd never felt so raw as I did watching them spiral last night. It hurt my fucking heart. The alcohol numbed the pain, just for a little while.

Now that the day had come, it hurt to string two thoughts together, and it tasted like somebody shit in my mouth. I was pretty sure I'd never get that wasted again.

It was hard to find anywhere to put my hand that wasn't an arm, leg, or torso. Atlas was under my head, Joaquin curled into his side with his hand on my thigh, and Kim was huddled against my back, doing his best to climb inside me.

We slept in a pile on the study floor.

Giving up, I used Atlas' stomach to push myself up. I winced at the pain in my stiff neck. He grunted, but didn't wake. Somehow, I extracted myself, and stretched.

My entire body ached. Even my heart. No, my heart was smashed to smithereens for them.

Quietly leaving the study, I closed the door gently behind me. Voices trickled through the hallway. Lake's was louder than the other, and he was pissed.

"I don't give a fuck what you have to do. I want that asshole dead!" Lake screamed, and the echo bounced inside my head.

Still, I walked closer. As far as I remembered he hadn't joined us last night.

I'd hit the edge of the kitchen as Gio started to answer. He stood with his back to me, his arms crossed as Lake berated him.

"It doesn't work like that. You don't think I would have done that myself years ago if I could have?" Gio's voice was calm. Cold even.

"That's because you and your ragtag team couldn't get anything done if it dick-smacked you in the face." Lake tossed out a hand and turned his face to the side. His nostrils flared as he seethed.

Then he pivoted to face Gio.

I sucked in a sharp breath. His eyes were swollen and ringed with dark circles. White-blond locks stood up in every direction as if he'd run his hands through it all night. Even his clothes were one big wrinkle.

Had he slept at all? He couldn't have.

"I'd watch that tone. It's because of me that you pricks have stayed alive. It's because of *me* that you have your girl, unwilling as she is."

Lake flinched at Gio's words.

"It's because of *me* that Parker decided you were worth the investment. We both know that you're a group of fucked-up boys who can't function in society without a little help."

Lake paled.

"Hey!" I shouted, stomping right up to Gio, placing myself between him and Lake. "Knock it the hell off. No one asked your opinion on anything!" I got up on my tiptoes, stabbing my finger toward his face.

Lake slid an arm around my waist and pulled me back.

Gio's eyes softened a fraction, but he didn't show any other reaction. "Sometimes the truth is the only thing that will help idiots."

"If you're not going to help, get the fuck out of here!" Lake shouted, spinning me around so Gio couldn't see me anymore.

"You know what, fine. You're on your own. I'll tell Parker he needs to find other babysitters for your asses. I'm done." Gio snarled as he started to spin. Then he stopped. "If you want to work, the offer still stands, Cressida. We could still use your help."

"Over my dead fucking body!" Lake covered my ear

with his hand as he pressed my head into his chest. His heart beat so furiously, it pounded against my cheek.

He held me for a few minutes before he loosened his hold. His heart never slowed down, but when I glanced around, Gio was gone.

The red-hot anger that had built so furiously, slowly leaked out of my pores, leaving me deflated. Sad.

The boys last night had seemed so broken.

Lake stepped away, placing his hands close to his head, but not touching as he moved to the window that looked out over the backyard. His hands shook as they hovered, then he finally curled them into fists and dug them into his temples.

He made a pained noise in his throat. Half-anger, half-torment.

The sound pressed down on my shoulders, trying to make me smaller. He was hurting, and I didn't know what to do. What would make it better?

I'd never comforted anyone, except for Kim that one time. But his upset was calm, quiet. Lake's was brimming with power like he was going to explode at any second.

What the hell did people do to help?

Carefully choosing my steps forward, I moved quietly. When I stood at his back, I touched his shoulder blade with my fingertips. "Are you okay?" I whispered.

What the fuck was that? No, he wasn't okay.

He spun around, knocking my hand down. His hair stood on end and his eyes were wild and bloodshot. "What the fuck is wrong with you, Beasty?"

I yanked back, hurt. I was trying to help him. Not fight with him.

"Tell me, Beasty, how did you watch my best friends fall apart last night and not *feel* it?" He threw out a hand in the direction of the study.

"I feel it Lake! I'm heartbroken! For Kim! Atlas! Even that asshole, Joaquin! What do you want me to do about it? I can't magically fix it or make it go away!" I yelled back, some instinct forcing me to match his tone even though I wasn't angry.

Seeing them like that, I was devastated for them, and so far out of my element I didn't know which way was up.

Lake grabbed my shoulders and shook me. "You know what you're supposed to do? Get pissed! Get fucking angry that someone wants to hurt us! Get livid that someone has this kind of power!" His words tumbled one after another, and each one was stronger than the last. "Promise that you'll do what you can so it never happens again!"

He sucked in a breath. "That's what we do! That's what *I* do, Beasty! I fix things! I make decisions so that no one will ever have the kind of power over us like Gates did! I make sure we're safe and happy as can fucking be! And when some fuckface tries to hurt us like this, I find out who I have to hurt and make an example out of them! For them. For you! And for my fucking self!"

He wheezed from panting so hard, his eyes searching my face looking for something.

"I..I don't know..." I whispered, but I could barely croak out the words. He dumped a tub of ice water over my head and I was still in shock.

"You don't know what, Beasty! What the fuck don't you know?" He gave me a slight shake.

"I don't know how to be angry." I blew out a harsh breath then shivered. "No, I..." I was angry. Angry that they were putting themselves in danger. Angry they didn't seem to hear me. But I had never been angry on my own behalf. Not really. And I'd never experienced the kind of anger Lake described.

When Megan or a bully at school tried to hurt me, I

pulled into myself. Told myself it didn't matter. That I'd be gone soon. Then it wouldn't matter.

At some point in my life, I started to stay in the hurt more than the anger. No, I stayed in denial, pushing all emotions out of my head and heart so I could function. Sure, I fought, but only as much as I had to. Especially after I met Books.

Raising two trembling fingers to my lips, I closed my eyes. Was I just as fucked up? Was I a bad person?

"What good does that do? Being furious because you were wronged doesn't solve anything! Moving on does. Removing yourself from the situation does." My vision wavered at the edges as I tried to make sense of my thoughts.

"Did you like seeing them like that last night?" Lake asked, dipping down to force me to meet his gaze.

"No," I whispered. "I feel bad for them."

His top lip pulled away from his teeth. He was so fucking disappointed.

"That's it? You feel bad for them?" His tone kept rising higher and higher. "You're not furious someone is doing that to them? You don't itch to make it better? Because I can tell you right now, every fucking one of us shredded ourselves to ribbons over that idiot Stevo putting you on the Pescis' radar," he growled.

Then like he couldn't stand to look at me anymore, he pushed himself away and spun around. The laugh that came next was broken, and ugly, and disbelieving.

"Shit. Maybe Joaquin's right. Maybe you don't want to be here. Maybe you're just a figment of my fucked-up imagination." He laughed again as tears started to fill my eyes.

Breathing became hard, and that spark of anger started in my stomach.

"Stop it!" I yelled as one tear fell. "Stop saying that!"

"Saying what?" When Lake turned around, his face was set in stone and the coldness slapped me in the face so hard I stumbled back.

No. "You don't get to judge me like this." I shook my head, not sure if I was trying to clear my head or shake some sense into myself.

"That's all you've done is judge us," he fired back, and I sucked in a breath. "Our choices, our careers, our associates, although you'd seemed to toss that all aside for Gio, and he's even worse than us." He sneered and turned away.

"No!" I yanked his arm until he faced me again. "You're fucking–" I screamed in frustration because he was right.

He was fucking right.

Even if I never would have worked with Gio, I used them. That wasn't different from what they were doing. Not where it counted.

"I have only ever been by myself. Alone, Lake. I've learned to handle my emotions and deal with life *alone*. You four have always had each other to lean on. Yes, your childhood was fucked up. Beyond fucked and twisted. No kid should have to deal with that, but you four are so lucky because you have each other and I've always been on the outside." I shook my head, trying to untangle my mess of thoughts.

"You have us, Beasty! You always have!" He pushed himself in my space until we were chest to chest, and he walked me backward.

"You lie!" I thrashed against him as he gathered me up in his arms and lifted me onto the kitchen counter. "You have held yourself so far away from me, I couldn't have touched you if I tried!"

"You're touching me now, Beasty." His voice dipped.

I was. I paused for just a minute to notice my hands splayed across his chest and my nails slicing into his T-shirt.

"Are you angry? Or do you just feel bad for us?" he asked softly, tipping my face up with a finger under my chin.

Breathing deep and blinking away the remnants of tears, I studied myself. Was I angry? I guess I never thought I could be or should be.

"If someone walked in here right now, tossing a pile of videos on the floor, saying they uploaded them on the internet, would you accept it? Would you just give Kim a hug and tell him it's going to be okay?"

I imagined what he said, if someone was hurting him right in front of me. I'd fight for him.

Just like I did all those years ago when I saved them.

The amount of fights I got into at school over them was insane.

But somewhere along the way, I'd started believing I couldn't, that to live the life I wanted to live, I had to be different. I changed who I was to get away.

Was that right? Was that my only option?

"I'd fuck him up. I couldn't watch him hurt any of you," I murmured the realization to myself.

"Then why is it so goddamned different when someone's hurting us but you can't see them?" There was a desperate note in his voice.

"I don't know!" I shouted, but not at him. At myself. Because I didn't understand it. Then I raked my hands down his chest.

He groaned, tipping his head back. With one hand, he reached behind him, grabbed the shirt and pulled it off. Already red welts appeared down the muscular planes of his chest and abs. They contracted as I watched.

"I need you now, Beasty. Are you going to fight me?"

Glancing up at him through my lashes, a flare of excitement fought for control with the sadness and confusion. I rolled my lips together. "Yes, I'll fight you."

"Then fucking fight me." He landed a hard slap against the outside of my thigh. It stung so bad, but it brought me to life. Woke me the hell up.

Then I started fighting back. I slapped him, raked my nails over his exposed skin, beating the hell out of him as he stripped me down and gathered me to his chest.

As he walked us up the stairs, I raged in his arms, biting his shoulder, screaming my frustration. He moaned and grunted in pleasure each time I attacked his skin.

This was liberating, releasing myself on him like this. The euphoria that zinged through me was like such a high, I was already soaked for Lake.

He didn't even bother shutting his door as he tossed me on the bed. He quickly stripped out of his pants, his hard, glorious cock bounced against his stomach.

Lake was a work of art. Thick and toned like a man at his peak condition. For someone who loved pain, his lightly tanned skin was strangely blemish free. Perfect, really.

He crawled on the bed and I laid back against the pillows. The potent scent of his cologne wafted around me, engulfing me, and invading my senses in the best way.

I loved the way he smelled. Sharp, musky, and delicious.

"Next time, we'll break out the toys. I have some that are more fun than you'd imagine. But right now, I need you." He swallowed and lowered his gaze to my chest. When he brought his gaze back to my eyes, he ground his teeth in determination. "I need you to fuck me up while I fuck you. I want you to make me bleed."

I nodded. I wanted to do this for him. He needed it, and I desperately needed him to know I could do it. I could fight for him in the only way I knew how. At least at this moment.

When Lake yanked my thigh up around his waist, I smacked his cheek so hard, his head snapped to the side. He slowly closed his eyes as his chest rose and fell with each breath.

Then Lake stuck his tongue out, tracing his bottom lip. "You busted my lip." He smiled darkly. "Perfect. You're fucking perfect, Beasty. Don't let me fuck with your head."

I couldn't take my gaze away from him as he adjusted himself, sliding the head of his warm cock up and down my folds. Biting my bottom lip, I got lost in the sensation of Lake's brand of intimacy.

He notched himself just inside when he dropped down overtop of me, catching my jaw and holding me still as he brought his mouth to mine.

Then Lake kissed me as he thrust inside. I yelled out, soaked, but not enough for his size. He didn't stop, swallowing my cry as he pulled back his hips then thrust forward.

On the third push, he was fully seated and the sting was gone.

I must be fucked up too. The bite of pain Lake always delivered lit my senses on fire and burned me up from the inside out. Adding to my pleasure when it should have dampened it.

Giving Lake exactly what he wanted, I bit his lip and scored my nails down his back. Gripping his ass cheeks so hard, I was sure he'd have bruises from my fingers and half-moon indents from my nails.

He kept hold of my face, squeezing just enough that it was uncomfortable as he devoured my mouth. Tilting my face when he wanted a different angle, pinching so that I would open my mouth wider, all while he held my thigh to his ribs.

We collided over and over again, our frustrations with

ourselves and each other spilling out between us in this wild fucking.

Ten minutes, two hours, we were outside of time.

He gripped my breast and massaged to the point of pain as he licked the fingers on his other hand and strummed my clit, never failing to crash his hips into mine. He fucked me so hard, it was like he wanted to fuse us together.

Without warning, I called out his name. Throwing my head back, I gasped as I milked the hell out of him.

White noise filled my ears as I rolled my head back on the pillow. When I came back to myself, glorious sounds filled the room. Lake's ragged breathing, the slap of our skin, and the headboard hitting the wall.

Then Lake grunted as he pistoned his hips, swelling inside me. He came on a fierce shout and gathered me up to his chest as he kept thrusting until he shivered, burying his face into my neck.

I was wrecked. Absolutely totally destroyed.

He laid us down as he traced shapes on my hip. We caught our breath in silence, until I broke it.

"What are we going to do now?" About the videos, about us, about life? I thought I knew exactly who I was but maybe I didn't. Maybe I hadn't even had the chance to figure it out.

"We're going to knock our enemies off the board," he whispered against my temple. "And we're going to set an example."

A day ago, I would have got caught up in how that wasn't what I wanted for myself–this kind of life. But right then, in the afterglow of sex and revelations, in a weird kind of way, they made me feel cared for as I drifted off to sleep.

One last thought passed through my mind before I gave into sleep completely.

Was this what love felt like?

Chapter Twenty-Nine

BEASTY - AGE 18

I jolted awake, my heart thumping hard against my ribcage.

The light was still on, and Kim had his back to me with my arm wrapped around his waist.

What time was it? Lifting my head, I looked for a clock, but I didn't see one. It could have been the middle of the night or just before dawn. I had no idea other than it was still dark outside.

I smiled, pressing my forehead lightly against Kim's back. He said he liked to hold me and always asked to put his arm around me on the couch, but when he went to sleep, he turned over and pulled my arm around him.

He liked being the little spoon.

I was sore and for the first time in my life, I felt normal. I'd had a typical experience, losing my virginity to a boy. One I liked. I loved?

Did he really love me?

Could we even know what love really was? We both had such unconventional childhoods.

There was a sound. It was muffled, and sounded like voices. Glancing at the window again, I strained to figure out what that was.

It was definitely a conversation.

My smile died. Lake said they weren't into bad stuff, and I wanted to believe him. I forced myself to, but now in the middle of the night, I couldn't escape my thoughts.

My gut told me he was lying. I wasn't stupid. I knew shady behavior when I saw it. Megan and Ed were prime examples.

Shifting back so I wasn't touching Kim, I froze, waiting to see if he would move. He didn't, staying fast asleep. I slipped from the bed, then on tiptoes, I went to the door. Before I twisted the handle, I turned the light out.

Then I carefully opened the door, letting out a sigh of relief when it didn't creak.

Lake's and Atlas' voices came from the living room. Holding my breath, I continued on tiptoes down the hallway. I couldn't get that close. The apartment was a decent size, but sound traveled here. Especially at night.

"We have to tell Beasty the truth. She's not going to take it well if she finds out from someone other than us," Atlas said.

Shit. I shot straight up, pressing my back to the cold wall.

"She can't find out. You heard her. She won't stay if she believes we're doing things that remind her of her childhood."

"What are we doing that reminds her of her childhood?" Joaquin asked, disgust coloring his words.

"We're not." Lake sighed, and I could imagine him pinching the bridge of his nose. "But we're not exactly on the up and up either."

"Then we have to get her to see things our way. We can explain it to her in a way that will make sense," Atlas reasoned with them. But there was no reasoning.

Illegal things were illegal things.

"Yeah? And how are you going to explain how much money we have?" Lake asked. "We drive top of the line cars, and we're going to buy a house soon. Not a small one. One we deserve."

"My gambling?" Joaquin offered. "I've always been good at it. That's not a secret."

A soft knock rapped on the front door.

Oh, no. They were going to catch me.

I ducked into the bathroom and got on my hands and knees. It was pitch dark in here. If they walked by and didn't go to the bathroom, then they wouldn't see me. If they did...

Someone opened the front door.

"It worked like a charm," a man said. He sounded familiar. Was this the man from last night?"

"No issues?" Joaquin asked so calmly, he could have been talking about Atlas' schedule for the day.

"I mean," the guy started, sounding like he was smiling. "There's always a little fight. But between the two jobs, they went smooth enough." There was a rustling. "Here's the cash. The weasel's pissed, and he said Atlas and Kim are now on the shit list, but that's one designer. Doesn't fucking matter unless the truth gets out."

"You counted it?" Joaquin asked as there was more rustling like Joaquin took a bag from him.

"It's all there," the guy confirmed. "As for the other job. The favor is secured, and he's not happy about it, but given the intel you have, he's not going to make a fuss. His firm is on the line."

"That's excellent," Lake murmured. "What about the Korvay job?"

I took a deep breath so I wouldn't have to breathe for a minute, and carefully stuck my head out of the bathroom. Being this low to the floor should be okay.

There were the boys, standing at the front door with another man. I couldn't see anything except his black, chunky boots.

Joaquin had a plastic bag under his arm, and they were chatting like middle of the night visits were normal.

"I think Sonia is better equipped for that one. I know Korvay and he'll respond better to her subtlety. And books are fine art type of things. They'd run as soon as they saw my big, tattooed ass coming."

They had a laugh like this was some hilarious inside joke. Then with a quick goodbye, the guy left and they returned to the couch. I ducked my head back inside the bathroom as I struggled to breathe.

I didn't even really comprehend what they were doing but it was illegal. There was no other way to explain it.

Whatever it was, it was so much worse than drugs.

I couldn't stay here.

My heart splintered at the thought of leaving. But I couldn't fucking stay here.

Books words floated through my head.

Your life started out as shit, and if you get sucked into the wrong crowd, you'll continue to live in shit. Greed and self-righteousness is a toxin in our veins. Once it's there, it continues to change everything about a person. Think of people like us as quicksand. Once you get involved, it's a slippery slope that you'll never be able to escape. Avoid it.

I didn't want to live in shit. That was the one thing I wanted for myself, to get away from all the crap in my childhood.

But the boys...

Tears blurred my vision and my nose started to run. I couldn't do this. Not here.

They were the only people I'd cared about growing up, and they'd never wanted me. Now they said they did, but who were they? They didn't even talk to me. Not really. Every time I entered a room they found a reason to leave. When I went with them to jobs, they were constantly busy unless it was to tell me when we'd leave. Even on the rare occasions we ate dinner together, they talked around me.

And it had been months!

They were still talking in the living room, but I wasn't paying attention anymore. I'd heard all I needed to. I got to my feet and quietly went to my room. I'd unpacked but I didn't have a lot. And somehow, I'd managed to put Kim off buying me a ton of new clothes, although he had bought a couple things.

Pulling my duffle bag from under the bed, I started yanking clothes off hangers, and everything out of the drawers, leaving only the new things. I had a pile of dirty clothes in the corner and I stuffed those in there too.

Five minutes was all it took to pack up every single item I owned. But I checked the pocket of the duffle bag. It was still there. The card and Visa gift card Books had given me.

Holding the card to my chest I chanted thank you over and over in my head.

I had a way out. Books made sure I was going to have a life free from everything. One day, I hoped I'd be able to thank him.

Opening the door, I took one step out into the hallway, but froze.

"Did Beasty come out here?" Kim asked, sleep in his voice.

I couldn't think about him. I did my best to block his face from my mind or how he was going to look when I left.

Wait. Did he...Did he want to sleep with me just to distract me? To tie me up in bliss so I'd forget about our dinner conversation?

I couldn't think like that. *I wouldn't.* It would tarnish what happened between Kim and me, and as much as I needed to leave, I didn't want to do that to something so beautiful.

Maybe I should wait until morning. Maybe I should wait until they all returned to bed. There were a million different ways to leave, but none of them seemed right. I needed to leave now.

What I'd just heard. What I'd listened too...

I was hot. Too hot. And it made thinking a struggle. Once I got outside and got fresh air, I'd be okay.

"Beasty." Kim was in front of me smiling, until his gaze dropped to the bag in my hand. He stepped back and I looked away.

It hurt too much to look at him.

"She's up?" Lake asked from the living room, then he walked up to us. He towered over us in a way that sucked the air from my lungs and I took a step back.

They'd never hurt me. I knew they wouldn't.

But I didn't know what they'd do when I told them I was leaving.

"What are you doing, Beasty?" Kim wore his heartbreak right there on the surface that even when I started to glance at him, I couldn't. It physically pained me.

I was hurting myself, and I was hurting them.

"You lied to me." I couldn't look any of them in the eye, but all four boys crowded my door.

"We didn't lie." Lake tried lying about lying.

"I–" I squeezed my eyes shut. I thought being here

would be good for me. But it's not. "The most important thing to me, the one thing I want for myself, is to get away from the past. From the bad people. What you guys are doing...I can't be a part of it."

"Beasty," Kim said as he took a step forward. "Last night, we made love. It was perfect." He sucked in a shaky breath and his words were thick. "You can't leave me after that."

I didn't want to leave.

The tears I'd been holding started spilling. It was ripping my heart out, but I had to choose myself. No one else would, so I needed to. And whatever they were doing, I wanted nothing to do with it.

But...

"Would you stop? If I...If I stayed, would you stop messing around with whatever it is you're doing?" My voice was small. Why would anyone do anything like that for me?

They exploded at once and I couldn't make out anything they said.

"Stop!" Lake yelled, slashing his hand through the air. "Beasty, we're not doing the things you think we're doing." He faced me, but I was already shaking my head. "Stop being ridiculous. Tell us what happened to make you want to leave in the middle of the night." He cut his gaze to Kim.

"Kim didn't do anything. It was..." I dropped my gaze to the floor. This was so weird, yet I didn't want them to think poorly of Kim. "We had a perfect night. But I can't stay with you." Taking a deep breath, I glanced up against my better judgment. "Will you tell me what it is you're doing?"

His jaw worked as he glanced away.

I nodded. That was fair. I expected that. It was still a blow to the one dream–living with the boys I'd idolized from a far–I had as a child. It was crumbling right before my very eyes.

But dreams weren't meant to last forever. They were only to get you to a better place, then you could concoct a different dream. That was what I told myself but it felt wrong and hollow.

Still. If I knew anything, it was that I didn't want to be tied to anything like Megan was mixed up in, and if they tried to say it wasn't, that was splitting hairs.

I mean, Megan tried to sell my body to pay off her debt. She didn't give a damn about my body, my life, or me. It would be devastating if I found out the boys could do that to me. So I needed to leave.

"Beasty, you can't go," Kim rushed out, raising his hands like he wanted to touch me but he didn't. Like he didn't know if he could.

It was probably for the best that he didn't. I'd break, and right now, for myself, I couldn't.

"You can't go. You fucking saved us and we want to take care of you." Lake stepped forward, his brows pulled low over his blue-hazel eyes.

Joaquin and Atlas just stood back, suddenly quiet.

"We're going to return the favor, Beasty. You're ours."

What did that even mean? They were helping me out of some sick sense of duty? Obligation?

"I can't stay here," I repeated in a hard voice, even though it wavered. Staying wasn't even a choice at this point. They'd never tell me what they were doing. They'd never stop. It wasn't like I was part of their group anyway. I'd always be on the outside.

I wouldn't be pulled back into the cycle. I was breaking the cycle. In my own way, and on my own terms.

Rubbing the fingers of my free hand together, I drew courage from it. "I have money saved up. So you don't have to worry I'll be homeless or anything."

"What the fuck?" Joaquin shouted. "You are never going

to be homeless again. I don't care if we have to drag you back here kicking and screaming." He started grumbling under his breath as he walked away.

"There will be nowhere you can hide from us. I swear to God if you become homeless, I'll–" Lake turned and raised his fists up beside his head.

My eyes widened and I took a step back.

Atlas watched me with an unreadable, unblinking stare. The stark attention made me uncomfortable, as if he could see just how hard this was. I glanced away from him too.

There was a soft sniffle, and I glanced at Kim. His eyes were shining bright with unshed tears and he watched me with so much desolation that I just...I couldn't do this anymore.

Turning back, Lake tried to control his voice. "You can't leave. This is all a misunderstanding." Raking a hand through his hair, he looked to the ceiling. "Wait until morning and we'll talk. All of us. Okay. Okay?" he repeated, making it more of a question.

I nodded. "I need some time to think. I'll see you in the morning."

Stepping back, I started closing the door. Kim stepped forward like he wanted to talk to me, but Lake shuffled him to the living room, all without touching him.

Once my door was closed, I stopped holding back the tears. I whined with each breath, like some sort of messed-up cat.

If I stayed with them, I'd end up just like Megan, justi-fying fucked up things and jobs all because it paid well. Sacrificing people's trust and pride because it got what I wanted or needed.

I couldn't be like that. I'd hate myself for it.

I'd hate the boys, and that might kill me faster.

They'd be in the living room. If they were anything like me, they'd assume I'd sneak out while they slept. I would.

I still was. But I had to find a different way. I went to the window, and opened the blinds. Flipping the lock, I slid it open. It made a small squeak, but there were no pounding footsteps in the hallway.

Sticking my head out, I breathed in the cool night air and glanced around.

There wasn't a balcony, but there was a rooftop right below the window. Maybe a seven-foot drop. If I could get there, I could go around the building and find another drop. That would only be one more story.

I could do that.

The pep talk sucked, but I didn't have any other option if I was actually going to leave. If I looked at Kim one more time, I'd cave. I'd sacrifice everything I wanted for myself.

I couldn't do that. I refused.

Dangling the duffle out the window, I held it as low as I could before dropping it. It landed with a soft thump.

Okay, this was it. I could do it.

I swung one leg out, sitting with my head and torso on the outside of the window. No, that wasn't going to work. My body needed to be inside as I worked my other leg outside. Rearranging myself, I got my stomach on the windowsill, grunting from the pressure. Slowly, I lowered myself, trying not to scrape my stomach too badly on the brick.

Then when I was holding on just by my hands, I let go. My feet hit the roof first, then I rolled back on my ass, hitting my head. It wasn't bad. I'd just have a slight bruise later.

I held still, waiting to see if anyone heard. I must have stayed on my back for five minutes. When no one came, I rolled to my feet, picked up my bag and worked my way around the building.

When I reached the end, just before the corner, I glanced back to the window. The light was on, and it was still open.

My heart squeezed. I was doing the right thing. This was the path I wanted.

The pain would go away with time. It had to.

How did Joaquin constantly fuck his head up like this?

I popped three pain relievers in my mouth and swallowed them down with a giant gulp of coconut water. I was so dehydrated that regular water, even the fancy shit Kim loved, wasn't going to cut it. I needed something better.

Coconut water was good enough for runners, it was good enough for me.

Next, I'd try some of Kim's ginger and lemon tea.

Kim and Joaquin sat at the table, their own drinks in front of them. Beasty and Lake were still in bed. Glancing at the clock, it was almost noon. I'd have been concerned if I hadn't rewound the footage and watched their fucking.

Jealousy bit me in the ass, but I had no energy to be irritated with him. For the first time in my life, I was drained. The urge to fuck with Joaquin was silent as was the drive to seek out a thrill.

Beasty didn't even know that side of me yet. I wanted to get her hooked on us first.

Grabbing two other coconut waters, I took them over to the guys. Kim never drank. That he did last night...

We had to make sure that didn't happen again. But from the look of desolation in his eyes, it was going to be an uphill battle. Then I glanced at Joaquin.

He was so fucked, I didn't have to do anything to help, he was taking care of it all on his own.

"Tell me what Gio said again?" Kim asked, staring at his tea with a vacant gaze. He didn't even acknowledge the water I set in front of him.

"You watched it just like I did." I pushed my phone to the middle of the table in case they wanted to watch it again.

I wasn't the only one who was shocked with how Beasty and Lake fucked it out. But the argument leading up to it was rough.

"Why are you asking about Gio? You know what's really bothering you." Joaquin laid his face in the crook of his arm on the table.

Kim sucked in a breath, his bottom lip quivering. But he didn't ask.

Not at first.

"Do you think Beasty doesn't actually care about us?" There it was. The troubling question in his trembling voice.

A snappy retort was on the tip of my tongue. Of course, she didn't. How could she when she left us right after she took Kim's virginity? We wanted someone who didn't exist.

But for once, I kept all that to myself. As much as I wanted to punish her, and I still did, I also didn't want to see her cry.

"She cares about us," Joaquin croaked as he rubbed his chest with his fist.

Kim shot a surprised look his way. Hell, I couldn't believe his words either. Not after he was a jackass to her.

"You think so?"

"You heard the rest of the conversation. I think..." Joaquin turned to look out the window. "I think we just don't understand each other, but she cares about us."

Nodding, Kim relaxed his shoulders. That was the validation he needed.

When no one reached for the phone, I pulled it back to me and turned on the camera in Lake's room. I bet he never thought I'd use it to spy on him. Then again, he had to know if he took Beasty in there, I'd be watching.

At first, Lake was molded tightly to her back, then he rolled over and scrubbed his face. She started to stir too. Glad they got to get some rest. Assholes.

I watched as they took turns pissing in the bathroom, I watched as they brushed their teeth, and I watched them descend the stairs. Only when they appeared in the kitchen did I turn the phone off.

Lake had a determined stride and an intense look of concentration on his face as he led Beasty to the seat next to Kim, and sat her down.

He started fucking with the coffee machine and made two coffees. "We're going to that show tonight."

"Like hell we are. The only place I'm going to is the bottom of a bottle, the Gold Room, or both."

I smacked the back of Joaquin's shoulder. "*Like hell* you will."

"What happened to keeping Beasty safe?" Kim peeked at Lake.

"Change of plan. We need to clean our house up. Get rid of that fucking weasel, make the Pescis a non-issue by knocking them off the board, and squash the video footage before anymore is released." He talked like we had a game board set up with all the players right out in the open.

I turned to Beasty. She wasn't making a fuss about

going and stealing a museum piece. If she was bothered at all she hid it well. There was a resolute look on her face as she stirred milk into the coffee Lake set in front of her.

"Even if we could get tickets, we'd never be ready in time. For Kim and Atlas, that takes hours to get them styled. They need designer outfits, preferably something they or anyone else hasn't worn before. It's too much." Joaquin fell back against his chair with a thump.

With a pained grimace, Kim shook his head. "We're not models anymore. I've stocked us with enough pieces that we can go in style and not stand out, but we don't have to live up to the same standards."

There was a *but* in there.

"And what?" I asked when he didn't continue.

Beasty took a sip of her coffee, seemingly lost in her thoughts. There was something different about her. Was Lake's brand of fucking so life changing? I almost sneered.

"I'm the charmer. People want to talk with me. Interview me. And I..." Kim sighed. "I just don't think I can handle it. I don't even want to go." He rolled his shoulders forward and dropped his head. He had to be as messed up as he said. There was not one lie there.

"I'll be with you. You won't have to talk to anyone you don't want to."

Everyone turned to Beasty.

"You realize that we're going there to do a job," Joaquin spoke with a measured tone. "We're not just going to support a good cause. This is a museum where there will be lots of guards protecting the statue Parker wants us to steal for him."

Beasty closed her eyes for a few seconds. When she opened them, her eyes flared and she pressed her lips together. "I'm aware," she said in a tone that dared him to argue with her.

Then she cut her gaze to Kim, and her face softened into something bordering sweet before her eyes crinkled in pain.

Kim and Beasty stared at each other, and for the first time since we woke up, Kim took a deep breath.

"I've called Parker. Renegotiated the terms of the job. He's going to help with both the Valencia mess and the Pescis, but we have to do this job and one more at a later time." Lake took his spot at the end of the table.

"What about the video?" Joaquin's voice wobbled, his gaze skating to me.

Now that I'd had time to sit on it, I was fine. But Joaquin never handled this shit well.

Lake hesitated, watching Beasty. "I called in a few markers to track down Donnie and the reporter he was speaking to."

"Do we know who she is?" Kim asked.

"No, but we will. What we do know is she works for the news station that's playing that video. Apparently, they were given exclusive rights to the footage."

That helped but I was sure people were sharing and resharing the video as we spoke.

Checking his watch, Lake rubbed his eyes. "We have two hours before we have to leave."

Tonight called for one of our stretch SUVs. These events were predictable. The only thing that mattered was who had the newest cars, the best outfits, the deepest purses. Basically a dick measuring contest in style.

There was no music and no conversation. Everyone was dead quiet.

But we looked good, not like we hadn't had our life upended for the fifth time last night, and got barely three hours sleep on the hardwood floor. Probably because it was the first time we all slept close to Beasty.

And partially because of what fashion had taught us. Or Kim, more specifically. How to hide our sins and secrets with highlighter and contour.

Beasty glanced up, catching me watching her. But I wasn't ashamed. This was my life's work. I'd do it until the day I died. She didn't look away. I narrowed my eyes and she responded in kind.

"What's this shit show of a plan? Do we even have a fucking plan?" Joaquin griped as he reached for the bar on the side. I smacked his hand and glared at him.

Last night was his pass. It was a pass for every single one of us. Now he was officially cut off as he dried out.

Lake pulled up a document on his phone. A map. "There's a statue in the Grecian room. Parker sent over pictures of the item, the blueprint, and guard rotation schedules. He's thorough." Lake sounded begrudgingly impressed.

He would hate that. He didn't like thinking anyone was smarter than we were.

"You all have it in your email."

I opened the doc on my phone to see if this was as detailed as Lake said it would be. It was and more, along with a write up of two different scenarios of the best way to get the statue out.

"Gio and his friends will be here?" I asked. They hadn't parted ways on the best terms this morning.

Lake snorted and Beasty shot him a glare.

"They didn't want to be, but when I spoke to Parker before we left, he assured me they would be there. Along with a couple friends of his to make sure we aren't caught with our asses out. He also said he'd take care of surveillance."

"Comforting," Joaquin snarked.

Kim didn't seem to be listening. He gazed at Beasty as if he was trying to figure her out, but also like he didn't believe she was really here. He was sitting so far from her, he was smashed up against the window.

Beasty had to see it, but she didn't address it.

Whatever. What was one more piece of dysfunction in our group?

Everyone read the write up. It was surprisingly simple. Parker had paired Beasty with Kim as if he knew they would be safer together. Lake was the bad guy, actually stealing the statue.

Then Joaquin and I were the distraction, starting an argument in the reception. Not a stretch, considering how much of an ass Joaquin had been lately.

We fell back into the awkward silence that was getting more uncomfortable each time. Like we were growing apart right in front of our own eyes.

Eventually, the car pulled up to the cue line. We could already see reporters camping out on the sidewalk. Flashes from cameras went off outside the car, along with questions from the reporters.

Beasty tensed and seemed to stop breathing. This wasn't even the entrance and she was nervous. I reached across the space and touched her knee. When she looked at me, I nodded. "It's going to be okay. You're worth ten of any of these assholes."

A ghost of a smile coasted across her face. Then she shook her head. "They're going to ask about the video."

"Let them." I shrugged. I didn't give a shit what they said. Although, I reached in my pocket and pulled out a box. Opening it, I dumped the contents in my hand and handed two to Joaquin and two to Kim.

You know what? Fuck it. I handed two more to Beasty.

"Earbuds?" Kim whispered, glancing at me.

"They're going to yell nasty shit to catch you off guard and get a reaction. We're pros, but we're also fucked up from last night. Take the earbuds and you can take them out as soon as you get inside.

The queue of cars wrapped around the corner, but when we reached it, our car didn't turn.

Instead, we started going faster.

Beasty, Joaquin, and Kim didn't notice as they put in their earbuds.

But Lake did. We exchanged a glance, then we each dove for doors on opposite sides of the vehicle. They were locked.

"God damnit!" Lake shouted. Beasty and Kim yelled as Lake laid over their laps to bang on the door.

The car sped up even more.

We all smashed our fists against the windows but they were bulletproof. The top of the line vehicle was to protect us. And fucking hold us prisoner.

Beasty had her hands up like she didn't know what to fucking do as Joaquin curled his body around hers.

Lake sat back up and tried to throw himself against the door, but it was pointless.

Kim started hyperventilating, and keeping a solid train of thought was getting hard for me too. I hadn't been trapped like this since...

This was not the fucking time.

I collected myself enough to notice we were on an empty road.

Trees passed and that rickety house in West Virginia flashed before my eyes. I shook my head.

A few buildings were here and there, then once again my vision was filled with Gates' house. What it looked like to stand just inside the front door.

Fuck! I didn't need this.

The buildings around us were all industrial, and all I could see was that damned chain-link fence.

There was no way in hell I could go back there. No fucking way. I couldn't.

Slouching down, I tried to kick at the glass on the other side of the car. It didn't work. Why the hell did my limbs feel like they weren't working?

I needed to get out of here. We would never go back there!

The car turned into a parking lot, as it started to pull through a bay door, a weird smell started seeping through the vents.

I glanced back, and every single one of us had drooping eyes.

This couldn't be happening. Not again...

"They're drug–" Lake tried to say, but I lost it as I fell into the darkness.

Epilogue

CRESSIDA, PRESENT DAY

My tongue was thick in my mouth and my head pulsed like a motherfucker.

There was also a bright light shining right in my face. I tried to blink my eyes open, but they seemed like they were glued shut.

I managed to roll over and rocks dug into my cheek. What the hell?

What happened? The last thing I remember was...Shit, I didn't even know. I had sex with Lake. I had some really uncomfortable realizations about myself. We got ready for the event.

It was almost our turn to get out. There were flashes in the windows. I hadn't dreamed that. Earbuds maybe?

Someone had their arm around me. Joaquin. He tried to protect me.

I finally got my eyes to crack, and hot black pavement filled my vision. Gasping, I shot up, then fell back down as my head spun.

Where the hell was I? Looking around, I was in an old

335

parking lot next to a rundown park. One no one had used in years.

Slapping my chest, I checked my dress.

I still had it. I still fucking had my phone. I pulled it out of my boobs, and the screen lit up. I'd never been so fucking thankful that I hated purses.

Shaking, I opened the messages. There were tons. Almost a hundred. All from the group chat with Gio and Adrian, or Adrian on his own.

GIO:

Where are you?

ADRIAN:

You should be here by now.

GIO:

Where the hell are you? You haven't even gotten on the carpet yet.

The messages got angrier and more urgent with each one. The last one was an hour ago at seven in the morning.

ADRIAN:

You better be alive. I was starting to like you and I'd hate to have to bury you. After I hunt down the asshole who took you.

I hit call, and Adrian picked up on the first ring.

"Where the fuck are you?" He screamed, no sign of the playful idiot.

"I don't know," I rasped. It sounded like I'd been partying my entire life. I sounded like Rona.

"Send me your location, right now," he demanded.

"Gio, Cressida is on the phone. I'm getting her location. Get Storm, we'll get on the road."

With clumsy fingers, I fumbled through the app and grabbed a pin of my location. He's lucky I even knew how to do this. Stevo had asked for my location once.

"Where are they?" I choked out. I knew they didn't know. How could they? They didn't know where I was. But I had to ask. I couldn't *not* ask.

He didn't answer.

"Where the hell are they?" I screamed, curling my other hand against my chest. "Where are they?" I cried. "Where are they?"

"Nowhere good," Adrian finally answered, his voice grim.

"We have to call the police. We have to–" I rambled.

"No. Listen to me, Beasty. Whoever has them, and we have our thoughts, aren't people the police will be able to save them from. If you want them alive, you cannot call the police."

I snapped my mouth shut, as I tried to comprehend what he was saying. But it was hard. I was tired, and thirsty, and my head throbbed.

"You cannot call the police. Do you understand me!" he barked and I jerked. "Do you want to see them alive?"

"Y-yes! Of course I do!" I sucked in air but it was like I couldn't take a full breath. I clawed at my throat, but it didn't help.

"If you won't help us, we have to lock you up." He tried to sound calm and understanding but I didn't need that right then.

I needed him to tell me he would stop at nothing to get them back safe and sound. "No! I want them back! We have to save them. They can't die. They can't. I can't lose them."

My words were one jumbled string, but Adrian had to understand me. That was the only option.

"Will you help us?" He was keeping his head on straight. That was good.

I knew what Adrian was asking of me. To draw out the Pescis. Be the bait. Work with criminals because in no world were Gio, Adrian, and Storm good men. What made a man good?

I knew what a bad man was. A bad man was Gates. The Pescis. Everything else?

My entire being was realigning as the blinders fell away from my eyes.

"I will. I want to help. I want to fight. For them."

Follow Beasty and the Fashion Boys in the next installment... Crazed.
Read here.

Afterword

Wowza.

We're on the other side and we're mostly in one piece! I'd love to tell you that these characters grew by leaps and bounds, but...

They're still learning about themselves. When people have lived lives as hard as they have, it's not a quick trip to self-discovery. It takes time, and experiences, and sometimes, okay, most times, a lot of heartbreak.

Don't worry, I have some big moments planned for the next book that I think you'll really love. We'll get to see some of these characters really come into themselves.

As for the preorder...

DON'T FREAK ABOUT THE PREORDER DATE.

I gave myself lots of breathing time to finished Crazed, but I will be moving the release date up once I'm done and satisfied with the story.

This is purely to protect my stress levels, but if you have any questions, please don't hesitate to reach out!

Oh and- Did you recognize any of the side characters? Asking for a friend.

If you want to chat all things Edged, come see me in my Facebook group Blake's Book Babes! There will be a spoiler post pinned!

If you want to keep up with me, you can join my newsletter for sneak peeks (and giveaways such as ARCs), random life hacks and survival skills, as well as news updates!

Specifically, if you want to see the Crazed cover EARLY, join the newsletter here.

And... If you're stalking game is strong, follow me here too!

Facebook Author Page <u>Bookbub</u> <u>TikTok</u> <u>Instagram</u> <u>Amazon</u>

Thanks for reading and I'll see you in the next book!

XOXO

Blake

Other titles

THE COLLECTION

Snatched
Edged
Bastard Brothers of Carnage Series
Addict
Convict
Killer
Psycho
Traitor

Mazza Series
Marks of the Mazza
Bonds of the Mazza
Secrets of the Mazza
War of the Mazza

Astrid Scott Series
Pretty Lies
Ugly Truths
Busted Dreams
Vivid Fears

Brittle Hope

Fragile Minds Duet
Fractured
Altered

Standalone RH Romance
Pin-up Girl

Co-Writes with my Co-wrifey
Cardinal Sins
Kill Song
First Chorus
High Note
Last Word

Standalone Series
Kiss of Fate
Taste of Karma

Standalone MF Romance
Full Glasses and Burju Shoes